SLEEPING MALICE

Adrian Spalding

Copyright

Copyright © Adrian Spalding 2018

Adrian Spalding has asserted his right to be identified as the author of this work.

All rights reserved. No part of this publication may be reproduced, stored in any retrieval system, or transmitted, in any form or by any means, electronic, mechanical, photocopying, recording or otherwise, without the prior permission of the author.

This book is a work of fiction. Names, characters, businesses, organisations, places and events other than those clearly in the public domain, are either the product of the author's imagination or are used fictitiously. Any resemblance to actual persons, living or dead, events or locales is entirely coincidental.

Books by Adrian Spalding

The Reluctant Detective
The Reluctant Detective Goes South
The Reluctant Detective Under Pressure
The Reluctant Detective Goes North

Sleeping Malice
Caught on Camera
The Night You Murder

www.adrianspalding.co.uk

Acknowledgements

This book would never have seen the light of day, but for the vast support from my friends and family. Especially those who went the whole extra mile to help, Claire, Heike, Anthony, Gavan, Brian and Peter, thank you.

A special thank you to my tolerant wife, listening to gruesome plots, pointing me in the right direction, editing the book, and having a never-ending faith that I could do it.

PREFACE.

Martin Jackson had less than two hours to live. He walked, head bowed into the wind, face shielded against the driving rain, as the lapwings etched their path across the grey sky. It was January in Brittany; ploughed fields sodden from days of non-stop rain. The lapwings were bouncing to earth in the gusts, waiting for some indistinguishable sign before, once again lifting themselves into the turbulent air.

Martin had been walking for an hour through the empty country lanes, but for the lapwings there was no one and nothing. He could feel the dampness of his rain-sodden clothes touching his chilled skin, his light summer-weight jacket no match for the driving rain and the grey French skies.

Martin estimated that he had at least another hour's walk in front of him. Just a few miles, which he could shorten by cutting across the fields, but which he had declined to do as the mud would slow him down. He stuck to the tarmac track. It would be dark soon. On such a moonless night, it would render him blind along the lonely road.

Martin thought of his earlier dry steps along the streets of Josselin. Standing in front of the antique shop, admiring the Roman statuette; a tourist souvenir with a broken lance, the shop owner had almost discarded it. House clearances always ended up with 'tat' that could be thrown out or put on display at a bargain price, someone might pay ten euros, a mere pittance in this day and age. The statuette had resided in the corner of the shop window, gathering dust for about a year. Shop owners had to be patient: trade was often brisk in the season and

Josselin was a tourist town. One statuette in the corner of the window did no harm. But it was Sunday and with heavy rain forecast, the streets were empty of tourists. Shopkeepers had all closed early, choosing to return home and plan for the summer trade.

Martin could not wait, he had come this far; tomorrow it could all be over. He punched the glass but it only flexed under the impact. He stood back, lifted his foot, and shoved his heel with as much strength as he could gather. The glass shattered, leaving an opening sufficiently large enough for him to insert his arm. Knocking to one side the antique diamond ring, with its four hundred euro price tag, he grasped the Roman soldier by the waist rammed it into his pocket and walked briskly away from the shop back to his rented car.

A few miles out of the medieval French town, a loud pop and jangling noise developed from the rear of the car. Standing beside the car, he felt the rain start to fall on his head. Martin looked at the punctured tyre; it gave a lopsided slant to the small Fiat 500. It was a car which gave the appearance that you could simply lift it up on its side and change the wheel without having to bend down. Martin had never been the technical sort, filling the screen washer would have been a challenge; a tyre was out of the question, even if he could lift the little car on its side. He started walking. The rain intensified, so did the wind; soon he was battling the elements which conspired against him.

The sun, hidden behind dark grey clouds, had now dropped below the horizon and the sky changed quickly towards the blackness of night. A starless night that would engulf the surrounding landscape. Before the darkness was complete, a single lamp came into view. It illuminated the door of La Belle Etoile, appearing so close he felt able to touch the yellow light. The weather offered no respite so Martin hurried to the door and rapped loudly on it with his cold fist. As the door opened, Martin felt the rush of heat and light almost overwhelm him. A tall figure blocked the way, his features lost in the shadows; his emotions could not be judged. For a moment both stood in silence, the visitor and inhabitant acting as though the other did not exist. Then the inhabitant asked,

"Do you have it?"

Martin did not speak. Instead he fumbled around in one of his deep sodden pockets for the statuette, pulled it from the clinging material and held it triumphantly aloft in the face of the inhabitant. Martin would have smiled had his lips not been so cold that they refused to move. Masculine hands took the statuette and examined it in the light that cascaded from the warm room, so tantalizingly close to Martin. "Very good Martin, it is just what I wanted, thank you." Phillip placed the statuette on a small table to the left of his front door. Martin watched and wondered if he would be invited in to share the warmth. He did not have to wait long to find out. From the table, Phillip picked up a long kitchen knife, its plain black handle sat comfortably in his large hand. In one sweeping movement the knife cut cleanly into Martin's neck. Simultaneously, a foot pushed into his chest, directing his crumpling body away from the door. Warm blood spurted from his neck, spraying away from the house, mixing in with the heavy rain. It did not take long, just a moment. Martin's exhausted legs gave way. His loosened head embedded itself into the thick mud. He lost consciousness and slipped into the arms of death.

THE CITY OF LONDON.

Helen Taylor stood outside the restaurant, nervously brushing down the imaginary creases on her newly dry cleaned navy business suit. She checked her reflection in the window. Her mole stood out below her high cheek bones. Over the years she had learnt to accept it, as she had her tall body with long legs that attracted the leering looks of men. She put her worries to one side, took a deep breath and walked in. The Thai restaurant was tucked away in one of those Dickensian lanes that were typical of the old city of London. Close to Cannon Street station, just a short walk from St Paul's, here you would be within just a stone's throw of tall bright modern offices. Buildings which appear to be made entirely out of glass, enabling the blocks to see themselves reflected in the mirror-like sides of their neighbours: vain buildings that wallowed in their own reflections. There were simple cubic office blocks close by others, more radical in shape: the Gherkin, the Walkie-Talkie, the Cheese Grater. Whatever their profile, all cast long shadows across the old cityscape. A cityscape with structures built centuries ago, now dwarfed amongst these Goliaths of the present day. However grand these new edifices looked, they did not hold the history or the wisdom of those older buildings. Livery halls, high spired churches that could boast historic celebrities, such as Dick Whittington amongst their congregations. These old buildings stood smugly within the forest of glass structures.

Helen was not often nervous. She normally had a confident air about her, that some said touched on arrogance. A young woman, she knew what she wanted. Here in this Thai restaurant with its fake furnishings, filled with be-suited businessmen, was the opportunity that she had been working towards. Her late father had been proud of her reaching Greenwich University, studying Modern English Literature and English Language. Communication and the written word were her first love. She could listen for hours, taking in what people were saying to her, sharing their experiences. Newspaper reporting was the only work she had ever wanted to do. Not long after leaving her studies she had secured a place on the Reading Observer. She quickly gained a reputation for incisive questions that encouraged controversial quotes, strong headlines and memorable stories.

She espied her lunch companion, wearing a white open-necked shirt, typing on his Blackberry phone, oblivious to the hustle and bustle around him. He looked just the same as the photograph she had seen on the website; research was a key weapon in the reporter's armoury. Mid-forties, with a smooth shaven angular jaw line, contrasting with his rounded dome of a head that was capped with longish, slightly wild, dark hair with grey appearing along the sides, like silver streaks. A colour that many women would have been happy to pay a small fortune for, he had it free of charge from nature. He was thinly built with long spider-like fingers tapping the phone keyboard; he looked up as he sensed her approach. His piercing blue eyes took her in and drew a conclusion in an instant.

"Helen, thanks for coming," he stood up, was a lot taller than she had imagined, and offered her his hand, which she shook.

"Pleased to meet you, Mr Mackintosh."

"It's Bruce, all my team call me Bruce, I hate being too formal."

He motioned for her to sit down and together they lunched. They talked about mundane current affairs, finding places to lunch in the City, as well as the merits of boot fairs, although Helen did not really understand how they managed to get on to that subject. That was the attraction of him, easy casual conversation that relaxed you, nothing that was contentious, and nothing that was solemn, just simple dialogue as they ate. Such a contrast to his reputation as a hard-nosed national newspaper editor.

Over coffee, he ordered a double espresso and Helen a skinny latte; Bruce moved the subject to the real purpose of his invitation.

"Helen Taylor, the daughter of Richard Taylor, who at one time worked for Barings?" She nodded in agreement, wondering why her father had been mentioned, "My father," he continued, "worked with your father for many years at Barings Bank, before my father took off and worked for Black Rock Investments. He always spoke very highly of your father, and said he taught him a lot about the banking business, the sorts of things that you just can't learn from books. You learn from experience, so when someone takes the time to share their experience with you, it builds a rather special friendship, a trusting friendship, built on mutual respect."

Helen had spent many an hour, as a young girl, sitting on her father's knee hearing him talk of the City of London, a city he loved, the integrity of bankers: doing business on the shake of a hand, honouring their word, understanding others and, in the end, making the best they could for their country. She had found it ironic, over the recent years, that the banking industry was now ridiculed and pilloried for the economic crisis that appeared in the UK. Maybe they were just the scapegoats this time, maybe the next time it would be another sector taking the blame; never the politicians, she thought.

"So when I received your letter and noticed your surname, I wondered about it. Did a little poking around, and found out you were indeed the daughter of Richard Taylor. I thought this might be an opportunity to repay the experience that your father shared with my father through their children; has a little synergy about it, don't you think? I now give you the wisdom of my experience and teach you things that books never could. That is assuming you are a good reporter. "

Helen looked at his eyes, wide open and full of enthusiasm with a kind of joy, as if he had found a long-lost sister,

"My father never mentioned your father that I recall. Of course, I know who you are, otherwise I wouldn't have written to you in the first place. This connection I honestly had no knowledge of at all."

"I guess your father would have nurtured and taken under his wing countless young bankers. Although he must have had you later in life, my father couldn't wait to start a family. I was one of five; well the first of five to be precise. Three boys came along first followed by two girls, which put paid to handing down clothes and football boots," he laughed, a warm laugh that endeared him to her.

"I was the younger of two girls," Helen contributed, "my father was a lot older than my mother, well ten years, but she was always considered to be old for her age. It is nice to hear you talk about my father with such kindness."

Helen held fond memories of her father, even though he was considered to be a 'weekend father'. He would spend most of his working week in the City, staying overnight in his small flat in Kensington. Every weekend, he would be home with his family, beside his two daughters; riding or walking across lush green fields, giving them financial advice and ribbing them about the fashions they wore. Then Monday morning arrived and he would return to his city life. Helen knew how unhappy her mother was, yet it was a subject that was never openly discussed. Mother had Harry to look after the garden and do odd jobs around their period manor house. Then there was Florence, a middle-aged Italian, who cooked and cleaned the home, enduring constant snipes from Mother, all of which seemed to just roll off Florence's slightly arched back.

"Can I just add," he interjected, "I was devastated when I heard what happened to your mother, it must have been such a shock for you."

"Thank you, but it has been many years since the accident."

"Even so, you would only have been a young girl when she died. How old were you exactly?"

Helen faltered, that sounded like a question a reporter would ask during the early stages of an interview, and Bruce was no ordinary reporter. Cautiously she answered,

"Twelve years old."

He nodded, "I know your father was devastated. At least that was what my father told me after the funeral. But being alone in the house with her when it happened, it must have been a terrible shock for a twelve-year-old girl who loved her mother?"

Another question; concern was welling up in Helen's mind. Was he really being generous inviting her to lunch on the strength of a speculative letter she had sent him asking for a job? Or was this something else? A manoeuvre to uncover more about her mother's death. Did he have doubts about the accident? Did he have new facts? She felt her palms dampen,

"It was a long time ago, but the memories are still very painful to me, as I'm sure you will understand. Could we change the subject?"

"Of course. I'm sorry for being a little blunt; journalists like us are naturally forward with our questions. So back to the reason we are here. Not looking at the past, but looking to the future. Although I will be taking you under my wing, I would rather you kept the fact that our fathers knew each other just between us. People will consider that I am doing you a favour, which I suppose I am, but I have seen the way you write and the way you handle stories so I am doing this for the benefit of my paper; my motives are purely selfish." He smiled, finished his coffee and continued, "So starting Monday, you'll be on some basic feature writing to begin with. Interesting, still important, no hard news as yet, which I know you are itching to get on to. I like my reporters to work up to hard news, to know just about every aspect of the paper first. That will give you a good foundation, plus, when you are on hard news, you know who does what and when at the paper, those who will help you through a story and who will drop you right in it."

"Starting Monday? Are you offering me an actual job?" Helen was enthused and relaxed as the subject had moved away from her mother.

"Well of course, I'm an editor of a national newspaper, I only do HR work on very special occasions, and you Miss Taylor, are one of those special occasions. So yes, you start Monday."

Maybe he was doing her a special favour. Part of her wanted to be proud and say that she secured the job because of her skills. Others, if they knew of the connection, would jibe her that it was only because of her father she was now being offered a post on the Daily Mirror. Either way, Helen did not care, this is what she wanted. Even if it was a favour, similar favours were being offered and taken across the city all the time. For Helen Taylor, this was her big opportunity and she was taking it, she had no concern about what anyone thought. The words of her father that came back to her were: "Dreams are the destinations that we plan to travel to." She hoped that her father was watching her now. He would have been so proud.

"I do need to give four weeks' notice," she added as a caveat.

"Helen," he leaned forward, held her hand in a fatherly sort of way, "you must know just how much of a small family journalism is, and a very close knit family at that. Your boss, Terry, we did our time on the same local paper. He was upset that I was going to steal one of his best reporters, but he still saw the bigger picture and there is just one condition attached to you starting next Monday, that is you plan your leaving do this

Friday, come what may, and buy him a double malt whisky. I thought that was a small price to pay. Welcome to the Daily Mirror!"

"Did he also tell you that I am away in France the week after next? I'm meeting an old friend from University that I haven't seen for a while. I can reschedule, see her later in the year," as the words left her lips, Helen regretted mentioning it, she should have just cancelled her leave, what was she thinking?

He interrupted her, "no problem at all Helen, I guess you have flights or ferries booked. Some things are worth waiting for, and I sense that you are one of those special reporters who come along once in a while, I can wait a week or two." Then he hesitated, thought for a moment, "I have an even better idea. Start Monday, spend a few days getting to know people and then off to France. Danny, our larger-than-life news editor, has been looking to do a feature on the retired English living in France. So perfect, that can be your first assignment. I'll tell Danny to arrange things."

LA BELLE ETOILE.

The following morning the hazy winter sun shone across the landscape, beginning its task of drying the French undergrowth and warming the land. Phillip had also risen early, excitement had interfered with his sleep, he had decided to rise soon after the sun and begin his day of activity. First would be breakfast, no day should start without breakfast. Time to reflect on what the day ahead might bring and what should be achieved during the daylight hours that were to follow. He breakfasted today on black coffee, brioche and myrtille confiture, it was a celebration breakfast. Before him stood the Roman Centurion that had been delivered last night. To an outsider, it still looked like a cheap tourist gift, yet in the deep blue eyes of Phillip it was more, so much more, a symbol of achievement, of ingenuity and not to put too fine a point on it, brilliance, that would have been how Phillip would have described it. For now, he just paid homage to his new craven idol. Once he had completed consuming his brioche, he stood, gathered the statuette in his clean hands then walked across the room towards the large fireplace. Once it had been an open fireplace, now it was home to a wood burning fire, which warmed the whole house with a dry, comforting heat. Above the wood burner, was a large black wooden beam that so often characterized period fireplaces in Brittany. It provided not only a cross member for the chimney, it also acted as a mantelpiece, upon which artefacts and souvenirs could be placed. Here Phillip placed carefully his latest trophy, adjusting the angle to which the centurion looked. He had decided that the Roman soldier should look slightly to his left, out of the window to keep watch on any strangers that might approach the house; not that anyone ever did visit. Keeping watch, Roman centurions were good at that, they were good at fighting as well; Phillip recalled that history was never a subject that greatly inspired him at school.

Phillip took a step back to admire his latest acquisition. Then ran his wide eyes over the other items on the mantelpiece. The statuette was the fourth item on the dark wooden beam. To the left, was a die-cast model of a London bus, a Routemaster, red and full of the scratches and marks that were made whilst the owner of the bus played with it during their childhood. The destination could still be seen, as could the route number, a 53 going to Piccadilly. That was something he had always meant to do, find out if the route 53 bus did in fact go to Piccadilly, he hoped it did. It would have been very cruel of the toy manufacturer to lead children to believe the 53 went to Piccadilly, when it might not have done. What if some poor child had jumped on a real 53 Routemaster bus, hoping to go to see Eros, then ended up goodness knows where, Ponders End? Which is a strange name in itself, the end of pondering, or just where all ponders end up. Sometimes Phillip thought of too many questions that always seemed to lead him to other questions. It was just such behaviour that made him stand out for the wrong reasons at university. Too many questions most of them awkward and difficult to answer, so his teachers dismissed them as stupid questions. Phillip never believed that any question could be stupid; it was just not all the answers had yet been thought of, or found. Teachers only ever wanted to hear the questions that they had the answers to, anything else was silly and stupid, and that was because, in Phillip's opinion, they had such limited knowledge. They had only learnt facts, parrot-fashion, which they then passed on to their pupils, imagination and invention were not elements that they would encourage. He picked up the Routemaster bus and caressed it in his hands.

Hands that were hardening, by working on his small holding, growing vegetables, keeping pigs and chickens, real toil. Working with nature and the spirits of the land to live, not like bus driving he thought. The city from which he had once earned a living held no hold over him, his life now totally immersed in the French countryside was all that he needed. Turning the bus over, he read the manufacturer's details, Matchbox. Now although he was not into history, he did recall that the original Matchbox toys were packaged in what looked to be matchboxes. Which again concerned him, that this manufacturer was encouraging young children to become comfortable with matchboxes. He wondered how many young children had opened a real matchbox, taking out the matches only to find out as they burnt their fingers or worse, that matchboxes were not real toys. Misdirecting children seemed to be the way this manufacturer played things. Maybe they had a dislike of children, maybe it was a 1950s government experiment, to confuse children. The 53 not going to Piccadilly, matchboxes that did not contain small die cast cars. He wondered how many times the public at large were misdirected and poorly guided by those who put themselves in charge.

He replaced the bus with precision to the exact spot that it had previously occupied. He remembered last night and Martin needed to be dealt with. He would still be stiff, hopefully no wild animal had started taking chunks out of him or had tried to drag him away. Phillip opened the door of his house, the early morning sunlight cascaded into the room behind, exposing every corner to intense light and just a hint of warmth.

From the doorway you could see the whole valley spread out before you, with the small single track road leading upwards to the lone house that stood on the ridge of the valley. Amongst the trees, coppices and farms that occupied the valley, the occasional white painted house could be seen, way off in the distance.

Phillip had not wanted to inherit anything at all from his parents, not the tall slim body, which he had inherited from his mother, or the angular jaw and prominent nose from his father's face, some things you could not control however much you wanted to. Yet Phillip had controlled Martin, who was lying as he had fallen last night, clothes wet and a dark patch of blood-soaked soil lying next to his head.

Martin, lying as he was on the ground, might be just visible to someone with a powerful pair of binoculars who had the urge to look up to the stone house that stood at the top of the valley. Phillip doubted that any of his French neighbours, none of whom he knew or encouraged to know him, would be bothered very much about an eccentric Englishman. They had their own lives to follow, although he did not doubt that he was mentioned in casual conversations from time to time. On the rare visits that he made to the village, his arrival would have been greeted by an inquisitive "Bonjour." Most of the local villagers that he had to have contact with, did not ask too many questions. They just let him get on with his life, which was what he liked about living here, he could live his own life and ask his own questions.

He pulled the stiff and rigid body of Martin towards the pig pen, dragging him across the wet grass. Then he set about removing the damp and dirty clothes from the body; the six pigs huddled in the corner of the large pen expectant and excited as to what was happening. Outside the pen, there was now a pile of clothes and inside the naked body of Martin, face down in the mire, his hands spread outwards and his legs making the figure four. The pigs edged forward with caution towards the naked trespasser to their territory. Phillip returned, pulled on the cord of the chainsaw, which burst into life with a high pitched buzz that scared the pigs back to the safety of their corner.

There was no skill needed to dismember the body with a petrol chainsaw. First a cut to the left knee, then the right knee, the amputated shins and feet were picked up without ceremony and thrown in the direction of the pigs who at first scattered as the limbs bumped in the sodden mixture of soils and faeces, before they cautiously edged back to the limbs, only to race away as a complete arm landed amongst them. This backwards and forwards movements of the pigs continued as body parts landed close to them, half an arm, a torso split into three parts, a head cut vertically, the brain matter splashing onto one now, not so brave, pig. Then there was silence as the chainsaw stopped and the tall man, who the pigs knew to fear, left. They could safely explore the food that had been left for them, the first such food they had had all week, today they would be happy to eat anything and everything.

Phillip knelt down beside Martin's discarded clothes and went through each pocket with care, exploring every corner that might conceal an item. Once thoroughly explored, the vestments were cast to one side in a pile. A wallet, a few credit cards, two ten pound notes, a hire car receipt and a Ryanair boarding card, nothing that could not be burnt there, so everything, even the cash was added to the pile of muddy rags ready to be incinerated. There was a large black car key with a Hertz logo on the key fob, so where was the car? Clearly Martin walked the last part of his journey. Phillip would need to take a trip through the village and the surrounding main roads, which would be a prudent task, to see just how close the car had got to his house. Car keys were put to one side. Next time he would need to instruct his victim to rendezvous somewhere away from his house. Phillip felt fortunate that Martin had not arrived last night in his hire car, that would have created a small problem of how to get the car away from his house, not an insurmountable problem, just part of the learning that Phillip enjoyed. Some loose change, a packet of sugar-free Polo mints and finally a pen, not much to bring abroad with you. Martin had a mission to accomplish, thought Phillip, with a wry smile on his face. A splash of petrol and a match marked the end of the clothes as they burst into flames. So, just a car key and a pair of shoes, shoes never burn well, but can be disposed of easily in the local charity recycling bin.

It was now time for Phillip's morning shower and this morning he needed it more than ever. Small fragments of bone and shreds of flesh were in his hair, peppered over his face; his working clothes were similarly adorned with remnants of the morning's labour. Phillip simply stood beside the smoky pyre and removed every item of his clothing, dropping each on to the flames until his naked body could feel the heat radiating from the bonfire. He turned and walked into the house, dropped the shoes beside the front door; the keys he deposited on the small table by the door. He continued towards the back of the house and walked into the shower, turned on the taps and felt the cleaning energy of the water flood over his body. Twenty five minutes later, he turned off the taps and began to dry his now thoroughly cleaned and rejuvenated body. Once dried, he applied moisturizer to almost every part that he could easily reach, then followed this with a dusting of talcum powder to prevent any chaffing, and finally a spray of antiperspirant. This strict regime had kept his skin supple, soft, and showing no signs of the ageing, which he would have expected as he was just about to enter his thirty-eighth year.

It was not long before he once again stopped in front of the mantelpiece and picked up the item to the left of the bus: a Lladro dancing horse. His mother had once owned one that she kept in a glass cabinet full of Lladro figures, but it was the dancing horse that always caught his attention. The galloping stance had convinced his young mind that the horse was getting ready to escape, burst through the glass and make a dash for the fields that surrounded his childhood home. He used to stare for hours at that horse, admiring its continued readiness to escape the confines of the pottery cabinet. As a child, Phillip too had wanted to escape, but unlike the horse, he would need more than a field to survive in. So he stayed, as any five-year-old would, and used his imagination to take him wherever he wanted to go.

Carefully, Phillip placed the horse back on the mantelpiece, and for the first time that morning, he spoke out loud. There was no living audience for his words, yet he knew that the trophies in front of him could hear him and take them in. "Ben, you did very well to get the horse to me in one piece, considering how clumsy you were." He turned away from the fireplace, ignoring the small Ninja Turtle toy with its dark memories. "Enough reminiscing, I have duties to do before lunch, and then to look for an abandoned hire car after it."

Lunch was simple and repeated each day. Phillip sat down at the table, a plate in front of him, with a single knife and a clean paper napkin. In the centre of the table were three other plates: the first held four slices of cheese, Emmental, neatly arranged on it, the second had two slices of ham, smoked with no rind or fat, the final plate had two quarters of a baguette. He took one quarter baguette, cut it in half across its length, placed one slice of cheese on the bread, followed by one slice of ham, neatly folded so that it would fit within the confines of the baguette, and finally, one more slice of cheese, then he closed the baguette around it and ate his creation. Once consumed the pattern was repeated with the second quarter baguette. All was washed down with a glass of water. Once each week there was an exception to this daily luncheon arrangement, due to the simple fact that one baguette lasted two days, therefore he bought three baguettes each week, which would last six days, but if he had bought the fourth baguette, he would have half a baguette left over at the end of the week. It did not sit well with his psyche to carry half a baguette over into the next week, so on Sunday, he had the cheeses and the ham as normal, but he replaced the bread part of the lunch with a dry cracker, which seemed to be a sensible sacrifice to make on such a religious day as Sunday.

Once lunch had been consumed and the utensils washed, dried and returned to their respective places in the kitchen cupboards, he left. Carefully Phillip locked the house door behind him, noticing that he should find some time to give it another coat of varnish. He eased himself into his silver-grey Land Rover Discovery and drove towards the village.

The sun was low casting long shadows in the winter afternoon, the blue sky had just a few hazy clouds traversing it. The surrounding fields were quiet and green; the crops that had been planted remained small and close to the ground, waiting till spring to burst forth. Soon these unobtrusive fields would be full of lush crops. Crops the farmers judged to be worth planting this year; the ones that would fetch the best price. Traffic was just about non-existent, as it was for most of the year. July would bring more traffic in the shape of tourists from around Europe, as well as a large contingent of French nationals touring and visiting the historic sights of Brittany. As he drove in the direction of Josselin where Martin would have come from, looking along the lanes for a parked or abandoned hire car, it only then occurred to Phillip that the statuette was not wrapped, it still had its ten euro price sticker on the underside of the base. Martin must have stolen the item from the shop, he couldn't have paid for it as it would at least have been carefully wrapped as any decent French gift shop would. Martin stealing the Roman Centurion, that thought, if true, added even more value to the piece. He smiled at the thought of Martin, sweet, good-as-gold Martin, actually stealing something, breaking the law, if only his friends could have seen him they would have been horrified.

He saw the Fiat 500, a small white car ahead of him, he lifted off the accelerator. It looked just like any hire car, clean, small and impractical for country life. It had been left leaning slightly into the ditch that ran alongside the road. Not that it was trapped in the ditch, just parked on the downward slope. He pressed the key remote he had found in Martin's pocket, the indicator lights flashed back in response, alongside a brief bleep, clearly that was the car. The shredded back wheel was testament as to why Martin had ended up walking the remainder of the way. At least the car was far enough away from Martin's final destination to avoid any direct link. Phillip continued on, taking a wide circular route back to his home. Driving, heater up full, the windows open, a cold breeze ruffling his hair, country odours of all descriptions filling his nostrils; he felt good. He speculated about the next time; who it might be and what he wanted from them; there was just as much fun in the planning as there was in the execution.

DEPTFORD.

Before Greg had sat down at his cluttered desk, he heard his name being called from across the open office, "Morning Greg! Throwing away a two-nil lead is getting to be a habit for Millwall! Lucky for you it was just a friendly."

Dean strolled towards Greg, a broad smile over his face.

Greg considered himself to be a lapsed member of the Millwall fan club, but even so, Tottenham fan Dean, could not resist rubbing last night's disastrous result into Greg's tired looking face. "I will be the first to admit the Lions defence is not as strong as it should be, but they're still young and lots to learn."

"Still three possible points down the drain," Dean dropped some messages in front of Greg's PC and walked off. "By the way, did you see Tottenham have gone top?" he smugly informed Greg.

Greg ignored the comment, powered up his PC and glanced through the yellow post-it notes. 'See Mike as soon as you get in.' that one sounded important. Mike, the Editor of the Deptford Chronicle, did not often summon any of his reporters in such a way. The normal procedure would be hearing your name being bellowed from his office. Greg was not the most popular reporter on the paper but he was the longest-serving. He started as a trainee and now fifteen years later, he was a senior reporter. Greg looked around the open plan office; just a couple of reporters were at their desks. Further away, the sales department were busy selling advertising space, a hive of activity, so different to the emptiness of the editorial desks, where just a couple of reporters lazily typed away at grimy keyboards. Yesterday most reporters had worked late to finish the weekly paper, today it was being printed and tomorrow it would be out on the streets. Today was down time for the journalists, so it surprised Greg that the editor was even in his office at this hour.

"Come in Greg, grab a seat."

"You wanted to see me?"

The office was neat, tidy, almost spotless, just a few sheets of A4 paper lay on the polished desk. Greg always thought it strange that an Editor should have such a tidy office. The previous three editors that Greg had worked under, seemed to have prided themselves on the apparent chaos that existed within their office space, piles of documents, newspapers, coffee cups everywhere and for one of them, a constant haze of cigarette smoke had hung in the air.

"Greg, you have been here at the Deptford Chronicle for fifteen years now and I know you well, after having worked with you for, what is it, five years. But as I look around all my reporters, for each of them I can name two or three good solid stories they have uncovered that stand out from the crowd. Good solid front page stories that make the public sit up and think, telling them like it is, stirring their emotions, that's what strong stories do. They start the debates across the dinner table, along the bars of local pubs; are the cause of discussion across countless works canteens. I look back at your work and I see nothing remotely close to a good front-page story." Mike paused, seeing if there was going to be a reaction from Greg, he guessed there would not be. Reporters listen, use the silence between people to let those with a loose tongue rush in and fill the void with a comment that can make a story.

"I know you can write well. I know you are a very able reporter. You fit in well with the whole team, but a good solid front-page byline for you, I have yet to see. Filler stories, short features, and then there are the suicides."

'Here we go,' Greg thought, 'bad news is coming'. He knew that if Mike repeatedly used the same phrase whilst talking, he was nervous and about to deliver bad news. Greg did not take well to any one saying that what he wrote was a waste of time. He listened camouflaging the anger that was welling up inside him.

"Your obsession on discovering the motives for suicides, digging deep often inappropriately for the reasons. Even when there is a suicide note you are still off like a hunting dog, sniffing out and tracking down a theory that to everyone else does not exist."

Greg interrupted, "Things are not always as they seem. I question the facts like any good reporter," Mike ignored his comment, so he continued, "they are questions that need to be asked."

"Let me give you an example of you overstepping the mark. Last year, the guy who walked into the Thames, the suicide; ring any bells? You questioned that one from every angle. Even the coroner has rung up and asked me just why you have such an intense interest in suicides."

"In my defence," Greg retaliated, "there was no suicide note; that odd scrap of paper that seems to rubber stamp the death and clear everyone's conscience of the real tragedy that has happened. So this one, as I said, no suicide note. He was well-off with no money worries, in a stable loving relationship, not a hint or sign of depression, which is, once again, another social sign of suicide, not a hint of anything that would suggest he would get up one morning and just walk into the Thames. If he is lucky, he might get a misadventure verdict, then at least his partner might get his mortgage paid off. People just don't walk into the Thames unless they are totally pissed, with alcohol that is, not pissed off, and then it is often the case that they just fall asleep on the foreshore and the tide consumes them. This young man was seen just walking straight into the water and just did not stop until he was halfway across and dead. It was no suicide!"

"There is not a story there. Why couldn't he have had a row with his boyfriend that morning and just decided enough was enough?" Mike asked.

"Because people do not just kill themselves on the spur of the moment; it is really that simple, Mike. So for those who did not plan to kill themselves, I like to see their story being told as it should." Greg no longer hid the anger from his voice.

"Well you might have that interest but I certainly do not and I doubt that many of our readers have either. People taking their own lives, suicide or otherwise, does not sit well on the pages of a local paper. You are no use to me Greg unless you are contributing to the paper, making a real contribution and filling those pages along with everyone else. At the moment you are just a hanger-on and living off the hard work of other reporters."

Greg leaned forward on his chair; there was now a realization of where this conversation was going. "At least I believe in those readers, and I still believe the reason I, no change that I don't just believe, I know that when I write a story I am writing it on behalf of the person whose voice cannot be heard above all those clamouring for attention. The little old lady with condensation running down her mildew-stained walls, who the council is ignoring, I speak for her! The single mother, robbed of the benefits that are rightfully hers, by a nonchalant state, I speak for her! Then I police those politicians who have bellicose voices that tell us what to do; councillors who take advantage of their position, maybe by claiming excessive expenses, maybe taking the odd bribe here and there, I police those places for all my readers! Then not forgetting those who have found the need to take their own life, I speak for them when they have no voice at all. So when I stand up and speak for those who have committed suicide, even though you have not the slightest understanding why anyone would, I am just doing exactly what I signed up for when I became a reporter, which you should have signed up for when you were a reporter. But that's all changed now, all your golden boys and girls out there, being very politically correct, reporting the right stories."

"Greg, .." Mike tried to interrupt as Greg's voice grew louder with anger.

"And you sitting in your executive suite like a fucking lord of the manor. Your only concern is that the accountants are happy with a bottom line and we are making money for the faceless shareholders. It's revenue and not rocking the boat that you worry about. Not the moral value or the moral power of the stories that fill the pages of the Deptford Chronicle, just the fucking financial value."

"Maybe you should have worked more with those old ladies and corrupt councillors, then I would not be asking you to pack up and go."

"If I did exactly as you asked," Greg pointed his finger at his editor, "I might well have a job, but I don't really want to work for a paper whose only priority for news is how much profit there is in the story? You lead an impotent paper, which for me shows no respect for the history of this great campaigning paper."

"I'm not sitting around here arguing with you all day, I do not have the time or the inclination. I don't want you around anymore Greg; I'm letting you go. You will be paid your notice and any holiday pay that we owe, but I don't want to see you in the office again after this meeting. Collect your stuff and go."

Greg stood up abruptly, his chair tumbling onto the floor, the abrupt movement caused Mike to shrink back into his chair, his eyes showing a hint of fear.

"Clearly you had already made up your mind, or the accountants have made it up for you, that suits me. Fuck you! Fuck the accountants! Fuck the shareholders!"

"There is nothing more to say Greg, you maybe were once a good reporter, you had your chances but this is the end of the road."

Greg turned and walked out of the office, "Bollocks!" he shouted to no one in particular.

As he returned to the open plan office, he sensed the two reporters looking at him, then the sounds of the busy side of the office occupied his hearing: telephones ringing, chatter of several people talking at the same time holding different conversations, keyboards being stabbed with fingers. Greg wondered when he might hear those sounds again as he walked over to his desk to collect his possessions. He could feel eyes, that he hoped were sympathetic, following him across the open office. As the final page turned closing this chapter in his life, he pondered on what lay ahead.

BROCKLEY.

Beverley Court, sandwiched between two declining areas, only held onto its own dignity thanks to the fact it was close to the green grassy slopes of Hilly Fields. This helped it maintain a value that set its residents apart. Not far apart, but at least it still had some sensible landlords, who having bought their flat in the eighties as an investment, continued to look after that investment being selective in their choice of residents. There were still a few professionals, or at least people who held down a job, that enabled them to pay the rent without the need to fall back onto the Welfare State to help them; it was a 'No benefits' type of block. Now only three people had actually bought their flat with a mortgage and lived in their own property, one of which was Greg, who now sat in his second floor flat, holding a lukewarm beer and wondering what he was going to do now his income had been severed.

You can be brave and bellicose, he thought, stand up for your principles, argue and debate with those around you for the right to have an opinion. Which is all well and good in a wine bar or over dinner with friends, who at the end you buy another round for, or serve the Crème Brulee and get on with your life pretty much as you did before standing up for your principles. It is another thing altogether when the person you are disagreeing with has the power to change your life by simply removing your main source of income at a stroke. Standing up for your principles in this situation means that you cannot get on with your life pretty much as you did before, from this moment on things will never be the same. Greg sat, lukewarm beer in hand, knowing that he did not know where the next few months or years might end. His ex-employers had given him a lump sum, plus his notice, plus his outstanding annual leave. The lump sum was on condition he agreed to leave. It was not a huge sum, but it would last him about three months, giving him time to decide what to do next. Some of his more legally-minded friends said that he should take them to an employment tribunal to fight for his rights; they could not just eject him like that even though he had agreed to go. But he had already stood up for his principles, and no amount of tribunals would get his job back. Well maybe they could, but did he want to go back there? Maybe not. Maybe just walk away and get on with life, wherever that might take him. Tonight, with so many maybes hanging over his head, he knew for certain that life was taking him to the Fox and Hounds in Lewisham, where he was holding his leaving do, well he guessed that it might be more of a wake, as he doubted that many of his colleagues would turn up, so he had taken the sensible precaution of inviting a few regular friends to bolster numbers.

The Fox and Hounds stood opposite Lewisham fire station. A pub which started life back in the early 1900s, it had been built to resemble an Elizabethan coaching inn, complete with half-timber exterior and low internal beams. When a 1960s fire station arrived opposite, it became the regular watering hole for off duty firemen, quenching their scorched throats after their shifts. That was how Greg started using the public bar of the Fox and Hounds for work on a regular basis, it was a hot bed of stories and gossip. Greg could sit there all night buying rounds and being bought drinks in return, all expenses paid. Once he had moved to Beverley Court, it was only a twenty minute walk away, so it quickly became his local, visiting three or four times a week until closing time and beyond, depending who was in the bar. That was back in the good old days, when those locked in the bar after closing time were mostly firemen, police officers and reporters, with just a couple of regular public drinkers. The police had joined them from the Victorian police station that stood on the next corner, and the mix of public services caused many a night of good banter, a few very rough arguments that on three occasions had turned into a full blown bar-room brawl. Yet, above all this, Greg got story after story and enjoyed every moment of it.

Then came the onset of political correctness, officers were moved around, and slowly things changed. Just a few die hard old-school drinkers remained trying to stem the tide of correctness that was sweeping the emergency services. So it was that in the 1990s the landlord moved on and then the new ones (two young men from the city) started an on-the-premises brewery: novel, interesting, but too expensive for the local population, so the landlords looked for and encouraged new clients to frequent the bar. Almost overnight it became a gay bar, with a new breed of drinker lining it. Greg, being one to stand by his principles, had no intention of moving out of his local and the beer was very good, albeit a little on the pricey side, but he was still on expenses so he stayed and befriended a whole new range of friends.

A lot of his friends and colleagues thought he was a bit strange to continue drinking at the Fox and Hounds, now that it was well known to be a gay bar. He suspected that a few of his work colleagues suspected him of being homosexual, not that that bothered him, they could think what they wanted. To those honest enough to ask the question, 'So you go to a gay bar; are you gay?' Greg would reply, 'You shop at the co-op; do you vote Labour?' Which was especially satisfying if he knew they were staunch Tory voters.

There were a just a couple of attendees sitting with Greg at the small round table at the Fox and Hounds. The atmosphere at the pedestal table was morbid and silent. Harry, a trainee reporter just out of his teens, knew of Greg's reputation, but had decided that he would come along tonight anyway, just for the experience of being in a gay pub. He thought of it as part of his training, so had collected the receipt for his round, with the express intention of claiming the cost back on his expenses. Donna sat close to Greg. She was attractive, and she made it obvious that she was attracted to Greg and wanted to go out with him. For Greg, it was not that he found her unattractive, it was just he did not go out with women.

"You would have thought that a couple of your fellow reporters would have come along for at least one drink; after all you have worked at the Deptford Chronicle for over fifteen years," Donna pointed out.

"Donna, thank you for pointing out that I have wasted the last fifteen years working with a bunch of self-centred wankers, but that is often the case with reporters." Greg gulped down his scotch and soda in one.

"When I started," Harry chimed in," everyone said you were a great reporter, top class and liked. Of course they mentioned your obsession with suicides, but everyone needs a specialist subject."

"Did I mention two-faced as well?" Greg added for his own satisfaction, "that's another trait of a reporter eager to climb the editorial ladder."

"You are just upset at being made redundant. Then being the man you are, kind and sensitive, you put on this macho persona." Donna stroked his arm sympathetically.

"Donna you are talking crap; it might sound like being made redundant but I was sacked. No one wants to admit that I was sacked because I am the only person willing to stand up and ask awkward questions when someone commits suicide. Question the reasons it ever happens. Young men are the most likely to commit suicide....."

"A whole generation is being blighted. Yes you have told us before," Harry added.

Donna glared at young Harry, with a look of 'don't push too many of Greg's buttons, he is not in the mood for jokes'.

Greg held up his empty glass, "I need a refill, same again?" Without waiting for an answer; he pulled away from Donna's caressing hands and strode towards the busy bar.

Donna leaned forward towards young Harry and explained her glare in case there was any confusion arising, "Tonight is not the night to wind him up, Greg is sweet, but he does have a temper on him. Let's move away from suicides and talk about football shall we?"

"Come on Donna, you have to admit, he does have an unhealthy obsession with suicides, everyone says so, yet no one knows why, or at least are not telling. You're good friends with him, do you know why?"

Donna emptied her half of cider and looked towards the bar to ensure Greg was still waiting to be served, "This is not for public consumption or to be spread around the office; I will kill you if this gets out," the look in Donna's eyes made Harry sure that her comment was not a joke, "his sister committed suicide when she was in her teens. There was no reason given, just a supposition it was the pressure of exams. I guess Greg has never really got over it. I can't imagine one of my brothers or sisters killing themselves. I am sure he blames himself somehow for what happened. Maybe he thinks he could have done more, seen signs of what she planned to do"

"Did he tell you that?"

"No, I found it out when looking through some news stories on line. Don't ask me to explain; just accept it and don't mention it to anyone."

"How did she kill herself, overdose?"

Donna gave the young reporter a glaring look, but before she could answer, another voice joined the conversation.

"What's this? A conspiracy?" Standing above them both, was a tall man. "Mind if I join you, I hear that Greg has left the Deptford Chronicle."

"They say redundant, Greg will tell you sacked," Harry explained to the stranger.

"That's sounds just like Greg; mind if I sit?"

The tall stranger, was Edward, a regular at the Fox and Hounds. Edward was in his forties, his grey hair brushed back from his rounded face showing the cleft on his chin. His face was tanned and exhibited just light fashionable stubble. Dressed in an open necked short sleeved shirt with jeans, he was smart with an air of confidence about him, but in his brown eyes were streaks of sadness.

Greg returned, his hands wrapped around three glasses damp with condensation.

"Edward, welcome to the wake. Drink?" Greg noticed an unusual sad tint in Edward's eyes.

"No thanks, I'm fully topped up. I hear that you might have some time on your hands, maybe I can ask a favour of you?"

"Fire away Edward, time is something I have plenty of now."

Edward lubricated his dry throat before starting:

"My partner, Martin, has left me; walked out, no note, no reason. I just got home last Thursday and Martin was not there. I waited until about ten. that night, having called his mobile a few times, before I got really worried. I then called our friends, my friends, his friends, none of them had heard from him. I looked around the apartment, he had taken nothing that he treasured; hadn't taken any clothes or a suitcase; the only thing I found to be missing was his passport. I called the police, and they were not interested in the least. As far as they were concerned he was an adult so could do whatever he liked until there was a body or something, they were not interested at all. So I have been out of my mind over the last week. Then, this morning our credit card statement came in, there was a charge for Ryanair. Of course I got onto them and asked about it and it would seem that he purchased a single ticket to Dinard in France. I just don't understand, he has never been to France in his life, save for a couple of duty free shopping day trips."

"Did you get back to the police?" Harry asked.

"Yes, I went back earlier today and they seemed to be even less interested now. I cannot imagine why he would have just walked out, flown to France without so much as a word, then nothing since. It has been over a week now. I know you are a good investigative reporter, and I know tonight is your leaving drink following your move from the Deptford Chronicle but I am happy to pay you, if you could find him for me. If he doesn't want to come back, that's fine; I just want to know that he is safe."

"I'm sorry," Greg responded, "I really don't think that I would be any good or help in that sort of investigation, but I'm sure you'll find someone to help you."

"Don't be stupid," Donna interrupted, "you've got time, you can dig out stories. Edward is asking for help, of course you can help him."

"Donna, what do I know about the French system? I can hardly speak French, missing persons is not what I do."

Even though Greg thought he was being firm, Donna could be very persuasive. The next day he found himself sitting on a plane taking off from Stansted for the French airport of Dinard, not really having any idea what or how he would find Martin, the missing boyfriend.

Last night in the Fox and Hounds Greg, putting aside the fact that he was not good at finding people, knew that lovers do have arguments, both gay and heterosexual, so, to a point and for most of the conversation, he was squarely taking the police point of view. Martin was an adult, so unless there was any evidence to the contrary, there was nothing to look into. If Martin wanted to contact Edward he would have done. Donna was not surprised at Greg's bluntness, she had seen that side of him before. Even when it was clear from the credit card statement that Martin had hired a car, Greg was still on the side of the police. As Edward, his voice wavering at times as emotion invaded his words, continued to plead with Greg, who was not fully paying attention. Greg's mind was beginning to turn to the problem of leaving the pub at the end of the evening without Donna either hanging on to his arm or shirt tails, or simply just following him at a safe distance.

It was when Edward described the vast excess charge that had been made by the hire company to cover the cost of recovering the car. They had charged for staff time for making the inquiries to find the car as well as the cost of collecting it, even though it was undamaged, it was a totally randomly large figure.

It was at that point that Greg forgot about Donna, "Abandoned the car you say?"

"Well, they told me it had a puncture, they even charged me for that, twenty-five euros would you believe. Well of course Martin would have left it; he would have not been able to drive the sodding thing; bloody French, just making money out of tourists."

It was then that Greg took a different view to the police. If your hire car develops a puncture, then you call the breakdown service that they all have, he reasoned. You do not just leave it beside the road, unless someone came to pick you up, but then why hire the car in the first place? Greg wanted to know a little more about the events leading up to the point when Martin just abandoned the hire car beside the road; as well as the practical question of what rate of pay Edward was thinking of.

BRITTANY, FRANCE.

Greg felt the surge of the Boeing 737-800 aircraft as it powered along the Stansted runway, building up speed to lift off and reach into the dull-grey cloudy sky that monotonously hung above the Essex airport. This was the moment when Greg's fear of flying realised itself through wet sweaty palms tightly gripping the armrests, his heart beating rapidly forcing his adrenaline-filled blood around his ever fearful body. All the while his brain grappling with the conundrum as to just how this heavy, lumbering mix of metals, plastic and humans was ever going to somehow lift off the rumbling runway. Greg had flown before so he knew, moments after he felt the plane tip back slightly, his stomach would jump as it lifted up. The wheels now turned silently as the plane rose up in to the sky. Somehow he could never fully believe the explanation that air pressure alone held this great weight, of which he was now a part, in the void of the sky. There just had to be another reason; another force exerting itself, maybe the willpower of all the passengers, praying it would take off and once there, stay there.

As everyone fully expected and hoped, the Boeing lifted off the concrete runway, packed away its undercarriage, banked right, ever climbing into the sky of broken clouds as it made its way to Dinard in Northern France. Then inevitably comes that equally fearful moment when the plane needs to land at its destination. For a number of years this brought a sense of relief to Greg, knowing this big chunk of metal would soon be safe on the ground. That was until a fellow journalist had described the landing as a 'controlled crash'. From that point on Greg faced the landing with the same trepidation as the take-off that did nothing to encourage him to be a relaxed traveller. He guessed he was not alone as the plane taxied towards the terminal at Dinard, following the tacky Ryanair arrival fanfare, a number of passengers burst into a spontaneous round of applause; maybe it was their way of thanking the heavens for letting them down safely.

Dinard Airport terminal is little more than a converted aircraft hangar, the Ryanair Boeing by far overshadowing it and most of the small light aircraft scattered around. Walking to the terminal, Greg could see the next batch of passengers already herded into the departure lounge, with its large windows that overlooked the tarmac, he wondered how many of them had clammy palms at this moment.

Once through passport control, Greg walked into the small public concourse of the airport.

The Europcar office was no more than a window in a wall, a neighbour of three other car hire firms. Two minutes off the plane and the work begins, Greg thought.

"Bonjour Monsieur, do you have a reservation?"

The heavy French accent was warm, friendly and inviting, Greg thought, you're going to love me, "Not exactly. I will want a car, but I do need some information first, and I was wondering if you could help me on both counts?"

"No problem, I can recommend good 'otels locally or maybe a restaurant, what do you want?"

"Actually, it's about a friend of mine, he left one of your cars in the countryside and you guys needed to collect it. I just want to know a bit more about what happened, I'm trying to find him."

"Ah the mad Englishman, so are you the police?" The Frenchman's tone changed.

"Reporter, Journalist." Greg explained.

"What journal do you work with?"

Now Greg had the feeling that this local Frenchman might not have heard of the Deptford Chronicle, although he didn't actually work for them anymore, so really he could say any newspaper and technically not be lying. "The Daily Telegraph newspaper, famous newspaper in the UK."

"So what do you want to know about the mad Englishman? I served him, gave him his car and we never heard from him again."

"Why was he mad?"

"He was 'bruyant', how you say, loud, banging the desk making much noise, wanting a car now, 'Lives depend on me' he kept saying. I gave him the car, even though he did not have the paper part of his licence; I just wanted him to go. I saw him take the car out of the airport; not a good driver, lucky it was only a little Fiat car. He only wanted it for the twenty-four hours, but after thirty-six hours, I called the Gendarmerie; I have to, they find the car and we get it back here."

"So what state was the car in?"

"State?"

"Oh, I mean - damaged, dirty, and anything wrong with it, any of his belongings in there?"

"Well the puncture we fixed. Dirty, but it had been found in a country road, some blood on the passenger seat..."

"Blood!" Greg's voice sounded more excited than he wanted it to sound.

"Un petit, a little, maybe he cut his finger maybe blood from le nez," he pointed to his nose.

"How many miles had the car travelled?"

"Kilometres monsieur, this is Europe," he smiled, "I can find out." He turned and opened a large filing cabinet behind him, and began flicking through small buff folders, with thin paper sticking out at odd angles, "Maybe you find him, if you do, tell the Gendarmes, they still have him as a voleur. A thief, I think in English."

"They are still looking for him then."

"Of course, he could not get back to England; his name will be on the list."

Maybe that was a good thing, Greg thought, at least Martin would not make it back to England, yet equally given the lack of border patrols across Europe, Martin could be just about anywhere.

"Here, he had driven one hundred and twenty-four kilometres when we found the car," producing a map he proceeded to point at a small road just north of a place called Josselin. Greg had never heard of it, but guessed he would soon be acquainted with the town.

"So, I now need a car, I have all the paperwork, I hope, and I will bring the car back."

"I hope you find him," the Frenchman said as he began completing paperwork for Martin's car, "I felt sorry for him; he was, I think the word is troubled, unhappy, I guess he should have been seeing a doctor not hiring a car."

It took Greg just over two long hours, as he was constantly stopping to consult the now much creased and used map he had purchased. Working his way through towns and villages with unpronounceable names and manoeuvring through crossroads and roundabouts which required driving in an opposite way to the way he was used to. The weather had been kind, dry and bright, so now he stood beside his hire car close to, or as near as he could work out to, where Martin had left the car, as indicated by the kindly French car hire man. He looked around at the green fields with Friesian cows gently munching their way across the lush fields; eating and barely interested in the man standing beside the car. Greg had driven north out of Josselin through a very large forest, before passing through a small village and arriving here on the D66; he wondered what to do next. Greg considered that maybe if he just waited there a while, someone would be bound to park beside him and ask if he was looking for the Englishman that dumped a car a few days previously, before proceeding to give Greg a whole list of clues and directions as to the whereabouts of Martin. That happened only in books. Here on the lonely D66 in the French countryside, Greg could not see a car, let alone a clue-laden Frenchman. He needed to do something, use some sort of logic. From his conversation with Martin's partner, he understood that Martin knew no French language, apart from the very basic school boy French. So what would Martin do? No car, yet having a place to go to, a target, a destination. He would start walking in the direction he had been travelling. So Greg got back into his car and slowly drove to see what he might find. In the end, it was no more than a kilometre before he saw the small cottage, surrounded by low well-trimmed laurel hedges and a woman, short of stature, hanging out washing under the now ever-increasing cloudy and grey Brittany sky.

*

Marie Hélène heard a car slow down. It was far too early for her husband, he would not be back for hours. So she turned and saw the car pull up beside her gate. A car she did not recognise, nor did she recognise the driver, clearly he was not from around these parts. Thankfully it was not the Gendarmes, at least her husband had not got himself into trouble again; once had been a misunderstanding, but the second time she was sure he knew perfectly well that the chainsaw was stolen. Since then, there had been so many times that she had lost count. Although the times he was away in prison, she did secretly enjoy the freedom of being without him. Marie's mother had warned her and she had not listened. Then the three children came along in quick succession and the time never seemed right to walk out on him. So here she was still hanging out washing, still looking over her shoulder expecting the Gendarmes to arrive.

The young man approached her with a look of hesitation, so she guessed he was not selling anything, maybe he was lost, not uncommon around here, "Bonjour!" she called out. He responded with the same word, but with a strong English accent that she recognised at once.

Greg took a deep breath and started using his schoolboy French, or at least what he remembered. "Pardon, je a regada une aimee, une voiture, la," he pointed back down the road. Greg saw her jumbled look before he said hopefully, "You don't speak English, by any chance?"

"Je suis desole, non." Which he thought was an odd reply if she didn't really understand English.

In fact Marie Hélène did know some words from her granddaughter, who was learning English at the local school, who often tested out newly learned words and phrases on her Grandmamma. Plus more words learned from the ever increasing number of English who were settling in this part of Brittany. Marie Helene knew more English than she would care to admit to, it was just speaking and understanding the fast-speaking English that confounded her and resulted in her remaining stoically French in her speech.

Greg looked at the woman, decided this had been a bad idea; he needed someone who could speak at least a little English to complement his little French. "Pardon, merci beaucoup." He said as he shrugged his shoulders, smiled and turned to leave the well-tended garden.

"Monsieur, venez," she was beckoning him into the house, "please," she spoke with a strong French accent.

Puzzled, Greg turned and followed her into the house. As he walked through the small porch way became a large kitchen-dining area. The room was dominated by a large, long wooden table covered with a bright floral plastic table cloth. Freshly-cut flowers stood proudly in the open fireplace and beyond the table with its eight oak chairs, was the kitchen, functional and to the point. Marie Helene was now talking into the phone, then handed the receiver to Greg, her smile warm and a little bit alluring. Greg cautiously took it and said a tentative 'Hello,' into the mouth piece, unsure of who was on the other end. To his relief, a very English feminine voice returned his greeting.

He was now talking to Faye. She was English, had lived on the other side of the village for a number of years, spoke French well and was part of village life, friends with many of those in the village and beyond. Faye listened intently as Greg explained his reason for being in Brittany and ending up in this French house. In true English style, some things just never leave your genes; Faye gave him directions to her house and invited him over at once for a cup of tea and to work out a way that she could help him. Proudly, Marie Helene waved her guest goodbye, glad of the diversion in her mundane life and looked forward to telling her neighbours about her lost Englishman and how she saved the day.

Even though Faye lived in her large French house, with her husband Ralph, in the middle of the Brittany countryside, the house and garden reminded Greg of the house where he had spent his childhood with his younger sister. From the choice of the flowers, the number of rose arches and garden furniture, to the unmistakably English interior of the kitchen with its Aga and banks of expensive looking kitchen units. The décor was colour-coordinated and there was the smell of freshly brewed coffee running through the house. Faye and Ralph sat across the large kitchen table, solid oak with a filigree cloth covering it; listening to Greg as he explained his quest while all drinking the coffee. Faye was in her late fifties, her husband maybe a couple of years older, and even though she was thin by Greg's standards, she looked healthy and alert, very tall, a height which only accentuated her lack of weight. Her eyes were bright and showing interest in Greg, observing him intently, taking in his attire, his manners and his stubble. Greg felt as though he was being assessed by a teacher; she had that 'teacher' quality about her. Ralph, her husband, also listened but more out of politeness than interest. He sat beside his wife, a tall, thin man with still a good head of greying hair but showing signs of receding, baldness was clearly in his family genes, his features weathered and framed by wrinkles across his face.

"To be honest Greg," said Faye, "I did hear about the Gendarmes hovering around a car recently, but I didn't hear much more and as far as I am aware there was no gossip about it, and trust me, if something exciting was happening it would have spread around the village like wildfire," she paused and considered the situation before offering a solution that in her eyes would be a good way of moving forward, "We know, not all, but most of the English around here, both those who live here and those who have holiday homes. I guess this Martin would have been seeking out an English family, all we can do is to give you some directions to other families and perhaps you can ask them, maybe he was just passing through, and no one needs to tell me if a friend just passes through. At least by speaking to others they might in turn be able to point you to other English families in the area."

Revived with coffee and biscuits, Greg set off again with a list of names and hamlets where he could find other English families. There were no numbers on houses to look for only the descriptions and locations that Faye had given him. La Heche was the name of the first hamlet and he was looking for the stone clad building, just past the bend, a house that had a large chestnut tree in the garden. Once he had identified what he thought was the house, he checked the name on the large green box that almost every house had beside their front gate, the mail box had the name Mr & Mrs Battener inscribed on it, clearly an

English name; already Greg was beginning to feel a little like a detective.

The Batteners were one of the oddest couples you might see, she was very tall and thin, gaunt in her appearance with long claw like fingers that ushered Greg in to the house. Her smile was pleasant but seemed to have an uneasy edge to it as she announced Greg to her husband, who was sitting in what clearly was an English styled front room; TV in the corner, large bulky three piece suite that just about filled the room, a large map of France on one wall and a large map of Atlantis on the other wall; Greg only knew it was Atlantis as it was clearly labelled as such in the bottom left hand corner. Mr Battener sat beside the fireplace, which instead of having space for burning logs, had an electric convector heater. Mr Battener had been sitting in a wheelchair reading the paper as his wife ushered their guest into the room; without hesitation he got up from the wheelchair and strode across the room to shake Greg firmly by the hand. If Greg had just witnessed a miracle no one else seemed that bothered, so Greg made no comment on what he had just seen. He was not offered any form of refreshment, which did not worry Greg, he was just asked 'what they can do for him', in such a way that he guessed they just wanted to give him his answers, say goodbye and then get on with their lives.

"Yes, heard about that little episode," Mr Battener said proudly, "I do one day a week in the English book shop in Josselin, marking up books, sifting through the piles of discarded books that we get given. It would seem that when some people move over here, they slim down the sometimes vast collection of books that they have, which they are sure will sell well, hence dumping them on the bookshop. As you can imagine, there are not a lot of French, who still make up the majority living here, that want to buy and read English books."

"Arthur, don't go off on a tangent, get back to the questions." That was the first time that Greg had heard his first name, previously he had only be referred to as Mr Battener. Berated, Arthur got back on track,

"Well on the Sunday, the day before they found the car, in Josselin there had been a.., well a good old fashioned smash and grab on the window display of the antique shop owned by Monsieur Feldus, who actually is German not French. He had owned an antique shop in Hamburg, then his wife left him..."

"Arthur!"

Her look and the tone of her voice was enough to snap Mr Batterner back to the subject,

"Oh yes. All they took was some stupid, little Roman statue worth next to nothing, well in fact I would say nothing, and then off they go. That car, the one they found over on the other side of the forest, that was the car, allegedly. Rumour has it that it was a hire car, hired by an Englishman, maybe the one you are looking for."

"It is the same car that Martin, the missing Englishman hired from Dinard airport, so it must have been part of a smash and grab."

"Yes, just not the sort of crime you hear about these days. Way back in the day, smash and grabs on jewellery stores seemed to be the height of fashion for any self-respecting robber. Now it's all drugs and gangs, not the same sense of excitement, well I don't think, and there are a lot less victims with a smash and grab, just the store owner and I guess he would just claim back his losses from the insurer, so clearly the owner would not be losing a great deal, even making a little bit on top if you get my drift."

Arthur Batterner had clearly made a strong case for the reintroduction of smash and grab raids on every high street, which might not endear him to many of the electorate, if he planned to add this to a manifesto.

"This Roman statue you say was stolen, nothing else, just the statue and it was worth nothing?"

"Just the one thing, a piece of junk, I would not have paid anything for it, but like all antique dealers looking to make a quick buck it had a ten euro price tag, well over the top if you ask me."

"And as far as you know the statue was not in the car?"

"Having spoken to Mr Feldus, the victim of the smash and grab, no, nothing, the car was empty. Which kind of worried him even more, as it raises the possibility that the so called ten euro Roman junk statue might be worth a lot more, now that would be funny, old Mr Feldus would be really upset having possibly let a priceless item through his greedy fingers, yes, that is what I think is really causing him sleepless nights."

"Well thanks for that, it all helps build a picture, I'm going to speak to some other English families, I am sure Martin will turn up."

Arthur Batterner placed himself back in the wheelchair., "Who is next on your list?"

"The Bashford family."

"Ah odd bunch that family."

"Arthur, that's not fair," Mrs Batterner once again reprimanded her husband. "They are just an ordinary family that tends to keep themselves to themselves."

"You may think that dear, I think they are a little too stuck up for their own good. Ask yourself, what they are doing over here, he doesn't work, never seem to go back to the UK and he is far too young to have retired, plus, always buying new cars, tell me where the money comes from?"

"It's none of our business Arthur."

"Drug dealers I would say, controlling a cartel from their French farmhouse. If you want a real scoop, that's where you'll find it Mr Auden, mark my words."

Greg strode back to his car and pondered the theft of the Roman statue whilst he drove to the next family. He could not find a valid or sensible reason for Martin to drop everything, fly to France, hire a car, steal an allegedly worthless figurine, before dumping the car and disappearing, unless it was not a worthless figurine. There were many imaginative and frankly, in terms of selling a story to a newspaper, many good reasons for the actions. Being part of an international smuggling ring could be one, and he had been kidnapped by a rival gang who wanted to get their hands on what turns out to be a multi-million pound artefact, but real life, Greg had learned from being on a local newspaper, life is rarely that exciting.

*

The Bashford family, who did not appear to be drug barons, greeted him warmly into their house which was just on the edge of the village. A long driveway led up to the front door of the white painted house, shielded from the road by a large hedge. The house looked a little like a fairy tale castle, with turret-like appendages to the roof, a wide downstairs window and surrounded by a lawn that had been manicured to within an inch of its life. They had been warned by Faye to expect Greg and at once apologised to Greg that they were about to eat so could not spare him too much time, but would help as much as they could.

His hair, which was jet black with just the merest hint of grey trying to spring up through the roots, made Greg think it had been dyed (men dying their hair just seemed so odd to Greg, but he knew that on his travels through life there would be many characters to try and understand), with half-framed glasses that he perched on the end of his thin nose, over which deep blue eyes looked as deep as they could into Greg, who nodded a simple 'Yes'.

"So what paper are you working for?"

"Well none really, I have recently gone freelance. Well, to be honest, I was kind of levered into it by being made redundant, so this is really a job, well more of a favour I am doing for a friend, not really a story as far as I can see."

"Must be a good friend to come all the way out here."

"Well," Greg admitted, "not what I would describe as a good friend, an acquaintance who is missing his partner and has asked me to help. I think most people think of journalists as investigative people, really I just did local news stories, but he is paying me, so it all helps."

The family sat in front of Greg in a semi-circular layout. Peter Bashford, the father next to his wife, Jane, a woman in her fifties and surprisingly still well dressed for someone who had lived in rural France; their two children, Reggie, fourteen and Paul, seventeen, sat dutifully next to their parents.

"How long have you been living out here Mr. Bashford?"

"A number of years now, it has been good for the children, both of them are bi-lingual, which in this internet connected world, is a valuable asset."

"So do you work over here?"

Peter did not answer spontaneously, but he did give an answer, "I'm retired."

"You don't look old enough to have retired on a state pension, maybe I should have been what you were in Britain, I could do with retiring early."

Greg heard Peter's voice become a little more defensive, "What does my status over here have to do with you finding your friend's missing boyfriend?"

Greg picked up on the clear reprimand and asked about the broken-down car, smash and grab theft, any gossip amongst the local English population? These questions seemed to relax both husband and wife, even though they could add nothing to Greg's search, he nevertheless made notes as they talked. He noticed just to his left a number of photographs, family photographs, close to where he was sitting.

"Your wedding photograph?" he pointed to a slightly faded photograph of a bride and groom, dressed in eighties fashion, the bride's dress white with a long flowing train which curved in front of them both.

There was a pause before Mrs Bashford answered with a simple, "Yes."

"And the school chess picture?" This time Greg leaned forward towards the black and white photograph, looking at the faces of the four boys and the plaque they were holding, "1990 chess champions," he read, "Wilmington school, is that in Kent?"

"I never went there," Peter answered, "just some very old friends, one of those silly things you keep. Well, as we can't really help you with your quest Mr Auden, if you would excuse us, we are about to have our evening meal." Peter Bashford spoke firmly.

Greg apologised for delaying their meal and thanked them for their help even though they had nothing to offer. Then he made his way to the next house, well he would have done had he not mislaid the instructions. He pulled over and consulted the map, looking for La Garenne, which seemed to be on the edge of the forest to the south of where he was. Light was slowly fading and he peered up at the signpost to ensure that he was about to head in the right direction. He watched as a car drove past, a French car, a silver grey Citroën C5 estate which had earlier been sitting in the drive of the Bashford's, and now was being driven by Mr. Bashford and his distinctive half framed glasses away from the house, and presumably from the evening meal that Greg had apparently been delaying. Some things in life you do without thinking or forethought, you just do them on the spur of the moment as they seem to be the right thing to do. Greg started the car, slipped into gear and followed in the wake of Mr Bashford's C5 Estate.

*

Peter Bashford had ignored his wife telling him to calm down, have dinner first then call later or even better in the morning. The reporter seemed genuine enough to her, and there was a car abandoned a while back, Faye had told her about it, so, "Let's just wait, there's no need to spoil dinner."

Peter would not listen, he grabbed his car keys, slipped into his padded jacket, "I am going to make the call, that was what we have been told to do and that is what I am doing, dinner can wait!" His children watched him leave, unclear of what was going on and just why the visit of the English reporter had inflamed the normally placid temperaments of their parents. Peter recalled the instructions had been clear and to the point, 'If any strangers arrive in the village asking questions about you, call, not from your house phone or from your mobile, not even a friend's phone, find a public payphone and call from there. It will most likely be nothing, just an odd coincidence, but we must always err on the side of caution, we are dealing with the lives of your whole family'. Those words had stuck in his mind, and now he was acting on that advice, by driving to the neighbouring village of Les Forges, with its lone payphone, a rare sight in the French countryside. Even in the half light of the sun that had now set, and darkness drawing its curtain across the day, Peter found the phone and dialled the number, a special number, which he had used before, once a month, just to check in and reassure everyone that he was alright.

*

Greg watched Peter Bashford walk away from the small payphone, having made a brief call, then return to his car, turn around and drive off. Greg stayed where he was, guessing Peter was going back to his cosy, family life. Greg needed to think.

Was the dash to the payphone an action that had already been planned? Was Peter calling a lover? Was he just keeping a random secret from his family? Or was it the arrival of Greg that prompted the need to make a telephone call that could not be traced or overheard? Greg sensed he had stirred something, but what it was, he was not sure, Arthur Batterner may well be right after all. Maybe Peter knew what had happened to Martin, but was not telling. Greg needed to learn more about the Bashford family. Yet now in the almost total darkness of this French village, a darkness broken only by a single street lamp, Greg had a more pressing need, a hotel with a comfortable bed in which he could rest and think what to do next.

LA VILLE DU BOIS.

Putting aside her normal reserve, Helen Taylor screamed a squeal of delight as she ran towards Justine; they had not seen each other in over five years. After being constant companions throughout their university years, they continued to stay in touch as they made their way through life. Justine was married within the first year of attaining her history graduate degree, and moved to France to be with her French husband. The two ex-students remained close over the years, while Helen followed her career and Justine started a family. They lived, taking such different paths, each on a different side of the English Channel.

"So is this really work?" Justine asked as they walked across the small airport car park at Dinard.

"An expenses-paid assignment here in rural Brittany, a bit of a result if you ask me."

*

Helen's first few days at the Daily Mirror were really about meeting people, learning who did what, where they sat and to make a few basic phone calls, before she sat down with her news editor, Danny, a loud east end boy whose cockney tones helped him stand out from the many graduates that inhabited the Newsroom. It was during that conversation, that Danny was pleased, on the advice of his Editor, to send Helen out to France on her first feature with Danny setting the scene as to what he expected the story should end up like.

"So all these middle class ex-pats sell up, buy a place ten times the size in France, and then act like the 'friggin' lord and lady of the manor, all the while living on a strong pound, which makes their pension look valuable. Now with the pound dropping and French prices rising, they now realise that all those acres of grassland that looked so tempting in the estate agent's bumph, takes a lot of cutting. They are not looking so smug, serves them right. So what about you going over and spending a few days with your friend's family, and see who of the ex-pats are coming back or struggling to make ends meet, or even the odd partner swap or love interest, could be lots out there, good chance for you to show me what you're made of. Putting it simply Helen, come back with a story about how mister stuck up middle class has fallen on his posh face, and if he is screwing one of the locals, or his wife has run off with the local French baker, so much the better, go get 'em girl."

*

Helen slipped into Justine's car, "Well, if I am going to have a first story I might as well be among friends."

They spent almost an hour and a half driving to Justine's house deep in the countryside, but the time flew by as they conversed incessantly. Knowing they could not cover everything they wanted to during the few days Helen would be spending in France, they decided it best to start as soon as possible.

It had been at Justine's hen party five years ago that they had last seen each other in person. Since then they had spoken often on the telephone, communicated via email, Skype and text, but nothing was like being together. Justine had married Laurent, a Frenchman who had studied naval history at Greenwich University, where they had first met. Marriage came soon afterwards, together with a move to France, where Laurent took up research in his spare time and earned his living managing a local drinks distribution depot. Two children had appeared during the last five years, with a third being a real possibility,

Justine confided. Justine, having once pledged to be a career girl, now revelled in the role of mother and wife, growing and cooking her own vegetables, she enjoyed the life-style. By mid-afternoon they had arrived at La Garenne, a small hamlet, where the residence of Laurent and Justine Vacher was situated.

A modest home, wider than it was deep, with two windows each side of the imposing front door. It looked like a wide bungalow but for the dormer windows set into the grey slate roof, three dormers, one for each bedroom. The front garden was as wide as the house but shallow, with just a few colourful shrubs. The rear garden, hidden from the front of the house, was equally wide but a lot longer, and was formed of a patio with a built in barbeque, garden chairs and a long simple oak table which could seat ten people with ease. Apart from a small band of grass, straddling the rear garden, with some flower beds, the main part of the garden was laid out as an allotment that was not barren; even in January there were pumpkins still laid in rows, all of differing sizes, leeks with their green paddle like leaves and onions half buried in the soil with sprigs of green moving in the light breeze.

It was late into the winter evening, the children had been safely put to bed, the dinner plates and dishes washed and put away. So now it was time for adults to relax, with a glass of wine, a little background music and the conversation to meander in different directions. Laurent had known of Helen and had of course met her on a few occasions, but still did not consider he knew her that well, so when the conversation started on family backgrounds, Laurent was keen to hear about Helen's childhood and how she arrived with such a real English voice. "Correctly spoken," as Justine always said.

"Well, I guess that some would say that I had a very privileged upbringing, I never went to boarding school, I think I would have hated it, although most of my education was private, day schools and such like, very serious and not a great deal of fun but it was nothing like some of the horrors that you hear from those who end up in boarding schools. So yes, big house in the country, weekend guests, I suppose a very middle class upbringing."

"Sounds more like an upper class sort of upbringing compared to my lowly education here in France." Laurent smiled, offering Helen more wine which she accepted, "So were your parents just rich like lords or ladies or rich from business?"

"Daddy was a banker, worked hard in the city and mostly came home at weekends, so I didn't see a great deal of him. Sadly that is the price children pay for all the benefits of a privileged life style."

"I'm sure your mother missed him as much," as Laurent finished his sentence, he sensed out of the corner of his eye a reproaching look from Justine, he wondered if he had asked the right question.

Helen continued regardless, "Mother, I think, was glad to get rid of him, there were often terrible loud disagreements and arguments at the weekends or when daddy was around. I suppose they had been in love at one time, they married after all, and I doubt if it was for the money. Daddy, when they first married, was not that high up at the bank and Mother's parents had money so they must have been in love, I am sure. It was just in their case absence did not make the heart grow fonder; it only drove a wedge between them. So as children, we might have appeared to have had a privileged childhood, but that privilege was peppered with hours of staying in our bedrooms away from the bickering and raised voices." Helen sipped her wine, thoughtfully,

"Justine said that you lost your mother when you were young, before University."

"Mother died when I was fourteen," Helen's voice was still tainted with grief, "It was a Thursday, both our cook and gardener have that day off. Mother used to like to cook on

Thursdays, I think she took the opportunity not to drink during the day as she wanted to remain reasonably able to cook dinner for her two daughters. Thursdays were good days, it was just the three females in the house, and on those days, we often laughed and giggled, as I am sure all mothers and daughters should and do. It was just that Thursday, my sister was out shopping with some school friends, I had decided to stay at home. As I recall, I was trying my hand at some watercolour painting in the garden, not that I recall what flowers I was painting, when I heard a scream from the house, naturally I rushed inside calling out to Mother to see if she was alright, she wasn't. I found her at the bottom of the stairs, I thought she was just unconscious, so I at once called an ambulance, but when the ambulance people arrived, she had died. There was a lot of fussing around, questions asked, 'was she drunk?' was the most asked question, but very little alcohol was found in her body and as I said Thursday was usually sober day, it was just a tragic accident. After that Daddy spent a lot more time at home, I think he took on less duties, or went part-time or some sort of adjustment to his hours, I suppose he felt that we should have at least one parent around us, or else we would feel like orphans."

"That is so sad!" Laurent commented, "Here I was thinking: rich young lady, having all the good things in life; I would never wish that on anyone."

"I am sure we all have our fair share of sadness and happiness, class background or how much you have in your bank account has little relationship to the difficulties that life throws at you." Helen emptied her glass, thrust it toward Laurent for a refill, and stated, "That is more than enough about me, I am working, don't forget, so I am looking for gossip, intrigue and all the bad things the English get up to when they are over here."

Between the three of them they dissected the reasons the English started crossing the Channel to live in the countryside of a natural enemy that went back many hundreds of years. In Brittany, one of the cheaper areas to live in France, the English there had sold up their semi-detached homes and purchased country houses with acres of space, good food and fresh air. In addition, those early English settlers to Brittany had spent a lot of time rebuilding the houses that the French had let go to ruin, hence starting a new business sector in France, that of the DIY store; the French soon learnt to join in with the English and 'do it yourself'. Then came the second wave, those who had retired early, and realised that the French Franc made their pensions go a lot further and once again they came across, having sold up and bought a house they could move straight into. The husband could make the first stop the garden centre, purchase a ride-on mower, a requirement for any Englishman living in France, and begin neatly trimming the many acres that came with the house. Yet however idyllic things might seem to be, no one is insulated from the winds of change. The Euro arrived, trimming the pension, then the economic down turn had brought the exchange rate almost on a par with the pound and the cost of living was no longer as attractive. Some saw the value of their monthly pension slashed and many decided to go back. They say if you stay seven years then you will be in for the long haul. Missing family, money concerns, or just not understanding why the French are just so French all frightened many of those who had invaded. Also, as many immigrants to a country do, they tended to stick close together, often leading to some villages in Brittany having a larger English population than the native French, which would not have been the end of the world but for, Laurent said,

"They actually wanted shops open on a Sunday, moaned about no fish and chip shops and many did not even bother to learn the language; the funny thing is that none of them thought of themselves as immigrants, they were English!" The three laughed, "Of course, not all the English are like that, many of them immerse themselves in French life avoiding other English at all costs, we even have an English person on our local council. The French are as tolerant as any other nation, but we do have our country and our values, which we want to hang on to. So we are happy for the English to come along, however mad they are, or even if they avoid everyone, like that man up at Belle Etoile. No one knows: who he is, what he is or what he does with his days. He turned up, I think last summer, and well the baker might see him once in a while, but otherwise he keeps himself to himself."

"Better than trying to start an English cricket team or demanding the local shop had cheddar cheese." Justine added.

Helen tilted her head sideways, "So this guy up at Belle Etoile you say, is he like a hermit?"

"Her Mit?"

"C'est la meme, "Justine translated, "ermite, vivre en solitaire."

"Ah," Laurent realised the word was the same in French, "Yes a 'ermite."

"Tell me more; he sounds different enough to make a story out of."

Justine began the story, or what there was of the story, which was not a lot. Maybe eight or nine months ago, someone noticed there was someone living at the house just to the east of La Belle Etoile, on the higher part of that landscape. The house had been empty for about two years, it had been owned by an English couple who had gone back to England when the husband's brother became terminally ill; so it was a bit of a surprise to see lights on in it. The village residents quickly started a rumour mill, deciding that whoever was there was most likely to be English, so Faye, one of the English in the village, was sent up to introduce herself and to find out a bit more. He was English, tall, good looking, in his thirties or so, but very much a 'Thank you, but no thank you,' when turning down invites to Faye's house for coffee or the social events that were being held in the village. Apart from that, he had been seen driving around a few times going to the bakers but apart from that, Faye had no idea, he hadn't even offered her his name, which was a little bit impolite to say the least.

"In that case, Justine & Laurent, I will make it my goal to find out more and report back to you, a service to my readers and to the village of La Ville du Bois. Cheers!"

They laughed and continued drinking and talking into the early hours of the morning.

NANTES BREST CANAL.

The early winter sunlight helped warm the dormitory-style room. It was a sparse, yet adequate hotel room, with a single bed, a small wooden effect wardrobe, plus a table and chair located next to the door leading to the tiny ensuite shower and toilet. Greg sat on the edge of the bed, its floral duvet creased and ruffled from the restless night that he had spent in room thirty-four, Hotel Chateau. The hotel overlooked the Nantes Brest Canal and afforded a superb view of Josselin's Chateau on the opposite bank. He felt the sun warm his back as he waited for an answer from the other end of his mobile phone. Being a reporter for the best part of fifteen years, Greg had an impressive address book of names and contacts that he had met during his time as a reporter. Valuable names and telephone numbers, that when the stories started to dry up, he could ring around and invariably a story would be uncovered. Like a fine wine, a reporter's contact book matures with age, gaining in value, as those clerks at local council offices you met many years ago, and whom you had kept in touch with, moved up their career ladder and possibly were now in a far higher position of authority and responsibility, with which comes better stories and better help.

"Carter," was the reply when the ringing tone had stopped. Fergus Carter worked in immigration, not strictly a newspaper contact, Fergus and Greg had been at the same school, not the closest of friends, but their paths often crossed and there were times they mutually exchanged information or Greg did a favour producing some copy that helped Fergus. Today's call, it was

Greg who was asking the favour, a simple question, yet one there would never have been an official answer to. The passports of Peter and Jane Bashford, what did it say about where they came from and what they did, that was all Greg wanted to know. For Fergus a simple check on the computer gave the answer.

"Well unless your Peter Bashford is twenty-one, sixty-eight or seventy-years-old, he doesn't have a passport. As for Jane, she is the seventeen-year-old sister of Peter, so unless they are both living there incestuously and that has aged them, I'm really sorry, I can't help you Greg. I also am looking at variations of the name, maybe they told you a little white lie when you asked their names," Fergus concluded.

Time for another call, another contact, "Henry, I need a favour." Henry, like Greg, also worked at a newspaper, the Guardian, working mostly on their educational supplement,

"I was at someone's house and I saw a photograph, a school type photograph, with four boys in school uniform pictured, it said Wilmington School Chess Champions 1990. There were four names, of the boys I guess, but I did not get a chance to read the names as they were so small and the person that I was interviewing must have noticed my vision hover on the photograph and moved in front of it."

"Yes, I'm sure about the name, as it reminded me of Wilma in the Flintstones."

"Thanks, I should be back in England in a couple of days and I'll buy you a coffee, or something stronger."

Apart from those two brief calls, Greg knew he would need to progress his search for Martin and visit a few more English houses today in the hope of turning something up before he had to return to England.

LA BELLE ETOILE.

Phillip made one final adjustment to the twelve music compact discs that he had neatly laid out on the table. They had been laid out in a line, with the cover picture facing upwards, this month they had been ordered by date of purchase (which was neatly written inside each sleeve). Phillip liked to vary the way he listened to music, so each month he would order the compact discs in different ways. This month he would start with the earliest music compact disc that he owned and during the course of the month work his way to the very latest purchase, then return back to the earliest. Last month they had been ordered in alphabetical arrangement by album title, which for him produced some interesting sequences of music. He was satisfied they had been correctly ordered, gathered them together and walked across the sunlit room to place them beside the very neat music player, that doubled as his radio. It would also play MP3, which according to the man in the shop was some sort of music that had been compacted by a computer; Phillip could not see the reason for such a process, so he stayed with his CD's. It was as he stood back from the music centre, to visually check everything was in place, that a loud knock at the door disturbed his concentration. Visitors to his house were very rare indeed. Apart from those that he had invited, the only callers were those irksome salespeople selling anything from tacky pictures, iced foods, double glazing and once asking about doing the garden. Fortunately, he only needed to answer the door and greet them in his native English language for them to soon decide it was not going to be worth their time, they usually grovelled a bit and then left.

The young woman standing at the door, who introduced herself as Helen, was not what he had expected, speaking in English; well spoken English at that, she was clearly not a salesperson. Dressed well and fashionably, she, he assumed, was not one of the latest immigrants to Brittany. She wore shoes that were clean and not very practical for walking around country lanes, her jeans, smartly creased, very clean and very tight on her long slender legs. Her jumper was fashionably large and engulfed her petite upper body, along with a large woollen multi-coloured scarf tied around her neck, she was not dressed for walking. He glanced over her shoulder and saw the French registered Renault Clio, a little too old and uncared for to be hers or hired, so she had borrowed it, she must be staying with friends, maybe nearby. He looked at her face, an attractive face with eyes that told a story, a very interesting story, a story that Phillip wanted to hear more about. This young lady was a curiosity, so he ushered her into the house, a rare, if not the first, visitor to this immaculate French property.

"Please sit down Helen, can I get you a drink at all?" She refused, which did not entirely offend him. "So you are interested in writing an article on an English person's experience of settling into French life. Would your readers really be interested in hearing about my tedious, uneventful life here in France?"

Part of his mind screamed out, 'why are you actually taking the time to speak to this person? Giving her the impression that you would be happy to discuss your life with her and the rest of the world! It has nothing to do with any of them, they are all worthless creatures fussing around their pointless lives and loves, in the end they all die, without making any sort of real impression on mankind.' There was another part of his mind, often drowned out and rarely listened to, that was speaking with a determination to be first for once. That voice was saying, 'she is a very attractive young lady; she has taste, or at least a reasonable amount of fashion sense, her voice is enchanting, her slim body, simply put, sexy. And her eyes. Her eyes enchanted that once timid part of his mind, eyes that hinted they were alike in so many ways.' It might not be described as love at first sight, it was more that the barriers were not at once raised as they usually were when any stranger touched his life. He was happy to be in her presence and listen to her speak.

Helen sat down in the very soft and comfortable sofa chair that she had been directed to. She had not expected to be invited into the house at the first asking, she had not even considered entering but he appeared so charming. Once inside, she was a little confused, the interior was nothing as she had expected, most of the men she had known did not take a great deal of pride in keeping their flats clean and tidy, not that they were dirty people, just a little disorganised and rather chaotic in the way they lived their lives. That was the type of environment that she was expecting to find, as she walked into the house, slightly knocking a small table that was beside the door, which did have a kitchen knife on it, which could be there for a number of reasons; maybe he was holding it when he answered the door or maybe he was just a little scared of who might call at the house. Helen looked at his body and doubted he would be the sort of person to be scared, his physique was impressive and would make many a man think twice before engaging in any sort of violence with him.

The room that she now found herself in was totally ordered, clean, and colour co-ordinated. There was a large fireplace, where the enclosed wood-burner flickered and crackled as it consumed wood, the mantelpiece above it held a collection of small items, lined up perfectly. To the left was a small table upon which stood a mini music centre, alongside, again lined neatly, were just a few CD's. To the right of the fireplace, there was a tall glass cabinet with colourful pottery figurines, lit by a single over head lamp set into it. Then moving further to the left was a longer settee, a three seater version of the two seater that Helen sat on. There he sat, with a low coffee table between them, upon which was a magazine either side of the centrally placed white octagonal fruit bowl which contained two bananas, two apples, two pears and four kiwi fruits.

" I am confident that your life is not tedious, I am sure living out here alone is challenging enough, sorry I didn't catch your name."

"That is because you never asked and I never ventured my name to you."

Helen smiled, "So your name is?"

"Does that really matter, there is nothing to write about in my life, whatever you might think. I do lead a very monotonous life here, which suits me, so if I give you my name it would be for purely social reasons, not professional. I do not want anything of my life in any magazine or newspaper."

"Ok, for social reasons, as friends, so at least I know whom I am talking to."

"Phillip."

"Well thank you for inviting me in Phillip, or do people call you Phil?"

"I just said my name is Phillip, if it was Phil I would have said Phil, you're Helen, so why would I call you Hel? I think not."

"Good point, but if you are being picky, one 'L' or two?" she retorted, not planning to be intimidated.

He smiled, "If I said I was born in the sixties, would that help?"

"Could be either but the two L version became popular in the sixties. So I would say two L's in your name."

"A good and accurate call."

"Thank you, so why have you ended up here in La Ville du Bois?"

"Helen, do you recall I did say I was not planning in sharing any part of my life with your readers, and to say I have ended up here, is not strictly true, unless of course I was to die in the next few minutes, you've never killed anyone, have you?" He watched her eyes for any sort of reaction, he already knew the answer to his question.

"No, I'm just a simple reporter."

Phillip smiled at the attractive young lady sitting opposite him, eyes never lie, there is a reason why people call them the window on the soul.

"Good, so if you are not planning on killing me then, La Ville du Bois is not where I might end up as you so plainly put it. It would seem a better question for me to ask is what brings you to my door?"

Helen told him, almost everything, not a total confession but more than she would normally have shared with a stranger that she had only just met. There again, she reasoned, if this meeting had taken place back in the UK, in a bar or night club, then she would no doubt have shared the same details with someone that she was attracted to, why wouldn't you? Phillip was attractive, maybe a few years older than her, certainly taller, maybe six feet, with a strong body, but without the bulging biceps of a body-builder, which Helen found could be very off-putting. Phillip's arms were clearly as strong as were his legs, or as much as she could tell through his jeans, although the jeans did show off his very firm, well-shaped bottom. His eyes were a deep blue, set above a very prominent nose, his jaw line was square and chiselled as were his cheek bones. Only his hair aged him a little, close cropped, jet black but for a few spikes of grey pushing their way through. Taking into account all the men that she had met, only a very select few she would ever put into the dating category, Phillip was one of those.

Once she had told Phillip, what she considered to be enough about her without going far too deep, she sat forward and declared that she should be going, thanked Phillip for his time, politely, yet honestly, saying it was a pleasure to have met him. She stood, tightened her scarf and offered her hand by way of saying goodbye. Instantly Phillip stood and from within his mind a voice, often subdued, sprang forth and on compulsion, took charge of his voice,

"I hope I can see you again, not for sharing any of my life with your readers, but I would be happy to share some of my life with you over dinner. I guess you will be going back to the UK soon, so what about tonight?" The usually dominant part of Phillip's mind shrank back in disgust, he was actually asking a woman for a date, how many times had that happened, twice he recalled, and then had his offers ever been accepted, never ever.

"I'd love that."

"Wonderful, let me know where you are staying and I will collect you at seven-thirty."

Helen left without a story, but did have a dinner date.

Phillip felt excited and wondered if he had found a kindred spirit.

LA GARENNE.

"Helen, you'll never guess who is in the kitchen?" was the question that Justine posed as her friend returned to the house. "Another reporter! You wait years for one to come along and then two turn up at the same time."

"Well I'm not in the league of a national reporter," the voice came from Greg, who was sitting at the long kitchen table holding a mug of coffee, beside which sat a plate of biscuits, which he was clearly working his way through with an unreserved enjoyment, "you must be Helen, I'm Greg." He stood offering his hand in a friendly greeting, his coffee still in his other hand.

"A reporter also. Are you working out here, if so what are you working on?" Helen asked after shaking his hand and joining Greg and Justine at the table.

"Well, as I was explaining to your friend Justine, not so much a story, just asking a few questions to see if I can help a friend find his partner, who appears to have come to France without any good reason and has seemingly disappeared."

Helen encouraged him to tell more, it sounded a lot more exciting than asking a bunch of ex-pats how they are getting on in France. Greg gave the basic account that he had given to the English families he had so far met. He mentioned the disappearance of Martin, his partner worried still more when the credit card statement showed that he had flown to France. The abandoned car led Greg to the general area of La Ville du Bois and the stolen Roman statue added a strange twist, although it was only alleged Martin's hire car was involved in the theft, innocent until proven guilty and all that. So far, no one knows anything of Martin, it seems he left the car and then disappeared.

"It's a big place, he could be lying dead for all we know," Greg admitted," and as I have found out nothing, I'll be back on the plane tomorrow having struck a dead end, but at least I have tried."

"But why would he come to this part of France, did he have any connection at all with this place?" Helen asked, the mystery of the disappearance stimulating her reporter's genes.

"Well, if his partner is telling the truth, and I can't see any reason that he might lie, then there is no reason, Martin just walked out with a credit card, passport and the clothes that he stood up in. Maybe, as it has been mentioned to me before, it was a lovers' tiff or he found another lover."

"And the stolen statue, a high value antique?"

"Worth ten euros, I am assured, not exactly high end art theft."

"Well," Helen offered, "if I hear anything when moving around the ex-pat community over the next couple of days, I'll let you know; do you have a card?"

Greg smiled, "Nothing as grand as that as yet, a scrap of paper will have to do for now."

Helen watched him write down his mobile number, but her mind was on the Roman statue that Greg had mentioned, "This cheap statue, what did it look like?"

Greg handed her his mobile number, as he considered her question for a moment, he had never seen the statute for himself, he had only had it described to him very loosely, so his description was just as vague, too vague for Helen to be sure of anything.

JOSSELIN.

Back in his small hotel room, Greg began the process of packing his few things. His flight was at five that evening, the hotel offered a late winter check out, this afforded him time to get on his way and be back home in his own bed tonight. If he had to be honest with himself, he never did have high hopes of locating Martin, it was more of a paid diversion which went a little way to coming to terms with his redundancy. He knew that soon he would need to do some real work, write some real stories that he could sell and earn his keep, but for now, life felt very different from that of reporting at the Deptford Chronicle, a rap at the door disturbed his torpid thought. Expecting the chambermaid to be ready to encourage his departure, he was surprised to be confronted with a young man, maybe mid-twenties in a large warm puffer jacket, a woolly hat in his hand, "Greg Auden?"

"Yes?" was more of a question than a statement.

"Mick Hayes, Accord Insurance Services, I understand that you have been asking about a Martin Jackson? It's just that I have some background on Martin which might be of help. Can I come in? Not the sort of thing I should be discussing out in a hotel corridor."

Mick walked into the room, looked around with a disdainful look, not the sort of hotel room that he was used to, his generous expense account unlocked the door to four-star luxury at least.

"I see that you are packing up, getting the five p.m. out of Dinard, I guess, so I won't keep you. Martin Jackson, yes, he has disappeared and for good reason in my books. He has been a little naughty in trying to screw his insurance company, well us at Accord Insurance Services to be precise, we're sorting out the dirty work for his insurance company. Mind if I sit down, thanks." He sat on the side of the bed, without waiting for a reply from Greg and unzipped his jacket, revealing a smart light-blue suit with a white open neck shirt. "We go after those who think it is good and right to tap their insurance company by making a dubious or, in many circumstances, a totally false claim. Some do get away with it, if they didn't manage to escape our clutches, then nobody would even think of trying to defraud their insurance company. But we all have a friend who has added a few items to a burglary claim; some go a little further, some a lot further. I'd put our mutual friend Martin in the middle sector, claimed he had lost a ring, a few grand, so not a cheap one, produced the receipt for it, plausible story, all very legit so far, and to be honest he would have got away with it, if it hadn't been just over the three thousand mark, and so a few more checks are done on the claimant. George Orwell and his '1984' would love what we can dig up about people, with a few simple clicks of a computer mouse. Turns out our Martin had done some community service for falsely claiming expenses when he was at Southwark Council. Don't you worry, I think you guys at newspapers have an understanding with your bosses about expenses, as do mine. So he has form for bending the rules, no pun intended." There was no reaction from Greg so Mick decided an explanation should be forthcoming for the barrack room jibe, "Bender, he's gay, bends over, never mind. So before writing the cheque, his insurance company speaks to the company whose receipt the alleged purchase is written on. Ah, now we have a problem, they have never sold such a ring let alone have a record of the sale. Scanned and altered a receipt, for what was most likely a cheap item; what you can do with computers nowadays only helps those thousands of budding fraudsters. So his insurance company hands it over to us, we confirm what they have found and ask the police to come along with us to go and arrest him. They plead lack of man power so there's a delay of a week, not the end of the world, insurance claims always take time, everyone knows that, don't they. So we are about to go knocking on his door, when it comes through the grapevine he is on his toes and decamped off to France. Hence you and I are here in a, frankly undersized hotel room, looking for a gay fraudster. So if you do find him, let me know." Mick handed a business card to Greg, who was still standing, a little surprised at what he had just heard. "His sweetheart, back in England, who is missing him, has no idea about this ring thing, but I'm happy if you tell him, there are no secrets about this now, Martin is clearly on the run, so if he wants to come back to the UK, then the best thing for him will be to hand himself in. I doubt to be honest we will ever see him again. Shame I didn't hear about you before, I could have saved you a journey, France in winter is not the best place to be. Now if he had decamped off to Ibiza, lots of gays there plus a lot of sunshine, that would have made the whole job a lot better." Mick stood, zipped up his jacket and made his way towards the door, "Have a good flight back."

"So how did you find out I was looking for Martin?" Greg asked, he felt that the explanation was a little too neat and convenient, life is never that simple.

Mick stopped in the doorway and turned around to face Greg, "That whippet of a French man at Dinard airport, the one who gave out Martin's car, I bet he got a slap from his bosses, letting the car go without the right paperwork. I bet he'll be more careful with the next Brit who turns up without both parts of their driving licence." He turned back to the door only to be stopped by another irksome question from Greg,

"So why go to all the trouble of finding me to tell me I'm not going to find Martin?"

"I'm spending another day here, as I am on expenses, then I am back to the UK and put this case away and start another, just suppose you do happen across him, well, I hope you'll give me a call and then I can close the case, we all win. Well maybe not his lover, I reckon our Martin will be spending some time inside on this occasion."

At that point Mick walked out the room, closing the door behind him, leaving Greg to finish his packing and let his mind race with thoughts. So the two hour wait in the departure lounge was spent on the phone, first was Edward, asking about the expenses fraud and the community service his partner might have served. To Greg's surprise, Edward hesitantly confirmed the community service his boyfriend Martin had served, clearly that was a part of Martin's life, which Edward was eager to point out was before he met up with Martin, but he could not understand the insurance fraud, that was a total shock to Edward. Martin never had need of money, and if he did, a quiet word to Edward would have been able to smooth out any money worries he might have had, that part seems so much out of character. Even though Edward thanked Greg for his time and promised to settle his account when he returned, Greg made it clear that he had not given up on finding Martin. The second call was to Accord Insurance Services, asking for Mick Hayes, the operator confirmed that he was out of the country and could not give any more details than that, but would be happy to take a message, which Greg declined to do. Finally he called Henry at the Guardian, asking if he had had any luck with the school photograph.

"You are eager Greg; I would have thought the laid back you would have waited until you got back. Well to start at the beginning, Wilmington School does exist, close to a place called Wilmington in Kent, a Grammar school with good results and a good online archive that I could dig into. In 1990, the Wilmington Chess Team, whipped the opposition, that opposition being other Grammar schools in Kent, hence they became the 1990 Kent Chess Champions, which I guess at the time made them the equivalent of today's geeks. The Team was made up of the following boys, all from the same form year: George Usher, Les Clarke, William Lynch and Dennis Jones. Where they are today I will leave that up to you, but I would add that none of them followed a career in chess. I hope that helps."

Greg wrote down the four names, "That's great! I'm not sure what it means but it must mean something. I'm about to get on the plane, so let's meet up soon."

Greg gripped the leather airline seat tightly as the jet powered up and raced down the runway before the nose wheel lifted up quickly, followed by the rest of the plane as it lifted into the air and traced its route across the Channel towards Stansted. However many thoughts he had running through his mind, none were strong enough to wipe the illogical fear of flying from his mind.

Once in the air, he wondered about the insurance man, something was not right, something was missing, not that Greg could put his finger on it, he was used to dealing with local councillors and local readers, not insurance investigators that turn up in your hotel room. Then there were the Bashfords, the warmth that went as Greg had asked questions about Peter Bashford's retirement and the work that he might have done in the UK, followed by an apparent dash to a payphone. What was most bizarre was there being no record of their passports, a whole family. Maybe Fergus had made a mistake, not surprising given his history, or maybe it was one of those clerical errors. The photograph, well, that might be some relation, a brother or sister, it could be anything or nothing. Greg was returning to the UK with more unanswered questions that he had left with.

*

Phillip was everything Helen imagined he might be at dinner, knowledgeable, considerate, easy to talk to and even exhibited some unusual habits as they ate their meal. He had chosen a majestic, yet traditional, restaurant in Josselin. Their table overlooked the canal, although a view of the fairytale-looking Château required leaning forward and cranking their necks to the left, which for the view it afforded from that angle, was not really worth the effort. Phillip was confident when faced with the range of cutlery, and glasses that made up each cover, he clearly was used to such swish surroundings. Helen was fascinated by one of his rituals. He had chosen for his main course, salmon with a herb sauce, served with sauteed potatoes and haricot beans. He first pushed each element on his plate away from each other, thus creating three distinct areas of food on the plate. Then he ate, first the beans, then the salmon and sauce, finally he ate the potatoes. This same process had also been applied to his pate starter, all the dressing and trimmings consumed first then the simple pate eaten last. He missed out on the dessert, maybe all of them were too mixed up and difficult for him to separate, Helen thought. Instead he had the cheese plate, again all eaten separately, Camembert, Chèrve, Paulin, St Agur, Helen thought in alphabetical order. For some this sort of behaviour would have been a little unnerving, maybe distressing, not for Helen, she almost felt a sense of relief, as she too had a strange habitual ritual around the dinner table, well to others it appeared odd. To her, it was normal to use hand gel to clean her hands between each course, starter consumed, a squirt of hand gel and her hands were refreshed, main course eaten and enjoyed, once again the hand gel would be pulled from her handbag and her hands restored and refreshed, the process repeated for each course. There had been times when she carried out her usual ritual, and had been questioned by friends around the table as to just why she was cleaning her hands at regular intervals. Her habit had become an embarrassment to her, so she more often than not prohibited herself from the hand gel syndrome, replacing it with at least two trips to the ladies toilet to wash her hands. There were some friends she felt comfortable enough to continue her hand cleaning at the table, and Phillip was now going to be placed in that category, as he too had special rituals at meal times. As they both began eating the cheese course, Helen commenced a conversation that would have major and intense consequences on her life. She knew the risk, but here she was sure there was a story, a big story waiting to be exposed and once written, the reporter would receive accolades for it and that reporter she wanted to be her.

"Yesterday you asked me if I had ever killed someone, it got me wondering, what it might be like to kill someone. What do you think it would be like to kill someone?"

Phillip looked at her, with those eyes that seemed to be able to look deep into her soul. She was a little unnerved, maybe a little scared, but she thought of that Roman statue on his mantelpiece. Maybe it was not the one that was stolen from the shop in Josselin, maybe it was a coincidence, but she still wondered how he would reply. Maybe that was the enigmatic part of him that she wanted to expose.

"What would it be like to kill someone? I will confess that is a strangely unusual question to ask when we have only known each other for a little over twelve hours, but it is a good question which deserves a good and thoughtful answer. First, what do you mean by kill someone? There are many ways in which you can kill another human being: solider fires a gun and an enemy solider falls to the ground lifeless, a driver, having drunk a little too much, slams into a bus shelter killing the little old lady he never knew. The chef here could make a terrible mistake, mixing cooked and raw meat in the fridge, killing one of his customers with food poisoning. I could have a row, drunken or otherwise, and use some sort of force to kill that person. All killing, or are you thinking of murder? Now that for me would be killing for a reason, a planned action that leads to the death of another human being. Totally different to just killing someone, so which were you thinking of?"

"Murder," Helen answered a little too quickly.

"Good choice, so your question now is: 'What would it be like to murder someone?' I would imagine empowering, giving you a God-like power over someone's fate. After all, in these circumstances, it is not just the misfortune of being in the wrong place at the wrong time to take the soldier's bullet, be hit by the drunk driver or consume the bug-infested food. You are going about your daily life and someone is planning for you to die at a certain point, maybe for a reason the victim might never know about. I think it would be good to murder someone, at the least it would leave you with a feeling of total supremacy, which I wonder if you could ever achieve again. Maybe it's like making love, the meeting, the build-up of foreplay, the expectation and then finally the orgasm as the person dies in front of you. One-sided love making, that reminds me of a few people I have known in the past," Phillip smiled warmly, "Does that help?"

"Possibly. The planning part intrigues me, but what about the reason? You must have a reason to extinguish someone's life."

"A reason, well of course, there will need to be a reason, that's why most murders are solved, as it is often a family member doing the killing and killing a relation, wife, husband, father, mother, rich uncle, the list could be endless, they are the simple reasons. It's the ones with the more complex reasons that end up being the unsolved murder, no direct link, no obvious reason, nobody. John Steinbeck once wrote, that 'if you are going to commit the perfect bank robbery, you should not spend any of the stolen money as that will just point the finger at you', so maybe that applies to the perfect murder, don't let it change your life. Killing your husband will change your life, giving you a reason, and thus no doubt leading to your conviction."

Helen had now finished her cheese plate, and was gelling her hands, an action which Phillip seemed to take no notice of.

"Yet, if you did kill someone, some stranger for instance, giving you such a big high, then wouldn't you want to share that experience with someone."

"Oh yes, using the sexual analogy, two lovers have really bed-rocking sex, then they share the experience reliving it in their conversation. In the murder situation your partner is dead, so you can't relive the moment with that person. So maybe you are right, sharing the experience would help you relive the sensations, but where does one find a suitably experienced murderer to discuss techniques and compare notes? Time Out magazine does not have a murderer to murderer small advert section, so no help there."

Phillip leaned forward on the table pushed his hand across and took her small hand and gripped it tightly into the palm of his cool soft hand, his eyes once again penetrating her very soul. The rhythm of Helen's heart changed, moving faster, she was sure it was fear making the change.

"It is getting a little late for us country folk, so I am going to pay the bill, take you back to your friends, wish you a good night, thank you for a very enjoyable evening, kiss you on both cheeks in a social way and then return to my house. If you really want to continue this discussion, I suggest that you come over to my place tomorrow morning at, say ten thirty, and we can, over a cup of decaffeinated coffee, discuss murder in more depth."

That was exactly how the night ended, as he had ordered.

LA VILLE DU BOIS.

In a village as small as La Ville du Bois (at the last count there were only four hundred and sixty-two residents), it is easy to avoid people but it is hard to be totally invisible to the other villagers, when just about all of them will go to the village bakers each day. The result is, if you want to know something, the baker will know the answer; who has arrived, who is leaving, who is ill, who has just lost their job, who had the most hideous hair style ever, and it is not just who, what the weather will be like, what the latest changes to government mean, what the economy will be doing, what time the fish van comes a calling. If you need to know something the village baker is the equivalent of the internet for finding things out. One of the many reasons is the footfall through the shop, so once the formal, 'Hello, how are you?' has been dealt with, there is an opportunity to exchange information, which in turn can be passed on where appropriate or deemed useful.

Jane Bashford enjoyed her leisurely walk to the bakers, it gave her time alone with just her thoughts away from the housekeeping; not that she was just a housekeeper to the family that she loved and cherished. She took pride in her garden, which she then was able to bring into the house by way of dramatic floral decorations, colourful and bold, such a contrast, she thought, to her own timid personality. Her floral skills were recognised by others in the village, so last year she had the honour of preparing and directing all the arrangements for the village church on the very special day in July, when the whole village celebrated their patron saint, St Anne. The pardon of St

Anne, started with a service in the decorated church, followed by a procession through the streets of the village before ending up at the Salle Polyvalente for a grand celebration meal. Jane recalled that hot July day and walking in the procession, such a contrast to the now chilly yet dry walk to the baker's, just Jane and her empty bag in which she would put her bread.

The baker's was a twenty minute walk from her house. It was quicker to drive, but time was something Jane had plenty of since moving to France; why drive, when you could walk along a quiet country lane. The first part afforded views on Jane's right side across the valley that lay to the west of La Ville du Bois, a wide vista of pastures sparsely populated with farmhouses and farm sheds. Over to her left, making up the horizon, was the large forest of Lanouee that stretched across the landscape. Upon entering the village, the start of which was determined by a name sign that was surrounded by flowers, Jane passed the sports field, home to the village football team, today, not being Sunday, it was quiet and serene, a reflection of village life. Jane often thought about her life here in France and the circumstances that saw her and her family deposited in a foreign country with all their UK ties cut forever. If she was honest, she did not miss her UK friends, not even her sisters, they had never really been that close, she did often wonder about her nieces and nephews growing up, and if they ever wondered what had happened to their Auntie Jane.

As she walked past the well-kept cemetery where generations of villagers were laid to rest, she thought how much she liked living without the stress that they had endured in the UK. Making ends meet, commuting, paying the mortgage and the rates, none of these now existed for her or her family, their generous allowance gave them a lifestyle many, including her sisters, would have been envious of. However idyllic a life might seem from the outside, every life has its darker or negative side. Crossing the empty road beside the Libre Service, that sold just about anything you could ever need, Jane looked up at the tall church steeple and recalled the shadow that hung over her family, a shadow that she felt darken last night with the arrival of an unexpected guest. The church towered over her as she stepped onto the pavement. The church stood at the centre of the village, the tallest structure for miles around and where all the village roads led to. Here at the heart of the village, beside the spiritual centre was the baker's, the social centre of the village.

Jane Bashford pulled open the door, the high pitched shrill bell tinkled as she went in. Mrs. Bashford went in each day for her bread, a Boule, a Baguette, and twice a week for cakes to go with afternoon tea. When they had first arrived in La Ville du Bois, she had also bought croissants for their daily breakfast, however, since her husband was found to have high cholesterol, Jane changed their breakfast to porridge and fruit each morning, the oats being good for her husband. She liked Annie the baker's wife and Annie liked Mrs. Bashford, she was always polite, spoke good French, always had a smile, also her children were very polite and well-behaved which Annie thought to be very important. Under the heading of 'the English should always know what the other English are doing', Annie proceeded to tell Mrs. Bashford about Justine's school friend who is visiting the village for a few days. A school friend who writes for a newspaper back in England and, Annie thought, was writing about life in a French village. Mrs. Bashford, gave the appearance that she was not that interested, just agreeing that she found life in a French village very tranquil indeed. Underneath her calm exterior, she was shocked to hear that another newspaper reporter was in the village, even though that reporter had not been in touch with them as yet. Annie, wondered if she had upset Mrs Bashford as the normally placid relaxed chat she was expecting to have, was truncated and Mrs

Bashford walked out of the shop, not even saying good morning to Madame Gestin as they passed in the shop doorway.

Last night she had told her husband that he was overreacting when a reporter had paid them a visit. The reason seemed genuine, there had been an abandoned car, it made sense that he would be asking questions of the English around the village, but now, another reporter. An abandoned car and a missing Englishman could not be that important, there must be something else, and she now feared that something of interest could be the Bashford family.

If Jane Bashford was being honest with her family, she would have told them that for the last eight years, ever since they left their modest semi-detached house in Hempstead, she had lived in fear. Fear of her husband's past catching up with him, fear that her children might be harmed, fear that her family would be taken away from her, or her from her family. Most of her fear was the uncertainty of what might happen if Peter's past caught up with them. She had succeeded in hiding her feelings of dread from her family, as she went about her day as a dutiful wife and mother, still full of good humour and appearing to be totally at peace with her new life in France. So last night, even though her heart had jumped when a stranger they had not invited passed over their threshold, she still smiled and remained outwardly composed, telling herself and her family it was just a simple coincidence. Even as she tried to tell her husband not to worry, she was terrified but held her fear in as she had always done. Yet now, she had heard from Annie, that there was someone else in the village, another stranger, another reporter, her fear brimmed over and gushed vocally at her husband as he tended his vegetable patch.

"Something is wrong, you don't get two reporters turn up in a back water of a French village, both just happening to be doing some vague story. Peter, I am now concerned something is really brewing up, I sense storm clouds on the horizon. You need to speak to London again, now."

Peter, partly out of breath from pulling the very large leeks from the ground, leaned against the spade and said, "Do you still think I overreacted when that other reporter paid us a visit last night?"

"One reporter is a different matter, and what he said about the abandoned car was a fact, so maybe he was actually looking for some missing Englishman, not you. Now there are two reporters, and how many more do you think might turn up? If they are on to us, heaven knows what will happen next."

"Look, as you know I spoke to London, and they said they will look into it. If there is any cause for concern they said, they would get back to me. Although a second reporter is a change of circumstances, maybe I should call London again just to keep them up to date. I'm sure it is just a coincidence, I'm just glad that you now agree that we should not be complacent. Now will these two leeks be enough? If so, I will go off and make a phone call."

Jane did not answer him, she hated it when he was being sarcastic, it was his way of saying he was right and she was wrong. She was tempted to call him by his real name, a name she had refrained from using for eight years, but she resisted the temptation, turned and walked back into the house.

MILLBANK, LONDON.

Christopher Davenport Wellington replaced the handset of the telephone carefully without emotion, his thoughts were too engaged elsewhere. William, or Peter Bashford as he is known now, had spent the last eight years living happily and quietly in France. Once a month, a check phone call arrives from him, a few pleasantries, the weather, maybe a brief chat about a news item, a few moments talking before goodbye until next month. Now in the space of twenty-four hours, two calls from Peter regarding the arrival of not just one, but two journalists, in what Christopher would contemptuously regard as an insignificant French village. Nothing obvious, nothing to the point, no direct questions to Peter, they are just there, like a wasp circling you as you lay out in the sunshine. There was no reason to suspect the wasp will sting you, even so you tense up just in case as you reason that it could. Christopher thought about the analogy, sit up and try and swipe the wasp and then it might well sting you out of spite. So if you are going to sit up and deal with the irritating wasp that is circling, then you should be decisive, destroy it to remove any risk that it will sting you. However you then run the danger of other wasps, hearing the pain of their fallen comrade coming to see what is occurring and then you will have numerous wasps circling you.

Logic told Christopher, that sitting back and letting the wasps circle the Bashford family would at this stage be the better option, less risk of stirring things up. Christopher liked to think that he always used logic; he always gave that impression to his staff. In reality he often liked to take action, attack being the best form of defence, call the shots and not just react to an ever changing situation. At this moment in time there was nothing that suggested that the reason there were two reporters in an innocuous French village was connected to Peter's previous life. For the second time in two days he called Mick Hayes, he wanted him back in France.

"I want you to go back tonight, stay nearby, and find out what the other journalist is up to."

"Can't I catch tomorrow's afternoon flight? It will be so much easier for me to stay in the UK tonight, I have only just got back, and I won't mind some time with a close friend, she has missed me."

At times Mick was exasperating, he never gave a simple yes, there was always something. It was just that he did his job well and people took to him, which is always useful when you are trying to wheedle out some secret or other.

"Take her with you, as your assistant, I just want you back in La Ville du Bois for the morning, so if that means driving down from Calais, that is the way it will have to be. There is now another journalist in the village, I want to know what she is doing there, the real reason. How long she plans to be there and if she has had any contact with the Bashford family. If you cannot be bothered to help me, I am sure I can find somewhere more local to deploy you."

Local deployment was very much a threat. Local deployment would be a nine till five office position in the centre of London doing very boring work and no expense account to inflate.

"Once you are there," Christopher was confident that his operative would be in France in the morning, "I need you to call me at the very least every twenty-four hours, and if anything significant happens call me sooner, is that clear?"

"I'll drive down alone tonight," Mick sounded exasperated, "my girlfriend would only spend the whole journey moaning at me so I would rather listen to my music. Call every day, unless something crops up, understood. Oh by the way. The other journalist is back in the UK safe and sound, although he did make a call to check me out, seemed like a nice guy, not what one would expect of a hard-nosed investigating journo."

"Leave the character references to me; you just put your ears to the ground."

Christopher leaned back into the deep buttoned green leather chair that his position allowed him to have, he looked around the wooden panelled room, a large room that resembled an Edwardian library. Originally his grand office belonged to the directors of ICI before the company moved out of their Millbank Headquarters. Now privileged civil servants and government ministers made use of the luxurious suite of offices. Offices that reflected, in Christopher's opinion, such a better time where values such as honesty meant something and the modern world had not yet been invented.

BROCKLEY.

Opening his front door in Beverley Court, Greg looked down at the small collection of mail that had been delivered in his absence. He stepped across the random letters and pizza menus before he closed the door behind him excluding the outside world from his private world, still painfully aware of the dominating silence within his flat. He had only been away a couple of days, yet the January evening chill had penetrated each of his rooms chilling the reception; his home felt cold, unwelcoming. Maybe it was because it was the first time he had arrived back from a holiday or a weekend break knowing that his break was going to continue tomorrow. There would be no Deptford Chronicle office to go to, no colleagues to greet to ask about the voyage that he had been on, what the weather was like, was the food as good as they say, was not that where some dictator or other had a winter retreat; a room full of journalists brought up the oddest and most obscure facts you could think of. This time that was not going to happen. Greg would get up in the morning, no alarm being set, have a slow and empty breakfast before doing what, he had no real idea, he was adrift and alone. It was not the first time he had found himself alone. He looked over at the white framed photograph that stood beside the telephone and PC screen. His mother, father and sister, and the young Greg at the very front, a holiday photograph taken in Cornwall, they had stayed at a caravan site close to Perranporth. Two weeks during the August school holidays, two sunny weeks, Mother and Father sitting in deck chairs, Father reading and Mother knitting, while Greg took his younger sister off rockpooling. Armed with bucket and two nets, they searched crevices and granite crags that had, until a couple of hours ago, been submerged under the sea water, now the tides had retreated across the expanses of sand. The two children searched out the crabs and crustaceans that had been left behind by the retreating tides and now waited patiently for those tides to return only to be scooped up in some child's net, then prodded, poked and laughed at for being funny looking. Just a few crabs would be taken back to the caravan to become pets for the duration of the holiday, to be fed on cheese and corned beef, none of which seemed to interest the sea creatures. Greg and his sister would spend hours on those rocks, their shorts and tee shirts getting wet, the brisk sea breeze overcoming the warmth of the midday sun to raise goose bumps on their skin. Then it was back to their relaxed parents for a sandwich, a plastic tumbler of lemonade, Mother would not allow any glass on the beach just in case it broke, then rushing back to the pools staying as long as possible before Father strode towards them telling them, in his very sharp commanding voice, it was time to come back to base camp and build sand castles, as the tide would soon be onto the rocks. There might be another hour or two of building sand castles and tunnels, then directed by Father, they would attempt to build an impregnable wall of sand, to keep the sea out of the castle grounds, each day they tried and each day they failed, the salt water eroding and spilling over their meagre defences. Even so it did not dampen their enthusiasm, the next day they would be there to try it all over again.

Greg touched the cold dusty glass of the photograph, sweet Brenda, his sister, five years younger than him, they spent hours together, laughing, playing, she liked all sorts of boys games and he, out of fairness, did occasionally play dolls with her, on the express understanding that she did not tell a soul, she kept her promise as she always did and never told a soul.

The last holiday he would spend with his family, was when Greg was eighteen years old, although he did not know at the time it was going to be the final holiday they would ever have together. Their caravan holiday was now at Caister in Norfolk, the sea was as blue as it had ever been, the sand felt the same as it had on the Cornish holidays. Now rock pools no longer held the same charm and attraction, Greg played tennis with his now thirteen-year-old sister, sand cricket, frisbee, active games between lazing in the warm sunshine. Brenda had shown no sign of what was going on in her mind. Unseen by the other family members, her mind was in turmoil and confusion. It was just three weeks after that family holiday on a Tuesday morning, a school day and Brenda was clearly over-sleeping. Mother went up to rouse her, whilst Father was putting his coat on and Greg was crunching toast and raspberry jam. The scream tore through the house but the tear was even greater on the family. Brenda was lying in her bed, looking like sleeping beauty, her hands crossed over her heart, her eyes closed and peaceful. The Coroner said it was an over-dose of everyday paracetamol, more than ten times the normal daily dose had given her kidney failure. There was no note, no message to indicate why she had decided to end her young life that was so full of promise. Even without an enigmatic message or obvious reason the Coroner passed a verdict of suicide. No one knew what had been going through her mind as she swallowed those fatal tablets.

Mother and Father tried to understand, tried to find a reason, examining small words, large actions before that fateful day, their own postmortem of Brenda's suicide only hastened their own deaths. Mother passed away almost a year to the day, she was out shopping when her heart decided it was broken enough and could not cope with the first anniversary of her daughter's death. Father followed eighteen months later, a growth in his side turned out to be liver cancer, he was not bothered about treatment, he just wanted to join his wife in heaven, which he did during one dark September night, with Greg beside him, shedding tears for all his family.

After that, his work colleagues became his family, sharing his downs, celebrating his ups, advising him on what to do, what to buy, commenting on his fashion and critique his writing. Now they too had gone, Greg was more alone than he had ever been.

Greg knew deep in his heart that he was a survivor, he could and would fight against any adversity that was sent his way and draw a strength from it. Maybe his mother and Father were not as strong, maybe that was why they gave up when Brenda died, which hurt Greg in a way he did not at the time fully understand. They were happy to die once their daughter had passed on, yet with their deaths they left Greg an orphan, a 20 year old orphan without family, no blood ties, all were gone. His parents had not thought enough of him to fight to be there for him, they just gave up, abandoning him to find escape in their own deaths.

Now Greg could not see much of a future for himself, he was at best a mediocre writer and reporter, who had been cast into a sea of top freelance writers whom he would need to compete against in order to pay his mortgage. He was in a sea full of rocks upon which he might run aground and where he could be eaten by the relations of those crabs he had tormented and captured all those years ago. Greg shivered from the chill in the air and his bitter thoughts, a single malt whisky was called for to warm the atmosphere.

It was as Greg consumed his third single malt whisky that there was a knock on his door. He walked across the small living room into the hallway, stepping over the mail still on the floor, before opening the door. Donna stood in front of him, smiling, holding a bottle of red wine.

"Welcome back to the United Kingdom and to the delights of South London," she thrust the bottle toward Greg by way of a present.

"Come in," Greg did not exactly smile as he opened the door wider for her to enter, but did not feel that he could just close the door on her.

"Everyone's missing you already, the place is just not the same without you. Actually before we open the wine, if that is scotch you're drinking, I do like a single malt as much as the next girl!"

"I've only been gone three days, I have had longer holidays." Greg said as he poured Donna a glass of his whisky, which she swirled around the glass, inhaling the aroma before taking a man size gulp.

"Mmmm nice, I always knew you had good taste Greg. Maybe it is only three days, I think it has just spooked everyone that you were just sent packing, without so much as a bye or leave. Rumour has it that you were sacked because of your suicide stories, but more of us know the real reason, money and cutbacks. There is talk that there will be more cuts on the way, so maybe it is good that you are out of it. Cheers!" They chinked glasses and Donna brought Greg up to date with the gossip that had happened over the last three days. Greg then reciprocated by telling Donna about his trip to France and the missing Martin and the defensive Bashford family.

Donna felt comfortable after her third glass and was excited at the prospect of actually being inside Greg's flat. She, of course, knew the address, had stood outside on many occasions, now here she was, on his black leather sofa sitting opposite him, almost like a couple. She contained her excitement and joy, knowing that if she started screaming and bouncing up and down on the sofa it would, no doubt, unnerve Greg.

"In all honesty, " Donna reasoned, " if this Peter Bashford is living an easy life, early retirement in France, then you turn up asking about a missing Englishman, and then start asking him how he can retire and live in France at such a young age, I think I would have asked you to leave as well. What's it got to do with you? Yeah, that would have been my response. Plus I do get what you are saying about the payphone telephone conversation, that I agree is unusual, but it might have been planned, he could have been phoning his mistress. After all if you are that young and retired, money would not be a problem, so a mistress, I think, could be on the cards." Donna concluded.

"And the school photograph?" Greg asked.

"Well, we all have odd photographs around our houses." Donna felt herself blush a little as she thought of the two photographs she had of Greg, hopefully he would think it was the whisky warming her cheeks. "Maybe there is a question to be asked, or maybe not. You are a good judge of character, hell Greg, you're a reporter, a good reporter that can judge people in the first five minutes. You have that gut feeling, that insight, however people dress or speak, you can see through the facade to the real person. What is your heart telling you?"

Greg paused a moment and thought about what Donna had said, then concluded.

"Peter Bashford is scared, that was what I felt sitting there in their room. I was just asking simple questions, which at first did not seem to worry them. Only when I turned to ask about their lives did they seem to tighten up, become more tense, a tension did swell up between them. Plus the passports, no record there, now that is odd."

Donna moved from her place and installed herself next to Greg, poured both him and herself another drink.

"That settles it for me, we need to look up those names in the photograph, and see what that brings, so let's get Googling."

The next morning Greg recalled calling out some names to Donna, yet that was all Greg remembered. He must have fallen asleep on the sofa, as that was where he woke up, pins and needles all down his leg from the awkward sleeping position. With a headache and a foul tasting mouth, he regretted the amount of single malt he had consumed, maybe there was a clue in the word single. He dragged his hung over body into the toilet, emptied his bladder, undressed, dropped all his clothes onto the floor and stepped into the shower. The hot water refreshed his body, and helped wipe the sleep from his eyes, alerting his mind as he recalled last night and his visitor, Donna. He felt guilty that he clearly was not able to ensure she got home safely, he hoped that she had. He need not have worried as, from the other side of the shower curtain, her voice echoed around the room over the noise of the shower.

"Don't look I'm having a pee."

"What are you doing in my bathroom?"

"I just told you, having a pee, I couldn't hold on any longer. If you had a separate toilet and bathroom this would have been a lot easier. Wow, we did drink a little too much last night didn't we? I still enjoyed a good evening, although we never did get around to that bottle of red, the whisky was too nice. Can I flush or will it interfere with your shower?"

"Fine, go ahead." Greg stood, he had stopped washing himself, thinking it rude to wash whilst in the presence of a guest. He need not have worried, the curtain was pulled to one side by Donna, who stood there naked, coolly she asked,

"Can I join you?"

Greg pulled the curtain back across the bath.

"No!"

"Ok, suit yourself. Give me a call when you have finished, don't rush, I'm not due in at work until eleven today."

Greg heard the door close and finished his ablutions as quickly as he could.

They sat across the breakfast table, Donna was now showered and dressed ready for work. Greg sat in loose fitting jogging bottoms and an old Bon Jovi tee-shirt.

"You're a real prude you know, I would have thought you being a single man, picking up women, wining, dining and bedding them, I just assumed sharing a shower with a work colleague, well ex-work colleague in reality, would have been no big deal."

Greg looked at her as she finished her coffee, preparing to leave for the Deptford Chronicle offices.

"I don't think I am a prude Donna, but I am sure it is not totally normal for work associates to shower together. They might do team bonding days and joint exercises, which I hear are very popular in Japan, but I have yet to hear of communal showering as a way of improving corporate efficiency. Let's say I was more shocked than being a prude, plus I would not have thought you were the type of girl to go showering with fellow workers."

"Don't get me wrong Greg, you're the only one I have ever considered showering with." She had thought of other things she could do with Greg, but for now she only mentioned showering. "I thought we did well last night, a real top team."

Greg looked at her with an expression which asked what exactly did we do as a team; Donna recognised the unspoken question.

"Don't worry," she stood and slipped on her coat, "I did sleep in your bed, just to be comfy, you were the one passed out on the settee, so I thought I would leave you. I thoughtfully put you in the recovery position just in case you vomited. The names, you don't remember do you? We searched out the names on that photograph and lucky for you we wrote it all down." She took a paper pad from the worktop close to the sink and handed it to Greg. "There was a lot of Directory Enquiry action last night, trawling through 192.com and plenty of searching, as well as a few glasses to help us through the night. But we thought we had a start, well I did, at that point you were about to slip into a total drunken stupour. Here we have the four names, plenty of addresses and telephone numbers, but I think, and you sort of agreed, that the first call should be to George Usher, not the singer that we found, but a George Usher who lives about two miles from the Wilmington school, good chance he could be the one. If not, there were not that many George Ushers in the UK, only thirty odd and the one in Kent is about the right age, if you believe 192.com. As I recall you said you would call him this morning whilst I am at work, which I must get off to now. I'd kiss you goodbye, but I think seeing me naked this morning is enough for now, bye."

LA BELLE ETOILE.

For a January morning, the sun was brighter and warmer than it ever seemed just a few miles across the channel. Helen wondered just why such a small stretch of water could make so much difference to the weather, was the sun really warmer here in France? She stopped for a moment and felt the warm rays take the morning chill from her cheeks. It was not really an early morning chill, but more a sense of anxiety as she stood outside Phillip's door at 10.30 a.m. as he had requested. She had considered overnight how wise was the decision she had made to go and see Phillip and talk more on the subject of murder that they had conversed about last night. She wanted to know more; she wanted to explore his strange mind. The Roman statue she had seen on his mantelpiece might not be the one that had been stolen from the Josselin shop by the missing Martin, but somehow she sensed and suspected that Phillip's eyes might have been the last that Martin saw and she hoped that that experience would not befall her. Yet in a strange sort of way she trusted Phillip, she felt she had some sort of connection to him, an empathetic understanding of what he was about. She, of course, had not mentioned any of this to Justine, as if she had the slightest notion that her university friend was going to visit the house of a potential murderer, then Justine would have flown into a wild panic, forbidding, maybe by force, Helen going anywhere near the house. A house that she now stood in front of ready to wrap firmly on the wood of the door with her hand to announce her arrival, she did not need to. Phillip, opened the door and smiled at her standing in front of him.

"I knew you could not resist, please come in and take a seat. Can I get you a coffee?"

Phillip brought in the cafetiere filled with the coffee he had freshly ground that morning, in celebration of his expected visitor. Together they used gel to clean their hands, Phillip waited until a small egg timer rang before he slowly pressed down the gauze filter, straining the coffee, before pouring the hot liquid into the waiting cups and saucers.

"Can I say, Helen, I really enjoyed our conversation last night. I thought it a most intriguing conversation, but to expand on the subject we touched upon, I think it is so much better to continue it in private." Phillip sat opposite her, the sun falling through the window spotlighting him like an actor in a dramatic play. "So why are you so interested in murder Helen? It is something I would have thought a well brought up young lady like you would not have much interest in, apart from reporting those tragic stories that you read about in the papers."

"Like we said last night, it intrigues me what goes through the mind of a murderer as they commit the crime. Even more I wonder about the planning, what it must be like to sit down and coldly, without emotion, plan to kill someone."

"My dear Helen, there is plenty of emotion throughout the whole process, from the moment you decide that someone is going to die, to the point of planning and working out the often complex logistics. The actual murder, which is then followed by disposal of the body and the removal of any potential evidence, all these chapters in the story are full of emotions, mixed sensations and feelings throughout the process. I assume." He added as an afterthought.

Helen turned and looked towards the mantelpiece, where among the other items she saw the Roman statue.

"And those?" She pointed in the general direction of the artifacts, "Do they have a meaning?"

"I would imagine your mother, like millions of other mothers, had bric-a-brac littering her house, each item a memory jogger, from a holiday, a gift from a relation, or a reminder of something special that might have happened in one's life. My mother had a glass gondola, it had a black hull, with green, yellow and red coloured glass for the canopy, I think an uncle must have bought it for her when he went to Venice. I know she held onto it and cried a lot when he died."

Bluntness and surprise can often unsettle the most confident of people, a blunt to the point question might rock the seemingly calm Phillip. "Did you murder Martin?" Helen asked.

Phillip finished his coffee in a deliberate and slow manner to allow him time to think about his answer.

"My mother always said, 'you should answer a question with another question'. I never really understood why you would do that, if everyone did the same you would never get an answer, so maybe that was the reason, to avoid answering a question you proffer another question. So Helen, here is my question to you, who have you killed?"

Helen looked at his eyes, they reached into her mind, picking out her memories as a mind reader might do. She had always believed that mind readers were theatrical tricksters, circus acts, yet here, alone with Phillip, she now believed that a human might well be able to read another's thoughts.

"I have never killed anyone," her answer felt uncomfortable.

"Come now Helen, you must think me silly, the questions you ask, the way you react. Consider, you are sitting there looking at me, I would guess you have taken a number of facts and information that you have collected, added them to some of answer and have convinced yourself that I have murdered before. Do not think that you are the only one capable of such a deduction, you have killed, of that I am convinced, maybe not a murder. Responsible for a death? Responsible for letting a life end? A life that you thought would be better off ending, to profit your own future."

"Your mother," he stated without emotion or any indication of where he would lead the conversation. Helen now found herself at the sharp end of a blunt question. Even so, Helen could not control those small independent muscles that must have twitched and moved in her face, they betrayed her buried emotions. "You told me last night that your mother fell down the stairs, could you have saved her? Could you have helped her or did you.....?"

"Stop!" Helen shouted, before calming slightly, "What do you know of what happened that day? Who do you think you are, insinuating that I killed my mother?"

Phillip corrected her.

"Perhaps not killed in the murder sense, maybe you just took control over her life. The very first time that you, sweet, innocent Helen who had always done exactly as she was told, worn the dresses and clothes that Mummy wanted her to, gone to bed when told, it was the first time you had control. Her life was in your hands. Call for help or not, it was you who had the supreme power over her at that moment. Nice feeling, wasn't it Helen? And yes, that was another question."

"Alright," she snapped back at him, "here's a question for you, have you killed anyone?"

Phillip stood and smiled at her as he walked towards the mantelpiece, "Actually as we discussed last night, I never killed anyone, I have murdered though. Another coffee?"

*

He walked out of the room, holding the tray of empty cups disappearing into the kitchen, calm and precise, without any hint of emotion. Helen could not believe her ears; he had just admitted he was a murderer. She was now on the edge of a story like no other, a double page spread, photographs and bylines, her byline telling the readers, over their breakfast, of her having coffee with a murderer. As scoops go this was a result for a rookie on the Daily Mirror, they would be proud of her, maybe not any Pulitzer Prize just yet, but clearly she would have laid down markers in the ground as to her potential, which the editors would be foolish to ignore. Another thought crossed her mind, why had he admitted to such a crime calmly over coffee, in front of a reporter, which was the first question she asked when he returned with more coffee, cafetiere cleaned and refilled, clean cups and saucers.

"Why did I admit to murder, to a reporter? Oh Helen, you can be so naïve at times. I have, I admit to you, committed four murders, and by the simple fact that I am telling you about them now here in my house and not in a prison cell must tell you that, as I have already told you, I plan and calculate everything so as not to get caught, which although I say so myself, does require a certain high level of intelligence. So ask yourself, I must feel very confident that whatever I tell you in this room will go no further. The conundrum for you is, does this mean I am going to make you my fifth victim or.....?" The timer rang out again and Phillip stopped talking to focus his attention on plunging down the filter and pouring coffee before he continued, "If you believe in love at first sight, then I suppose that is why I told you."

"Love?"

"Not in the man, woman sex type love, but if you believe in love at first sight, you believe that two people can meet and have an instant connection. We have a connection, a connection in the way we enjoy having supreme power and control over people's lives. Your mother, I could sense it from the moment we mentioned killing and murder. Your eyes gave you away, you contributed to your mother's death and frankly you liked the experience, didn't you? And you are wondering if you could ever do it again. So the moment you met me you saw that connection too, we are from the same mould Helen, so tell me how did you kill your mother?"

*

Helen recalled the day. She had been sitting on the warm summer grass, her watercolour pad laid on her lap, as she drew with her pencil the outline of some flowers, she thought they were some sort of iris, although she was no garden expert. It was a Thursday, both the cook and the gardener had their days off. Her sister had gone to town shopping and Helen remained to draw in the garden, a favourite pastime of hers. Her mother stayed in the house, maybe having a sleep, one of her afternoon naps, which she often had following lunch and two or three glasses of wine. Helen liked those times, she was alone, no one to critic her, no one to tell her how ugly she was, no one to say 'just because she was Daddy's favourite'. Mother seemed to take it out on both Helen and her sister for their father being away so much; deep down Helen guessed he preferred to be in the City away from Mother's moaning, complaining and drinking. So here in the garden alone with just the insects, flowers and the cordial sunshine, Helen felt she was in paradise.

Thursdays were often a pleasurable day, Mother would cook for her two daughters and they would talk around the dinner table. Mother would not drink as much as normal and for a few hours they giggled and gossiped like females so often do. But other Thursdays she would be tense, often not cooking, hiding away in her room, maybe spending the whole day hidden away whilst her daughters went about their lives caring for themselves. Today had been one of those bad Thursdays, she had hardly seen her mother and Helen had lunched on toast and left over pate. Her sister had gone shopping so without her for company, Helen had secreted herself in the garden amongst the flowers.

But that Thursday afternoon everything would change as a scream came from the house and tore along the garden dragging Helen from her blissful isolation, it was instinct that took Helen, as fast as she could, into the house and her mother's cries for her daughter to attend to her.

"Helen! Helen! Where are you, stupid girl, I need you now!"

Helen arrived out of breath, panting heavily from the run, to discover her mother lying at the bottom of the stairs, her leg clearly broken, the white of the bone was pushing through the skin, her arm was twisted awkwardly behind her, and at the side of her head, blood flowed fast from a large gash. Helen stood, looking shocked.

"Helen, get me the doctor. Don't just stand there like a lemon, ring the fucking doctor I'm in pain, look at my sodding leg, get me a doctor first, then a glass of scotch."

Helen did not move, the shock transfixed her, her mother was lying helpless and at her mercy. It was then, as her mother brushed her hair back with her hand, that she felt the warm liquid spilling from her head,

"Oh shit, I'm bleeding! God, it's pouring! Helen, don't just stand there like an idiot, get the phone, call the doctor; now, you fool, do it now and get me a towel or something to stop this blood ruining the carpet."

Helen stopped in the doorway, looked at her mother, her now helpless mother, injured yet still unable to be kind, still treating her daughter like some low class servant. Helen walked away from her mother and picked up the telephone that was close to the kitchen, then replaced the receiver, walked back to her mother and stared at her in silence.

"You stupid bitch, call a fucking doctor!"

Her mother was now trying to crawl away from the stairs, blood still gushing from her head, through which Helen could see the white of her mother's skull, however bad it might look, it was possible it was worse than Helen suspected. Without speaking Helen returned to the telephone, unplugged it and took it out into the garden with her. Her sister was going for a meal after shopping so she would not be back for many hours. Helen returned to her drawing pad on the warm summer grass, her mother's pleading voice growing weaker as Helen moved further away until blood loss and pain started to impinge on Mother's ability to stay conscious. Helen recalled that it was for the best part of forty minutes that her mother shouted, abusing her daughter, her only chance of survival, she still called obscenities at the daughter that she could not see. Two hours later, well after the shouting had stopped, Helen walked back into the house, her mother was lying on the floor, breathing very faintly in a pool of blood. Helen went outside again to her drawing, blue irises are complex to draw and get just right. It was just after six o'clock that evening, when she once more returned to the silent house, her mother's breathing had stopped. Helen held the limp wrist, there was no pulse, her jaw hung loose, she held a mirror to her mother's mouth, no condensation, no breath, just to be sure she waited beside her mother for another thirty minutes. She noticed her mother had soiled herself and had not moved at all, the blood had stopped falling from her skull. Then and only then did Helen plug the phone back in and call for an ambulance.

*

"Well Helen, I'm interested I'll ask you again how did you kill your mother?"

She looked across the room at Phillip, who now sat leaning slightly forward, looking at her like a little boy lost, inquiring, wide eyed and waiting for her to speak. She had never told anyone the truth of what had happened during that afternoon when her mother had fallen down the stairs, she knew at the time she had done wrong, wrong in the normal sense of what a mother and daughter relationship should be. Helen hated her mother, because her mother hated her, but that would have been too hard to explain if she had told the whole truth about that afternoon. As a teenager, she always confided in herself that she had just let things take their course, she had not pushed her mother, her mother had fallen, so just not helping was not killing someone really; Mother might have lived, it had been God's will to let her die, Helen just helped the process. She knew she could never tell anyone, modern society would still consider her actions to be manslaughter at the least, she would never have made university, never become a reporter, and would, no doubt, have been banished by her family. So here she was in a foreign country, sitting opposite a man she barely knew and she was about to tell him everything, it just felt the right thing to do. Her mouth opened as she began to confess and she knew her life could never be the same again.

Helen told him each graphic detail, the fall, the leaving her at the bottom of the stairs, the regular walk to the foot of the stairs to see how far her mother had deteriorated, how she was glad to see her mother dying, for once she, Helen, was in control and the superlative human being in the family house.

"And that secret, you have held inside you all these years Helen, you must be so strong and have so much will-power. Plus such strength of mind, that is a big burden to carry, yet I hope that now you have shared your special secret with me, you might feel better, more relaxed, a weight off your shoulders."

She smiled at him warmly and agreed she did feel better.

"So, maybe," he continued, "not full blown murder but certainly that feeling of euphoria when you realise that you have had control over when someone lives or dies. I guess Helen, you are interested in total murder, if so, you have come to the right place, let's go for walk." He beckoned her to follow him as he went out through the kitchen and outside to the large garden with its vegetable patch, collection of haphazard sheds and small buildings and the noise of pigs as they approached the animal pens.

She followed him, wondering just what he was going to show her or do to her. Maybe she should have been fearful, alone with a man in the middle of almost nowhere who had already said that he had murdered four people; was he lying, or was he telling the truth and about to remove the only witness to his confession?

MEOPHAM, KENT.

Christopher's mind was not on the afternoon meeting with three of his young enthusiastic aides, who were all trying to convince their superior that tracking the movements of a Junior Minster, might not be considered to be in the public interest. Christopher's thoughts had regressed eight years, to the last time he had seen William Lynch or Peter Bashford as he was now known. He began to recall in his mind, the last lunch they had together.

*

"So just why exactly have you dragged me all the way up from Devon just to have lunch in this restaurant in the middle of the Kent countryside?" asked a very agitated William Lynch.

Irritated by the question, Christopher Davenport Wellington slowly moved the menu away from his field of vision and looked over his frameless glasses towards his lunch companion opposite. William Lynch had no interest, at this stage, in the contents of the lunchtime menu, he wanted an explanation. Their table was located in what had been for many years an unprofitable public house, until the brewery closed it down and the empty pub had been taken over by two enterprising young men, who saw the potential for a restaurant with high standards, in the affluent village of Meopham.

"Look at the menu William, they have some very interesting dishes, all cooked with an excellence that is hard to find in some London establishments, plus there is not that awful lunchtime crush of office workers having a raucous lunch. This is a lot more civilized, I am sure you will agree. In addition, as you can imagine, it would be foolish of me to be seen having lunch with you, people would start asking difficult questions. Now, don't worry yourself about why we are here, order first, I am ravenous."

His work colleagues suspected that Christopher Davenport Wellington was not his real name. Those who tried to find out came up against a barrier of secret files, missing links, unconfirmed stories and general tittle-tattle. Christopher himself avoided or ignored direct questions about his lineage, although he did secretly enjoy the discussions around his name. The general consensus of those who took part in the Christopher name debate, was that he was an actual direct blood relation to the Duke of Wellington. One of Christopher's distant relatives then fell out with the Duke, and hence began the Davenport-Wellington name, adding a distinct naval flavour to the army side of the family, and further annoying the Wellington branch. Others less sympathetic to Christopher, and his arrogant management manner, described him as 'the bastard offspring of a Portsmouth whore who could not be sure if Christopher's father was a sailor or a solider.' In the event neither hypothesis was correct.

As they ate, William tried to bring the conversation back to why they were at a discreet countryside restaurant but Christopher would not be distracted from enjoying his spatchcock; pausing between mouthfuls, only to continue offering his unwelcome opinion on the way the current Tory government were still squeezing the Civil Service, to a point where officials like Christopher, would be unable to carry out their work with the degree of skill required. Christopher had been a civil servant all his life and had no intention of letting any government, left, centre or right, interfere with his chosen profession.

"So how have you been since the unfortunate incident William, family alright with the accommodation?" The question came without warning as Christopher stirred his coffee. William waited a moment to compose himself before answering.

"For an intelligent man that is an incredibly stupid question to ask. I am devastated. I lost my work colleagues, I lost my work, and I lost my purpose, in a split second. An explosion and everything was gone. Not forgetting being forced by you to give up my house, my relatives and friends, and now you have me on some sort of gardening leave, so I clearly have no future with you people, unless you have some special plans for me?"

"William, you just don't see how lucky you are. Imagine if you had not gone out to your dreary driveway and seen that nasty flat tyre, you would have arrived at work in plenty of time to be killed. Being the scientist that you are, changing a tyre is a lot more challenging for you than splitting molecular structures, so the Automobile Association needed to be called to carry out the task for you. Then, and this is the bit I really like, you ring your friend Tony, ask him to tell everyone that you have arrived but are throwing up in the toilet, because you knew that if you were not present at that essential staff meeting, you would have been in the very deepest of trouble. Having already been given a final warning, that flat tyre could have been the end of your employment with the Government, explosion or no explosion."

Christopher adjusted his glasses, then sipped his coffee and waited for his words to sink in, before continuing,

"So, when that terrible accident happened, you had a very lucky escape. We wouldn't be sitting here talking, would we?"

"We are only talking here today because I have something you want."

Christopher did not respond, he just opened the small dark chocolate bar that came with his coffee and smiled.

William pushed his empty coffee cup to one side, leaned on the table bringing his face closer to Christopher's plump rounded face.

"Maybe I should not have called in and told that little white lie but I couldn't afford to lose my job for not turning up for an 'essential' staff meeting. All the previous meetings I had been to were a total waste of time, yet you would have still used it to get rid of me, and my face that didn't fit. But I did tell a little white lie, and the consequence was, I lived. I also know a little too much about what went on in Sevenoaks, fortunately, that knowledge is my insurance. If I should die, everything I know becomes public."

"Oh, if life was that simple, William, the more strings one holds onto the more likely they are of getting tangled and knotted. To be honest, you are holding onto some interesting strings, so I am not going to re-employ you, sack you, let you go, or anything as easy as that. I have decided I'm giving you a new life, a new start and really for a man of thirty-seven years of age, you have won the equivalent of the lottery."

Christopher drank the last of his coffee before waving arrogantly to a passing waiter for another black Americano.

"William, since the explosion, you have been on gardening leave away from the prying eyes of the press and others for reasons you are fully aware of. Imagine for a moment if we had talked of the lucky escape of one worker who, fortuitously, had a flat tyre and escaped death. All those boring tabloids would be humming round you like a horde of excited honey bees. Then the questions they would ask: about your family, your AA membership, you and your work, what sort of work you did at the site? There we have a little bit of an issue being that it is secret, so do we lie? We certainly do not tell the truth. So we have to fudge, and history has shown time and time again that fudging does not work. So, we just kept you out of the limelight and told the truth. Those at the site had indeed all died, which of course we honestly thought at the time was true, and no journalist ever thought to ask about if there were any other workers, from the innocent, almost boring factory, who survived. The newspapers, they told their story, dreary stories. They told everyone the plant was processing chemicals for a small company that now would maybe face bankruptcy following a tragic accident. You see William, we had to keep you away from the limelight, not just for now, but forever. We cannot afford you being discovered by the press or anyone else for that matter."

"So how do you plan to give me a new life? Lock me up somewhere?"

Christopher ignored the question, which was what he always did if he was asked a question that he did not want to, or could not, answer.

"Don't worry, it does not include concrete boots in the Thames. It involves a French farmhouse, plus a substantial living allowance until both you and your lovely wife pass away. There, of course, will be the usual cost of living allowance increase every year, all paid directly into your French bank account in Euros."

"I don't have a French bank account."

"Oh you do now, and a French farmhouse, all the paperwork has been taken care of. If you really hate it, then you can always ask me and I will arrange another location for you to spend lazy days at the expense of the Government. Just one word of warning, if you decide to go missing, I will track you down, and maybe next time my solution will not be that beneficial to you."

"Is that a threat?"

Christopher grinned,

"Very much so."

"Let me be clear on this," William had now leaned back in his chair, totally surprised at what he had heard. He always knew that Christopher would have a plan, this just sounded too good to be true, even with the clear threat at the end, "you want me and my family to go and live in France with your Tory government paying for everything, keeping me to a ripe old age. Why?"

"Well the Tory Government will currently be footing the bill. So will any subsequent Government, I guess that Labour will be back sometime in the future. The why part is a little more difficult to explain, nevertheless I guess you want me to try. Look upon this as a witness protection scheme, not to put too fine a point on the situation, there are some who, as you are fully aware, would prefer you dead. I support, as I am sure you do, the opposite view, in which you should live to a ripe old age, living in France away from those prying eyes. So this means you get to draw your pension very early."

"Do I have any option in this plan of yours?

"Not unless you are happy to die at a young age. That is not a threat from me, you understand, just a prediction of what could happen should you not take up my generous offer. You know that you have enough tangible knowledge of what was going on in Sevenoaks, to be of value to anyone who wanted to restart the project. The UK government does not want to restart it and the very last thing they want is some grubby third rate country getting their soiled hands on you. Under those circumstances, I cannot see you making old age. At the very least, you will end up working in some dirty, hot laboratory in the middle of the desert with your family being held as insurance so that you continue on with your work. On balance, I would say a new name and a new life in the French countryside is not a bad option."

LA BELLE ETOILE.

"My pigs are such a treat to watch. I do eat ham but would never eat any of my special friends here. They are my accomplices in homicide, a part they play which they enjoy so much."

Together Helen and Phillip leaned on the weathered, waist high fence that boxed in the six pigs. Their pungent smell disgusted Helen, even so she refrained from making any comment, Phillip was clearly proud of his pigs as he introduced each one of them to her by name.

"My last victim ended up in this pen. His body is now gone, totally consumed by my pigs and then spread over the pen in the form of shit or, as us country folk like to say, manure."

He laughed at his own joke.

"Good for the soil and not a million miles away from a dull vicar declaring, 'ashes to ashes, dust to dust'. It just proves to me, that one way or another, we all end up back in mother Earth from whence we came. I suppose I could tell you about my victims, but I'm sure you would not get a real sense of the total power I have over people, choosing them, planning how I am going to kill and then dispose of the lifeless body. I'm not scaring you am I Helen?"

She was not going to show it, but she did at that moment, seeing the excitement in his eyes, feel like she was potentially going to become the pigs' next meal. However, she did not flinch or panic, she just continued to lean in a lazy manner against the fence looking at the pigs ferreting around the pen for food.

"No, but I would like to hear more."

"Helen."

He turned to her with the excited look of a child when it realized that it was Christmas Eve and Santa Claus would soon be visiting with his bags of presents and parcels. He squeezed her cold hand, pulling her slightly closer to his chest; they were now so close she could feel his warm, clean breath on her flushed cheeks. Helen was not sure what she expected next, a kiss, an embrace, or his hands around her neck.

"I'm going to show you, just how good I am at what I do. How easy it is to kill. You aren't returning to the UK yet, are you?"

His voice was that of a concerned child who was worried that Santa might pass by missing his house leaving him without any presents.

"I don't plan to go back for a couple of days yet."

"Thank goodness, let's go back inside or else you might start getting a chill."

They both returned to the warmth of the fire, again sitting on a settee but this time Phillip sat next to Helen, their knees touching. He took from the side table a red address book, flicked through the pages and selected a page. He pointed to a line and grunted in a satisfied way, leaned across and picked up the telephone, dialed a number and waited. He looked at Helen with excited proud eyes, he seemed to be reveling in showing off to her, but she was not sure exactly what she was watching being played out; she listened to one side of the conversation.

"Dougie, how are you? It's Phillip."

"Yes from the club. What a wild night that was, how could I forget you were totally, well, you just were."

Helen heard a muffled voice from the cordless phone, before Phillip continued.

"Yes I'm fine thanks, enjoying life in France or as they say, *'Je sais que quand tu rêves, tu n'entends que ma voix.'*"

Phillip remained silent for a moment, there was no muffled sound that Helen could hear, then Phillip took up the conversation.

"Dougie, I need a very special favour from a very special friend as you are to me. Could you bring to me by tomorrow night at the latest, a pie funnel, shaped like a black bird, I really do need one urgently."

Once again, Helen heard a muffled reply.

"Yes I am in France, you will have to fly to Dinard airport, there you will hire a car from Avis and drive to their office in Loudéac, returning the car to them. I will meet you there, outside their office and bring you to my house. Now repeat those instructions please."

Phillip nodded his head as Dougie confirmed what he had been told to do.

"Thank you, Dougie. I will look forward to seeing you tomorrow night. There is no need for you to tell anyone what you are doing. Goodbye and take care."

Phillip put down the phone and turned to Helen, smiling broadly.

"Well now do you believe that I have power over people?"

"Did you just ask that person – Dougie - to bring you a pie funnel from the UK and be here tomorrow night, from England?"

Phillip nodded

"You sound surprised Helen. Didn't you believe me when I said that I had the power to make people do things, and ultimately have the power of life and death over them? Tomorrow night he will be here. Assuming the flight is on time, then about an hour and a half drive to Loudéac, plus my getting him here to the house, so come back tomorrow night, say about half past eight, and you can meet Dougie in person."

"And then?"

"I kill him, why else would I invite him over? You will learn so much Helen. It is now almost lunchtime and I would rather eat alone today, so maybe you had better go."

Helen drove away from the house, wondering if she had really heard the conversation correctly, or if she was dreaming and about to wake up in a warm, cosy bed, having had the weirdest dream ever. Yet driving through the country lanes felt real and arriving at Justine's house looked real enough. The smell of cooking, as she walked through the door, seemed normal enough. The lunch she consumed with her friend was certainly real. Helen had to conclude that she had not dreamt the morning, it was all real.

The story she was being drawn into seemed to be just getting bigger and bigger, an extraordinary story, with her byline, that she could soon be writing. Or could she? Helen felt something else inside her deepest, darkest feelings, she could not think of words to describe or explain the feeling. What she did know was that tomorrow night she was going to witness a murder, and that thought excited her.

WILMINGTON, KENT.

Greg lied, he knew he had to, there were always times when it was better to tell a small white lie at the very start when assuming that it would better for all in the end. So when he had telephoned George Usher, George was understandably out at work, his wife, Emily answered the telephone and listened politely to Greg with growing interest as he explained that he was writing a history of grammar schools in Kent. That was the small white lie. He then went on to tell her that during his research, - not so much a white lie, more slight variation from the truth - he had found an interesting photograph of the 1990 chess champions at Wilmington school - now back on track and telling the truth - and he had thought it would make an interesting chapter if he traced those four former chess champions - maybe half-truth - half lie. Greg was assuming, he admitted to Emily, that the George Usher he was telephoning was the same one as in the photograph.

"How very fascinating Mr Auden."

"Please do call me Greg." He responded quickly.

"Well Greg, my George did go to Wilmington and the photograph you discovered, I am looking at it right now, well one of the copies at least, on our side board with our other family photographs. Too many of the grandchildren." she added jokingly. "George has always been proud of that photograph, the only time he really won anything of any importance. He tells everyone that when he met me, I distracted him from his interest in chess. He tells everyone, with that big Cheshire cat grin he has, that England missed out on a World Chess Champion. I know he doesn't really believe that, but he does like to tease me and our friends."

Emily was sure that her husband would love to meet with Greg, to talk about the chess champions. Greg and Emily between them arranged a time that evening of just after eight o'clock, once the Ushers had finished their dinner and washed up. Emily seemed very keen to make sure all the dinner plates were washed and put away before her guest arrived. They would look forward to spending the evening reminiscing, an excited Emily was looking forward, she admitted, to surprising her husband with the news when he returned from work.

The house was, even on the dark January night, a very tidy, organized semi-detached house, with pebble-dashed bright white walls and a garden of neatly cut back shrubs for the winter. Lawn edges were trimmed and tidy and a freshly cream painted doorway surrounded a PVC door that matched the double glazed windows of the house. The interior, as Emily showed her guest in, was equally tidy, not a speck of dust to be seen, ornaments placed carefully with thought, not one appeared to be out of place. Greg imagined that everything in their home had its own place. A soft floral fragrance hung in the hallway, Greg suspected that it had been only recently hoovered in preparation for their guest. They went into the living room, as Emily described it, a warm, inviting room of beige shades, a selection of table and standard lamps were lit around the room giving a diffused soft lighting. George stood up from his armchair located to the left of the fireplace with its faux flames and imitation coals; on the right hand side was another single sofa chair with knitting laid on it, obviously Emily's chair, and set between the two a longer three seater sofa. Greg thought it strange that the chairs all faced the fireplace, as opposed to towards the television, so often the focus of sitting areas, which was demoted to a corner of the room. Greg suspected the room reflected their personalities, neat and tidy, precise and placed, nothing unexpected, no surprises.

Introductions concluded, tea offered and accepted, arrived with a selection of biscuits on a plate decorated with some pretty flowers in yellow and pink. Emily Usher knew how to make people welcome.

Greg stuck to his small white lie of researching a history book on Kent Grammar schools, which if he kept to his timetable should be out late next year. At the back of his mind he wondered if that might not be a bad project to begin now that he was without work.

George proudly showed the framed photograph to Greg.

"It was the first time the school had won the inter-school competition. I think our headmaster, Mr Dunnett, was over the moon at his young boys getting to the final let alone winning it. Between you and me I would imagine that the competition was a source of great rivalry between all the headmasters. So when we brought back the trophy in 1990, we were welcomed into the school hall like conquering heroes."

"Have you kept in touch with your fellow champions, or as so often happens with school friends over the years, lost touch?" Greg asked, making faux notes as George recalled the heady days of being in the 1990 winning chess team.

"Well, sadly Les Clarke died about three years ago; had a very bad stroke and soon after that his heart just stopped. We had kept in touch from time to time, not great friends, but we still went to the funeral, didn't we Emily."

Emily nodded in agreement and offered Greg another cup of tea which he refused this time.

"I suppose William, William Lynch was a bit like that, not dead, we kept in touch through Christmas cards and the like for a number of years, but of late we have not heard from him, so I can't give you any contact details. But Dennis, now he only lives around the corner, we often have a drink and last year he and his wife joined us for a two week break in Portugal, which was really good, great weather; once or twice Emily got a little tipsy on the rosé wine."

He smiled at his wife, who coyly smiled back. Greg doubted that getting really pissed out of their heads was something Mr and Mrs Usher ever did. Greg was beginning to think that might be a good idea as he tried to recall some of the events of last night, passing out in the same flat as your stalker might be considered by many, as dangerous. He wondered if Donna had, despite what she said, taken advantage of his inability, although she might have denied it, she was after all his stalker. He might need to question her further later on, although deep down, Greg could never really see Donna as being anything but honest.

George started explaining to a partly interested Greg, how he had to first become part of the Wilmington chess team through an internal schools competition which resulted in, as everyone had assumed, friends Dennis and George to be in the team as it was widely accepted that they were the two best chess players in Wilmington High School at that time. William and Les were almost in the same league, but even so they found the internal matches harder. Emily pointed out that her husband was always vain when it came to his chess playing, he and Dennis spent hours in Portugal playing each other.

"So Dennis lives around the corner, what does he do for a living?" Greg asked.

"Planning department at Kent County Council, prepares planning applications for the Councillors, getting the plans, all the objections and comments and the absolute reams of paperwork that goes into a planning application. Both of us have been there since we left school, although I'm not in planning, I am in the rates and revenue department, which can be a challenge at times as well, you won't believe some of the stories that people come up with to get out of paying their rates."

"Did William work at the council as well?"

"No William was more of a science geek, Dennis and I were maths geeks, give us an equation and we were more than happy, William preferred mixing chemicals and such like."

"So where did William live and work?"

"Only went to his house once, over the other side of the A2, near Hempstead, he lived with his wife and children, as I say mostly Christmas card correspondence. You know the sort of thing, 'Happy Christmas, hope you are all well and we must meet up next year sometime' and you know you never do. Not like Dennis and I, we are always meeting up, well not surprising as we only work a few floors away," George laughed.

"William's work?"

George shook his head, "Never really said that much about it, some sort of science thing down in Sevenoaks, that's all he really told us, I guess working out how much cereal is safe for us to eat. Don't you think that science is mad, on the one hand they will tell you that five fruits a day is good for you and then in the next breath they say the sugar in those five fruits is bad for you, tell me Greg who should we believe?" Before Greg could answer, George answered his own question, "No one, just do your own thing, as the saying goes just a little of what you fancy does you good."

Greg nodded in agreement as he turned the conversation back to William. "So you say you have lost touch, any idea where he might be so I can possibly talk to him?"

"Sent a card to him one Christmas, Emily always insists that we put one of those address stickers on the back. Got them from the Heart Foundation so supporting a good cause as well. That way the post office know where to return the card to. It came back 'gone away' without a forwarding address, what could we do, maybe he'll contact us one day."

Greg felt a little disappointed he was sure this meeting would have shed some light on the Bashford's, maybe it would turn out to be a dead end after all, or maybe the Lynch family and the Bashford family were the same.

"It was about seven or eight years ago as I recall." Emily who had been almost silent throughout the evening added the small fact, "There had been some sort of fire explosion at the place where William worked, a few were killed."

"Testing plastics, that's right Emily, you have such a good memory, she says mine is too filled up with chess moves. That was it, there had been an accident and we weren't sure, but it sounded like the place where William might have been working, although we could never be certain, the papers said it was a plastic testing facility, whatever that might be. So we read the reports as best we could and there was no mention of William being on the list of those who died. How could I have forgotten about that, it must be my age, we're all getting older. Anyway we called, as we had his phone number, just to see if he was OK, but no reply so we left a message but they never came back to us, always was a little on the snobby side if I'm honest. Then it was the following Christmas that the card comes back to us. Now Dennis will have some stories about the chess and Wilmington school which I am sure will go well in your book."

"So William did or did not work at this place that caught fire?"

Emily looked at George then George looked at Emily, wondering if each other had the answer, it was Emily who answered,

"Well to be honest we don't know for sure. When we talked to William about his job he was always very vague, he implied that it was some sort of research place in Sevenoaks and as I recall the papers described it as a research place also so we just assumed, in a way that's why we called, but they said everyone at the site lost their lives, so I guess William could not have worked there."

"There was no one named Bashford at your school was there?"

"Not that I know of, why do you ask?"

"Nothing really."

"Let me tell you..." George began, "about the time that Dennis and I tried to start a chess club at the local council."

Greg half listened appearing to write in his notebook as George shared some, what he considered to be wacky, council stories. All the time Greg was thinking that maybe Peter Bashford was not in that chess photograph after all, maybe he was chasing ghosts, in rooms filled with smoke and mirrors. Yet William Lynch the chess champion had vanished, and there was the photograph link.

"Just one other question before I go, only to add some human interest to my chapter on the chess champions, how many children do you have?"

"Just the one," Emily answered, "Jason, now married with three lovely children."

"And the others?"

This time George answered, "Dennis has three, Lucy, Lesley and Michael, Les had the one, Harry, nice boy, doing a great job looking after his mum, and William has two boys, as I recall Neil was the oldest and David the youngest, or maybe the other way round, I forget."

There are always coincidences Greg thought, someone disappears from a circle of friends and someone appears in France about the same time, people have two children, which is far from uncommon, then there are facts, a photograph of schoolboys with a chess trophy, a small link. Then there is the question, just how this might all be related to the disappearance of Martin? Greg knew he had a lot of work to do if he was ever going to find out.

LA BELLE ETOILE.

"Helen, can I introduce you to Dougie? Dougie, this is Helen."

The young man stood up politely, shaking her hand. He looked casual and calm, dressed in faded blue jeans, brown brogue shoes, and a lightweight black jumper over a white tee shirt. Helen judged him to be about twenty-five maybe a little older. Smooth skin with a rounded jaw, covered in just a hint of stubble, not entirely fashionable as yet, maybe just a long time since he had shaved.

"So pleased to meet you, Phillip has told me a lot about you. I am so impressed meeting a real live national journalist, yours must be such an exciting job."

Helen was not at that moment sure how to answer him. He had a surprisingly firm hand shake given his childlike features, his hands were cool and dry. Being a journalist she knew the work could be exciting, yet at the present time it was weird and confusing, today bordering on nightmarish.

Helen had laid awake all night as she tried to imagine just what was going to happen today. Maybe she was the victim of a very sick joke. Phillip would produce a knife, pretend to murder Dougie, then when Helen screamed, they would all roll around laughing at her expense. Even though she had known Phillip for a very short time, she doubted he was the sort of person who would roll around laughing, let alone enjoy playing a childish trick on someone. Then what could be the other options? Phillip seemed serious enough, he was frank in telling her he had murdered people before, and he seemed overly keen to display his talents to her. Was Dougie really going to die? Was she really going to witness a murder? Helen was starting to realise that she was not so much doubting what could happen over the next couple of hours, but she was scared of her reaction to it.

"Being a reporter is not always as exciting as it sounds, often the stories are pretty mundane."

They all sat down. The blackbird pie funnel stood on the coffee table. The strange gift that Dougie had brought across the Channel, following the simple phone call that Phillip had made.

"Coffee, Helen?" Phillip offered and poured without waiting for an answer from her, he was very much taking control of everyone in the room.

The three of them chatted, Helen adding little to the mundane conversation, her thoughts were muddled. The natural human reaction should be to stop this madness now, warn Dougie of what was planned; convincing him would be another matter. Or call for help and stop this in its tracks, murder was wrong; a crime, one of the seven deadly sins. She could not allow another human being to die for no reason. Yet she had doubts that echoed around her mind. It was not the first time that she had contributed to a death. Her own mother, lying injured on the floor, asking for help, a request Helen had totally ignored. For a vindictive reason, Helen had allowed the death. If murder was justifiable, then Helen would have pleaded that her mother was cruel, that it was a natural reaction to repay for all that unkindness. Maybe that was how she was able to live with the secret for so long. That was until she had shared her secret with Phillip. He who had opened up another possibility for her actions that day, that holding the power of life and death over someone was the attraction. Was that the real reason that Helen let her mother die? Helen could no longer be sure. Now here, waiting for a murder to happen, as if it was the start of a West End play, Helen began to feel anticipation and anxiety rising within her.

"Helen, are you OK?" Phillip asked, "You seem very quiet."

"I was just thinking, thinking about you, Dougie, coming all this way to bring Phillip a pie funnel, you must think a lot of Phillip. I'm sure a lesser friend would have just posted it, save the expense of paying out for a flight to France."

"Phillip is a good friend, we have not known each other long, yet I just had to bring the pie funnel over when he asked for it. That's what friends do."

Helen looked at what appeared to be innocent eyes, staring hopefully at Helen.

"So when are you going back to the UK?"

"When Phillip has finished with me, I think he still has a use for me." Dougie turned to look at Phillip and they smiled at each other. Helen wanted to ask, did he know what was going to happen to him? But she could not bring herself to ask the question.

"If I asked you to come back with me to England, would you?"

"As I mentioned, if that was cool with Phillip."

Deep within Helen she knew that she should stop this whole nightmare, call the authorities, save Dougie from his fate that was the right thing to do, the humane action of any ordinary person. Yet she knew she could not, something within her wanted to see this scene played out to the gruesome end. That something that had laid deep within her, was now rising to the surface. Phillip was right about her; Helen did have a dark side, a side of her that wanted to be present at a murder.

"Dougie be a dear, could you go out and wait beside the pigs for a moment? Helen and I will be out in a moment, I just want to have a word with her in private."

Dutifully Dougie stood up, left the room via the kitchen door and walked out into the chilly night air.

"He is so sweet don't you think?" Phillip spoke like a proud father or brother. Picking up the pie funnel he walked towards the fireplace and placed it carefully alongside the other mementos that stood there, "Sweet though he is, he is all mine, totally, until the day he dies, which happens to be today." Phillip grinned, and looked at Helen, "Do you want to come out and watch? Actually, I know you won't be able to resist, you are that drawn into the whole exercise, intrigued and fascinated."

"Does he know he is going to die?"

Phillip stopped making his way towards the kitchen door, turned towards Helen and looked her in the eye with an intense stare.

"I doubt it, he has no idea why he is here or why he even came, he cannot understand what compelled him to come here, with a stupid pie funnel in his hand. Yet whatever he is thinking, his physical actions override any of his thoughts, they are worthless, he is in my power. Come let's go or he'll catch his death of cold, which would spoil all the fun." Phillip laughed at his own pun as he started to walk outside.

"Is this some sort of very sick joke?"

Once more he stopped and looked at Helen.

"Far from it, my dear Helen, this is very much the real thing. Dougie will not be alive to see tomorrow's dawn, or midnight for that matter. He will shortly be deceased, at a time of my choosing."

"Why do you have to kill him? Can't you just let him go home, you've proved your point clearly."

Phillip again stopped and turned to Helen, looking at her standing in the middle of the room, confused and unsure.

"Helen, prove the point?" his voice sounded irritated, "You are the one missing the point, I have to kill him, it is the natural conclusion to what I do. My control over people is their lives. I take their lives, that is what spurs me on. You might recall?" he asked sarcastically, "we likened murder to sexual intercourse; controlling Dougie to come here is very much the foreplay, and without the coitus it will have been a total waste of time. Not only that, not to kill him would require a change of plan and that is very dangerous. Letting him go now, waving goodbye to him as he flies back to the UK, is not a good idea. Think about it, Helen. I can wipe the memory of this trip from his mind, but what I cannot do is erase the transactions on his credit card statement. I cannot predict or control the questions his friends will ask. Questions that would potentially lead back to me, then expose me to the World and the discovery of my special hobby. Your journalist friend is only here in France asking questions about Martin, because of a credit card transaction. Those financial records brought him to France, that's why I always evolve my plans. Dougie drove to Loudeac, where I picked him up on a quiet street and the connection is broken. That is why I am so successful at what I do, I make a plan, that takes into account all eventualities and stick to it. That is one lesson you will need to learn."

Phillip turned away from her and walked through the kitchen and into the garden, on his way collecting a large carving knife that was on the worktop. Helen now knew that she could not resist following him, seeing first hand a cold blooded murder, someone dying violently. The thoughts that now ran through her darkened mind had become a melange of excitement, anticipation, trepidation, all tainted with a little anxiety. As she followed Phillip out into the garden, she instinctively picked up a small kitchen knife, why? Helen could not be sure of the reason, it was either as a form of self defence or a hope that she might contribute to a murder.

Helen stood about ten feet away from the two men. Dougie was standing looking at the excited pigs, Phillip beside him within arm's length, his back to the pig pen looking and smiling at Helen. The trio bathed in an intense brightness provided by a security light that had illuminated in response to the activity that was going on beneath it.

"Helen, this is what you wanted to see for yourself, not just following up after someone had fallen down the stairs, this is real power. My decision, my choice, my victim. Acting like a deity choosing life or death, what do you think Helen, feel good? Not that whatever you might say would have any influence on me, things cannot go back now, we are close to the climax, Dougie is now in too deep as are you now, no pun intended."

"Can he hear us?"

"Yes, he can hear. I doubt if he can understand what we are saying. He is doing as I told him, waiting beside the pigs. So until I give him another instruction, here he will stand."

"Doesn't his conformity make it a little too easy, where is the challenge?"

"Ah," Phillip responded, "that would be your upbringing asking that question. High class fox hunting needs the thrill of the chase; the speed, the mud, a frightened fox fleeing through woods, pursued by a pack of dogs and potbellied men dressed in hunting uniforms on horseback. The fox endures a couple of hours of terror, trying to outrun or outmanoeuvre those pursuing him, before, as in most cases, he is cornered, he knows death is next and death is painful as he experiences being torn apart by dogs. Now Dougie here, has no inkling what is going to happen to him, not the slightest clue, it is as if he is sedated. Even when I strike, he will not fully understand what is happening to him, and yes, he might feel pain, just for a minute or so, before he passes out. So tell me, who is the most inhumane? The challenge for me is in the planning, the meticulous attention to detail, the success of the kill and the avoidance of detection. Does that answer your question?"

Without any sort of preparation or warning, Phillip's arm, that had been hanging lazily beside him, almost took flight travelling upwards, his hand moving towards the neck of Dougie. Then in the white light of the security lamp, the kitchen blade glinted. Without stopping Phillip slashed it across the front of Dougie's neck, the young man stood without flinching as the knife tore through first skin, then muscle, then arteries.

"Always kick them away from you Helen, remember, avoid the blood spurting over you." He was right as Phillip pushed Dougie in the chest with his foot, spinning the young man away from his killer, the first spurt of blood shot across the ground, firing out from his neck, the others following in a regular beat as his heart pumped blood out. With nothing coming back in to be recirculated around the body, Dougie's knees bent then started to fold into the ground. "There we go Helen, not rocket science, simple really. Let's go back inside, as there is not much to watch now, unless you want to watch the life flow out of him."

Phillip held onto her hand and almost dragged a light-headed Helen back into the warmth of the house. She had just witnessed a real murder, of that she was clear; euphoria started to fill her mind, but her natural revulsion and disgust numbed and confused her.

Phillip poured Helen a glass of red wine.

"This is a St Emillion, Helen, a very nice red, which I like to drink on special occasions. Have a good mouthful, and it will help, I would suspect that you feel a little confused, upset, even a touch nauseous."

Helen swallowed a large mouthful of the wine, warming her chilled body. Although she was partly disgusted and horrified at what she had witnessed, there was certainly in her psyche a feeling of euphoria that was rising ever closer to the surface. She had seen a man have total power over another man, choosing the time of death, the method of death and carrying out the whole deed without showing any sort of emotion. She wondered what it would have felt like to have held that knife.

"So what happens next, do you just leave him?"

"Before I get into the practical side of things Helen, can I just say thank you for being there to see what I did. Comparing it to sexual acts, which we have previously discussed, that would count as one hell of an orgasm, the first time anyone witnessed what I can do, seen the power I hold over an ordinary human being, Thank you Helen. One day I am sure I will do the same for you."

Phillip gently sipped his wine savouring the bouquet before he stood up and walked to the blackbird pie funnel and adjusted its position.

"Next Helen, we savour the moment, recall and relive it all, which we can do this evening. I will leave Dougie out there until the morning, no one will be passing by this desolate house. By morning he will have bled out totally, Dougie will be dead, cold and very stiff, then I conclude my plan, I remove all his clothes, leaving him totally naked. The next step, and this is a little bit on the messy side, I take a chainsaw to him, head off, arms off, legs off. This is not the sort of thing I would talk about at dinner, as it could easily put you off your food. The limbs are then cut in half again and thrown into the pig pen, followed by the torso which I try and cut into three pieces, it gives the chance for the pigs to get in amongst all the entrails. After that, a small fire to burn all the clothes, that is once I have emptied all the pockets, wallet, coins, keys that sort of thing. Most of that gets thrown into bins across a number of Bretagne tourist sites, just dropped in the rubbish bins. Then lastly the shoes, difficult to burn and stand out like a sore thumb in rubbish bins so I give then to charity, pop them in those clothing bins that you see at so many recycling locations. See, every cloud has a silver lining."

Phillip spoke in such a way that he could have been telling Helen about how to bake a cake, the essential ingredients of what to do after you have committed murder. The wine had helped Helen settle her wild, confused thoughts.

"The fear of getting caught, is it nowhere in your vocabulary at all?"

"Well to be truly honest Helen, it is a little, so I neatly tie up all the loose ends. By tomorrow night, the body will have gone, save for a few bones, which I will add to a rubbish bin far away from here, so they will also be gone by the end of the week into some large landfill site, also by which time personal effects and shoes will have gone. This time next week, maybe a good forensic team might find some small DNA trace of Dougie, but they will need to look over my house with a fine tooth-comb, also they will need to have reason to look here in the first place."

Phillip returned to his seat, "Think about it for a moment, Dougie will be reported missing in England soon, if not already. The police will say to themselves, 'missing adult', do we really care, adults can go off and do what they like. Maybe, just maybe, they will from border records, credit cards and the like see that he had travelled to France. So in that case, the British police drop the French police an email with the details of the missing man requesting their help. At that point, the French police have no real interest at all, why should they bother, no kudos for them if he is found, dead or alive. The French, just like the British police, need to reach their targets, looking for some Englishman, who has more than likely gone on an extended holiday, does not help their figures. So it is very, very unlikely the forensic team will ever turn up here. Finally I adapt and evolve, Martin was my first cross channel victim, he hired a car, there I made a small error, I had given him my address. So lucky for me it broke down before he reached my house, so there was no direct connection to me, hence no 'sat-navs' allowed. I now give very good directions to a place away from La Ville du Bois. See I adapt, evolve like all good species do, Dougie took the car to Loudéac, where he handed it back to the hire company with a one-way hire. I just picked him up afterwards a little way away from the car hire office, so again a dead end for any potential investigators. The murder, the knife across the throat is exciting, but the planning, the covering of the trail is just as challenging and as rewarding. More wine?"

Helen accepted his offer, as if they were at a middle class dinner party, sipping wine and discussing politics.

"So the first three were in England, did you dispose of them in the same way?"

"I lived in a flat, now I can give you a number of cases where a killer has cut up their victims in a flat and then placed them in plastic bags in the communal rubbish bins, only to be uncovered by foxes first, then with human limbs poking out of a black rubbish bag, the police are called. They don't have to look far, maybe the second floor of the flat at most. So no, I used a different technique, which I am sure you can imagine was clever and ingenious, as I have not been caught or detected as yet. My activities are not listed as murders, which is always a good way of avoiding detection. Yet, I could see you could only go so long before, in the overcrowded world of a city, someone might see something that would start those in police uniforms to ask questions that might be difficult to answer. Hence the move to this quaint corner of France, where I Imagine I could do a few more before moving off to another part. There are only so many men that go through Dinard airport never to return, before someone will start asking serious questions."

Phillip stood up and walked towards the kitchen door,

"I think a light supper is called for. Are you a little peckish Helen? I am sure you must be, and then we need to talk about how your first murder might be carried out. 'Helen, my young apprentice', that has such a warm, family feel to it, don't you think?"

Helen did not reply, she knew without doubt, she was now a very different person to the one who had arrived at Dinard Airport just two days ago.

LEWISHAM.

The first thing Greg did after eating his simple, but easy to prepare breakfast of toast and lime marmalade, was to call his friend, Fergus, at the Passport Office. This time asking about any passports that might have been issued to William Lynch.

"Easy one this time, Greg," was the surprisingly swift reply from Fergus, speaking in what had become his trademark emotionless voice. "Date of birth is about right, address in Hempstead, the one in Kent, there are not too many Hempsteads around. William Lynch last used his passport eight years ago coming into Gatwick, south terminal. Due for renewal five years ago, but never renewed, maybe they decided that English holidays were better. I don't like going abroad, too complex going through all those security checks; plus, I never really trust foreign people any more."

Greg understood and sympathised with why Fergus no longer trusted foreign people. Secondly, Greg called Donna. That call was partly against his better judgement, but he needed her help, that was the excuse he used to himself for calling.

"So," she said over the crackly telephone line, sounding suspicious of what the true motive might be. "Just to be clear, you want me to help you," she emphasised the 'you', "by getting as much information as I can about a fire at a plastic works in Sevenoaks. Then to bring it around to your flat tonight and we can discuss anything that I might have found over dinner?"

Greg agreed that was what he wanted, part of him was still unsure about asking her, but now it was too late.

Everyone that day at the Deptford Chronicle office was amazed how good a mood Donna was in as she went about digging through old microfilm and making telephone calls. No one was sure exactly what she was doing, no one wanted to ask, just in case it turned her back to her normal blunt self.

At lunchtime, Greg made his way to the Fox and Hounds pub to meet Edward to expand on their earlier telephone conversation, and to share what he had found out about Martin so far, which was very little. Greg was expecting his first freelance pay check, as well as hoping for a free lunch.

Midday, the Fox and Hounds is at its quietest; there were empty tables, the atmosphere of gentle conversations rippled through the bar, nothing raucous happening, just lunchtime conversations, some based on business, some founded on friendships. Greg, sat opposite Edward, working his way through a BLT, lubricating his speech with a glass of bitter, and began telling his story in between mouthfuls. Greg shared the key points; the conversation with the car hire company at Dinard, the trip down to where the car was found with its flat tyre, the meeting up with the French farmer's wife and then meeting the first English couple. Moving on to the other English families that he met, talking about the 'smash and grab' which allegedly was connected to the car. That part Edward listened to in disbelief, only briefly commenting,

"That sounds nothing like Martin," before allowing Greg to continue with his story.

The interaction with the Bashford family was glossed over for now. Then the hotel visit by the insurance recovery agent was repeated to Edward, who leaned forward in his chair and spoke in hushed tones to Greg,

"Well yes, as I told you, Martin once did some community service, having been charged and found guilty of fraud, only a minor fraud, nothing on a grand scale, it was when he was at Southwark Council, years ago. I wouldn't say they were trumped up charges, Martin did tell me that he was a little overzealous and creative with his expenses, even so, I am sure he was not the only one and I still suspect, although Martin was adamant that I was wrong when I said, it was just because of his sexuality, there can be so much discrimination within large organisations. Okay they have their policies and things, but it's individual members of staff that either make it or break it."

"So the insurance claim for the ring, do you think it could be true?"

"He did it once so maybe you think he could do it again?" Edward reluctantly admitted, "A lot of people would also agree with you, I am sure. But I know Martin, he was not short of money and I was always there to provide for him in that respect if he wanted it and I did help him out a lot buying things; clothes, shoes, paying for nights out, as I earn a lot more than him, so I can't see why he would do that. Maybe I should call this investigator up and speak to him."

"Well, I think maybe I should ask him a few more questions, if you have had no suspicions of Martin taking a chance and defrauding an insurance company. So there you have it Edward, a dead end, I have no idea whatsoever where Martin will have gone after he left the car beside the road, I'm sorry I tried. There is just one question, did Martin know, or you for that matter know, a William Lynch or Peter Bashford?"

Edward searched his memory for a moment or two before saying,

"No, those names mean nothing to me. Why do you ask?"

"Maybe it's nothing, it was one of the families that I asked about Martin, well there was something strange, but I'm not sure it has anything to do with Martin disappearing, maybe they thought I was from the Inland Revenue."

"Well you would be the best judge of that. Thanks Greg, I do appreciate what you have done, I know you have tried your best. Just one other favour I want to ask of you Greg, well maybe not a favour, there is someone who wants to talk to you and I think you might want to listen to what he has to say."

Edward looked across into the corner of the sparsely populated bar as the lunchtime customers drifted back to their work, he beckoned a man over to join them. Greg watched as the man, in maybe his early thirties, tall with a shaven head, an AC/DC tee shirt, bleached jeans with chunky army type boots, over one arm was a jacket and in his other hand a pint glass of beer, half consumed, made his way over to them. When he smiled as he joined them, distinct dimples appeared on his cheeks.

"Greg, I would like to introduce Alistair to you, he knows about your trip to France looking for Martin."

They shook hands, Alistair's large, rough hand almost crushing Greg's hand.

"I know Alistair socially," Edward admitted, "we have met a few times in bars and clubs, also I use one of the many gyms that Alistair frequents. I think you might be interested in hearing his story."

Edward gestured Alistair to begin now that he had been introduced as if he was some sort of cabaret act. His voice was higher in tone than Greg had imagined, seeing the size of his biceps and the stretched tee shirt fabric containing his sculptured chest, clearly a man who could drive women crazy, unless he was gay, a question he cleared up in his first sentence.

"I have been living with Dougie for about two years now. He is only three years younger than me. We first met at a club where he worked, the Angel Wings in Gravesend." Greg nodded in recognition; Greg recalled that he had written a story relating to the club just last year, a young man committed suicide, drowning himself in the River Thames.

"We have been getting along fine, just the occasional angry word, but show me a couple who doesn't disagree from time to time. Yesterday I went off to work, I'm a physical trainer, men in mid-life crisis seek my help to retain their youthful bodies, and on the whole I can do a reasonable job with them. Dougie, I guess would have left the flat about midday to go to his job at Angel Wings, serving behind the bar making all types of weird and wonderful cocktails. He has a real skill mixing alcohol into all sorts of exotic colours. Normally he finishes about midnight and gets home by twelve thirty, one o'clock at the latest. So when he was not back by two in the morning, I was concerned, so I phoned the club, there is normally a few late night drinkers there with the owner. Anyway I called, only to be told that he hadn't arrived for work, they had even tried to call him, as he has never taken a day off in all the time he has worked there. Anyway there was no reply from his phone I, of course, tried a few times; it just went to voice mail. I was so worried, I just couldn't sleep, I phoned the hospitals, called the police, I must have sounded like a crazed poof, but I had this horrible feeling that something had happened to him."

Alistair paused, took a large glug of his beer before continuing. Greg suspected it was a way to try to compose himself.

"I was out of my mind; I had no idea where to start looking. First, I tried a couple of friends who given that it was four in the morning were so kind and considerate. They said the right things but had no idea where he might be. So I thought about what they do in the films and documentaries, and went on line and checked out his credit and bank cards, we share everything you understand. I wanted to see if he had drawn out any cash or gone off clubbing somewhere, I was just desperate for a clue as to where he might be."

Alistair felt it was a justification for looking at his partner's online banking.

"Well, there they were, some transactions for that very day. First Ryanair, two hundred pounds and then Avis, one hundred and twenty pounds for a hire car. So then I checked his emails, and he had taken a single flight to Dinard, then appears to have hired a car for only a one-way rental, leaving it at a French town called..." Alistair consulted a sheet of paper, "Loudéac, it's in Brittany."

Greg felt a tingling down his back, almost a repeat of Martin's disappearance, same airport and Loudéac, Greg recalled, was not that far from where he had been earlier that week.

"Do Dougie and Martin know one another?"

"Well yes," Edward interrupted, "we all meet up socially so we all know each other, but they have not eloped if that's what you're thinking."

That was exactly what Greg was thinking, even the denial did not convince him entirely, sex, Greg knew to his cost, could lead people into strange and difficult situations.

"So what do you want me to do?"

Again Edward stepped into the conversation.

"Go back to France, ask more questions, maybe you will have better luck looking for Dougie, we'll pay all your expenses and pay you for being there. They cannot have just disappeared into thin air, there must be an answer. Even if it does turn out they are living together, we would both want to know and then we could talk to them to find answers."

"Well, easier than you make out, but first I'll ask a few questions at the club, see if I can get any other information or clues before I go off to France again."

Greg was not going to admit it, but he truly thought that after a few questions at the club he would uncover a clandestine romance between Dougie and Martin, which he guessed was also clearly lurking at the back of both Edward's and Alistair's minds. Another reason was Greg did not relish the thought of travelling by plane again so soon.

GRAVESEND, KENT.

In Victorian times Gravesend in Kent was the destination of choice for the rich and semi famous. It had a beach, bear pits, formal gardens and a paddle steamer that took Victorian holiday makers along the Thames estuary, which in the days of Queen Victoria was wide and bustling with boats of all shapes and sizes. Days out there were a highlight for many families, traders and professionals, who were happy to take their families out of the stink of the city. Since those heady days, Gravesend has continually slipped way down the holiday league table. Today the beach is just a mud flat, the remaining bear pit no more than an archaeological curiosity in a housing development. The only tourists that find themselves in Gravesend are there to look at the grave of Pocahontas. The fine Victorian architecture is now tired and weather beaten, old pubs have been converted into flats or, in the case of the Angel Wings, a modern night club catering for a certain section of the community.

Greg knew the club. He had visited it about a year ago, following the story in which a man had simply walked through some public gardens onto the foreshore and continued walking into the Thames without stopping. The Coroner had recorded the death as suicide; Greg had guessed that it had been an action that had been prompted by excessive alcohol.

The Club had not changed. He walked in through the main door into the dark lobby with its black walls and stale odour of sweaty bodies. Once your eyes had adjusted to the darkness, you walked into the main club area, where a long polished wooden bar took up one complete wall. But for a compact stage, built-in alcoves for intimate contact and conversations lined the remainder of the wall space. Where Greg stood overlooking the empty dance floor, on his right was the compact stage where a tall lanky man was setting up his record decks ready for the evening's entertainment, and to Greg's left was the bar comprising of a semi-circle lit with gaudy coloured lights which reflected off the many optics that lined the back of the bar. Here at just after six in the evening, there were a few people milling around, drinking and chatting over low level background music. The bar staff were themselves preparing for the evening rush that would start to gain momentum in a couple of hours.

"Drink sir?" Greg was asked as he approached the bar. Greg surveyed the branded pumps in front of him.

"Just a half of Doom Bar and a little information if you can."

At once the barman frowned.

"If you're the Police, I know nothing but how to serve drinks, OK?"

"I'm a reporter who is not publishing anything but working for a friend of a friend. I'm looking for Dougie, I'm told he worked behind the bar here."

Instantly the aggressive confrontational look went out of the barman's eyes and was replaced with a look of sadness,

"Who's the friend of a friend?"

"Well, actually it is two people: Alistair and Edward, they both want to know about their partners."

"Maybe we all would like to know the truth, there are a few nervous people around here I can tell you. Totally weird, Dougie one day working here as normal, said good bye and see you tomorrow to him at the end of the night, then nothing, he has just gone off somewhere. Someone said that he had just taken himself off to France, is that true?"

"So it appears. Can you think of any reason for him to go over there or if there is someone he might have gone off there with?"

The barman pushed a half pint of Doom Bar bitter towards Greg, then leaned on the clean bar.

"No idea. I knew Dougie well, or I thought I did. We've worked together for the best part of three years now, he was a real hard worker, enjoyed his job and was really sociable. But for all that he was a 'one man' man, only eyes for his Alistair. Trust me on this one, he was attractive, I tried, not even a one-nighter, Dougie was as faithful as the day is long. So if he went to France it was not for love, of that I'm as sure as I can be, but as my mother said, when I told her I was gay, and told her she would never see me walk down the aisle, 'Never say never,' that's what she said. Now look at me, getting married to my partner in two month's time, and my mother will be at the front of the church, just dying to tell me as I walk past, 'Told you so; never say never!"

Greg took a refreshing drink from his glass.

"So no hint that he was going to go off to France, didn't pop out to get any Euros, check his passport or the time of planes between customers?"

"No mention of anything out of the ordinary. It was honestly a complete shock, I thought at first he was off sick or something; even being off sick would have been unusual for Dougie.

But then there was that other guy, Martin, Eddie's partner, or should I say Edward which he prefers, being the snob he is, he also went off to France. People tried to put two and two together and come up with five, but France is a big place and Martin was a bit more of a lad, so you wouldn't put it past him to take off somewhere, but not Dougie, I'm sure."

"Also," Greg added, "I was here last year reporting on the death of that guy who walked into the Thames, he had a Scottish name as I recall." Greg reminded the barman.

"Nathan White, not Scottish, although a lot of people called him Scottie, he loved Star Trek. Well at least we knew where he had gone; they found him three days later floating near Tilbury. But that was rubbish wasn't it? No way would Nathan have committed suicide, as the police said. Drugs or too many poppers or something like that, maybe, Nathan was a wild one. But he was seen actually just walking into the water as if it did not exist, he just kept walking. By the time anyone could get close to him he was up to his neck, they just couldn't get to him before he walked under the water."

The barman poured himself a tonic, ignoring the turmoil going on around him as others filled shelves with bottled beer and stacked glasses overhead.

"You're a reporter, I remember you now, you were here asking questions about Nathan, you too took it as being odd, killing yourself by drowning, far easier to throw yourself in front of a train, and a lot quicker I guess."

Greg smiled, however before he could answer, the barman continued,

"To be honest," he leaned forward and even closer to Greg in preparation to share gossip, "there is talk that this club is jinxed. Think about it, Nathan in the Thames, both Dougie and Martin disappearing abroad, then there was Ben, did you hear about him? That was two years ago, drinking here most of the night, a regular was Ben, last seen drinking here, leaves about one in the morning but never got home. Then they find him two days later, his body burnt and dumped off the dual carriageway in Thamesmead. So that makes four strange instances in two years; does nothing for the reputation of the club as I'm sure you can imagine."

"Was that the one where they found the petrol can and lighter next to his body, coroner decided death by misadventure?"

"Don't ask me what the verdict was, but if it was misadventure, tell me why a grown man like that was playing around with petrol and a lighter beside a busy road? It was a frightening time I can tell you, homophobia is still around, and showing no signs of going away. I reckon that once people start hearing about Dougie they will find other clubs to frequent."

"So, you don't think Dougie will be found?"

"What do you think? Not saying that he is dead; he might have had his own reasons to disappear. Either way the Angel Wings gets the bad P.R."

Greg finished his drink of Doom Bar and left the club; stepped out into the late January sunshine and walked through the stationary traffic to his parked car. There he sat trying to piece together what linked two dead men with two missing men from the same club. Could a family living under false names in France be connected? Then there was the schoolboy chess team, one of whom appeared to have escaped a fatal explosion. He could not see the connection or even if there was one. He hoped that maybe Donna had been able to turn something up.

BROCKLEY.

Greg greeted the smart young man at his door and handed over the cash in exchange for a large white plastic bag filled with the Chinese food that Donna had ordered earlier. Donna was acting as the perfect housewife, not that Greg really wanted a perfect housewife around his flat. Donna, after taking the dinner plates out of the cupboard, had inspected them and decided that another wash would be good for them. Now happy with their condition, she continued to prepare the table, laid place mats on the oak table, cutlery, napkins and two wine glasses. She had opened a bottle of Merlot wine, after Greg seemed indifferent to which bottle she should choose from the wooden wine rack that sat in a gap between the kitchen cupboards. Two nights in a row, Donna had found herself at Greg's flat. Things she felt were getting interesting, although she planned not to let him have so much alcohol tonight. She had half considered digging out some decorative red candles that she had noticed tucked away in the cutlery drawer but in the end she had decided that that might be a step too far.

First tonight, during dinner, she had to report back on what she had found out. Greg listened, biting into a spare rib as Donna spoke and referred once in a while to a small note pad that she had next to her. She had spent most of the day as instructed researching the fatal fire at a plastic works in Sevenoaks in July 2004. She had learned from news clippings that the fire had gutted the R.G. Plastics building, following a significant explosion that left no survivors. Seven people had been killed when a compressor exploded after failing to turn off due to a fault with the safety mechanism. The compressor explosion, although not fatal in itself, was close to a vat of highly flammable liquid, which had a long name that Donna had written down but could no more pronounce than understand just what it was exactly. This created an even bigger fireball that took out most of the building. Just one door down from this fire ball were all seven people who worked there, having a staff meeting. None of them survived, their charred bodies only identified by DNA and dental records. The building was located away from residential areas, a condition of the planning permission given the nature of the volatile chemicals they held there. Although it was on an industrial area, it was tucked away in a corner, its neighbours had lost four Luton Vans, which Donna thought were those big box looking ones. Greg informed her that she was correct.

"There was some sort of official inquiry into the tragedy, a Health and Safety Executive report, but it would just seem to have been a tragic accident. Someone had left the compressor on and its safety valve had failed, it just happened to be next to liquid that went whoosh; that's my description not the official report you understand."

Greg smiled spontaneously at her, "So the official report says that everyone was killed who were on the site at the time?"

"According to the papers and the very in depth and partly - no change that, the totally boring Health and Safety investigation."

"It didn't mention any staff that might not have been at the place?"

Donna finished her crab claw, having fallen behind Greg in consuming Chinese food.

"Not a thing about other people, everything I read seemed to imply that all the staff were killed. Maybe the report was not concerned with those that were not there."

"The report would have mentioned other staff to understand what was going on at the site. No mention of anyone else?"

Donna flicked through the bound report that she had acquired from where or how Greg was not concerned.

"The only other names mentioned with the report were the owners of R.G. Plastics. They were not there at the time but did give some background information to the report. I then looked to see if the company was still operating. Companies House records show that it ceased business after the explosion and that the two directors and owners of the company, Gerry and Ron Moss, no longer live at the address that Companies House have for them, and I can't find a forwarding address either. The telephone directory gives one hundred and sixty-two results for Ron Moss, not impossible but time consuming."

"What about the names of those who died, was there a Bashford or a Lynch among them?" Greg asked, scooping up the last of the egg fried rice.

"I'm afraid not. Is it worth finding relatives?"

"I doubt it. George Usher only thought that the William Lynch in the photograph worked at the place in Sevenoaks that went up in flames, he didn't know for certain. William could have worked somewhere else and just moved like people do, and not wanted to stay in touch with his old school mates. Again, nothing concrete, maybe Peter Bashford is not William Lynch."

"Who is Peter Bashford?"

It was now Greg's turn to tell Donna about France in addition to the two deaths and two missing men from Angel Wings. He was not telling her in any expectation that she would solve the confusion that he was feeling; it was more a way of helping to bring his thoughts into focus. However much he thought about it or talked to Donna it always came back to the reaction from Peter Bashford when he had visited. There had been a look of fear in his eyes that Greg sensed, and there was the chess photograph in which he was not mentioned yet stood on his sideboard, together with the fact that one of the participants from the Chess Champions at Wilmington school was no longer in touch with friends and no longer had a passport. A nervous man living in France, a gay club developing a reputation for giving out bad luck, nothing made any sense. There were no clear connections, just suppositions and suspicions.

Both of them had finished eating. Donna began to clear away the dishes talking as she went.

"Go back to France, go and see this Peter Bashford and ask him, why is he so scared of a reporter and why does he have a photo of school children in his house?"

"Wait!" Donna called from the kitchen. She returned to Greg, tea towel in hand. "You said that William Lynch had not used his passport since the fire at R.G. Plastics. What if Peter Bashford is the William Lynch who we think, or at least have been told, worked at R.G. Plastics, maybe he should have carried out some checks on the compressor that blew a gasket. So not doing those safety checks caused the explosion, manslaughter on that scale carriers a long mandatory prison sentence, I think I'd do a runner, wouldn't you?"

"Well Donna, if they had suspected someone of failing in their responsibilities, that fact should have been included in the official report. But there again you have a point, it could be a reason. There are still a lot of ifs and buts. And don't forget, I am meant to be looking for this Martin chap and now Dougie, neither of which have any connection with the Sevenoaks factory."

Donna returned the place mats from where she had taken them, alongside a photograph of Greg and his family. She looked at the black and white photograph and questions arose in her mind, that she should never have asked.

"Do you find me attractive?" she asked as she continued to stare at the photograph.

"That's a question out of the blue."

"Yesterday, in the shower, we both stood naked looking at each other. I was happy to join you but you declined. I'm sure there can't be many men who would turn down such an offer, unless of course, you don't find me attractive."

"You're attractive Donna, of course you are, it's just we are, or at least were, colleagues, it just doesn't seem right."

She rejoined him at the table, this time holding the photograph, then filled her glass and continued her questions.

"Have you ever had a girlfriend? You've never spoken of one, past or present, I always imagined someone like you would have a regular girlfriend."

"Relationships can take hours and days and weeks of hard work just to get close enough to someone who might be your life partner. Most end in heartbreak, so what's the point? I've just learned to live without a life partner."

"So you have had girlfriends?"

"Does it matter?"

"To me it does."

"Donna, you're mad, what's it got to do with you? Nothing. We're just friends, who help out each other from time to time. Whether I have or I have not had girlfriends is totally my business."

Greg's voice was becoming irritated, he snatched the photograph from her and returned it to the sideboard.

Donna guessed that he did not want to admit to never having had a girlfriend. She wondered what could be wrong with him, a virgin at his age, odd, yet she found it strangely enthralling. She decided to move onto another question.

"You did look sweet as a young boy. Is that your sister?"

Greg looked back across to the table where she sat finishing her wine, "Yes."

"I can't imagine losing any of my family in such circumstances, I suppose that is why you have such an interest in suicides, kind of making amends."

"Amends!" he exclaimed loudly, "What are you talking about? What do I need to make amends for? She killed herself, she decided that enough was enough and took enough pills to down a horse, let alone a teenage girl."

"I just meant," Donna tried to retract the remark that had changed Greg's mood from agitated to aggressive in an instant. "That looking into suicides, like you do, helps with the pain of losing your sister."

"Donna, what the fuck do you know about losing a sister? When you have been there, you can talk to me about it, until then, shut up."

"Maybe talking about it would do you good." Donna was not one to back down after a bit of abuse had been thrown at her. "Bottling things up inside only eats away at you, until you are not the person that you should or could be. Did your parents take account of what her suicide might do to you?"

Greg emptied his glass, appearing to savour the red wine for a moment before making an angry retort.

"It has nothing to do with you at all Donna, what's done is done. So you can stop interfering and get back to your mundane life."

"Charming. So I take it neither parent put their arm around you to comfort you. Maybe your mother did but your father looks like he could be more than just a little stern."

"Donna, both of them are dead, in fact all my family are dead. What they were, they are no longer, so I have just got on with my life."

Donna stood close to him and looked into his angry eyes.

"But you haven't have you? The coroner could find no reason for her taking her life, no note, no indication. You still carry an open wound, did you have any suspicion at all as to why she might have killed herself?" As soon as Donna asked that question she regretted it, maybe that was a little too blunt, even for a Donna question.

"If only I'd...." Greg stopped abruptly and looked down at the table.

"If only you'd what?"

"If only I'd not invited you around tonight, my evening would have been a lot more relaxed."

"Then you would have known sweet F.A. about a boring burnt out plastics factory in Sevenoaks." Donna retorted.

"I'm sorry, that was cruel of me, I do appreciate your help." The anger had shifted out of his eyes. "My father was not the sort to put an arm around you to comfort you, you had to be tough, be a man, or else you were just a pussy in his eyes. If I'd been tougher maybe things would have been different. The past cannot be changed, however much we try to change it in our minds. I don't want to talk about it Donna. Thanks for your help, but it's best you go."

Greg stood up, warmly hugged Donna, the anger gone from him, "You could still be my very own Velda."

Even though Donna had never heard of Velda, the much loved secretary to fictional detective Mike Hammer, standing in the hallway as Greg closed the door on her, she still took it to be a compliment. As she started to walk away, she thought she heard sobbing, and hoped she was mistaken.

MARSHAM STREET.

Routine was a key element in the daily life of Fergus Carter, Executive Officer at Her Majesty's Passport office. In the three years that he had worked there he arrived promptly at 8.50 a.m, switched on his computer, walked to the small kitchenette that was alongside the photocopier machine, put one spoonful of instant coffee in his plain white mug, followed by one spoonful of sugar, then filled the mug with hot water from the instant hot water machine on the wall. Fergus guessed that the instant hot water machine might well have a slightly more technical name, but had decided he had no need to know it. After putting just a dash of semi-skimmed milk into the coffee, he returned to his desk, put the mug to the right of his screen, sat down, logged on and then began work, just a minute or so before nine. Routine would then dictate that at 12noon he would have a cheese and Branston pickle sandwich (no supermarket brand, it could only be Branston) and eat at his desk. The sandwich would then be followed by a thirty-minute walk around the neighbouring streets. Three-thirty would be the time for his second mug of coffee of the day and then he would leave the office at five p.m. His working day was spent processing passport information from an application, and then forwarding that information to another section, which produced the passport, ready to be sent back to the applicant. Ever since his nervous breakdown, a well-planned life was what Fergus liked and how he had lived for the past three years.

The call came that morning without warning, a request to step into the team leader's office, where a man stood looking solemn and serious. The team's leader, as instructed, stood outside, leaving Fergus to the mercy of the man.

Prior to being an obscure executive officer in the Passport Office, Fergus Carter was an immigration officer, not one that stood at airport gateways checking incoming tourists, he was part of a team, all dressed in black leather jackets, that made unannounced visits to places of employment to ensure all those employed there were legally permitted to work in the United Kingdom. The fact that he was making a surprise visit usually was the result of intelligence that had been acquired and was thus being acted upon. He and his team visited private residential properties to make sure all those living there had valid visas and passports. He had been knocking on doors, surprising people for almost ten years, yet that all changed for him when at 5am one grey July morning, he entered a scruffy council flat in Tower Hamlets with four of his team. The bleary-eyed woman nervously let them traipse into the flat, which stank of curry and stale body odour. All five moved from room to room, shouting out their presence intimidating the sleepy waiters and casual workers that arose from the mattresses on the floor. As Fergus walked into a small cubby hole of a room crammed with a bunk bed, dirty curtains and a smell he did not wish to identify, he felt a sweaty arm wrap tightly around his neck, a cold metal object against his temple.

"I'll fucking kill you cop, I'll fucking kill you!" was the loud shout which seemed to be almost inside his ear.

The panting bad breath of the assailant enclosed Fergus and together they stumbled and fell to the floor, the gun still pushed against his temple, the arm tighter than ever around his neck.

"Fucking stay still or I kill you!" was the next shout, the noise bringing the rest of Fergus's team towards the crammed room.

The first of Fergus's partners at the doorway was greeted by a gunshot that crashed into the yellowed paintwork of the door frame, sending all the team away from the door for cover. Fergus was now on the floor, the weight of his assailant on top of him, arm still crushing his neck and now the acrid smell of the gun shot mixed with the bad breath.

"I kill you all! I fucking kill you all!" was now a scream, a scream of panic and the irrational behaviour of a person with limited language, which did not bode well for any negotiations that might be held. Fergus squeezed out some words from his constricted throat.

"Think about what you're doing, there is no way out, don't make things worse for yourself."

"I fucking kill you all!" was the only response that came back with the same fear in the voice.

Without any sort of warning Fergus felt his throat be released from the hold, the weight left his back, as the man stood up, Fergus turned to look up, only to see a young muscular boy pointing the gun at Fergus. In the next second everything changed, the boy fired two shots at Fergus, somehow missing him, the boy then placed the barrel of the gun into his mouth and there followed, in an instant, an eruption of noise, blood, flesh and other bodily materials that Fergus did not want to think from where they had originated. The body with its bloody shattered head crumpled forward onto the splayed form of Fergus. The now dead, even heavier weight, pinned him to the floor and its shattered head leached across his face. Fergus screamed and continued to scream hysterically well after the dead body was pulled away from him.

There then followed countless nights of sweats, when peaceful sleep became an impossible dream, replaced by just a maelstrom of nightmares, together with a fear of going anywhere outside the safety of his small flat. Weeks turned into months of counselling and support, to bring back Fergus into what was only a shadow of the person he had been before. Clinging to the security that strict routine brings, Fergus was able to move out into the world and take on a job, a routine job that did not touch his now very vulnerable and tender emotions.

Now standing here in the small office facing a stranger, Fergus felt tense and scared. As soon as the door closed, without offering him a seat or any form of sympathy, the stranger launched into questions.

"Fergus, yesterday morning you carried out a search for the name William Lynch. Who asked you to? Why did you carry out that search?"

The old Fergus, the one who pushed down doors, strode into backstreet factories, pinned potential suspects against walls, would have told him to: 'Piss off'; asked for a warrant and told him 'what's it got to do with you?' was no longer there to answer. The meek and mild Fergus could do no more than offer contrite answers.

"A local reporter called Greg Auden. I have known him for a number of years."

"So why did he want to know more about the passport of William Lynch?"

"I didn't ask. It was just a favour I did for him, he is a friend, a good friend."

The questioner noted the name and as requested Fergus gave, the mobile number that he had for Greg, together with the name of the paper he worked for. Fergus hoped to pacify things by saying that Greg only worked for a local newspaper. The man seemed unmoved, took the number and left without saying anything else.

Fergus stood in the office slightly confused before he was told by his team leader to go back to his desk.

During lunch Fergus walked for a bit longer than thirty minutes around the neighbouring streets, his mind vexed. He hoped that he had not got Greg into too much trouble. They had never been that close at school and had only partly kept in touch. But after Fergus had suffered his nervous breakdown, he often found Greg at his front door, coming in, cooking him a meal and talking, or just talking and being there. They were never going to be close friends but Fergus knew that he could always rely on Greg for help or support. So the thought of getting Greg into trouble worried Fergus so much that he had been walking for over forty-five minutes that lunch time. He was so delayed that his team leader was once again waiting for his return in order to tell him,

"Two more people want a word with you alone. What on earth have you been up to?"

Maybe, Fergus thought, they were going to dismiss him from his job. They most likely could do that as he felt sure that he had broken some rule or regulation by passing on information, however bland that information might be. They were different people, two men, dressed in grey suits, one wearing a tie the other an open-necked shirt, both had shirts with double cuffs, that peeked out from the sleeves of their jackets. Fergus noticed that they both wore the same cufflinks, square cufflinks with the design of a black and white chess board, he knew it was a chess board and not a draughts board as overlaid on the cufflink was a black rook. This time they asked Fergus to sit down, he sensed bad news.

"You carried out a search on the passport of William Lynch yesterday, Fergus. Today, I am here just to understand why you did that, and who, if anyone, asked you to carry out that search. Now you know and I know that you have breached a number of regulations, not least of which is breaching the Official Secrets Act, which you of course signed up to when you joined, by sharing this information outside the office. But if you are totally honest with me now, I am sure we can look upon your co-operation as a positive."

Fergus was a little confused, these were the same questions he had been asked during the morning, of that he was sure. Even so, he thought it best that he should humour them,

"A local reporter, Greg Auden, called me and asked me if I could tell him when the passport of William Lynch was last used. He gave me an area where he thought this William Lynch lived, and there was one on the system in the right area and about the right age, so I told him when that was last used and that it has not been renewed." Fergus thought that by giving a little more information this time it might help him if they were considering firing him.

"Did this Greg, the reporter say why he wanted this particular information, what sort of story he was working on?"

"No, from time to time he has asked me the odd question or for a piece of information." Fergus regretted confessing to other times that he had shared information, the old Fergus would never have made such a slip, he had been trained in interview techniques, the old Fergus was a lot sharper and more savvy.

"So he has asked you for other names, or information on other names. What other ones has he asked about recently?"

Fergus wanted to appease these men, so quickly owned up to what he knew, albeit a little too quick.

"I have not spoken to him for a while, or given him any information until recently, when he asked me for information on a Mr. and Mrs. Bashford. I could not help him as they did not exist or at least have passports. Before that it was years and years ago. Are you going to fire me?"

The one without the tie answered.

"Not at the moment, your co-operation has been noted and appreciated, thank you Fergus. If Greg contacts you again, don't tell him we have spoken but give him what he asks for, although I would recommend you call us straight afterwards; here is my card. Thank you, Fergus, you can go back to work now."

Obediently Fergus stood up turned, thanked the two men, and returned to his desk and once again continued his work, it would soon be time for his afternoon cup of coffee.

MILLBANK, LONDON.

The dark wood-paneled office was very reminiscent of the 1930's for the simple reason that that was exactly when it had been designed and built for an executive director of Imperial Chemical Industries. At that time ICI was one of the great companies of the world, they were pioneers in chemical products. Thus their offices on the Millbank of London not only stretched across Horseferry Road, but the interior and exterior proclaimed the opulence of the golden age of the British Empire and that was the reason Christopher Davenport Wellington liked his office. Yes, it was on the fifth floor, the very top of the Millbank Building; yes, it did overlook the Thames beside Lambeth Bridge, yet for all that, it was the smell of the wood-paneling, the squeak of the fine oriental carpets as you trod on them and the space around his large desk that made Christopher feel secure. Secure in the knowledge that some values had not been lost but just lay dormant. Christopher was very much an old school civil servant; old values, gentlemen's agreements and a stern belief that whatever government was in power at the time, it was the civil servants like Christopher, who knew the right way forward for the good of the country. Politicians came and went; MP's spoke out in public with phrases that might appease voters and encourage those undecided to cast their votes. Yet for all the rhetoric, Christopher knew that he held a longer-term responsibility to his country and Queen. Whatever the political party of the day might say. Christopher was proud to hold dear that ideology, which now was ridiculed by so many of today's modern generation, old fashioned values and a strong civil service make a country great.

He never took his responsibilities lightly; he was in at 7 a.m. and then would stay often until after eight in the evening. His personal staff comprised of two personal assistants, one would start at 6 a.m., enabling her to clear the post tray, prepare a morning dossier for Christopher, as well as prepare his morning coffee, which would be on his desk as he arrived at 7 a.m. At one o'clock in the afternoon, the second of the personal assistants took over, this changeover happening whilst Christopher was lunching, to save him any inconvenience. His responsibilities were vague, to say the least, he did not have a direct Minister. His post stood to the side of the top civil servant, but he gave direction and guidance to the whole of the civil service, without being a public-facing person. When pressed, as he often was at dinner parties and social functions, he would describe his job as "the grease monkey of the Civil Service, I ensure all the cogs and wheels are suitably oiled to ensure the politicians have as few or as many cock-ups as we plan for them."

Just three years away from retirement, Christopher was divorced, no children and not looking forward to a life without being able to attend his grand office each day.

His afternoon personal assistant opened the door to his office and peered around the door.

"Sir Christopher, I have Harry for you, he would like a word."

"Send him in, please."

Harry was described in his job description as an executive assistant to Sir Christopher. Although it sounded mundane, everyone knew that Harry did the dirty work for Sir Christopher: speaking to people, overhearing conversations, to ensure that Christopher knew everything that was going on.

Christopher listened closely to Harry as he reported back on his latest mission, a mission he had been set earlier that morning, it was now after lunch. Harry was young, enthusiastic and keen to climb the ladder by any means possible. Christopher nodded when Harry finished, before summarising what he had heard, a habit he liked that annoyed many others.

Earlier that morning alongside Christopher's black coffee, his morning dossier contained a wide varied range of messages, memos, reports and general paperwork. One report he always took an especial interest in was the DD report, or as some people out of earshot of Christopher would describe it as the 'big tits report'. Christopher had a range of names of people that he took an interest in and whenever they showed up in IT conversations or searches, their activity was reported back to him. It helped him to keep an eye on those around him. The reports came from a range of sources, he smiled as he read through today's report. A well-known MP had been seen entering a known drug den that was currently under police surveillance, advice was being sought from the Deputy Commissioner, who had now sought the guidance of the Deputy PM. The car of a certain business leader was parked outside a city bar, for many hours before he staggered out to his car and drove home. All this information Christopher could carefully squirrel away and make use of when it suited him. There was one other report that he had not expected to see. One of the names on his list was that of William Lynch; eight years ago he had placed that name on his watch list. Today for the very first time it appeared to have an activity, a passport officer had conducted a search on the name. Christopher knew full well that the passport no longer existed. So who was interested in that name, it would not have been someone at passport control. Hence within moments, Harry had been summoned and told to look into who exactly asked for the search, then find out why they were so interested.

"So Harry, let me be clear on this matter, a misunderstanding would not be helpful. This person Fergus, a lowly data operative was asked by a reporter, as a favour, clearly it is not departmental policy, to see if William Lynch was on the passport database, which he was. That was it, just the basic details and the reporter, Greg Auden, you say, was happy."

Christopher paused and thought for a moment before he continued.

"Thank you, that seems simple enough, your warning to Fergus should be sufficient. Wisely you have pre-empted my request and carried out a search on Greg Auden, who is on a plane, well plans to be on a plane later today bound for Dinard, strange sounding place."

"Yes, Sir Christopher, in Brittany on the north coast of France. Do you want him stopped at the airport?"

"Interfere with the press, heaven forbid we should do such a thing to the free press, no, for now our knowing is sufficient. I'll take it from here Harry. Thank you, you may go."

Once he was alone, Christopher leaned back into his chesterfield chair, the green leather creaking softly. Using his mobile phone, Christopher called his man in France, Mick Hayes, with the simple instruction to watch and track the movements of Greg Auden, who was arriving at Dinard Airport on the afternoon flight. Christopher could do no more than wait to see if the wasp would decide to sting. Only time would tell how much of a problem this reporter, Greg Auden, might be.

ALBERT EMBANKMENT.

Later that same day, three quarters of a mile away in a tall modern glass-walled office, Reece Campbell stood in front of his floor to ceiling window that overlooked the River Thames. His hands behind his back, almost standing to attention, shoulders back, seventeen years in the Highlanders regiment instilled that into you. His six foot six broad frame towered over the bookcases either side of him. He had enjoyed his lunch, sushi with green tea, eaten in his office as he did every day. Now what he was being told was interfering with his normally regular digestion. Without looking at the two men who stood formally in front of his glass and metal minimalist desk, he found the Thames more interesting, he harangued their message:

"Was the man stupid, giving this reporter information like that?"

"It was only to find if a name had a passport Sir." Reece spoke as he continued to look at the passing Cory tugs pulling rubbish in larger containers away from the City to landfill sites somewhere in Essex.

"You're a dick head!" his Scottish accent sounding irritated. "You have no idea what such information might mean, you have no understanding of what the whole scenario is behind a name, so don't give me shit about only a name. You are both simple messengers, I decide what is and what is not important. So, the Lynch name I know. What about the stupid passport prat, Fergus and this reporter, Greg Auden you say? Then there was another search for a Bashford for the same reporter a few days ago, what is Fergus, for fuck's sake, directory enquiries! So who are they, Greg Auden and Peter Bashford?"

He turned and looked over his glasses at the two men in a clearly threatening manner. "Have you checked?"

They both knew Mr. Campbell well enough to have already gathered the information that he was bound to ask them for, if they did not have it to hand, they would not have been in his best books, and the last place any person who worked with Recce Campbell would want to be is outside of his best books. The shorter of the two men answered.

"Greg Auden is, as we mentioned a reporter, nothing on him, but for a request to make a statement years ago following his sister's death. The only current item of interest is, he is going to France later this afternoon. Been there recently, during the past week in fact, and apart from that, everything else is boring and mundane." The shorter man waited, just in case there was a reaction from Reece, there was none, so he continued. "Peter Bashford, nothing at all, and we mean nothing, not even a passport or parking fine, he is well under the radar, not even got a vote. Possibly a cover of some sort."

"The reporter, the request for a statement, did he give it and how did his sister die?"

The shorter man fiddled with his note book, his chess board cuff links glinting in the rays of the afternoon sun as it came through the window. "She committed suicide, and the statement, if it was made, was never filed anywhere."

"Thank you, interesting. Well, get yourselves off and join Greg on his trip to France, let me know where he goes, whom he contacts and call me in twenty-four hours, now off you go."

Dutifully they left the office, while Reece returned to looking at the river Thames as it ebbed along.

It had been eight years since he had heard the name William Lynch, eight long years of waiting and now his patience was paying off. He smiled, William Lynch, the lucky researcher who missed out on getting caught up in a tragic accident all those years ago, who then disappeared off the face of the earth. Reece doubted that anyone as much of a geek as William would be able to disappear, create a new identity for himself, obtain a false passport then maybe leave the country. William could not have done that without some help, maybe not from the criminal underworld, maybe from inside a government office and Reece could guess whose office that might have been.

BRITTANY, FRANCE.

If he had to be honest with himself, Greg was not totally sure just why he was enduring for the second time this week the unpleasant, partly alarming, sensation of the Boeing 727 taking off from Stansted en route to Dinard. He had considered the futile attempt he had made at finding Martin last week, which had resulted in nothing but a few weird facts. All right, he told himself, the Bashford family were not totally welcoming but, there again, Mr. & Mrs. Battener were not what you would describe as fully functioning in a social sense. So what could you make of that, nothing! Justine and her French husband seemed normal enough, as did her friend, Helen, even though she did not fit the experience that he had personally had of Fleet Street reporters. Fleet Street reporters, such an old term, now all the national newspapers had left Fleet Street for the outer suburbs and cheaper rents. So the term was as redundant as were the thousand or so printers that had found themselves out of a job, as newspapers took up modern computerised technology. All the Fleet Street reporters that he had ever met were arrogant and convinced the World should revolve around them. They had a reputation to live up to, hard drinking and living life in the fast lane. Greg recalled one he had met, together they had worked on a story in the sleepy seaside village of Whitstable. He had been from the News of the World, at the time one of the biggest selling newspapers in the country. He had a new top of the range Ford Sierra, dressed in well-tailored suits, ordered the hottest curries, drank wine by the bottle and anything else he wanted, sometimes prefixing his orders by making it clear he worked for the News of the World. Although during the course of the evening that Greg shared with him, it became increasingly clear, he was struggling to pay his large mortgage as well as a car loan, and the curry had, Greg found out at breakfast, kept him awake all night with heartburn. Greg might not have been that fashionable only ordering a mild korma, but at least he had slept like a baby all night.

Maybe Helen was that new breed of journalist that was evolving in response to the digital age, copy no longer being phoned in to stenographic listeners, it was now just zipped across the internet in a split second. She wore sensible clothes, he guessed she would eat healthy food, have the occasional glass of wine and maybe run regularly at least five kilometres in order to keep healthy. Maybe she had the bravado, maybe not; maybe it did not really matter. What Greg did know was that the plane was going to land soon and his hand gripped tightly to the arm rest in preparation. Maybe he should change his approach, maybe he needed to look towards the gay community in France, if there was such a thing in such a rural area as La Ville du Bois, maybe Loudéac held the key. Greg felt himself adrift; all he had in mind was to go to the Avis outlet in Loudéac, ask about Dougie returning the car and if anyone had picked him up, together with anything else he could think of to ask. He guessed it would be a dead end there, he very much doubted they would give him a forwarding address. A dead end, a point where the trail runs cold and stops, that could be the biggest indication that there was something connecting the two missing men. Also Greg was planning to go and see the Bashfords again, hopefully to talk about the photograph, sitting innocently on the sideboard, the 1990's chess champions, and William Lynch, who had not used or renewed his passport, a pseudo dead end? Either way, Greg set himself a target of two days, before he was going back to the UK with the express intention of finding some real work, local reporting, small articles, the bread and butter of what he knew and was more than capable of doing. Investigation, he was beginning to think, was not a skill he should put on his CV.

His mobile phone rang as he was settling himself into his Fiat 500 hire car at Dinard airport, adjusting seat mirrors and cursing that he had to remember the gear stick was on the wrong side for an English driver.

"Fergus, what can I do for you?"

"I'm sorry Greg, I really am, I had no choice, it was a surprise and they so unnerved me that I just said everything, I really had to or it might have been the end of my job and I do so need that job and the pension that is at the end...."

"Whoah Fergus, take a breath!" Greg interrupted, hoping to calm down a clearly very flustered Fergus, "What's happened, tell me about it slowly?"

"It was just before lunch, I was called into the office and he asked me why I had searched the name of William Lynch, he was, I am sure, going to sack me, so I told him that you had asked me."

'Thanks', Greg thought, 'for dropping me right in it', what he said was "That's OK Fergus. Do you know why they wanted to know?"

"He didn't say, just asked who had asked me and that was it, he let me go back to work, but the others...."

"Others?"

"Yes, after lunch two other men asked who I had done the search on William Lynch for, so I told them, and this time they asked for your number and where you worked."

"So, to be clear, they came back after lunch and then asked for my number and where I worked?"

"They were only there after lunch, the other was before lunch, different, the ones after lunch were a lot more friendly, the morning man seemed very sinister, like a grumpy immigration official and I know how grumpy they are." Fergus tried to make a joke but did not seem to respond to his own humour.

"Two different sets of people both asked you who had asked you to search for William Lynch?"

Fergus agreed that was the upshot, then Greg continued,

"Do you know if they were from the same department or what department they were from?"

"Sorry Greg, I don't know, I think they said internal affairs, if we have one, I wasn't really listening as I was worried when they called me in. I'm sure they will be in contact with you soon."

"Fergus, they were onto you within twenty-four hours of my request, why would that happen, and how would they know you weren't doing it for legitimate reasons? There must be thousands of inquiries a day."

Fergus thought in silence for a moment before answering, "There must be some sort of alert on the name, like you get at passport control; it would give instructions on what to do with the person, arrest them, question them, who needs to be searched, hold all passengers travelling with them, let them through and call someone, all sorts of instructions, depending on what the person is suspected of."

"But William Lynch has not had a passport for a long time, he has not been on an electoral roll for a number of years, so why would they be interested?"

"There could be a hundred reasons, they might tell you when they contact you."

Greg doubted he would get such a call and at the same time, he felt sorry for Fergus, who was now just the shadow of the man he had been.

Greg left the Dinard Airport Car Hire car park, twice forgetting that the gear stick was to his right, he was too preoccupied with why the passport office were so interested in William Lynch, one dead end was possibly beginning to open up.

The young lady who greeted him at the Loudéac branch of Avis, was clearly excited to be asked questions. The fact that she might be breaking company regulations did not seem to bother her in the least, she was taking part in an international investigation. Plus, she was able to practice her language skills, speaking in English to an English person. She had since her school education spoken a little English, but then working for Avis, she started to pick up English words that were connected to car hire, so helpful when the English arrived to hire cars, but today she was able to use the vocabulary that she had been learning from evening classes at the local Salle des Fetes.

"A man named Douglas Scott left the car here at eighteen thirty-five, handed over the keys, all signed off then left. It was close to closing time, we shut at nineteen hundred, by the time he left, he had no luggage except for a plastic bag. He waits outside, then turned left to the town centre, when I shut door to close up he was about twenty metres gone, still waiting, I then locked the door, I look again, he had gone, that is all."

"So what about when you were locking up, was there a lot of traffic going past?"

"No, that time of night, this road, it is very quiet, I think a car did pass behind me when I was locking the door, yes, as I looked for him, there was a car turning right, up close to the...," she hesitated as she searched for the English word "traffic lights." she said with a smug smile.

Greg left, so now there was a semi dead end, he wondered if it was William driving that car, or even Peter Bashford, which was his next planned visit.

A dark figure with a shrewd pair of blue eyes watched Greg as he got into the small Fiat and pulled away from the Avis office and disappeared into the cold night.

LA VILLE DU BOIS

By the time that Greg pulled up outside the Bashford house in La Ville du Bois, it was after eight in the evening. The sun had long since set and the darkness was now complete, only broken by the small porch lamp that illuminated the Bashford's front door. All the window shutters had been closed, with no light escaping from any windows that lay behind them. The garden looked ghost-like in the light from the single outside lamp, as did the walls of the house, now a deep grey, no longer the bright white they were when illuminated by the sun. As the door opened, Greg felt a wave of warm air rush over him; it was Mr Bashford who had answered the door, holding a cloth napkin in his hand. Greg clearly saw the look of surprise on Peter Bashford's face as if his worst nightmare had just returned.

"I need to ask you some questions, Mr Bashford,"

"No," was the blunt instant answer which interrupted Greg, "I told you before, I have nothing to say to the likes of you, just leave."

"Just two minutes, a couple of simple questions and this whole misunderstanding will be sorted out."

"Misunderstanding, the only thing that you are misunderstanding is when I said no before I meant it, good night!" Peter tried to push the door closed but it jammed on Greg's leg which he had placed just over the threshold.

"Wilmington school chess champions, that photograph you have, where is William Lynch?"

Peter tried using his foot to push the reporter's leg out of the way of the door closing, the rising voices had brought his wife, Jane, to the door.

"What's happening?" her voice was concerned, uninvited night-time visitors were a very rare occurrence out in the French countryside.

"I'm just trying to find out what has happened to some friends who are missing. But Mr Bashford why don't you have a passport on record? And where is Mr Lynch who has not used his passport in years, not since R.G. Plastics closed down, in fact?"

"Peter, get rid of him," his wife instructed, her voice becoming spiky and laced with panic, clearly not noticing that her husband was pushing harder and harder against the door.

"I am not talking to you, get out before I decide to really hurt...."

"Have you something to hide Mr Bashford?"

It was at that point that Peter Bashford landed a strong kick to the shin of Greg, whose instinctive reaction was to pull his leg back away from the door, giving Peter Bashford the opportunity to slam the door shut, Greg heard the door being locked behind it. The outside light was turned off, leaving Greg grasping his painful shin in total darkness.

"I'll be back, I am not giving up until I find out all about William Lynch!" Greg retreated carefully from the garden, almost having to feel his way. They had turned off the outside light through spite, leaving him with only a glimmer of moonlight that appeared and disappeared between clouds, just giving enough light to find his way back to the car.

*

Inside the now secured house, the family gathered round the dinner table where their dinner of roast chicken had been interrupted and now lay going cold on their plates. The two teenage boys were sitting looking at their parents.

"He knows Peter, he knows all about us. You've got to call London now, before it's too late," Jane said, now verging on hysteria.

"Maybe he made a lucky guess, if he'd known more, he would have said. He just has a couple of names," Peter tried to sound reassuring.

"Not just any names, our names, your workplace, maybe he knows everything. Peter, we need protection, not just on the other side of the Channel, but people alongside us who will protect us here." She turned to her now worried teenage sons, both sitting silently at the table. They knew the barest details of the reasons why they had suddenly moved to France; they had never been told to expect such fear from their normally placid caring parents.

"I'll go and call London." He looked at the worried looks on the faces of his family. "Maybe it would be better if we put together a few things and then search out a hotel for the next few nights. We could go down to the south coast, there will be plenty of empty hotel rooms at this time of year and that will put us out of harm's way until London tells us what to do. Boys, go upstairs, pack a bag each for a couple of nights. Jane you do the same for us. I'll go and call London, then we'll go off tonight. Whatever they say, if we end up sleeping in the car tonight it will be better than waiting here for the doorbell to ring again."

"Dad," Paul, the oldest boy who resembled his mother but was already taller than her, asked, "are we in danger, I mean real danger."

Peter held the hands of both his boys close, "Not yet, but that's why we are going to slip away tonight, just to be on the safe side. Now you two get going upstairs and get packed. I'll be half an hour or so." He kissed his wife and slipped on a heavy jacket, picked up his car keys from the vintage stand beside the door, "Love you all, see you soon."

*

Greg played a hunch and parked his car a few metres away from the Bashford's house. It was not long before in his rear view mirror he saw the porch light come on again, the door opened and a moment later, Peter's Citroen sped past the innocent looking Fiat. Peter paid no attention to the car, he was too busy focusing on getting to the payphone in Les Forges. The dark field edged lanes were empty at this time of night, his headlamps were the only light, apart from the few porch lights scattered around the landscape. It was colder than he thought it might have been and he shivered as he increased the temperature of the heater, wishing the car would warm up more quickly. He followed the winding lane, clipped part of a grass verge and slipped a little too close to the ditch on the other side. "Shit" he said out loud, realising that he was now driving following two sherries, plus a number of glasses of red wine with his half-eaten dinner. He felt light-headed, not drunk, so it would be fine. He continued driving towards and then into the forest of Lanouee, following the long straight road to the crossroads. The winter skeletons of the trees illuminated in the car headlamps passed by faster and faster. Peter was concentrating on the situation at home, someone mentioning William Lynch and Peter Bashford in the same breath as R.G. Plastics, not on his driving. He approached the crossroads quicker than he expected, braking heavily so that the car's wheels began to lose grip on the moist road surface. He corrected the steering one way, then the other, a little too much over correction and the car slid to an uncontrolled halt just to the left of the crossroads, thankfully, he thought, still on tarmac. Once again, he pressed the accelerator and turned right to the long forest road which led to the village of Les Forges.

In his confused, preoccupied mind he had not noticed the headlights a little way behind. Peter's mind returned once more to the reporter whose name he could not think of, why had he used the pretence of his missing friends, when he must have known all along, why tonight? What else had he found out, what else had changed? He hoped Christopher would be able to help him once again. A new identity, a new country, a new life, it was still running but what choice did they have? The speed he was driving at was once more creeping up, unnoticed by him, as the alcohol had dulled his reactions. The fear of discovery was clouding his judgment, the road, but for his headlamps, was cloaked in total darkness. The short, winding lane, close to the village of Les Forges, was bordered by a deep ditch that carried excessive rain from the road and into the nearby river. He had driven this road hundreds of times, shopping trips, days out with his family, now he was looking at leaving again to go anywhere where he and his family could not be found. The payphone was just ahead a few hundred metres when he clipped the grass verge, his steering juddered, then continued along the road. In his befuddled mind he had forgotten about the crossroads and the stop sign at the entrance to it. It only occurred to him that he was on the crossroads when the lights of the articulated lorry travelling downhill, with its trailer full of pre-packed eggs going to the supermarket distribution depot, appeared to his left. The French Police decided in their subsequent investigation that he was travelling a little faster than he should have been and could not easily stop on the slippery road, and therefore had caused the accident. Even if the unlucky lorry driver had had any sort of warning that a car would race out of the forest at that time of night and at that speed, ignoring the crossroads and the stop sign, there would have been nothing that he could do to avoid the accident.

Somehow fate had brought them together at that precise moment in time, a second either side of that moment and the impact would never have occurred. It was a heavy deafening impact, an impact that embedded the Citroen, squashing it like a fly into the grill of the Mercedes truck from Transport Renard. Peter did not die instantly, his body was totally entangled in the twisted metal, with deflated white, ineffective air bags all around him, warm blood rolled across his face. It might have been the alcohol, the fear of leaving his family behind or the pain that now began to engulf his body that made him delirious. He recalled a children's story he used to tell his two boys when they were a lot younger, 'just like Chicken Licken', Peter thought, he did not get to the telephone to tell the King that the sky was falling down. That was his last earthly thought.

LA BELLE ETOILE.

The table looked as though it had been laid out with a theodolite, the plates so consistently located on the table. Stainless steel cutlery arranged perfectly alongside the smoked glass place setting. Two glasses to the right of Helen's plate, a tall wide-bowled red wine glass alongside a tumbler for water, both so clean they sparkled. Opposite to Helen's, was a mirror image place setting. She looked at Phillip, as he cleaned his hands with antiseptic gel, a recently acquired habit, Helen joined him in the same ritual. Across the centre of the table, within easy reach of each of those eating were three plates: the first had eight slices of Emmental cheese, the second had four slices of ham, smoked with no rind or fat, the final plate had a whole baguette cut into four pieces. Double Phillip's normal lunch fare, to accommodate his guest. In terms of Phillip's shopping habits, this additional mouth to feed, would upset the system that he had developed. He did carefully think about that aspect when inviting Helen over for lunch, he even toyed, momentarily, with having a different type of lunch. The problem he could not conclude was what he could substitute his lunch with that would meet his expectations and also please Helen. So in the end he decided to stick to his regular lunch, just using twice the quantities. He had bought an extra baguette and planned to substitute half a baguette for the crackers that normally accompanied his lunch every Sunday. That all fitted in perfectly. The other concession he made to his visitor was the addition of a glass of red wine with lunch, as well as his usual tumbler of water.

Helen began to eat, she was not exactly sure why she had accepted Phillip's invitation to lunch, he seemed to be captivating her, intriguing her beyond her sensible reasoning. Even though she told herself she was following a powerful news story, in her heart she felt that was now a lie. Last night he had in cold blood, killed a young man. She had watched as he proudly ripped the life from Dougie, as if she was some Roman empress, he, her champion, crushing his opponent. She had seen all that, Dougie talking to her normally, following him out into the garden, seeing him die. Then afterwards she calmly had a drink with his killer, munched on crackers and soft cheese for a supper with an actual murderer and then left. She had slept soundly that night and had now returned in the cold light of the winter's day to share lunch with him and to hear more gruesome details and boasts from this pleasant looking man sitting across the table from her. Perhaps he was right, that she had a warped gene within her DNA that allowed her to cross the moral barrier and kill. Maybe leaving her mother at the foot of the stairs to slowly die, could be blamed on that defective gene. Meeting Phillip and seeing him kill had now awoken that dormant gene. Now she was just waiting for the right circumstances, to no longer just leave murder to chance. If her mother had not fallen down the stairs, would Helen have taken steps to kill her, she thought possibly not, but now that last night had happened, the lust to kill had now been encouraged and nurtured by Phillip to swell up and cascade over her thoughts. As obsessive as cleaning of her hands was, she had learned to control the habit in company so as not to appear strange, Phillip was teaching her the freedom to let go of those inhibitions and be true to herself.

"It was so good of you to come over today for lunch. After last night, I really did want to continue talking about it, it helps to maintain the euphoric high I get, to actually talk to someone who was with me. I cleaned up this morning, so the pigs are having a good feast, more than we are," he laughed, Helen smiled. "I need to get rid of the shoes and a few silly items that he was carrying; the pie funnel as you can see is my latest addition. His passport was burnt this morning as were the weird scraps of paper he kept in his wallet, cocktail recipes I think they looked like. He was a barman, well, he always liked to think of himself as a cocktail waiter, he was in fact, in my opinion, a humble barman. The credit cards went the same way as the passport, with the wallet going in the rubbish, along with a watch and a couple of those cheap friendship bands that are so popular now. But I have kept a little gift for you."

Phillip placed on the table beside Helen a traditional waiter's friend, with corkscrew, foil knife & lever with crown cap remover,

"Before you say anything, I have no idea how he got that on the plane, I'm sure airplane security is totally hit or miss. It was in his pocket, maybe, but even so, if he'd been a terrorist, that is not the sort of thing you want to see on an airplane. That is one of the reasons I am not a great one for using airlines. Those so called security guards that check your luggage and watch you go through scanners, well they are so badly paid and work such long hours, I'm not that surprised the odd little weapon gets through from time to time."

Helen picked it up. "It's engraved 'with love, Alistair.'"

"His older sugar daddy, thinks he is so grand and fit, does the gym, has the muscles, well he is still ageing, which is clear looking at his skin."

Helen looked up from her plate of ham and cheese, still holding the waiter's friend in her hand, "How well did you know them, Dougie and Alistair?"

"Only socially, I used to go to a club, music and drinking, they were often there. Well Dougie was behind the bar there, so he was there most nights, his guardian angel and chief financier, Alistair, was there some nights, but not always." He leaned across and refilled her wine glass. "It was a gay club, but

I'm not gay, well for that matter I'm not heterosexual either. I suppose one might describe me as androgynous, no interest in conventional sex. Not that that should be of any interest to you either way; I'm just keen for you to better understand me. Understand that I am not a monster from some X-rated movie, I am just me with a few unusual traits, trying to live my life."

"Why would you want that, you don't seem to be the sort of person who needs people to understand him, I would have said you were very much an independent sort of person."

"A loner is society's description of me, for the simple reason I do not adhere to social rules and conventions. I am me, God made me and if people think I am weird, then they are being disrespectful to God. That being said Helen, I do want you to understand me, see what drives me, it will help you mature into the person God chose you to be. Not the one that society deems you should be. Look upon me as the person who will liberate you. So do you have any ideas as to whom you might murder?"

Helen was totally sure that this was the first time she had ever been asked such a question over lunch and in fact any time before, in any situation, she felt a tingle of excitement ripple through her body, just who would she murder? But first she had a question for her emerging master.

"So you knew Dougie, if he was a friend or even an acquaintance, doesn't that lead to the possibility you might become a suspect?"

"Not friends, Helen, my victims. Can I get you some fruit?"

Helen declined the offer of her choice from the fruit bowl, Phillip chose a conference pear, which he proceeded to slice and eat.

"These were all chosen victims, people I have no affection for, just casual people that I conversed with briefly. The club, in Gravesend, the Angel Wings, a gay night club, full of potential victims, living lives that are not conventional, men come and go all the time through the doors of the club. I paid four casual visits to the club and struck up conversations with some of the men there, took a phone number and a name, they are then on my potential victim list. As you saw, Dougie was happy to talk to me on the telephone and come over and see me. As I said, I went to the club four times, then, never again, I was just a passing male, one of maybe thousands."

"So you said that you murdered five people, I know Dougie, you have already mentioned Martin, so who were the others?"

He wiped his hands of pear juice, then used the antiseptic gel to clean them further, removing some of the sweet stickiness that contaminated his fingers.

"The last four have been from the club. There was Dougie and Martin, as you quite rightly mention, then Nathan White, that was truly good, he drowned in the Thames, and Ben Murray, a can of petrol and a lighter can be very dangerous." Phillip laughed, a warm infectious laugh.

"And the fifth?" Helen asked.

"Technically, that was Dougie; you want to know about my first, well, Helen my love, even a man like myself needs some secrets. Let's go and see how the pigs have been doing, unless you'd rather not?"

Helen rather would, she thought. She felt able to ask any question of this man, a self-proclaimed murderer, who had confidence in her and was pleased to boast about his victims even though she was a national newspaper reporter, which she now felt she was. She was starting to become the arrogant, self-possessed person she knew she would have to become, sensing it had started this morning when she phoned Danny, her news editor, asking him if she could stay longer in France. As she walked towards the pig pen alongside Phillip, she recalled her conversation with Danny.

"Babe," She hated him calling her that, even though it was the term he used for all the female reporters, most of whom accepted that it was just Danny's way. "If you want to stay, you've got to give me a good reason, a sensible reason that will end up with a story."

"I told you before, I just don't want to say at this moment in time. It's big, very big, it will blow your mind, sell thousands more copies and make great PR for the Mirror, the scoop of the century, but you have to trust me and give me more time."

"Babe, you're a novice, a 'newbie', out in another country. All I wanted were a couple of stories about old English 'farts' who are having a tough time in France. You're not on the local rag where the Mayor dunking his digestive biscuit and losing it in his tea makes news, you're on a National paper, the very best in the country. I doubt your scoop will turn a hair on my head, so what's this great story you have?"

"I told you, I'm not saying and I'm staying here. I might have worked for a local rag, but I was handpicked, and I am bloody good, so just to let you know, I am staying."

"Great, when the paper has a load of blank pages, I'll tell the boss, all the staff have decided to stay out searching out big stories, but they aren't telling me what they are! I'd be mincemeat, Helen. Helen, stop arseing around and fucking tell me!"

"If you have a problem then speak to your boss, he's giving me a chance, and this is my chance and I'm taking it. Ask him, if he calls me back, I might tell him, but not you Danny."

The line was quiet for a moment.

"Yes well, we all know that you were hand picked out by the boss, which you can use to your advantage once in a while Helen. But just be careful using that friendship or else people will start asking just why the friendship exists, and I can tell you, some journalists have some very dirty minds. I'll give you an extra day and then I want to hear from you about what you are doing or see you back in the office, writing the story up, and it had better be a bloody good story as well, if it doesn't make the front page, you'll be in the shit."

The thought of him becoming her first victim did come to mind, but she guessed that killing the news editor of a national paper was not the best way to start a career in journalism. She was pleased that she had stood up to Danny and got a couple more days to sort this whole thing out one way or another.

"They have overeaten, I suppose we would expect that of pigs, so now they are sleeping it off, I'll give them an hour before they start again."

Helen looked into the pen, it looked at first sight like any other muddy pig pen, smelly, dirty and full of pigs. It was only as she looked around that she saw a bone, maybe a leg bone with tissue and muscles, partly eaten but some were still attached, then she saw some ribs, a foot, a couple of fingers, all in various states of consumption. The gruesome sight made her a little fuzzy as she pictured Dougie, sitting sweetly on the chair last night, introducing himself to her.

"So how do I go about killing another human being?" Helen asked the question automatically, with a coldness that would have shocked her closest friends.

"I have, in most cases, found identifying a victim a very rewarding part of the procedure. Someone who is not close to you, although you will need to know them up to a point, for no other reason than you will need to plan the actual murder, so it goes without saying you will have to know something about them. Then you need to look at the skills you might have that could be used to entice the intended victim into the situation that will lead to their murder, and for that you will need to look closely at yourself and discern what skills you can utilise. A pretty female can have an advantage, and before you go all sexist on me, I thought I might be and I am attractive to some gay men, I used that sexual attraction to get to know my victim better. I wouldn't go to bed with any of them, heaven forbid, but I used the temptation to lure them towards me in order to learn a little more about them. Then you must consider, just how to kill and dispose of them. I must say I am really pleased with the way I can get them out of the country and over here, that has helped so much, in fact murdering in foreign countries is not too difficult, but you must always ensure they are not local, no point going off and killing one of the English in the village, the police would soon be on to you. Look, I'm getting ahead of myself and getting excited. Think about, not who you are going to kill, think about how you wish to entice and then kill. From there, I am sure, between us we can come up with an amazing strategy to succeed. Let's go back inside."

Helen went inside knowing she would get another invitation to this house of death and would then be pressed about how she planned to kill. She realised she would soon be arriving at a crossroads, where not to kill would only put her in a danger greater than she had ever faced. Back tomorrow evening for dinner and Phillip would begin to groom her, his apprentice to plan and then in time, commit her first murder, whoever and wherever that might be. Once Helen was at that crossroads she would have to make a decision. Walking away from the house, she realised that whatever route she took, she would never be the Helen Taylor that left the Reading Observer, just a few weeks ago. She would either be a murderer or would have been murdered herself. She had already discounted writing the news story.

LA GARENNE.

Greg had decided not to follow Peter last night, he guessed he was off to the same pay phone to call whoever he calls, instead he had a light meal at the Hotel Chateau in Josselin, before making a couple of telephone calls. The owner of the small antiques shop that had had the statue stolen, was happy to speak to Greg, although not until the afternoon. Then, for some strange inexplicable reason, he found himself calling Donna for no better reason, he told her, than to speak to someone friendly about mundane subjects, Donna doubted and hoped that was not the only reason.

The more he thought about it the more he believed that Martin had picked up Dougie from the Avis office, and if that was the case, then there was a good chance they were staying nearby. If they were an eloping couple, which seemed to Greg to be the most logical answer, it could now be they were leaving for warmer climates or were planning to very soon. Yet when Greg thought more about people eloping, running away, escaping from their existing lives, he thought they would probably choose a more romantically attractive destination in the first place. La Ville du Bois in the middle of winter would not be his first choice for a romantic destination. There had to be a reason for choosing this area of Brittany, a remote country destination, where you needed a car; but both Martin and Dougie had left their hired cars behind. When Dougie was picked up, presumably by Martin, then Martin must have had access to a motor car here in France. Logically, both of them must have some sort of a connection to someone here in France, already living in the rolling French countryside and able to provide a car. The most likely candidate to Greg had to be Peter Bashford, who clearly had something to hide.

In a foreign country, you have to find someone to trust and Greg decided he would put his trust in Justine and her French husband, so he called from his mobile, spoke to Justine and asked if he could pop around in the morning for a coffee and a chat about the people living in and around the village, she readily agreed.

With Laurent at work, Greg and Justine sat around the long dining table, holding cups of coffee. Greg explained his dilemma; his lack of knowledge about French village life was hindering him.

"Two gay men turning up in the vicinity of La Ville du Bois, they must have some sort of connection to the village or at least somewhere around here. Do you know of any other gay men living around here?"

"To be honest Greg," Justine answered with a smile on her face, she could see the funny side of the question, her smile lighting up, what Greg considered to be an attractive face, even with her hair tied back in a bun as she had not bothered to wash it that morning. "That is one of the oddest questions I have ever been asked. Where is the local gay scene in La Ville du Bois? I very much doubt if there is one, I would think you would need to go off to Loudéac or Rennes maybe, to find gay clubs and sexually orientated night life like that. What about searching the internet, there must be some websites for visiting gay tourists."

"Maybe I could borrow your computer for that one; I wouldn't feel that comfortable about Googling gay clubs in an internet café, it might attract the wrong sort of attention. Also, I guess the site would be in French and I'm not that good at French, I can order food, but not state sexual preferences."

"I see your point there Greg, although most websites in France have an English version, the French are very open minded that way, children are taught it at a very young age, and most of the services, like the gas, electric and telephone companies have very good English speaking operators. This is a pity really as it makes some of the Brits who come over here to live very lazy and does not force them into learning the French language."

Greg finished his coffee and refused the offer of a second, "So does anyone spring into your mind who might take in two gay escapees from England?"

Justine refilled her cup and spoke as she stirred in her one spoonful of sugar.

"Listening to what you have told me, I am in agreement that both Martin and Dougie cannot be too far from La Ville du Bois. With Martin leaving his car on a lonely country lane, it means that he was either able to walk to his destination, or he could have called whoever he was meeting, and they came and collected him. There are just two things that bother me, first; the stolen statue, I cannot see why Martin would have smashed a plate glass shop window to remove a cheap statue. Then the other thing is, are we getting too obsessed with the fact they are both gay, is that really anything to do with this? It might be, but I'm just saying their sexuality might not have anything at all to do with this story."

Justine sipped her coffee, before continuing,

"I am sure if two strangers turned up in the village someone would have noticed, unless of course they have been kept inside someone's house, and have not seen the light of day. None of the families that I know, both French and English, appear to be into stashing men away in their back rooms!"

Before Greg could respond, Helen walked into the kitchen,

"Mmm, coffee smells wonderful, just what I need. Hello Greg, How are you?"

"Still looking for my gay men."

"Plural, have you lost another one?" She joked as she joined them at the table sitting alongside Justine as Greg explained about Dougie. Greg wasn't sure, it was maybe just her natural concern for a missing person, but her mood changed ever so slightly.

"Eloped," she concluded, "without a doubt and probably miles away."

Helen looked at Greg, he was about to speak when Justine spoke first,

"If they were here in the village, I am sure, as I said to Greg, that their presence would have been noticed, not much happens in La Ville du Bois without someone noticing and telling someone else, be it the arrival of a different car, or a guest at a farmhouse, the baker would have heard and passed that information on. So I think we can safely assume that they have taken their friend's car and gone off, either to the south of France or somewhere else in Europe, neither of these two men will be in La Ville du Bois any longer."

Helen looked at Justine,

"Friend's car, what is all that about? I thought Martin had left his car, wasn't that what started this all off."

"Yes, but if when Martin was over here, he left his car beside the road, as Justine said earlier before you were here, he must have either walked somewhere or a friend picked him up and took him some place. Don't forget, Dougie was picked up by a car, and Martin, having left his car behind, was wanted by the French police so I doubt that he would have been able to hire another car."

"So," Justine added, enjoying being part of the increasing excitement that had arrived in La Ville du Bois, a normally sleepy French village, "we think that both of them must have made contact with someone around the village. So when you came in, we were going through likely candidates for having two gay men in their house." Justine joked, but Helen did not smile, she seemed preoccupied.

"The Bashfords, what do you know about them?" Greg asked Justine as she stood up and walked over to the fire, opening the glass door and pushing two large logs into the cavity of burning embers, allowing wood smoke to escape into the room. She brushed her hands, removing traces of the splintered wood from them, not caring too much about the floor, wood fires meant the tiled floor around it was almost always ashen and odd small chips of wood were scattered over it. She had resolved early on just to sweep that part of the floor once a day.

"I was surprised that he was a bit off with you he has always, whenever I've met him, been the most polite of men, chatty, happy just to talk about mundane stuff. Although they have never invited us over there, not all couples are sociable, others are just too sociable, always inviting people over for dinner, think they are the ones that are bored with their own company. All I know about the Bashfords is that they have lived here for about eight years, came over from southern England. I don't think they have ever told me anymore, or at least I have not asked. The children attend school and seem to have settled in well, polite, pleasant children, both of them are totally bilingual; I think one wants to be a pharmacist, a very good trade to have in France. As far as I know Mr Bashford senior does no sort of work, he always describes himself as unemployed and happy, as he says he is too young to be retired. I have spoken to the wife a few times, when our paths have crossed mainly at the bakery, again, very much keeps herself to herself. Just because we are immigrants it doesn't mean we have to stick close to the English. That guy that you visit Helen, no one knows anything about him at all, although now you and he have a thing we might learn a bit more." Justine smiled as she teased Helen who did not react as her school friend might have expected, there was no humour in her voice.

"There's nothing between us, it's just a story and he is giving me some good copy."

"Who's that?" Greg asked.

"Just an English guy who is a bit of a, loner, he'll be the main part of my story on ex-pats, so please forgive me if I don't say too much about him."

"I'm sure Greg could pop in and ask him if he has seen either Martin or Dougie."

"No," Helen snapped back at her friend, "I've been to his house a couple of times and I have not seen anyone but him there."

"Well at least let me ask him the question, he might have known them and lent them a car to elope. If that is what is at the bottom of this, I would be able to tell their jilted partners back home that their partners have gone off, they'll be upset, but at least they would know they are okay and out living another life. As we have all said, they could be miles away somewhere in a love nest by now."

"I told you," Helen reiterated, "he lives all alone, there was no one there but him, and I'm sure he would have mentioned it if he had had any recent visitors."

"Well, just ask him, that's all I'm asking you. Ask if he has heard of these guys, please."

Greg sensed that Helen wanted to shout back at him, but she composed herself and spoke calmly.

"I'll ask him next time I see him." she conceded, but Greg was not convinced she would.

"OK well maybe next time, could you ask him if he has seen any lone Englishmen wandering around the countryside. Or maybe I could visit him, where about does he live?" Greg deliberately taunted her.

"I told you he's my contact, my story, I'll ask him, right," Helen stated it forcefully so that there could be no misunderstanding that she was not going to extend an invitation for Greg to visit Phillip.

Greg knew that reporters competing for stories often held their contacts close to their chest, but Greg felt that Helen was reacting in an excessive way. Even so, Greg put her reaction to one side, he had only recently met Helen maybe she was just like that, time would tell. Justine sensed the tension and tried to move the conversation away from the subject of Phillip.

"We are of course assuming they came over here to meet up with English residents, but as I recall, the nearest home to where the car was found was French, Marie Helene and her husband, who is a bit of a rum character, screw down your valuables when he is around."

Her light-hearted comment made little impression to the tense atmosphere that had descended over her kitchen.

At that point the phone rang in another room and Justine left the table to answer it. There was an uncomfortable silence between Helen and Greg while they waited for the return of their host. Greg broke the silence.

"Ok, I only asked. If you want to keep him to yourself, that's fine, trust me Helen, I am not about to steal any story that you are building I'm only looking for the two missing men and ..." he stopped as he heard Justine mention his name.

"Yes, Greg is here, do you want to speak to him?"

The room was silent as Justine returned still talking on the telephone, her face creased into a look of anguish.

"Oh no that is so terrible for you, if there is anything I can do, just ask. Yes, I'll ask him, I'm sure he will help you, take care."

"Someone wants me?" Greg asked as Justine stood in the kitchen, the phone still in her hand.

"That was Jane, Jane Bashford, her husband Peter was killed last night in a car crash, and she wants you to go and see her."

LES LOGES.

Jane Bashford sat on the settee with its dark blue floral pattern that had a very English country feel about it. It was the first time that Greg had really noticed the pattern, he realised that, as Jane sat composing herself, having explained the circumstances of her husband's death, the whole house had an English feel to it. Greg had time to look around the room; previously he had been briefly engaged in a heavy conversation with Peter. The tall oak bookcase, filled with old dusty looking tomes, Dickens, Shakespeare, Faraday, autobiographies as well as large reference books, 'Rickards Classic Chess Moves', 'Physics a Science without boundaries', interspersed with classic fiction, Steinbeck, PG Woodhouse, Wilkie Collins. Book titles that added weight to Greg's thoughts that Peter Bashford is, or was, the same person as William Lynch. Alongside the bookcase was a matching oak buffet, with photographs in a variety of different shaped frames, family photographs, mostly of latter days of their life in France, the two exceptions being a faded colour wedding photograph of what looked to be a young Jane and Peter, alongside which was the school chess photograph. In it, George Usher looked a lot younger than the man whom Greg had recently interviewed, he looked closely at the William Lynch in the photograph trying to compare it with the facial features he recalled for Peter Bashford, his only conclusion was that maybe teenage boys transform into different mature men. The log burner in the corner of the room was full of cold ashes, having been left since last night. The grey cinders were all that remained of what must have been a roaring fire while the

Bashfords ate their dinner, Jane unaware that she was sharing the last few minutes of her husband's life.

"I suppose you are thinking it strange that I have asked you to come over to see me at such a difficult time. Given that neither Peter or myself have exactly welcomed you into our house last night, with good reason, I should add."

"I must admit your invitation did surprise me."

"Well, now that my dear husband is dead, circumstances are very different and more difficult for me."

She sipped some water before continuing,

"I have two teenage children that I will need to take care of, so I trust you will respect me and answer my questions with an honesty that maybe your profession does not always reflect."

Greg felt that he was being spoken to by a stern school governess not a newly widowed woman, whose eyes were still swollen and red, having cried themselves out and now empty of tears. She fidgeted with a handkerchief, her hair loose and unbrushed, a face void of any make up, her skin pale and blotchy.

"So Mr Auden, why did you visit us in the first place?"

"I told you at the time, there was a man whose partner, for no apparent reason, flew over to Dinard, hired a car, which was found not two miles from here. No body, no message, not the slightest indication of why or where he had gone. I was asking questions of all the families I could, in case they might have seen or even knew of him."

"Then your second visit?"

Greg wondered how blunt he should be with Peter's widow. He recalled what he had said last night, so could not avoid that. She wanted honesty so he had better give it to her. At that moment Greg felt he had nothing to hide from her. It reminded him of the time his father had asked a difficult question of him; of when you have to make the choice of adding to the lie, strengthening the wrongdoing which might land you in trouble, or just admit everything in the hope your honesty will not hurt anyone. Last time he had added to the lie he had already told and that had not turned out well, so this time he spoke the truth.

"Well the first time I visited and I started to ask questions about your husband retiring, what he did back in England, those questions provoked a very strong unexpected reaction from you both; a most unexpected reaction that surprised me. Don't forget, I was looking for a missing man, your husband's reaction aroused doubt in me; were you both being honest with me? I had also noticed the photograph."

Greg pointed to the chess photograph which Jane also looked at with a wistful glance, seeing in the photograph the man she still loved even beyond death. Greg continued, "I researched the photo, found out which school it was, and also found out that a Peter Bashford was not in the photograph. Of the four boys, I could account for everyone but for William Lynch, who seems to have disappeared. Then add to that that Peter Bashford has never, according to official records, had a passport. I'm sure you can understand why I came back to clear up just why that photograph shares pride of place with your wedding photograph."

"I'll be honest, Mr Auden, I do not trust reporters. I have learned, through necessity over the last few years, to trust as few people as possible. The thing is, as I have mentioned, I have two teenage children whom I will need to provide for financially and now that my husband is dead, I am not sure what my future holds."

Jane leant forward to the small round side table that had been placed in front of her, where there was an empty cup and saucer, a half-filled glass of water, a box of tissues, a packet of aspirins, and also a white A5 envelope which clearly had been opened. Jane picked it up and clasped it tightly in both her slim hands before handing it to Greg. She looked across at the faded wedding photograph.

"I married William Lynch many years ago. Soon I will be burying Peter Bashford, the same man, just different circumstances. For as long as I have known William, he worked in research. Please don't ask me exactly what sort as he never told me the finer details and I never asked. The research was for Her Majesty's Government, so I guessed it was secret, or at least not for any public consumption. We had a good life. We had a house, a comfortable income, beautiful children, close friends, and even relations and in-laws. Very much a typical middle-class English couple. Often I wondered what I had done to deserve such a secure, enviable life, I could not imagine it ever changing. Then one day, it did change."

Jane paused, straightened her skirt in a nervous way. She appeared to be composing herself.

"William's car had broken down and the AA had arrived to fix it, so he was going to be late for work. No big problem, he did not have to clock in or out. Once the car was fixed but before he made his way to work, we heard on the news that there had been a serious fire in Sevenoaks. William worked in Sevenoaks so I asked him if it was near where he worked, as he had become very concerned with the news report. My husband nodded to confirm that it was his place of work that was on fire. The report was saying that all the personnel on the site had been killed. Well, it would not surprise anyone that William was becoming very upset, colleagues and friends killed tragically. What I thought was odd was that he made no telephone calls or any attempt to contact anyone from his management. Maybe he just thought they had all been killed and the shock had almost sent him into total silence, he just sat in front of the TV waiting for the news reports to update. Later that day a man called at our house and spoke to William on the doorstep, they chatted for a while, I had no idea who he was, I just assumed it was to do with work. Once the door had shut and the visitor had left, William came into the living room and said that we had to move. Of course it was a bit of a shock, but at first I was excited, thinking that he was being moved to another location, bigger house, bigger garden, space for a vegetable patch, a chance to change some furnishings. I now realise I did not fully comprehend at the time what his exact meaning was. William was not saying move like most people do, not being relocated to another facility, selling and buying another house. William was saying leave the house, our home, that very night, collect some items and just go. I said he was mad, and asked 'why did we need to?' how could we just walk out with our children, people cannot just leave a house, there are bills to be paid, you need to tell the council, the gas people. I told him, it was the shock of the fire and losing his colleagues. 'No,' he insisted, and was very resolute, I also saw the fear in his eyes, so we packed up there and then. 'We had to leave that night, find a hotel as a temporary measure before we are given something more permanent', he said.

I suppose when I took my wedding vows, this was the 'for worse' part coming up. He assured me that the house would be taken care of, there would not be gas and electric men chasing us for unpaid bills, there was someone who would tie up all the loose ends for us, we just had to go at once . Clearly it was to do with his work, and he did not wish to tell me more. I had to trust him, which I did; as a family we always trusted William to do the right thing. We spent three nights in a hotel; I must say it was a very nice hotel, in Waltham Abbey. The children thought it a great adventure, no school, all day playing in a hotel room or swimming in the indoor pool. Then a car collected us and we found ourselves in a furnished house in Dorset, or at least I think it was Dorset. We could not leave the premises or the grounds, on William's insistence. Food and supplies were delivered to us by the local shop and we stayed there for almost three weeks. Still I had no real idea why we were living under such circumstances, however many times I asked William, all he would say was that we were in danger and the Government were protecting us and would not let anything happen to us. He said the less I knew the better it would be for me and the children. I, of course, was not happy, but he was my husband, the man I loved and trusted and yes, I was happy for his work to be secret. I was very much involved, so I yearned to learn more, nevertheless he would not share with me exactly why we were in hiding.

His parents had died years before, and his only brother lived in New Zealand and they never spoke. My elderly mother was already in a nursing home and my two sisters, well, what was I going to say to them. As William would say, for the moment we had to avoid all contact. Well, we moved again, this time we stayed at, what was to be fair, a very pleasant country house, for a further two weeks before we once again began moving, this time to Portsmouth in a French registered car that had been delivered to the country house. It was only then that William explained to us that we were all going to live in France. He told us that he could never explain the true reason, just that the Government thought it best for us. I had a new name, Jane Bashford, and I should forget about ever being Jane Lynch."

She paused and sipped her water. Jane looked deep into Greg's eyes,

"I was, deep down, very upset and scared for me and the children. I am sure you can imagine, but I wanted to be the faithful wife and I trusted that William, whatever he was doing, was doing it for the best reasons and with the best interests of his family in mind. So my upset was buried within me. We arrived here, to find all our belongings, neatly boxed and stacked, as if we had ordered the removal people ourselves. So we began our new life. The children loved the open space, found it odd that no one spoke English at school. Children are so adaptable aren't they, they quickly got the hang of it, a lot quicker than I ever could. So here we have remained, for almost eight years, living a very easy life, of which I am sure many people would be envious. Each month a payment would appear in our bank account, more than William ever earned in the UK. We are fully in the French health system, we contribute to their tax system, our children enjoy the life here and I have lived, not really knowing what I am doing here or why I had to leave my two sisters behind; what must they think of me? Well I don't know what they think of me, I have not spoken to them in eight years. William said it was just too dangerous, again refusing to give me an explanation. Once a month he called a man in London, but if we were worried about anything, he could call him anytime. That all changed this week, when we invited you into our house, now I am not sure what I have, I know I no longer have a husband."

"So why did Peter, or William, have to go to Les Forges to call this man in London?"

"Secrecy, so that his call could not be traced I presume. You know Mr Auden, I decided it was best just to accept the situation instead of constantly badgering my husband to tell me what was happening, I trusted him, and so I got on with life.

That envelope I have given you, it contains the phone number of the man in London and some other numbers and letters. I don't want to call it, but I thought you might. The worst case, I suppose, is that you are from the side we were hiding from, if there is a side we are hiding from, maybe you will kill me, maybe not, I have no idea. All I want to do is to keep my children safe, maybe now that William is dead, the children and I are no longer in danger and we will be able to go back to the UK, I really do not know."

Greg opened the envelope, there was, as Jane had said, a telephone number, it was a London telephone number, and a string of letters and digits that meant nothing to Greg.

"Don't call from here, go elsewhere. I am, I guess, still in hiding."

"Was your husband killed last night or was it an accident?"

"The police seem to think it was an accident. He had been drinking and was driving too fast, he didn't stop at the crossroads and was hit by a bloody great lorry. I am assuming it was a tragic accident, so maybe I am still safe and hidden, that is, assuming you are being honest with me. Equally his death could have been constructed, he could have been murdered, I just don't know."

Greg refolded the paper and replaced it into the envelope.

"Your husband worked for R.G. Plastics, was that some sort of cover for a government department or facility?"

Jane slipped two aspirins into her mouth and washed them down with the remaining water in her glass.

"This might come as a bit of a shock to you Mr Auden, but I have no idea, all I knew was that my husband worked as some sort of scientist for the government in the Sevenoaks area of Kent. I know that the plastic factory, as highlighted on the news, was burnt down, I know little else. Of course when he first started, I did ask questions, lots of them but William never shared his work with me, he maintained that the work he was doing was top secret so could never discuss anything with me. Our dinner conversations about his work was a simple 'did you have a good day?' Yes or no, even if it was no, that was the end of the conversation. If you tell me he worked for R.G. Plastics, well then you possibly have better information than I ever had."

Greg was not sure if he was impressed by her composure or frankly disgusted that she was here discussing her husband in cold tones less than twenty-four hours after his death. He seriously wondered if she really was the type of woman who would ever take anything less than the full answer, yet her husband for many years, according to her was part enigma.

"Why do you want me to call this man in London? Doesn't it make sense for you to call him yourself and then I am sure he would make arrangements for you to continue to be safe and well provided for."

"I had thought about that, the issue I have with following that route is that I will once again be reliant on some sort of government department. I do not like being beholden to others, Mr Auden, we have some money behind us and I am seriously considering just moving out of here and starting a new life, not as affluent perhaps, but somewhere else in France or maybe back in England. I do not want to spend the rest of my life living off the state, and I am not talking about welfare handouts."

"Do you know anything about the explosion and fire at R.G. Plastics?"

"I told you before, Mr Auden, that I know nothing, just what is public knowledge. William said nothing, and I mean nothing, about his work."

"Yet he told you that should he die, you needed to open this envelope."

For a moment Jane hesitated, maybe a little too defensive.

"Please use your common sense, Mr Auden. I knew that we were hiding from something, my whole family was in danger, so between William and myself we made a plan should anything happen to him. That envelope you now hold is part of that plan. The remaining part is a sum of money that I have access to that will enable me to move out of here. It is not a lot, but it will keep the children and myself going for a while."

"I don't think you are being totally honest with me. There are things that you are not telling me."

"Mr Auden, I have no clear idea whatsoever exactly what my late husband did, or why we had to flee across the channel. So how can I know what is relevant or not? I haven't yet explained how to make a courgette and pumpkin fritter because I have no idea if that is relevant or not," she said sarcastically, "I have given you as much as I can guess at to be relevant, which I know from your viewpoint is not a lot."

As Greg left the morbid house, he turned to Jane before she closed the door behind him,

"I'll let you know what was said by the man in London."
Jane shrugged her shoulders,
"That's up to you. Good day, Mr Auden."

LA BELLE ETOILE.

Taking a deep breath, Greg turned on the engine of his small hired car and wondered why Jane Bashford-Lynch, or whatever she wanted to call herself, had decided that he should have the pleasure of calling a 'secret number' and speaking to someone unknown at the other end. He only assumed that that someone was a man, but maybe it was William Lynch's' lover and a woman would answer and that would be an interesting turn of events. In fact, more and more Greg started to feel he was finding interesting things about the village and its inhabitants, the mysterious English person that Helen was visiting, sounded just the sort of person that Greg should speak to in the search for two missing men. He understood that people might want to avoid too much company, why else would you want to move to an isolated French village? But to attract the interest of a Daily Mirror reporter, however green around the gills that reporter purports to be, there must be something of interest. So Greg went to the town information centre, also known as the baker's, bought a large pain au raisin and asked, in very broken French, about the lone Englishman and where he lived. Following excellent directions and a map drawn on the back of a paper bag, he was now pulling up outside the isolated house at Belle Etoile. There are very few secrets in village life that cannot be uncovered.

"Puis-je vous aider?"

Greg turned to see who was speaking to him, he locked the car out of habit not necessity. Walking towards Greg was a tall well-built man, dressed in blue slim jeans, a plain red polo shirt, with a discreet Ralph Lauren logo, both items too clean and well pressed to be working clothes. The man walked towards Greg wiping his hands with what appeared to be a torn piece of white sheeting.

"Are you Phillip?"

"An English voice, how refreshing, yes indeed you are speaking to Phillip and to whom am I talking?"

"Greg, Greg Auden," he offered his hand, and they shook hands. "Nice place you have here, I have a one-bedroom flat back in the UK, so I am envious of your house, land and the view that you have."

"You should never be jealous of what anyone else has or does not have, many material possessions only mask pain and hurt. What can I do for you?"

Greg stood looking across the wide vista that surrounded him, even for a dull winter's day with some broken clouds, the view was impressive. Fields and woodland dominated the view, with houses few and remote, far away their chimneys spiralling wood smoke up into the sky.

"Back in the UK I have some friends whose partners have taken a trip to France but have not been seen or heard of since. I'm here trying to help find them, so I wondered," Greg turned and faced Phillip, "if you had seen or heard anything recently? The first one left his car not too far from here. Did he perhaps knock on your door for help, to use your phone to get help or call the person he was going to see? The second man dropped off his hire car in Loudéac and was then picked up by someone unknown. After that the trail goes cold."

"Maybe they have eloped together, gay men and their lovers have the strangest of habits."

Greg pulled his jacket closed against the cool wind that was increasing its strength.

"Did I mention they were gay?"

"No Greg, but you said his car broke down and then the second one dropped off his hire car, add to that that you began this conversation by saying you were looking for friends' partners, I just assumed that the most obvious reason for these two would be eloping. I only assumed they were gay; I guess I am right. However, returning to your question, no strangers, or at least male strangers, have called here for months and months. How long ago did they elope?"

"Recently disappeared, not eloped, well not as far as I know. No gossip from the village that you have heard, seen odd lights at night, any cars driving past."

"Greg, I am not sure of your background, but I think you are getting a little too over the top. I live here far from the madding crowd and well away from the village that I have very little contact with. I like it that way, I'm a loner, a social loner because I like it that way."

Greg had now decided he disliked Phillip. He was a 'prick', that was going to be Greg's description of Phillip if anyone asked, a 'conceited prick' who looked down his nose at everyone and thought himself better than the world.

"Although I heard you have had a female visitor here recently so you can't be that much of a loner."

Phillip smiled, now having finished wiping his hands on the rag held loosely in one hand, it fluttered in the still increasing wind.

"I never said there had not been female strangers here. Well, to be honest, we have got to know each other well, and I just assumed that a woman visitor to my humble abode would not be of interest to you." Phillip's smile was now very much of the smug variety. "Helen did mention you. We are working on a story together, an interesting piece, which of course as you are also a journalist, I am sure you will appreciate, I don't want to discuss with you. Have you asked, well you must have asked Helen about the gay men you are looking for. I'm sorry I cannot be of help to you Greg; I do honestly wish you luck and hope you find your gay men. I must now continue with my chores, running a small holding like this on one's own does not leave much time to be sociable. Goodbye."

Phillip did not wait for any further response from Greg, he simply turned his back and walked away leaving Greg alone in the gusty wind.

"Phillip, before moving to France, what part of the UK did you come from?"

The wind now howled between the two men, far away the wood smoke left chimneys at a severe angle. Phillip stopped and turned back to his uninvited guest.

"Kent."

"That's a big county, which part?"

"I moved around a lot; I could not settle down anywhere. With hindsight, I suspect I was longing to be alone in the countryside, something which is very hard to do in even such a green county as Kent, the 'Garden of England' they call it," Phillip stopped, almost daring Greg to press him further, which he did.

"So where were you living when you left England for the open spaces of Brittany?"

"A small, slightly seedy, I am ashamed to say, one bedroom flat in a converted house on East Hill, Dartford. I am sure you can imagine this is far and away a better environment, now I must be going. Goodbye Greg and once again, good luck searching for your gay men."

This time Greg turned away and took four short steps back to his car, unlocked the door and sat inside away from the chilling wind, the sun had now retreated behind the ever-increasing cloud cover. Phillip was, no doubt, a very interesting character and Greg wanted to know a little more about him. Maybe he would need to hold out a sort of peace offering to Helen, take her to dinner and see what she might say after a couple of glasses of wine, as Greg felt sure it was not the first time he had seen those penetrating eyes of Phillip's.

*

As hotel rooms go, the room that Greg had been assigned on his second visit to the Hotel Chateau was a lot more spacious than his previous one. Not only did it have a wooden framed double bed with a very loud floral duvet cover, it also contained a desk and chair close to the window that over looked the Nante-Brest canal, the view dominated by the Chateau that made Josselin so famous. So now in the late afternoon winter sun, Greg once again withdrew the folded A4 sheet from the envelope that Jane had given him and looked at the mixture of numbers and letters that were below an obvious London telephone number: '020 7248 7171', followed by a woman's name: '*Theresa Quinn*'. The letters and numbers: '*e4 e5 Nf3 Nc6 Bb5 552649 172601*' meant nothing to him. The third and fourth lines seemed to Greg to be more random, yet for William they must have held some meaning for someone, maybe calling the number might help explain everything. Holding his mobile phone, he wondered just who he would be calling, taking a deep breath he pressed the green connect button on his touch screen, a few mechanical clicks later the ringing tone sounded out in his ear.

MILLBANK, LONDON.

The lighting in his office was not the best, having been designed for an Edwardian Company Director; at the time electric light had been a new invention and florescent lighting many years away. So even in modern times with the installation of energy efficient LED lighting, Christopher's Office looked dull, and even more so at three o'clock on a grey winters afternoon in London with low cloud and fine, annoying drizzle. Most of the traffic passing his office, five floors down, had headlights on. He typed away at his computer keyboard, giving suggestions of ways that the Home Office should reply to some testing questions, that had been asked by a Member of Parliament, of the Under Secretary, questions which by their nature and phrasing would not have originated in the mind of this particular MP, whose sharp, razor like mind had been well and truly blunted in childhood.

The telephone beside him interrupted him, it was his personal telephone, only close friends and certain business associates had access to.

"Hello," Christopher answered, leaning back into his chair away from the desk.

"Who am I speaking to?" Greg asked.

"If you are asking that question, I would presume it is highly likely that you have the incorrect number."

"I was asked to call this number by a Mr Bashford. Is a Theresa Quinn there?"

Christopher sat up, leaned forward and minimised the word document he had been writing, returned to the screen desktop and double clicked on a small icon marked: 'Pinpoint'.

"Mr Bashford, you say, why did he ask you to call this number?"

"Well, it was not exactly him, it was his widow."

Christopher tensed slightly; 'widow' implied that she no longer had a living husband.

"His widow, you say, so how are you related to Mr. or Mrs. Bashford?"

"I would feel more comfortable knowing who I am talking to."

"Christopher, and you are?"

"Greg, a friend of the family. Following Mr. Bashford's tragic accident I was asked by his distraught wife to call you."

Christopher smiled, so this is the investigating reporter who is calling, how considerate.

"Well Greg, thank you but I do think there has been some misunderstanding; the name Bashford has no connection with this telephone number or office as far as I am aware. I honestly think there might have been some sort of mistake here. Did he say, or did his wife say why you should call this number?"

"Maybe the name William Lynch will help you?"

"No, sorry. "

"R.G. Plastics, he worked for them at one time."

"Not a company I have heard of. I think we are going around in circles here, you must have the wrong number. Or maybe, can I suggest, that we are a new company and that British telecom have assigned a number that once belonged to the company Mr Bashford worked for."

"In that case Christopher, I am sorry to have troubled you, as you will clearly have no interest in what is written below the telephone number that I have just dialled."

Christopher thought that William Lynch would not have been so stupid as to just write out all the information on a scrap of paper and then add Christopher's personal number to that paper. However, Christopher could not discount that William might have made some sort of arrangement in the case of his death. If he was dead, until Christopher had heard it from a trusted source, he would not assume anything. Christopher was desperate to find out, the moment he could end this conversation, he would be on the telephone to Mick Hayes, his so called 'eyes and ears' in France, to ask why it was down to some humble reporter to tell him, if it was true, about William Lynch's death.

"Well, it might give some clue as to why you were asked to call this number. What is written below the number? Is it a reference number or something like that?"

"Maybe if you told me the nature of your business, it might then all become clear."

"I doubt you would understand, Greg, derivatives and other very obtuse financial dealings."

"Maybe I do have the wrong number, sorry to have troubled you."

At that, the telephone went dead. Christopher looked at the pinpoint window that had opened up, there were about twenty different telephone numbers representing all those desk phones that were assigned to his office. He double clicked on 020 7248 7171, the one that was beside him, the last call it showed was from a mobile, an English mobile, with its full number and location simply showing as being from the European Union. The English government were still to agree a protocol for tracing telephone calls across the EU. Although on this occasion, the failure in information technology was more than compensated for by Christopher's knowledge of where Greg Auden was.

"Mr Hayes?" Christopher asked by way of introducing himself, the field agent sounded a little hung over and tired.

"Sir."

"I have just been reliably informed, by the person that you are meant to be keeping an eye on, that Peter Bashford, the person we are meant to be looking after, has just died. Find out why, when, who, where and call me back in four hours. There is also a piece of paper in the hands of that reporter, with my telephone number on it. I want that paper or, at the very least, whatever is written on it. I trust you will not be distracted from these simple tasks by anything or anyone, however attractive they might be?"

Mick Hayes pulled himself up from the bed, disturbing the young woman lying next to him, dressed himself and then left. She wasn't bothered about his departure, simply turned over and snuggled down under the warm duvet; she always made sure her clients paid up front.

*

Reece Campbell listened to the voice at the other end of the telephone, calling him from a small village in France, with the latest news of what had been an eventful twenty-four hours. The visit by Greg to the Avis Car Hire in Loudéac, then to a house in the village of La Ville du Bois that he never went inside, but appeared to talk in a very animated style, possibly there had been a disagreement. After which the man from the house got into his car, which was followed until it met with a tragic accident just on the other side of the large forest that bordered La Ville du Bois. At that point, the field agent returned to the hotel, Greg was already back there safe and sound. This morning, news from the bakery was that Peter Bashford, an Englishman, was killed last night when his car hit a very big lorry; first reports seemed to blame the accident on drink. It was generally agreed between the two that the Peter Bashford killed last night was the same one that had been searched out through the passport office. Reece gave Jason some more instructions for the next twenty-four hours and informed him that if there were any unexpected developments he should call in at once. Things were very delicate and needed to be handled correctly.

JOSSELIN.

"So why have you invited me out to dinner?" Helen asked as the waiter handed them menus.

They sat, opposite each other, in the grand, ornate medieval-styled dining room of the hotel Château. A high oak beamed ceiling, with replica jousting shields and swords hung on the walls of the imposing dining room, at least fifty feet long and some twenty feet wide. To the left, as you entered the room, on the far wall were tall windows, allowing an uninterrupted view of the flood-lit Château. To the right, just past the chill cabinets crammed with luxurious desserts and fruits, was a majestic medieval looking fireplace, which tonight had a roaring fire, consuming logs with the same gusto as the customers showed when falling upon and devouring the food courses that were laid before them.

Greg poured a glass of water that Helen lifted from the table and drank from. It had been a simple yet firm invitation from him. He wanted to see her to talk about what was developing in the village following the death of Peter Bashford. He needed to share some of what had happened with her as he wanted, and was possibly going to need, her help. She thought Greg's invitation was a little unexpected, however, as Helen was unsure of what might come from it, she had accepted it anyway. After having dinner with a multiple murderer, Greg seemed to offer no threat. Plus, he might have some story that she could use to placate her irksome news editor.

As Greg sipped his water he watched with a degree of amusement, which he hoped he had concealed from Helen, as she withdrew a small bottle of hand gel from her hand bag and proceeded to sanitise her hands, rubbing the Aloe Vera gel in between her fingers.

"I invited you for two distinct reasons, first, social and secondly, someone to help me make sense of what is happening here in La Ville du Bois."

"I like to ensure all those street germs get nowhere near my food," she explained, ignoring his answer to her question, having seen the odd look that he was giving her.

Greg just nodded; he was very much of the opinion that odd habits are only odd to other people. If she wanted to wash her hands every few minutes that was entirely up to her, it caused him no concern at first, only as the meal went on and she regularly gelled and cleaned her hands had Greg moved it from the category of odd behaviour into bordering on the weird.

The meal began with a simple green-salad plate. Greg commenced his story, by telling Helen about the odd way that Jane Bashford, who the night before would have been happy to see him thrown out of her house into the silage, following the death of her husband had treated him like a long-lost confidant.

"She didn't even know where he worked until the place blew up and was plastered all over the news. She never asked any questions of him, just followed him to France like a faithful dog, all she has is this piece of paper."

Greg handed it across to Helen, who looked at it with a puzzled look on her face.

"I called the obvious telephone number, there was a man called Christopher who answered. Unsurprisingly, he gave nothing away, denied any knowledge of Peter or the Theresa mentioned on the paper. That is all that seems to be happening here, nothing. There are small teasing tidbits, odd actions, strange coincidences, nothing that gives me the slightest idea what is actually going on."

She handed the paper back to him and filled first his wine glass and then her own, before cleaning her hands once more.

"Well I have no idea about your experiences of reporting, for me I know, in my experience, the story is never clear at first. We get sent out to an incident or hear a piece of gossip or a request and we talk to people, talk to some more, maybe do a bit of research and then the story starts to become clear." She leaned forward as she finished her entrée, "So let's review the facts so far, we have two missing men, ignore for a moment they are gay, as that could be sending us off down the wrong path. Let's assume they are unconnected and have not just eloped."

Greg wiped his plate with his bread.

"That is a big assumption to make, they were both gay, both had connections to the same night club in Gravesend, which in itself prompts me to think their disappearances are connected in some way."

"No, it's practical not to look at the obvious as we have two dead ends with them, so put them to one side and it should make things clearer. Now that just leaves Peter Bashford, who we now know a lot more about. From what his wife has told us, Peter Bashford was William Lynch, a scientist who worked for the Government on something so secret, that even his wife did not know about it. Then they get sent over here, not working, just sent over here, clearly according to the wife, still on the Government payroll, let's not forget, our taxes have been keeping him in this very comfortable lifestyle. So why would the government send him over here? Following, what we understand from some old school friends and his wife, was an explosion at the place we think, or maybe should assume, he worked. Someone is hiding him. They appear to be all facts to me which we can build on."

"Why hide him?"

"Well that's to be found out. I'm sure it's safe to say, that the call he had to make every month was more of a check-in call. Then if they were worried about something, they could call anytime, hence Peter calling when you first arrived; again some facts that we can work with. Those numbers must be some sort of clue, to what, don't even think of asking me but I will tell you one thing, the answer will not be here in France, I am sure it will be back in England, maybe go back to his school friends, we know his name in England, William Lynch, and well, I'm sure we can do some poking around, find the sisters or other friends and family and see what they know."

"Makes sense, look at it from a cryptic puzzle point of view, sensible. But where do those two missing men come into the equation, how do they fit into the puzzle? They must have a connection to the village, that seems to me to be logical, even though Jane Bashford denies knowing them."

Helen gelled her hands before starting on her main course, poached salmon in a sorrel sauce. "The car of the first guy, Martin, it was found near the village, I'll give you that. Although the second man seems to have been collected from Loudeac, a twenty-minute drive from here. What's to say his final destination is not miles from here? Martin could also have been picked up and taken anywhere around here, we have no idea. That's why it seems to you that you have hit a dead end, because you have. You should also consider that the Bashford Family are more than a little enigmatic as well, there could well be a connection between the Bashfords and the two men, you just have to find that connection."

Greg picked at his food as Helen continued to add to her ideas: 'first speak to his remaining school friends back in England', 'maybe make contact with some of William's friends', 'those who might have been neighbours and might be able to shed some light on the person behind the mask." Greg half-listened to Helen, wondering if he should mention his visit to Phillip and the fact that Phillip had lived not a million miles from the Angel Wings Club in Gravesend, for Greg, that was a strong connection.

"So," Helen began probing Greg's personal life as they ate the lemon tarts they had both ordered for dessert, "you are no longer employed at all, just a freelance, that must have been so hard. How long were you at the Deptford Chronicle?"

"Fifteen years in all, started there and never got around to going anywhere else, maybe I just got a little too comfortable, maybe my ambition was not as driving as I first thought it might have been. So when the time came, the 'Steady Eddie' of Greg the reporter, was to be the first sacrifice on the altar of economics."

"Had you always wanted to be a reporter, I know I did."

Greg thought a moment before answering, "I guess I never really knew what I wanted to do, my late teens were a difficult time. There were only a few years between being a hormonal teenager and an orphan. First, my sister died, she took her own life, that set off a chain reaction which destroyed my parents' relationship and broke their hearts. They died within a few years of my sister. I was just twenty when I found myself alone. I suppose I joined the newspaper for no better reason than to spy on other peoples' mishaps and heart break, to maybe find mine were not as bad as I had imagined, there is always someone worse off than you, that sort of thing."

"Maybe that is the voyeur in all reporters. And did you find anything worse?"

"No, people still have bad things that happen to them, but nothing seemed to be as cutting as what had happened to me. I still could not find any solace in reporting all the bad things that happen, murder, deaths, poverty, violence, nothing eroded the hurt that I still felt. It was only when I was sent to report on a suicide, that I sensed a sort of understanding, an empathy which was not surprising. I began to find a purpose in looking for the real root of why a person takes their own life, and that helped me. I was looking for the root cause of the suicide, the underlying reasons. Ultimately that was to lead to the demise of my journalistic career at the Deptford Chronicle." Greg stopped for a pause, surprised at himself for being so open with a person he had only met a day or so ago.

"It must have been a terrible shock, your sister's suicide, had she suffered from depression previously? Had she mentioned suicide before?"

"Us reporters can never switch off can we?" Greg gave a sardonic smile, "There were no clues, no history of depression or any sort of indication that she was planning to take her own life. Maybe we were all too wrapped up in our own lives to realise that someone so close was unravelling and falling apart from the inside. Maybe it's proof that we often do not really know those so close to us."

"Was there ever a reason?"

Greg was silent as thoughts passed through his mind. Helen looked at him and saw that his eyes saw nothing around him but appeared to be lost in those memories that haunted and tormented him.

"Nothing," Greg replied.

Even though she hardly knew Greg, she was a good reporter, she was able to read between the lines of speech, helping her to dig down and find the real story. She naturally understood body language, those tiny movements of eye lids and eyes that shied away from investigative gaze. Helen was good at reading people and telling when they were being honest and when they were not. Helen knew that Greg had lied to her, she also believed that he knew why his sister took her own life, he just was not ready or willing to share that knowledge with her.

"That must be the worst part, not knowing why she took her life. I bet you have tried to guess at some reasons, what would they have been?"

"I cannot imagine what the reason might have been."

"Didn't the coroner make any comments?"

"She was dead Helen, there is no point in trying to find the reason, the result could not be changed. Let's change the subject shall we?"

"If she had shown no suicidal tendencies before, there must have been something really traumatic for her to take her own life, and not to tell people why, that must be cruel."

"Not as cruel as the way you are being to me, talking about it."

"I'm sorry Greg, it's just, well I sensed you know, or think you might know, why she took her life. Maybe sharing those thoughts might help."

Greg pushed his dessert plate to one side, leaned forward on his elbows until his face was just a few inches from Helen's. A casual observer of the couple might have thought he was about to kiss her.

"Helen, you might be a good reporter, but let me tell you one thing, you are a shit psychologist. Let's change the subject, how about newsprint in a digital age?"

Reluctantly Helen changed the subject of their conversation and talked about the economics of newspapers in an ever-changing world. Then as coffee was served to their table Helen, as she replaced her hand gel into her handbag, changed the subject once more.

"I do hope your visit to Phillip earlier today was purely asking about missing men and nothing to do with trying to find out what my story is?"

"Well," Greg smiled, "to be honest maybe part of me hoped I would stumble across your story, but he was not giving much away. A real weird one that Phillip, odd way of speaking and phrasing things, plus, he used to live not a million miles from the night club connecting a number of men who have died or disappeared. Oh, he also knew the club, had been there a few times. So maybe there is a connection here in La Ville du Bois," he tried to sound sarcastic, it sounded more like a threat to Helen.

"I am sure if you took a five-mile radius around the club, then there would be a few potential suspects."

"Maybe, I had that same thought, then I thought about it a bit more and it occurred to me that two of those men from that club, have now disappeared not five miles again from where Phillip lives. That's odd, but what it means I have no idea yet, do you?"

Helen looked into her coffee, avoiding any eye contact with Greg, she had no idea where the conversation might lead, so she changed the direction.

"There is no story that I am building at Phillip's, it is purely two people who like each other's company, I do not work twenty-four hours a day I have a life outside of writing news stories."

"Well, I can see why you might like each other, you both seem to have a lot in common." Greg wanted to say that you both seem a little weird but was too polite to mention that.

"So is there a connection with Phillip and two missing men from Gravesend, or are you too close to the situation to give an honest answer?"

"He has odd habits, maybe to an outsider a bit of a weird loner. Let me assure you once you get to know the real Phillip, he is a wonderful man. He is not a murderer." Helen defended Phillip.

"I never mentioned murder, but it is an interesting thought."

They parted in the hotel reception, watched by the hotel manager sitting behind his small desk, surrounded by tourist leaflets and reading a newspaper. Following an awkward formal farewell handshake, Greg went up the wide carpeted staircase to his room. Helen left via the glass doors at the hotel entrance. She had half hoped that he might invite her up to his room for a night cap. She only wanted the invite so that she could then snub him, vindictive yet satisfying. Why she felt the need to refuse him she wasn't sure, maybe she just wanted to hurt his feelings, show herself to be superior. Whatever the reason, the lack of an invitation was just as much a snub to her as she felt her refusal would have been to him.

As Helen walked across the road to the car park, she began to worry that Greg was beginning to show an interest in the activities of Phillip. She was sure that she had not helped to quell his interest by mentioning murder but had only succeeded to fan the fires of suspicion that were, no doubt, building in Greg's mind. Helen wondered what her father might advise, he had always been one to give good advice. She might need to stay close to Greg to know what he was thinking and doing. She could not afford to allow Phillip's activities to come to light, now she was his accomplice.

Helen walked through the cold, damp night air, pulling her coat closer around her body, holding in the warmth from the restaurant. A slight mist was starting to build beside the still waters of the canal. The hotel car park was almost full of cars, yet, like the small narrow streets around her, devoid of any people. In the dim light she unlocked the car door.

Sitting beside her father when she was younger reminded her of those warm summer evenings, helping with a crossword in the evening paper, he, encouraging her with additional clues to the words. They were the times that helped her develop her love of words. He had tried to talk her through the chess puzzles in the paper, without much success; the game of chess seemed outdated and a little pointless.

Her mind suddenly jumped back to the present as the thought suddenly came to her. The first row of numbers and letters, she had seen something similar, not the same, but she now realised what the notation was.

e4 e5 Nf3 Nc6 Bb5

e4, a pawn to e4, then a pawn to e5, knight to f3, knight to c6, chess notations, it was a set of chess moves, bishop to square b5. Her father talking her through the chess puzzle in the Evening News all those years ago, trying to teach her the chess move notations. She locked the car door, she needed to tell Greg at once. It would be a good distraction if he was lying awake thinking about how Phillip was linked to the two missing men. The intriguing Bashford family was the best diversion she could offer Greg.

*

She turned and hurried her steps back to the hotel. The receptionist, still casually reading his newspaper, glanced up at her. With a knowing smile when she asked, he freely gave her Greg's room number, 213 on the second floor. She walked briskly up the two flights of stairs, with memories of her father encouraging her to understand chess, she always did and still did prefer crosswords. Moving along the slightly dusty corridor looking at the numbers, 213 was going to be on the left four doors along. Yes, Helen recalled, her mother always hated the way her daughters clung to her husband whenever he was home. Helen was surprised that her mother could not see that it was his scarcity that made her and her sister overdose themselves on their father when he was there.

Chambre 210, chambre 211. Before she could see the number on the door, Helen realised that the dark polished wood door of chambre 213 was slightly open. As she approached the door she heard muffled noises coming from the room, she quickened her pace, sensing something was wrong. Standing in the doorway, she saw two men rolling around the floor struggling with each other. The bigger man was astride Greg and pinning him to the floor; his gloved hands clasped around Greg's throat attempting and succeeding to shut off his air supply. Greg was having no success with his efforts to pull the stronger hands away from his throat. He could make no more of a sound than a low, choking noise as he fought for his breath and his life. His bulging eyes saw Helen standing at the doorway and pleaded with her to help, do anything to swing the fight in his favour.

Helen stood transfixed, unable to move. All she could see was her mother, sprawled at the bottom of the stairs looking up at her daughter pleading for help. Her mother's pleading voice echoed in Helen's mind.

*

"Please darling, help me, I've hurt my leg, I think I may have broken it, please help."

Helen, then a teenage girl, had always believed that her mother's drinking and arguing nature was the root cause of her father's absence during weekdays. There was someone else that Helen also laid the blame on, a suppressed suspicion of a person that she did not know.

"Was he here?" There was venom in the way she pronounced 'he'.

"Darling, please help me first, we can talk later. I think I may need an ambulance."

Helen ignored her mother's request.

"Was he here, your fancy man?"

"Does it matter?"

"Yes it does matter. Why can't he help you, he's your favourite. Get him to help you. I can still smell his aftershave, so he has been here. Left early today, has he?"

Her mother started to drag herself with her broken leg towards the mahogany telephone bench, there the trimphone waited tantalisingly close.

"He had an important meeting, so had to leave, alright." she retorted, "Now use the phone, get me some help, please Helen."

Helen looked down at her mother, she felt for the first time in her childhood a sense of power over her. So often she had been scared of her mother, now the tables were turned, Helen had the upper hand, Helen was dominant.

"What does he have that father does not? What makes your lover so special?"

It was the first time Helen had ever used the word 'lover' to describe the man that often appeared at their house to spend time with Mother alone in her room.

"Honesty," her mother's voice was now elevated above her pain, "is that what you want Helen, honesty? If that's what you want then here we go. Your father is never here because he is, no doubt, shagging some young tart in the City. Picking off the secretaries one by one. Power and money does that to men. They go off and screw around because they can afford to, and those young 'made-up bimbos' are happy to spread their legs for a man who can splash money all over them. So I languish here alone and unloved. Now tell me, why shouldn't I find a man who loves and cares for me? Don't judge me Helen, in life you have to make harsh choices sometimes to ensure you hold onto your happiness. Now get me some help."

"You're lying, Father would never be unfaithful to you."

"Oh, you are so young, naïve and stupid. One day you'll learn, your father is not the perfect parent you think he is. He is a tough, callous businessman who makes lots of money. Money that buys him a hedonistic life in the City. I know more about your father than you could ever imagine, all bad things. Call him now, see if he answers his phone, I doubt he will, this afternoon he will be drinking Laurent-Perrier champagne while screwing two prostitutes. If nothing else your father is a creature of habit."

"Don't lie to me, you're making all this up."

"Call him, see if I'm right. I know I am right; do you want me to tell you the hotel he is at?"

"You're lying, like you always do," Helen's voice was now close to hysterical. Her body tense and enraged, a wrath like she had never felt. Yet for all the anger, all the pain she was feeling, she was still able to think with a cold logic, planning what she should do.

The large wooden round newel cap had always been loose, often it fell off or came away in your hand as you walked downstairs holding onto the banister. Helen looked at it, considered a course of action and acted without any hesitation. Stepping over her mother, she stood on the first stair, pulled the oak newel cap from its location and stepped back towards her mother and knelt down beside her.

"I will help you just this once Mother."

"Thank you darling."

"I will help you die, you foul mouthed bitch." Helen brought the heavy wooden cap down on her mother's head in one swift, sweeping motion, cracking her skull open, blood started to stream from the wound. Although Helen was enraged with her mother, the teenager had a logical side that gave out calm mature instructions, 'just hit Mother once, then replace the cap from where it came making it appear as if she had fallen down the stairs, hit her head on the knob, before bouncing further down the stairs and landing on the floor with a broken leg and a cracked and bleeding skull'. Helen obeyed her analytical mind, then unplugged the trimphone, and carried it out to the garden, leaving her mother to die alone.

*

To Greg, Helen seemed to stand looking over him and his assailant for minutes, but it was really just for a second or two, while he fought to draw any sort of air into his lungs. He tried to cry out with his eyes for her to help him.

There was a part of Helen that suggested taking no action, Greg would die, with him would die the notion that there was a connection between two missing men and Phillip. But there was another part of her mind that reasoned that with Greg dead, the assailant, who seemed to have the upper hand, would turn his attention to her. She would then need to escape and whatever happened, the whole affair would end up in the hands of the police. She would not be able to avoid being questioned, as one of the last people to see Greg alive. She had had dinner with him and been seen going up to his room, after having said goodnight to him. Her presence here was leaving forensic traces that would be found. On balance, Greg living, for now, was the better, safer option.

Helen looked around the room hoping to see a suitable weapon to distract the assailant. There was a grey-green telephone sitting on a small table close to the door. She pulled the cable out from the phone socket close to the cream skirting board and gathered the thin wire, ignoring the telephone dangling uselessly at one end. In one brief slick action Helen looped the thin strong cord around the assailant's neck, then pulled with all her strength. In an instant the large man, surprised, let go of Greg, who gave out a loud gasp as air flooded back into his lungs. The assailant, his fingers desperately trying to squeeze between his neck and the ever-increasing tightness of the thin telephone cable, tried lifting his body up in an attempt to throw Helen off him, her knee firmly lodged in the small of his back served to increase the pressure on his neck as he tried to lift. He laboured to turn around; he tried to wriggle his body free from her grip. The strength of her position over him and his ever-decreasing oxygen intake all conspired against him.

Greg had no choice with the weight of two people above him, but to lie on the floor and watch a man fight for his life in front of him. Spittle hitting his face as the choking man shook and struggled.

"It's OK, Helen," Greg still snatched breaths between the words, "we've got him. Relax. Let go a bit."

She could not or would not hear what Greg was saying. To her, there was only her and a man who she was killing. She was enjoying doing so and she had no intention of stopping until the man with the cord around his neck went limp and lifeless. Only then would she even start to consider letting go.

"Helen, he's out for the fucking count, let him go!" Greg was tempted to try and pry her hands away but fear of the man reviving prevented him. Helen had a look of a determined woman, who was not going to change her mind. Still in total silence and with eyes that concentrated on holding that noose tight, she was in a world of her own.

"For Christ's sake Helen let go of him, you're going to kill him."

That was her goal and blocking out Greg's pleading voice, she held the noose until the hands tugging at the wire stopped tugging, flopping forward, his head no longer straining against the pressure. The back once so strong and now so arched, deflated. Only then did Helen let go and stand up looking triumphant as she stepped away from the body, the telephone wire still tight around the deceased's neck. Greg pushed the body off him and rolled away from the slaughter.

"Fucking hell Helen, you killed him, you fucking killed him!"

Helen walked back to the door and closed it. She turned and looked at Greg.

"Calm down and lower your voice. It might have escaped your notice Greg," Helen spoke with a very cold detached voice, "that he was trying to kill you, so what would you have rather me do, just let him get on with garrotting you or just leave you to it? Maybe you had it all under control and I simply misunderstood the whole situation."

"Helen, you killed him, he is dead."

"Yes, I killed him, he is dead, lifeless. A bit like he was trying to do to you. It was the only way to ensure both of us would see tomorrow's earthly sunrise."

Greg stood, snatched his mobile from his pocket.

"Shit, the screen has broken, and it's only three months old. Result! It appears to be working fine, what's the French equivalent of 999?"

Helen assertively walked over to Greg and pulled the phone from his hand, looking at him with an intense commanding stare, she spoke calmly to him.

"Greg let's just take stock of what we have here for a moment before you go calling in the French police. First, explain exactly why you were rolling around on the floor with a man trying to throttle you?"

Greg slumped onto the bed like a child who was being reprimanded by a parent.

"I left you downstairs and came up here to my room, unlocked the door, walked in and that guy," pointing to the lifeless body on the floor, "had my suitcase open and going through my stuff. He turns and looks at me, I recognise him as the insurance man who is looking for Martin. So I am standing there thinking, why is he back and going through my stuff? He then throws himself at me dragging me into the room and we start to tussle on the floor. After a moment or two he is on top of me, hands round my throat strangling me, I'm just glad you walked in when you did."

Helen sat on the bed beside Greg,

"The same insurance investigator; the one who said he was looking for Martin?" Greg nodded yes in answer to her question. "Well, not many insurance companies hire killers to do their investigating."

Helen walked across to the body and knelt down beside her victim. With her back to Greg, she allowed herself a very small smile of satisfaction. She started to search through his pockets as she spoke to Greg, placing each object she found on the floor beside her.

"So let's think just why he was looking through your stuff before wanting to kill you. The fact that you recognised him would seem to suggest he took a split-second decision to kill you, not the reaction you would expect from an innocent insurance agent, even if he was turning over your room. I seem to recall us discussing a research scientist that worked for the government, whose contact you called today to mention that he was dead. I think you may have stirred someone into action. So calling the French police at this moment in time might not be the best course of action. Here we go," she opened the passport that was tucked in the back pocket of the man, "Mick Hayes, well at least he has a name."

She handed the passport to Greg who looked at the photograph.

"That's the name he gave me, he told me that Martin had run off because he was being chased after for an insurance fraud. So why would he be going through my stuff?"

"I would doubt that Mick Hayes is his real name."

Helen opened the mobile phone that was in the front pocket of the deceased's jeans along with a hotel key and a hire car key fob. She looked through the call history and then handed it over to show Greg.

"Recognise that number?" Greg looked at the number.

"The London one I called this morning?"

Helen nodded and slipped the phone back into Mick Hayes's pocket.

"So there is no doubt now, you call the guy in London and then hours later you get a visit from Mick Hayes, who is happy to go through your room and once you recognise him, feels he needs to kill you. I think we are getting into something very dark and clearly dangerous. It would be good for us to make ourselves scarce, get back to the UK to see what we can find out about that dead scientist and if this man has any sort of background. But first we need to get rid of his body."

"Get rid of his body! Shouldn't we call the police?"

"We do that, and I suspect before long you and I will be in police custody. I did just kill him, and I do not plan to stand trial for saving your life. Until we know exactly what is happening, we need our freedom."

"Well, we can't just slip him into our suitcase, take him outside and tip him into the canal. Or can we?"

"I know a better way; let's get him to my car. First we'll need to get past reception. Lift him up and each of us put one of his arms round our neck and then we can drag him downstairs, making it look as though he is drunk beyond belief."

Between them, they struggled with the lifeless body down the flight of carpeted stairs into the reception area. They passed the guarded eyes of the owner, who looked at the trio, the petite woman; the out of breath Englishman and the drunken man, they were moving through and out of the hotel. At least, he thought, they were quiet and not disturbing other guests. He quickly left the sanctuary of his desk to open the door for them to effect an easier exit. He did not want a drunk Englishman in his hotel, it would not do his reputation any good at all.

"Merci," Helen said, "je suis desole, beaucoup de vin rouge."

The desk clerk smiled and nodded in agreement then watched as they walked across the road, damp with the night air, to the car park. Satisfied they were on their way, he closed the glass door before amusing himself as he watched the trio struggle to the small Renault Clio and roll the drunk man onto the back seats. The couple stood together talking, so he went back to his desk and his newspaper.

"So what are you going to do with him?" Greg asked, his breath condensing in the cold night air.

"Don't worry, I have a plan, and the less you know the better. Go back to your room, smile at that little Frenchman, and then we both need to go back to the UK."

Helen got into the driver's seat and started the Renault, eager to get the warmth from the engine into the car. Winding down the window she continued to talk to Greg, although he felt it was more like an instruction.

"My news editor is starting to have kittens, so I have to go back for a while. I'll call you when I get back to the UK and we can then meet up somewhere and make a plan. Actually, if you have someone in the UK, call them before you leave to tell them you are on your way home, and if you are not back by a certain time, ask them to call me and I'll do the same."

Greg looked at her with concern in his eyes,

"Are you expecting that one or both of us might not make it back to the UK?"

"Well, I am sure we will get back, it's just possible that we might have our names on some sort of list and might get stopped at passport control. Maybe not, I'm just saying, how many times do you get a murderous insurance agent in your hotel room? Tomorrow, we'll also be on the only flight going back."

"Do you want a lift?"

Helen thought for a moment.

"It's a hire car isn't it?" she did not wait for a reply, "drop me off at the terminal and then drop the car off, that way we can avoid any contact at the terminal and during the flight. I hope we both get on the plane without any difficult questions. If we are on any list, I am sure the UK government would want us under their jurisdiction and not have to go through an extradition process."

Helen then added as an afterthought, "Oh, by the way, the reason I was coming back to your room. That odd selection of letters and numbers, they are chess notations, I am sure. The rest is a mystery, but I'm sure once we are back on the other side of the channel, there will be people we can ask, and somehow we will figure it out."

Greg watched her drive into the night, past the illuminated medieval chateau before slipping into the darkness of the night in her little car with a body on the back seat. Greg wondered what she was going to do with the dead Mick Hayes and what on earth was going on around him.

LA BELLE ETOILE.

The book was one of Phillip's favourite books, a novel by eighteenth century French author, Emile Zola, who many critics described as a French version of Charles Dickens. Phillip thought him better and more in tune with the common people of Paris in the late eighteen hundreds. "L'Assommoir" was the story of a simple laundress, Gervaise, who had high hopes yet with an innocent kindness, that clouded her life decisions, to the point that she ended up dying alone and penniless, under the stairs of a shabby garret in the Paris slums. Phillip liked the moral of the story, that you could easily fall from grace and find yourself in the gutter, because a set of circumstances overtook you. He saw a lot of his own mother in Gervaise, kindness that led her down a pathway that she could not exit from. Gervaise had a daughter, Nana, who was the subject of another Zola book. The daughter was more pragmatic, just as Phillip was. Both of them escaping the quagmire of poverty to forge their own lives in their own way, a way their parents would not have agreed with. Phillip had read L'Assommoir four times, this was his fifth, he knew it was one of those novels that he could never tire of. Closing the book, he looked towards the log fire and thanked that he had the inner strength to decide his own destiny, find and follow his own special niche in life. Here alone in France, he felt satisfied and contented. His parents had divorced when he was fifteen. Living with his mother, they moved from the large family home, in which Phillip had been born, to a rented house first, then to a flat, a pleasant spacious flat with a garden in which he helped, aged ten, to plant strawberry plants with his mother. He never managed to taste those strawberries, as by the summer they had to move again, this time to a top floor flat, a simple council flat. Through all these moves, he recalled only seeing his father once or twice but each day he watched his mother drink until she could no longer care for her young son, who, by his late teens, was a consummate housekeeper, despising the woman that often laid in her own vomit. Yes, his mother was Gervaise and he was the Nana equivalent, using his skills to forge a life so much better than his mother could ever dream of.

His reminiscence was broken by the headlights that reflected across the room; a car was approaching. Phillip was going to have a late-night visitor, a rare almost non-existent occurrence at any time of the day. He looked out of the window, and watched the small dirty looking Renault Clio stop and Helen step out of the car. He waited until she had come to his door and knocked hard. He opened the door to a dishevelled and tense looking Helen. The full consequences of her earlier actions she now grasped during her drive to Phillip's. The relaxed confidence that had attracted him to her was gone, now hidden behind eyes that were lined with anxiety.

"I need your help."

Phillip felt like saying he could clearly see that she was in need of some sort of assistance, he however resisted,

"What on earth is the problem Helen?"

"You need to see what I have in the car," she gestured towards the isolated Clio, the small doorway light reflecting off the dull muddy metal panels of the car. He automatically followed her, in keeping with her request as she walked towards the car.

Expecting that she needed his help and expertise with a problem she had with the car, which he assumed she would have guessed might not be his strength, he nevertheless continued towards the car. Phillip could not see anyone inside the car, the car clearly worked, it had arrived at his door, he wondered what the problem might be. For a moment he tensed, not from the chilled night air, an uncomfortable thought came into his mind, a journalist she was first and foremost, was this a trap? Was his trust in her misguided? Had he taken her too far into his confidence and his own self-regulating world? Phillip gave a nervous glance around; he could not see anything or anyone else in the graduated darkness that surrounded his house. Maybe she had schemed and tricked her way into his world and now the trap had been set and was out there in the darkness. TV crews, press photographers laid in wait for him to appear and be confronted; be made to justify his version of reality. Helen opened the rear door of the car and with total relief in his mind, he saw the lifeless body. He relaxed, his distrust in her was totally unfounded, had he really doubted his skill and ability in reading people.

"Helen, my love, my successful apprentice, is he really your very first real kill? How exciting, I think I must feel like a proud parent who sees their child go from crawling to those first few steps and then walking. You must tell me all, his name, why you chose him, how you killed him, close the car door, he'll be safe there and let's go inside. I'll crack open one of my very best bottles of St Émilion to celebrate, my special intern coming of age."

Once inside Phillip listened attentively as Helen explained to him about her first murder and recalled the day's events. The death of Peter Bashford, now known to be William Lynch., the intriguing story his wife had given Greg and the sheet of paper with the odd notations on, the telephone number that Greg had called, then the intruder in the room and the death, which Phillip encouraged more detail of.

"Tell me Helen; relate how you felt as you were pulling tighter and tighter on that wire?"

Helen stood beside the ebbing flames of the fire, drinking her wine a little quicker than normal, shivering, not through being cold, of that she was sure, it was the first tremor of her actions that she was now coming to terms with. Although she was not disgusted or frightened, she was satisfied and thrilled she had crossed a line that only a few ever knowingly do.

"I suppose at first it was a natural defensive reaction when I saw what was happening, Greg was clearly in danger, so I had to get this person off him somehow, which was not going to happen by simply pulling him off, he looked too strong for me. I thought about grabbing an object, any heavy object and then just hitting him again and again with it, but nothing that I could see appeared to be suitable for the job, then I thought of the telephone wire."

"Small but so effective, continue please."

"Really at first, I only meant to use it around his neck to deter or just distract him from throttling Greg, he was bound to remove his hands from Greg's throat and pull at the wire that I had wrapped around his neck to stop him being strangled. I guess I hoped that at that point Greg would be able to fight back and together we could tackle him. Although once I had it around his neck and I twisted it tighter something within me encouraged me not to stop, go further, pull it tighter, squeeze that neck, then I could see I had full command of this person's life between my hands, he was going to die, or maybe not, the choice was mine. It was a powerful, intoxicating feeling, that I did not want to stop, even though I knew that by not stopping I was going to kill him. It just did not matter, I needed to maintain the intoxicating high that had enveloped me, dare I say, almost like the most incredible orgasm, one could imagine having."

"There you felt it, it's just indescribable, you just cannot find adequate words to explain the sensation to anyone, unless like ourselves they have been there. A toast, to Helen, your first homicide, congratulations!"

As they both imbibed from their wine glasses, a voice spoke up in Phillip's mind, advising him of what he might be getting into. A murder without planning, weighing up the risks, closing any doors that could connect you back to the victim. The body now lying outside in the back of the Renault Clio, was the result of a spur of the moment action, something that went against the grain of Phillip's essence.

"So who exactly is that young man outside, who was so intent on killing your friend Greg?"

"His name, as far as we are aware, is Mick Hayes, he might be some sort of civil servant as he seems to be taking instructions from the other side of the channel. This might give us some clue, it was what Mrs Bashford gave us, a puzzle of sorts I think," she offered Phillip the slip of paper.

Like a child given a new toy, Phillip adored puzzles, the more cryptic the better the challenge, the voice that had expressed concern was, for the moment, pushed to one side.

Phillip looked at the paper on which Helen had copied the information that Greg had given her, and offered her own explanation of the middle part, e4 e5 Nf3 Nc6 Bb5.

"I'm sure that they are chess moves, whatever they mean, I have not played chess since I was a teenager, with my father."

Phillip smiled,

"White pawn to e4, black pawn to e5, white knight to f3, black knight to c6 and white bishop to b5, the classic opening described as the Ruy Lopez opening, a common opening for players across the world, nothing too special in that. The name Theresa Quinn that is below the telephone number that Greg called they didn't say she was at that number?"

"The man at the other end said just about nothing of any use."

"Then two banks of six numbers, interesting, 552649 172601," Phillip considered them for a moment before he spoke again, "well I do like a puzzle, yet I can see no obvious relationship between the numbers, they could be a code of some sort, a combination for a safe. In isolation, they are just about meaningless, unless you had some inkling as to what they might represent. Yet, maybe, if we do not take them in isolation, thinking what they might be, not a phone number as I would have expected a bank of eleven numbers, so even bringing them together does not present any sort of basis for a telephone number. Ordnance survey, they use banks of six numbers to give an eastings and northings, but they would be missing. Got it!" he snapped, "An ordnance survey grid reference, not on their own, they are missing two letters, but take the initials of Theresa Quinn, TQ put that before the numbers," now he walked over towards his computer that was alert waiting to be used, as it was always, sitting in a discreet corner of his room, " that would give us a complete grid reference, TQ552649 172601, so if I am correct, it should give us a place in the UK."

Helen looked over his shoulder as he first Googled the reference and then clicked a link that took him to a map with a small marker on it.

"Well, it is a place, a piece of woodland in Kent."

"Not any woodland but look" she pointed towards a cluster of buildings north east of the woods, "Wilmington School, which was where William Lynch went to school."

"Well, in that case I would say we have solved the clue, yet what is in the wood, or why the deceased William Lynch placed that grid reference on that piece of paper will no doubt be a mystery until you go and visit the woods. But first we should go and remove the body from your car, before full rigor mortis sets in, the last thing we want is a stiff body trapped in your car."

Before he reached the door, Helen, who was following behind, spoke in a tone that any listener might have thought they detected a hint of sadness.

"I leave for England tomorrow afternoon, I have to go back and show my face to my news desk."

Phillip stopped and turned to face her, taking one of her hands he rubbed his thumb over her soft skin.

"You have a lot to do back in England, not least to solve the mystery of the school woods, and I am sure you will be back, your lessons here have only just begun."

MILLBANK, LONDON.

Christopher threw the DD report across his desk in anger and snatched the phone from its cradle and dialled the mobile number for Mick Hayes. It rang several times before going to voice mail,

"Hi, this is Mick, can't take your call just now, but if you leave a number, I'll get back to you. Cheers!"

As soon as the computerised female voice had given her instructions as to how to leave a message, Christopher began his curt, short message.

"It's me, call me at once."

Christopher's wrath had arisen as he was reading his regular morning DD report on activity and people that he took an interest in. Brief notes, comments, observations populated the report in short paragraphs. Christopher was in good humour as he began reading:

'Gavin Henderson. Mayfair Casino. Arrived 22.15 decamped 04.34 with unidentified female.'

That image had entertained Christopher. Mr Henderson was hoping to become a board member of a well-known city bank following his forthcoming retirement from the Civil Service. Gavin's nighttime activities with gambling and females would be a useful weapon for Christopher to have in his armoury.

It was the next item that instantly riled him:

'Gregory Auden. Booked on 16.30 Dinard – Stansted Ryanair flight.'

Christopher knew any such booking would have needed to take place yesterday in order for it to be listed in his DD report today. So it should have been yesterday that Mick Hayes called to share the information with him.

Mick Hayes used to be a good reliable operative who was shrewd as well, nothing got past him and he was a wise field man. But that seemed to have all changed when he met a young woman, three years his junior, with a small child of her own; it soon became obvious she was a distraction from his work. Even though Christopher was more than aware that when Mick Hayes was out in the field running errands, he did have a wandering eye and hands, casual relationships had never interfered with his work. However much he maintained he was in love, Christopher knew the truth, being with a woman and a small child in a longer term relationship was scaring Mick, it was too much like being married.

They had only spoken yesterday; he had been tasked with confirming that what Greg had said about the car accident killing William Lynch was true. Christopher wanted to know as much as he could about Greg and what he was really doing in Brittany. Christopher knew that would involve his field operative riffling through a hotel room, something he never relished doing.

Christopher dialled the hotel where Mick was staying. It was early, even so a bright Frenchman answered the phone, and was more than happy to speak in English. He was pleased to confirm that Mick had not returned last night, his car was nowhere around the hotel, and he could not help at all. This only frustrated Christopher more, if a woman had once again distracted him, this could well be his last assignment before being given more local duties.

The next call was made to a close contact in MI6. Christopher gave the English registration mark of Mick's car and asked if they had any trace of it in the Brittany area of France. They were not going to be able to give an immediate answer but in five or six hours they would get back to him.

He made his next telephone call later that morning to a Mrs Jane Lynch. She did not answer the phone, a woman with a heavy French accent did. Whoever it was that answered confirmed for Christopher the tragic circumstances of Peter Bashford's death. Christopher gave his condolences without giving his name. At least the rogue reporter had not lied about that. So now he leaned back in his chair, his anger subsiding as he wondered just what or who Theresa Quinn could be. Then his thoughts turned to what else might be on that paper that William had left behind.

So, Greg was coming back to the UK, Christopher wondered just how much Jane had told him, he suspected enough to arouse his suspicions. It was now time for Christopher to act and resurrect the espionage skills he had put to such good use many years ago. He could not afford anyone else to find out the secret of R.G. Plastics.

LONDON STANSTED.

Greg looked across the Dinard departure lounge at Helen who was sitting calmly sipping her water and reading from her mobile phone. He wondered how she could look so contented; she was an escaping murderer. Their journey to Dinard Airport was for the most part completed in silence. Greg asked if she had slept well, Helen replied that she had and certainly she looked fresh and relaxed. Greg had spent the night turning over the events of the day in his mind. His hotel bedroom had been a constant reminder of the killing that he had been part of.

Greg parked the car outside the small airport terminal. Helen turned to him and reminded him of her plan and the contingency should they be pulled over when they arrived at UK passport control at Stansted. Part of Greg thought she was being a little too dramatic, she was describing the sort of scenario that you see in spy films or read about in dramatic books. It was then that he reminded himself that he had witnessed Helen killing a man yesterday in cold blood and then going to dispose of the body somewhere. All of which seemed a weird nightmare that played out while he was trying to sleep, only it was not a nightmare at all but had really happened, so maybe she wasn't being over-cautious after all. Then Greg started to think beyond the passport control desk, it would be bad enough to be taken to one side and questioned, but what if they walked through passport control without the passport officer batting an eyelid, what then? Helen had still killed a man, who it would appear, was connected to some sort of organisation potentially linked to the Government. Greg could not see them letting that go and just writing it off as one of those things. Greg was thinking that he would need to be constantly looking over his shoulder and lying asleep with one eye open. He wondered if he could live like that, maybe it would be preferable to be taken to a small room when they arrived at Stansted Airport and get it over with.

"So which car park is it?" Helen asked, looking at Greg's vacant stare. "Greg, you didn't hear a word of what I just said did you. You have to play your part, know what you need to do. I'll tell you again, so pay attention and listen," her tone was impatient, laced with tension. "I will go off to check in on my own, while you return the keys and the documents for the car. Then you'll check in and I should, by that time, have already gone through security and be in the departure lounge. Once you are through security and in the departure lounge, do not acknowledge me. Sit away from me and try to look like any other bored passenger. When we queue up to board, let's try and keep well apart, and that is what we'll do all the way. Make sure we are separate at the passport check in desks, and then follow the same pattern as we go through customs and out into the free flow part of Stansted, so my question is, which car park is your car in, so that I can get on the right coach?"

Greg shuffled through his wallet and pulled out the car park ticket.

"If we make it that far without being questioned, do we need to keep an eye out in case we are followed? Long stay, zone E, bus stop three."

Helen wrote down the car park information.

"Makes sense to keep an eye out for anyone boarding the bus without luggage. Once we get off the coach, I'll follow you back to your car and then off we go. Now, do you have the number that you need to call if I don't join you on the coach?"

"I have it here." Greg pulled another creased slip of paper form his wallet, "Danny, your news editor, tell him all, everything including the death part."

"It was in self-defence, just remember that. If you don't make it, then I will be contacting Donna and talking to her. Finally if neither of us makes it through and Justine does not hear that we have arrived safely, then she will call Danny, and say that we have gone missing."

"Didn't she ask why?"

"No, I just told her it was common practice in national newspapers, which she accepted without question. Ready?"

"See you on the other side…. of the channel that is."

Now he sat watching her, Helen appearing calm and collected. Greg knew he was just the opposite, clammy and confused. It reminded him of his teenage years, studying his younger sister, Brenda, as she read the tall, laminated menu in her hands, while the waitress stood over her waiting to take their order.

*

The Fairwell restaurant, from its shiny Formica tables to its encrusted sauce bottle tops, everyone knew it was just a simple high street cafe serving greasy food cheaply and quickly. Brenda had ordered egg on toast, she seemed more uneasy than normal. The last few weeks she had been tense and anxious and snapped at those around her. Greg ordered a full English breakfast, without the black pudding, just the thought of it made him feel ill. As they waited for their food, he had a deeper, darker feeling in the pit of his stomach. Brenda had sworn him to secrecy about their meeting, not to tell anyone, that was not a good sign. They were big brother and little sister, they could be seen out, they could be friends who were just meeting up, they could go off shopping or work out at the gym together, their parents would not mind. So why the secrecy Greg had asked himself, but he could not bring himself to ask Brenda, she had not been herself over the last few months. During their recent holiday, her mood had been dark and depressed. He had, at the time, just put it down to her being a moody teenager, her time of the month. Even his mother had quietly asked him if he knew what was wrong with Brenda, but he could add nothing. He simply told his mother, 'well ask her,' but neither of them could. Now in the cafe, he had the feeling he was about to find out. The way she looked at her mug of steaming tea, stirring it aimlessly, did not fill Greg with optimism. He was right, she shared her secret with him, he dismissed her fears as over exaggeration, she raised her voice. He put down her concerns, at one point calling her stupid, which did nothing to help her aggression towards him.

"I'm going to do it Greg, I have to. There is no other way. And you're going to have to help me, like it or not, you're my brother, my big brother who should be protecting me."

She left her meal, left her tea, left the restaurant, left Greg confused. Her last words echoed in his mind as she left slamming the glass restaurant door, the bell above it tinkling across the cafe. Other diners looked up at what they guessed could have been a lovers' tiff.

Greg felt embarrassed as he felt the eyes of the other diners regard him with what he guessed might have been disgust, assuming it was his behaviour that had forced the sweet young girl to leave her food. He finished his full English breakfast, trying to make sense of what he had heard. He now felt that same fear of what the future might bring in his stomach as the Stansted flight was called and he lined up nervously to board.

*

Greg negotiated the Stansted airport traffic aware that Helen was looking around his car with an inspecting eye. What she was looking for he had no idea. The flight from Dinard had been straightforward and tedious. Flying always left Greg tense, today it was the baggage reclaim, a place he normally felt relieved to be back at and on 'terra firma', that increased the tension, his heart pounding as he handed his passport to the uniformed border control officer. Still pounding as he walked through the green customs channel, avoiding eye contact with anyone in any sort of uniform.

Helen had spent her time above the channel making notes about the Bashford family hoping that would further deflect Greg's thoughts from Phillip. The walk-through passport control and customs she found exciting, she knew she had the ability to kill, the ultimate action over another human being. She felt special and untouchable, she had no trouble smiling at the customs officers, almost daring them to stop her. She looked around the coach taking her and Greg back to where his car was parked, no one looked to be following them, this was going to be easier than she had thought. Maybe the authorities had yet to learn of the death of one of their own in France. Helen smiled to herself, they had better hurry up, before the pigs have their fill.

Greg flicked the indicator on his VW Polo and joined the busy London bound M11, the early evening winter darkness had already fallen across the motorway.

"What exactly are you looking for?"

Helen turned to him with a questioning look on her face.

"Is this your car? Or a hire car?"

"Mine. Why?"

"It's just so clean and tidy looking, not what I would expect from a male reporter, or at least not from the ones that I have known. Do you spend all Sunday afternoon cleaning and polishing your pride and joy?"

"Don't mock me and don't judge all men to be the same; I'm just a tidy person, there's nothing wrong with that. And you're one to talk, cleaning your hands at every opportunity, that is something I would not expect from a normal female reporter, or at least the ones I have known."

Helen decided to change the subject, the last thing she wanted was to get into an argument whilst stuck in a car. So she dug out the notes that she had made on the plane.

"Right, let's see what we have. The Peter Bashford who lived in France with his family, was in fact a government scientist according to his wife. He had worked at some sort of research facility in Sevenoaks called R.G. Plastics. We know that place was destroyed by a fire and explosion which killed all the personnel there but for Peter Bashford, who at the time was called William Lynch. Following the explosion, the Lynch family were whisked into hiding and moved around the country for a few weeks, before ending up in France and the little village of La Ville du Bois. Which I think you will agree is pretty much factual all the way along the line according to his wife and your research."

Greg nodded.

"Pretty much all that does come from his widow, Jane, so unless she has a reason to lie, which we should not discount although it seems unlikely, it all appears to be true. What does trouble me is the fact that she didn't seem to take much interest in her husband's work. I find that odd."

"Well, if it was a secret type thing, maybe she was happy not to pressure him into telling her. Plus, someone is paying them a handsome monthly wage to stay in France. We know William needed to call in each month, so he had a friendly contact in the UK to help him if need be. So when you turned up, prying into just how he was retired and what had he done back in the UK, the first thing he appeared to do, was call that London number. So that tells me he was protecting something, and someone had an interest in protecting him."

"But he could have just lied to me, he could have told me that very first day when I spoke to Peter, William, whatever he was called at the time, he could have simply told me one big fib, told me he won the lottery, inherited money, big golden handshake, anything really."

"But," Helen added, looking across at Greg's face that was being illuminated by the passing headlights.

The automatic windscreen wipers began wiping away the first spots of wintry rain, smearing the wind shield turning the tail-lights ahead into a kaleidoscope of red and amber.

"All those things you could easily check up on. And don't forget, he could not know how much you already knew about him. If there was something he was hiding, then by the sheer definition there must be someone wanting to find what has been hidden."

"Good point" Greg conceded.

"Then he goes and dies, in what seems to be an innocent road accident. A real accident, we are led to believe, prompting Mrs. Lynch or Bashford to quickly hand over some instructions that she held in the event of his death. So therefore he must want her or someone to learn the secret, so the bit of paper she gave you with odd bits and pieces has to mean something significant."

Greg slowed the car as he approached a large lorry driving slowly in lane one, he checked his mirror to see a line of headlights, he would have to wait for the moment behind the tail lights of this lumbering lorry.

"Let's make a deal first off about names. Shall we from this moment on refer to their real names, Mr. & Mrs. Lynch, William and Jane?"

"Deal"

"Right, on that paper we have a telephone number, which upon calling, I get a cold shoulder from the other end, so from that we can deduce the person on the other end was not eager to talk. Secret squirrel stuff again?"

"Could be." Helen agreed before adding, "Then the opening chess move, nothing odd about that. A famous opening any half decent chess player would use, but as to its significance, I have no idea whatsoever. Next, we have an Ordnance Survey grid reference, which happens to be just yards away from Wilmington school, where Peter, sorry William Lynch went to school and was a chess champion."

"The picture that started all this off," Greg spoke as he indicated and moved into lane two, causing a large Land Rover Discovery to brake hard and flash his lights in anger. Greg was sorry about that, but he had had enough of watching the red tail lights of the Asda articulated lorry in front of him.

"I vote for going to see that guy, the school friend you met before, he might have some idea of what that copse might be, or not be. Whatever it is, Wilmington school seems to be at the centre of this mystery."

"And what about Martin and Dougie?" Greg asked.

"Solve one and I'm sure we will solve the other," Helen lied.

Four cars behind Greg was an ageing Vauxhall Zafira with a sticker in the back window informing other drivers that there was a 'baby on board'; the Zafira also pulled out and over took the Asda lorry. Alongside the baby sticker was another decal, this time of Eeyore, with the caption 'get off my tail'. There was even a baby seat fixed to the rear seats, a typical family car, that's what they wanted you to think. The two suited men in the front seat sat silently as they moved through the traffic, all the time watching the Volkswagen Polo. The passenger's telephone rang:

"We are London-bound on the M11."

But for the drone of the engine and the traffic around them, there was silence in the Zafira.

"Just the two of them."

The passenger listened to his instructions.

"The first opportunity, affirmative," he pressed the red button on his mobile as he returned it to his pocket and turned to the driver.

"We are to stop them at the first opportunity and then bring them and their car back to east London."

"The car as well, what do they want the bloody car for? Just being difficult I guess. They're not going to follow us without a good reason, are they? So we'll need to split up, one in here and one in their car."

"That's fine, I'll go in their car, you follow, it'll be fine."

"What do we tell them, were you told that?"

"Of course not, if we were told exactly what to do and things go wrong, our masters get the blame. If we have to use our own initiative, then we're the ones for the high jump. Lose, lose, that's what we are paid to do. Let's see when and where they stop, we'll make a call then. Just don't lose them."

*

The traffic continued to build as Greg and Helen approached the outskirts of London. Greg joined the M25, taking the clockwise route towards the Queen Elizabeth Bridge, then planned to pick up the A2 towards the home of George Usher. The Vauxhall continued to follow them. Inside, the two men travelled in silence, neither had any idea where the Volkswagen Polo's final destination might be. If they had known, they would have wondered why he did not go through the City and Blackwall tunnel but that would have been with the benefit of hindsight. With that hindsight, they would have decided they should have had a better plan to stop them.

Greg saw the blue road sign for motorway services. They were approaching the Queen Elizabeth Bridge at the Dartford Crossing; the traffic had now lightened and they were making good progress. It was the motorway service sign that prompted Greg to announce,

"I'm hungry, I think I need to eat before we start talking to Mr. Usher. You peckish?"

Helen looked across at him with an accusing look and said, "I'm just being practical and thinking about time, you know, avoiding knocking on their door at midnight."

"I'm not thinking a three-course meal, although that would not go amiss. I am thinking more a burger and chips."

"In that case, nothing for me."

Greg was not going to be put off, at least his stomach was not going to let him be as it reminded him of its emptiness, by cramping and tightening, just in case he might be dissuaded from stopping for food.

"OK a compromise, there is a drive through Burger King near the shopping centre at Lakeside, just after the services, we'll pull in there, I'll have a whopper and fries while you drive, and still get to Mr. Usher at a reasonable time. Is that a deal?"

To Helen, that seemed fair, so she accepted the offer and within five minutes, she was in the driving seat. Greg had returned with his burger and fries all contained within a brown paper bag. Helen watched him settle into his seat, he had also purchased two coffees which she had readily agreed to, predicting that it might be a long night at the end of a long day.

They remained for a few minutes parked in the Burger King Car park, Helen had decided to drink some of her coffee before setting off.

"That smells horrible. Shall I tell you what parts of the animal they use for those burgers?"

"You can," Greg swallowed a mouthful of burger, "yet I doubt you will put me off, it tastes good to me, so whichever part it happens to be, it suits me. They tell me it's a hundred percent beef, which it is, so let's not ask the question which part of the animal does this burger originate from, I can eat while you're driving, I have a tough tummy."

"You must have to eat that stuff."

"I've eaten worse, trust me."

Helen started the car and slipped into first gear, but before she could release the hand brake a man tapped on her window. Instinctively she pressed the button and the window opened, cold air flowing into the car. Helen wondered what this man could want with them in the middle of a Burger King car park, if it was directions he was out of luck, she was not used to this side of London.

"Good evening," his breath reeked of garlic, an odour that Helen could not escape as she was so close to the man. "To save us all a very long conversation, I know that you have been in contact with William Lynch, who I know was recently killed in a car crash in France. Mr. Lynch, was of interest to Her Majesty's Government. The same government which employs me and has asked that we go with you, to a small office, to talk about what you know and maybe what you should not know. Once that has been established, we can ask you to sign something called the Official Secrets Act so that her Majesty's Government can rest assured that her secrets are all safe and well."

"My mother always warned me not to go with strangers. A rule I still adhere to even though I am a lot older and some say wiser."

"Clearly," said garlic breath, "not much wiser, you are coming with us, whatever your mother might say." His head nodded towards the front of the car where a man, arms folded, stood. He looked just like an ordinary security guard that you get on the door of a late-night drinking club, to ensure only the right people are allowed in. "Can I suggest in the interests of safety for all of us, that you and your friend with the burger do as you are told, and I'll drive, you can sit in the back. My friend will follow in our car. Happy or not that is what is going to happen."

"Shouldn't you show some sort of identification at least, if the Queen herself has sent you to collect us?" Greg asked, having finished his interrupted mouthful of one hundred percent beef parts.

"You just get on with your burger, let's get moving, shall we?" Garlic breath began to open the door, which Helen pulled back.

"Tell your friend to move, as I am not stopping for anyone and certainly not letting you drive."

"The only way you are going to drive away will be over my friend, so just get out and let's get moving, shall we? I have had a long day and my patience is wearing thin." This time he tugged at the door and Helen could not counter his strength.

"If that's the way it needs to be done, so be it."

She gunned the engine, released the hand brake, dropped the clutch and let the car fire forward in a burst of acceleration. The wheels took a moment to grip the car park surface, possibly made slippery through years of French fries ending up on the floor, or maybe it was just the dampness from the earlier rain shower that had passed by. Whatever the reason the tyres did grip after a very brief moment, too quick for the man standing in front of the car. His eyes widened when he realised the car was being driven at him. He never imagined the sweet young girl behind the wheel was going to drive straight at him. But she was and before he could react and leap out of the way, he felt the impact of the car bumper on his shins, sending him forwards onto the bonnet, his head ramming into the metal, denting it out of shape and breaking the skin across his forehead. The warm blood started to flow as he then somersaulted, his upper back hitting the windscreen. Amongst his confusion, the car stopped sharply sending him forward, back onto the ground, rolling forward and tearing his trousers, grazing the skin around his knees. For a moment he lay there, a little dazed, but not feeling as though he had been badly injured, just a few scrapes, a bit like he used to get when he was young and into fighting other young men after the pubs had closed on a Saturday night. His surprise turned first to indignation and then anger at having been struck by the car. He was going to make her pay for her actions and decided she would get a couple of slaps before he handed her over to his boss. He rolled onto his knees, and tried to get up. His anger quickly transformed into panic, as he heard the noise of the car engine scream out again as it launched forward. Coming closer. Too close. He could not move quickly enough. The front offside wheel ran over both his legs breaking his bones in several places. The pain shot through him like hot spikes running through his head. Through the pain he heard the car stop and accelerate again. He wondered in his muddled mind just why she would stop and then drive off. A fraction of a second later, he had his answer. The pain and his thoughts stopped, as the rear offside wheel ran over his head, turning it into a rhomboid, killing him almost in an instant. Garlic breath was left standing in the middle of the dark car park, watching the Polo drive off, unable to comprehend what he had just witnessed.

Greg was not sure who was now driving his Volkswagen, Helen the reporter or a Helen capable of taking another human's life away in the same way Greg killed spiders, which when he did, he often felt pangs of guilt.

"Jesus, Helen, you've just run over that guy! You've got to stop he might need some help. What on earth were you thinking?" Greg turned in his seat looking back as 'garlic breath' went to see what he could do for his partner. Greg's burger was falling apart in his hand, with sauce and pieces of bun and meat dropping onto the upholstery and the carpet. "He looks badly hurt."

"Most likely, and you've made a mess on the carpet." Helen spoke coldly, as she continued driving away from the car park. "I felt a bump in the steering which, I guess, must have been his head, so I doubt if he will be getting up for a while. And Greg just what is in that burger? Whatever it is, it has made you stupid. Do you really think those guys were going to have a quiet chat with us? Get real Greg, we are in the middle of a shitload of trouble and we need to look after ourselves."

"Helen, you killed someone yesterday with your bare hands, you have just run over a guy without so much as turning a hair or batting one of your pretty eyelashes, who the hell are you, a reporter or a crazed killer?" Greg watched as Helen twisted and turned the steering wheel, cutting in and out of traffic, bringing them onto the Queen Elizabeth Bridge. "Are you even aware of what you have fucking done? Not a twinge of guilt or remorse?"

"First you need to give me directions, as I have no idea whatsoever where Mr. Usher lives. Secondly, why should I feel guilt, yesterday that guy wanted to kill you, I think we are both clear on that one, you had an even greater interest in my distracting him from throttling you. As for the car park man, he had a choice, I was moving, he could have got out the way, oh no, he being an arrogant bastard thought he was better then everyone around him. Everyone should do his bidding; do exactly as they are told. Well he chose the wrong person for a confrontation."

"Knocking him down is one thing. But reversing over him is....take the next junction, London bound A2..." Greg interrupted himself to give Helen directions before continuing, "Reversing over him is plain murder, nothing less, you meant to kill him. Of that any judge would find you guilty."

"Why should I feel guilty, what sort of law have I violated, penal, moral? I stopped a chain of events that could have easily, not just easily but would have, ended up with us being the victims of a violation of our human rights. They would have taken our freedom away just because it suited them, because they think they have a greater moral right, just because they work for the government and we are just the drones that need to do exactly as we are told and accept that whatever they say is right. And would it have stopped at our freedom, have you never heard of torture and pain to extract information from people? I'm not guilty Greg, I am in control of my own destiny."

"Jesus, Helen you scare the crap out of me. That is no way to live in a civilised society."

"The government tells us we live in a civilised society, yet do we Greg? Do we really?"

WILMINGTON, KENT.

"You do realise," Helen began speaking as they approached the pebble-dashed semi-detached house of Mr. & Mrs. Usher, "we are going to have to break the bad news to them both that William is dead. They have met you, so best if it comes from you." It sounded like an order.

Apart from Greg giving a series of directions to the Ushers' house, they had travelled in silence. Helen did not want to get into a big discussion about the rights and wrongs of killing people and Greg was just not sure who he was talking to anymore.

The rain had not stopped, it had just become less intense and was now no more than a fine heavy mist that clung to your clothes. Greg pressed the door chimes.

"I doubt if they will be that upset, they haven't seen him for years and from what I gathered on the last visit, they were not close to the Lynch family."

George answered the door, as man and protector of the house, it was his duty to answer the door after seven in the evening, unless guests were expected. He would protect his wife from demons, devils and door to door salesmen. He looked at Helen first and then Greg, was just about to say 'no thank you' to whatever they were offering when a spark of recognition washed over his ruddy face.

"The book writer, grammar school, Greg, that's it, what can I do for you?"

"May we come in for a moment, I wanted to ask you a couple of questions and give you some news. By the way, this is Helen, my assistant." Greg could not see them, but he felt the daggers as Helen looked at him, he hoped they were not going to be real daggers.

Emily served tea to her guests without any hesitation, while her husband exchanged pleasantries with their unexpected, nocturnal visitors. Emily was not going to be deterred from being the perfect host, so she would not take no for an answer when they at first refused the offer of tea, she then offered biscuits as well.

First Greg explained that he had traced William only to learn that he had been tragically killed in a car accident in France, where he and his wife and children had been living for the past few years. As he had predicted, George did not show any great emotion, just respect for a school friend who had passed on. His wife appeared to wipe a tear from her eye, although once again Greg thought she was only being polite and doing what was expected of her.

"Funny," George said, picking up the chess champion photograph and examining the young faces in the picture, "two out of the four have now gone, half of the champions, who knows how long it will be before none of us are left."

"Don't be so morbid George, we have years in us yet."

"Well I do hope so dear, yet none of us really know what is waiting for us around the next corner, time is tempting and fickle."

Greg thought of the man who Helen had turned into a speed hump and guessed he had never expected that when he left home that morning, it would be for the last time. Now, not for the first time that day, Greg felt hungry and the ginger nut biscuits on the floral-patterned plate were tempting, although he knew how hard they could be and his teeth were not the type you would see on a toothpaste advert. Without thinking he took one, dunked it into his tea and consumed the softened biscuit. He caught a look of disapproval out of the corner of his eye from both Helen and Emily. Once he had finished, he spoke, to help him resist the temptation to have another one.

"When we spoke to his wife, Jane, after the accident, she gave us a piece of paper that he wanted her to have if he died. She did not know what it was or what it meant so asked us for help."

At that point Helen chimed in, as Greg chose a custard cream, leaving the ginger nuts to one side.

Helen handed the paper to George, who glanced over the writing.

"This is what she gave us, the telephone number does not exist," she lied, which in turn drew a disapproving look of surprise from Greg. "The notations, I am sure you can see, are chess moves," before she could explain more, George proudly interrupted her.

"Classic Ruy Lopez opening move. Obvious just about to any chess player. I don't suppose there is a chess player out there who has not played that opening, although not all of them could tell you it was the Ruy Lopez opening. Well to be precise his name was Ruy Lopez de Segura, a priest who studied chess and wrote a book way back in 1561. Although the move was first noted in a chess book around 1490, so he was not really the first person to use it. Even so it is Ruy whose name people use for the move, or 'Spanish Opening' as it is often called. Although Theresa Quinn is not a name I know, Emily, do you know a Theresa Quinn?"

Emily sat upright in her chair, stirring her tea, "No dear."

Helen began her explanation of what they thought the initials of the name stood for when added to the numbers and that it then gave the ordnance survey reference for a small wood next to George's old school. George nodded recalling the fenced in wood that he had often visited with school friends.

"Wilmer's Wood, I'm not sure if that is the correct name. It was the name that we gave the wood, as teenage boys do, claiming the land for ourselves."

"Did it ever have any significance for William?" Greg asked as he picked up another custard cream and received another disapproving look from Emily Usher. She considered two biscuits as being polite, now that Greg was consuming his fourth, she felt that to be a little rude.

"Wilmer's wood," George smiled, "it was an important part of all our lives, well at least the teenage growing up years. As eleven year olds, when we first went to Wilmington Grammar school, the woods were where we would go after lessons and act out adventures. Climbing trees, hiding from imaginary enemies and protecting the land from aliens from far away planets. We also often just sat around talking, drinking lemonade out of cans and eating sausage rolls straight from the wrapper. Of course we played chess as well there amongst the moss and the fallen leaves. Then, young boys turn into teenagers, fighting acne and hormones, often at different times. So in our early teens, when Dennis and I were still sipping lemonade and eating sausage rolls, William and Les had moved onto beer and cigarettes. Although it was only a short fad, neither of them really enjoyed those two evils, but you had to try them, if you didn't, you were not going to be a true teenager. Dennis and I also tried the beer, which was not bad, but the cigarettes made us cough and it left a smell on your clothes that led to us being caught out on a number of occasions. But we still continued to visit the woods and still played chess, our true passion, in the sunlit glades. I say true passion, as we grew up other passions surfaced and Wilmers Wood became the perfect place to take young ladies walking, holding hands, stealing a kiss and proudly show them a kingdom in which they could be a queen. I often wondered who actually owned the woods, we never saw anyone else there, there was only us four boys. Although I can't imagine we were the only visitors, but for us four boys it was ours."

"You never took me there," Emily told more than asked.

"Dear, I met you a long time after I was a teenager. Once we left school, I don't think any of us ever went back, I suppose until you just mentioned it, it had been only a distant dim memory. But to answer your question, apart from being a fond childhood memory, I cannot think of any reason that William would hold that place in any special regard, let alone add it to a set of cryptic clues."

"George," Emily spoke as though she was asking permission to speak, which she was not granted as George continued at once.

"Maybe he buried something there. You say that it might have something to do with his research work, yet pre-empting your question, there was never any particular spot there, I would not have the faintest idea. In our later years, as I mentioned to you before, Dennis and I were close friends and William seemed to socialise more with Les."

"That was what I was going to say dear," all eyes turned to Emily, "don't you remember when Les died, his wife, distraught as she was, came around and asked if we knew where William was living. We, of course, could not help as we had lost contact by then, we had the Hempstead address, but Christmas cards had been returned, 'addressee gone away'. The reason, she told me, was that she had an envelope that she had to give to William should Les ever die."

"An envelope?" Greg and Helen spoke together, which seemed a little too dramatic.

"Yes, a letter addressed to William, I suppose she still has it, she might have thrown it away, although she never appeared to be the sort of person to throw anything away. The house always looked a mess." Emily had a habit of putting people down who did not adhere to her own standards of behaviour.

Emily also liked the way her visitors now buzzed around her like bees around a honey pot, leaving George just listening. She thought it best if they were going to visit if she called Les's widow, Alice, first to see if she still had the envelope, and to warn her, as it was getting late, that she was having some visitors.

Emily did like to organise people, even though she tried to be discreet, she noticed Greg pick up the last two custard creams as he left. He didn't see the frown on Emily's face, he was too busy thinking about the letter that Les had left for William. It could well have been a close friend offering some last thoughts before death, yet Greg had a gut feeling it was going to be more than that.

*

Together they walked in the sodium light of the street lights towards Greg's parked car. The drizzle had now stopped, the wet pavement reflected the street lights, there was still a January chill in the air. They did not say a word to each other, Helen pulled her coat closer to her to keep out the cold and keep in the warmth. Once in the car and on their way to see Alice Clarke, they would have time to talk.

"Mr. Auden," a male voice called from behind them.

Greg stopped as did Helen and they both turned around. Two men were walking towards them, their features indistinguishable in the shadows cast by the street lights, they were both of similar height, one dressed in a long overcoat, the second in a short bomber jacket. Helen and Greg looked at each other, each knew what the other was thinking: 'do we run?' Instead, they stood like rabbits trapped in headlights, as the two men approached and finally stood close enough for Greg to see one was clean shaven while the other wore a trimmed, fashionable stubble.

"This is Detective Sergeant Smith, I am Detective Inspector Williams," they both offered their warrant cards as proof of who they were.

"Gregory Auden," DI Williams began, "I am arresting you on suspicion of causing death by dangerous driving. You do not have to say anything....."

Greg shook his head interrupting,

"I think there has been some mistake."

The inspector ignored him and continued, "But it may harm your defence if you do not mention when questioned something which you later rely on in court. Anything you do say may be given in evidence."

The Inspector then continued, "that's what they all say at first. The car you own was reported as being in collision with a male in a fast-food car park earlier this evening. The male has since died from his injuries."

The ever so slightly shorter one with the long coat stepped forward taking advantage of Greg's confusion to securely handcuff his hands. Helen looked down at the manacles in disbelief, and then decided to be defensive.

"What sort of evidence do you...?"

The slightly taller one with the bomber jacket interrupted her,

"Helen Taylor, I am arresting you on suspicion of causing death by dangerous driving......," this time he pulled her hands from her body and placed handcuffs around her wrists. "....you do not have to say anything but anything you do...," he continued with the caution as Helen protested

"This is ridiculous."

"I am sure, if there has been some sort of misunderstanding then once we are down at the station it will all be sorted out, but for now you are coming with us."

Both of them were led past Greg's car which was untouched and parked sensibly under a street light. A few yards behind a car alarm beeped as the taller man disarmed it and opened the rear door.

Greg wondered why they had walked past his car, wouldn't they need that as evidence? Greg could see the dented bonnet, the cracked headlight and the smears of blood but they had not taken any steps to protect it. Something was wrong, nothing over the last few days had been what it had seemed.

First Helen got into the police car and then Greg was placed on the back seat too.

"Don't worry Helen, I'm sure we will sort this all out once we are at the police station," Greg didn't really believe what he was saying, "and we get to call a lawyer or someone. The man you killed was trying to abduct us after all."

"If they are the police." Helen was not certain they were, already the handcuffs were rubbing her wrist, being shackled was not one of her favourite pastimes.

The slightly shorter one leaned towards them before closing the door and then spoke softly, "I wouldn't say too much at present, just leave the talking for when we get you away from here."

As he was about to close the door a third voice called from just behind the car. Both detectives looked up and saw a man, maybe in his early sixties, it was hard to tell in the street lights, he wore a cashmere coat and a trilby hat and was walking towards them.

"Detectives, please, I do think there has been some sort of error in this matter."

"Sir, please let us deal with this, it is a police matter."

"Oh, I very much doubt that young man, real warrant cards are issued to real police officers, the Queen's Warrant as I am sure you are aware."

Greg crooked his neck to try and see, without success, who this man was. He was now standing alongside the rear door that remained open. The two detectives, if that was what they were, stood looking at the elderly man who pulled a small wallet from his coat pocket and showed it to them.

"See, I think you will find that this trumps both your not fully legal warrant cards, and also the other form of identification that you should be carrying with you. So I refer you to my earlier statement, there has been an error in this matter. Mr. Campbell asked you to collect these two young people, well there has now been a change of plan. Your destination has been compromised so I need to remove them swiftly to a place of safety. If you could take them to my car over there, the Volkswagen Golf, then I can be on my way. You need to return as planned but just be aware that about a mile from your destination, a car will pick you up and try to follow you. We do not want that to happen, once you have identified the car, drive anywhere but the destination. Call into Mr. Campbell and give him the details of the car, he will instruct you from there. Please, we do not have a lot of time. If you could take these two to my car."

The slightly taller one with the fashionable stubble examined the small wallet he had been shown.

"Sir, no disrespect, but we only take orders from Mr. Campbell, I will need to call him first."

"How do you think they are aware of where you are going? Communications somehow have been compromised; hence I have been dragged out of a warm comfortable office in Whitehall to drive all the way out into the countryside, on what is, frankly, a cold and totally ghastly night, in order to inform you personally as I have the clear authority and my presence should indicate to you that this is of the highest priority."

This time it was the turn of the shorter detective to voice his doubts, "I still would like to call just to be sure."

"Fine," the older man took a phone from his pocket, "use my telephone or your own it does not matter one bit, you make a call and they will track where we are. Mr. Campbell will answer and mostly likely fire you on the spot, worse still he might invite you to his office tomorrow and kick your stupid mind right out of your head and right through the window of his very plush office into the Thames. Let's be honest young man, you know and I know what he is capable of. So please go ahead and either call Mr. Campbell or take those people to my car."

They both looked at one another and then the slightly taller one nodded. Greg and Helen were led handcuffed to a VW Golf parked a hundred yards or so behind them. Again they were placed in the back, still handcuffed. The older man sat in the driver's seat, removed his trilby hat, started the car and spoke to the men through the open window, that was allowing the light rain that had once again started to fall, into the car.

"Don't forget, about a mile from the destination, if our intelligence is correct, it will be a Vauxhall Astra, only then call Mr. Campbell when you are being followed."

Without waiting for any sort of answer, the VW Golf was driven off leaving two pretend detectives standing on the pavement getting wet in the increasing rain.

The three drove in silence for about five minutes before the driver threw his trilby backwards landing it between them.

"You'll find a key to the handcuffs in the brim, between you both you should be able to release those handcuffs. They can be so painful if they are not placed correctly, clearly that is entertaining for some criminals, for journalists like you, not so entertaining. Well Mr. Auden and Miss Taylor, where are we going?"

Greg, undid his handcuffs and then freed Helen, wondering if he had heard the question correctly.

"I think you will find that you were taking us somewhere."

"Strictly speaking, I am taking you away from a potentially difficult situation for you both. So now I have done that, I will need some direction from you two. Can I suggest that we make use of this McDonalds car park and we can have a friendly chat."

Both Greg and Helen wondered what a friendly chat might be exactly.

LA BELLE ETOILE.

The lapwings flew across the clear blue skies of Brittany, a large flock, squealing and clacking wings moving in unison, heading west towards the setting sun. Below them at Belle Etoile, the lapwings were not concerned that a naked man stood over a fully clothed, lifeless body. The lapwings took no notice, they just continued their unhurried flight westwards, the man far below was no threat to them.

Phillip looked down at the dead body of Mick Hayes. It was now time to turn the body into pig fodder. A body that Phillip had not drained life from but instead his newly acquired apprentice, Helen, had carried out the deed. He did not feel the cold wind on his naked skin, his own vanity warmed him. His pride in being able to detect that homicidal flaw within a person's psyche. A flaw that allowed them to cross the moral line from just wanting to kill someone, which many people thought about, to actually making it happen, snubbing out a human life. He was being totally honest and critical, the way Helen described it, she had started out being purely defensive for her friend. But then that dark pulsating vein of flawed blood, the blood of the executioner within her rose up and engulfed her, until she was no longer acting defensively but had continued her actions until Mick Hayes was lying dead in her arms, a killer's arms, a killer's hands, a killer's fingers. But all pupils need direction from their tutors, however talented they might be. Learning takes time, he could not expect her to dispose of the body herself, not just yet that would be for next time. Yes, he knew there would be a next time. He knew all too well that

Helen would reflect and relive that moment when the body she held fell limp and lifeless, she would relive and recall that many times, and each time a small voice would ask when and who would be next. That pleading inner voice would ask again and again, each time getting louder and louder, until Helen could no longer resist the call within her and she would seek out another person to squeeze the life out of.

Phillip turned the body over, removed the over jacket, cut the thick jumper away, unbuttoned and removed the striped shirt, finally the slightly off-white tee shirt, leaving a naked torso. Then the shoes were pulled off, followed by the socks, trousers and finally black boxer shorts, all the vestments of the deceased he placed into a small pile. He then tugged at the cord of the chainsaw, allowing it to burst into life, its high-pitched sound exciting the pigs, who knew that soon they would be feasting on fresh meat.

Phillip began the dismembering process with his methodical coldness, just as a butcher would turn a carcass into saleable pieces. As he cut through the knee joint, Phillip thought of Helen. He was sorry that she had to go, he would have liked to show her his dexterity at dismembering a human body. The deft movement of the spinning chain cutting through skin, muscle and bone. For the first time in his life, he missed another human being, he felt the void that is left when a human you have feelings for departs. Loneliness was a feeling he had never really experienced before, always happy to be on his own, lacking any tolerance for those around him. Maybe, he wondered, if this was what love was all about, maybe love was just a feeling that without the other person you are a little less of a person. Not that Phillip had ever felt inferior to other people, but now he did feel that something was missing, something which had been there when Helen had been with him, across a table, beside him on the settee. Those times he felt complete or at least more complete than he had been before. He realised that before he had met Helen, he had something missing from his life, it was just that he had never known it.

His parents had never shown any love to each other, they were just there in the house with him, three people leading lives that could as easily have been played out in three separate homes. Phillip, when he looked back at his childhood, saw that he was treated with the same lack of love his parents gave to the decorations and furniture in the house. They needed a chair to sit at the table and they needed the table to be able to eat, they had to eat to continue living, so they endured having table and chairs in the house. The table and chairs were not cared for, but were scorched, old, unpolished, and food stained. The furniture had to be endured, the consequence would be not eating. Now Phillip looked back, with an adult's eye, he saw that he was just like those table and chairs. His parents did not really want or need him, it was just that all the families along the street had children. In the same way they had a table and chairs, his parents needed to have a child to fit in. Maybe that was when he first thought about the logic that his parents used. What if we did not need to eat, then we would not need a table to eat at and we would not need a chair to sit on at the table. So was it better not to have those things in your life that you did not love? Surely we lived to love, that was what he had been taught at Sunday church. Snub out the life that does not love and then all those tables, chairs and children would either not have to suffer the endurance of a loveless life, or they could find love elsewhere.

He threw an amputated limb into the pen. The pigs scurried around and fought over the first limb that arrived from the air. They had no obvious morals; this was food arriving and food was to be eaten.

He halted the motor on the chainsaw, rested for a moment, wondering if she had felt the same about him. Love was something that was not necessarily shared between people but maybe it was given one to the other and then replicated. How would he consider telling her how he felt, that would be a defining moment in such a blossoming relationship. He could sit her down, hold her hand and tell her how much he had missed her. How deep the void was when she left, how he wanted to spend every instant of his life next to her. He was now thinking thoughts that he had ridiculed before when people had spoken of such things, he brushed them aside as being stupid, wasteful thoughts. Why love anyone? Was there any point? Now he had reconsidered and seemingly altered, Helen had somehow, in some way changed him. He hoped that when he came to tell her, that she would tell him she felt the same void, the same emptiness when he was not around. Then together they could share new experiences: new deaths, the planning, committing and concealing, a couple with shared interests. However much those interests might be outside of what society might decree as normal, he knew they were real. He hoped she would not be away too long, maybe at last he could live to love, just as he had been taught in that cold, bleak church of his childhood.

Above the heightening south-easterly wind and with the sun now lowering into the horizon, Phillip heard the metallic tone of a phone, a mobile phone ringing close by. Surprised, he tensed up, listened, looked around him for a person nearby. The ring continued, his ears located the source from within the discarded pile of clothes that lay beside him, a melody that resembled some classic symphony. He then recognized it as the Coppelia overture, an odd choice for a ring tone he thought. He would not have imagined the semi-dismembered body lying before him was a ballet lover. Although to be fair, Phillip only knew of him in death and based all his assumptions on his clothes and possessions. Phillip rummaged around the clothes, sinking his hands into each pocket, but he found nothing. The phone was clearly ringing from within the jacket. A second examination of the pockets revealed a torn lining, Phillip recovered the mobile phone from it, a slim touch screen mobile phone, ringing, displaying the caller, Christopher. Whoever Christopher might be, he was not going to get an answer, after four more rings, the phone became silent, and the display showed one missed call.

It then fully occurred to Phillip that he did not really know just who Mick Hayes had been in life. He knew in death that he was burgling a hotel room in Josselin, but just who he was in life, Phillip could not be sure. Perhaps he had connections in the United Kingdom, who might want to find him and where he had gone. When Phillip murdered, the victims background he knew and could plan to put a moat between himself and his victim. He wondered if there might be such a moat between Helen and her victim, he could not be sure.

He had also felt something else in the lining of the jacket next to the mobile phone, he retrieved a small, plastic identity card that displayed a photo of the dead man, now naked on the muddy ground, his name, Michael Hayes, beside an emblem of the Government Crown. Clearly Helen was correct in her assumption that he was a civil servant, a worrying aspect, the voice in his mind once again spoke up. Calmly Phillip pulled the back off the telephone, removed the battery and dropped it to the floor. In that moment he knew he could no longer risk staying at Belle Etoile. Mobile phones could be traced, he knew, to within a few hundred yards and with so sparse a scattering of houses, Belle Etoile would soon potentially be the subject of a visit from some official as it became necessary for authorities to find Mick Hayes, which, without doubt, it would.

Without any sign of panic, Phillip finished cutting up the lifeless body throwing the parts to his pet pigs. He poured petrol over the clothes and set light to them, leaving them to burn and taking the phone into the house. He began to shower, knowing that his young female scholar had made a grave error. A mistake that potentially could mean he would not only need to leave France as soon as possible, he would also have to either consider taking Helen with him or contemplate another solution.

ELTHAM.

Looking at his apprehensive passengers via the rear-view mirror was not the politest way of holding any sort of conversation. Even so, Christopher reasoned it was the best option for him as turning to talk to them might only make his aching back worse. He had gone through a period of pain during recent weeks and was only now starting to feel that it was getting better, twisting around would not help it to continue healing. He could have stood outside with the two of them and carried out a conversation, but the rain had once again started to fall in large drops and with the ever-increasing wind it had become a driving cold January rain, so that option was dismissed. They were parked in the car park of a McDonald's fast food restaurant, which could be an option with its warm, dry seats as well as refreshments on hand. For Christopher it was the least acceptable choice as although he had never actually been inside a McDonald's fast food restaurant, he based his opinion of it on what he had heard second hand and his own perception of the people who frequented such establishments. Children, however well-behaved, were just not acceptable in any form of restaurant, including fast food restaurants, which only seem to attract loud, ill-behaved children. Then there were the adults, who by the sheer fact were in McDonald's was a clear indication that they were not going to be people like Christopher. He preferred to be close to people from a similar background to his own. Anyone who would even consider eating out of brown paper bags would not be his type of person. So he had no intention of entering the warm and dry restaurant whose car park they were now situated in.

"So," Christopher began, watching the nervous eyes of his passengers in the rear-view mirror, "where do you want me to take you?"

"I think you kidnapped us," Helen answered, "unless you have a different view on the situation."

"My dear, let us all be clear. Both of you were about to be kidnapped by the two gentlemen, until I persuaded them to hand over both of you to my care. I agreed that in that moment you might well have been under the impression that you were still being abducted. Yet, consider where we are now, you no longer have handcuffs, I have allowed you to be released. The doors beside you are unlocked, you could, if you wish, simply open the door and leave. You are free to go. Therefore captives, you are most certainly not. In fact, it is the opposite, I am at your disposal, hence my question where do you want to go?"

Helen leaned forward and closer to the older man that had driven them to the car park. She noticed his aftershave – familiar. She recalled it from somewhere, maybe an old boyfriend, or a man standing close to her in the tube; at that moment, she could not quite place it.

"So we can just walk away from your car and lose ourselves in the night?"

Even with his tender back, Christopher twisted around in his seat to look at Helen, she was attractive and Christopher liked attractive young women. So worth a dull ache in his lower back to look closely at her face.

"Yes, although to be honest, I doubt if you would actually lose yourselves in the night. I guess, even as we speak, those two gentlemen we left behind, might well have now realised that they have been hoodwinked. So they will be back looking for you again, and trust me, dear Helen, no matter how good you think you are, they are better, a lot better. Staying with me will be a benefit to all of us."

"How do you know my name?" Helen retorted indignantly.

Christopher feared this was going to be a long conversation and an explanation was required. However uncomfortable it was going to be to hold that conversation in the confines of the Volkswagen Golf, it was still better than entering the McDonald's restaurant with its noisy children and abrasive adults.

"I do not just save random people from danger, if I did, I suppose I would be considered a super hero, which I am not. I know your friend Greg; we spoke on the telephone recently. I have followed some of your progress around France. I know you are very interested in the life of William Lynch. I know he is sadly dead. I know you are looking for something. I also know that neither of you know what you are looking for, which makes things a little difficult for you both. Yet that is something I could help you with. I also know that the person who instructed those two men to collect you on his behalf, would possibly kill you. I wager you did not know that. I also know that sitting here talking to you is uncomfortable and could potentially get a lot more uncomfortable if our two kidnappers start looking and find us. So before you both start asking a lot of questions, most of which I am sure I can answer, we need to be on our way. You left that house, I am guessing, with the intention of going somewhere, I am happy to take you there."

There was, for a moment, silence between the three of them, Helen sat back into her seat and Christopher turned to face forwards and resumed looking at then in the rear-view mirror.

"The number that William called each month that was you?" Greg asked.

"Yes, and I do not want to get into a long comprehensive conversation here for the reasons I have already adequately explained. If you will not give me any directions, I will just start driving. It is a lot safer to keep moving."

"You weren't very forthcoming during that telephone conversation either, so I am for leaving right now."

Greg released the door, opening it and a cold blast of wind and droplets of wintry rain entered the car. Helen also pulled back the lever opening her door, she was with Greg on this one, at least being away from this person, whoever he was, they would be able to make their own fate.

"Bad choice Helen, your father would not be impressed."

She stopped, leaving the door half open, the wind blowing her hair and chilling her fingers. The interior lights had come on, reflecting off their faces a cold yellow light.

"My father, how do you know my father?"

"You are Helen Taylor. I knew your father, Richard, worked at Barings Bank, very nice chap, very old school, we belonged to the same gentleman's club. Also a few times I visited your wonderful house at the weekend. If he was alive now, he would trust me, just as you should."

She closed her door with a loud thud, the noise of the wind stopped at once.

"You visited our house?"

"A few times, in the main I spent time with your father in the City."

The mention of those weekends when her father invited his friends, evoked strong, wonderful memories for Helen. She recalled those weekends with her father, and that they were fun weekends. Playtime and games in the garden, new adults to talk to, laughter, so much laughter. Much more exciting than the boring weekdays with just her mother and sister, and in that moment she felt a connection with her much-loved father.

"It is possible that my father knew you, he knew a lot of people in his business life and his personal life. We had many dinner parties on our terrace at the side of the house under the awning, so you could well have been there. Greg, maybe we should trust our driver, what other option do we have."

Christopher interrupted,

"Helen, you are so much like your father, slipping simple tests into your conversation. You know as well as I do that your father hated eating outside, even on that wonderful patio which was, in fact, at the rear of the house overlooking those beds of red hot pokers. Richard never once ate outside, not even a sandwich with afternoon tea. 'Neanderthal man may have eaten outside' he used to say, 'I'm modern man, and that is why we build dining rooms'."

"That sounds just like my father. I am now more inclined to believe you are telling the truth about your friendship with him."

"Hang on Helen, are you saying you know this man?"

"We were going to see Alice Clark, Holly Tree Cottage, Wotton Road, about five miles from here. She has something that might help us find what we are looking for. Close the door Greg, I think we need to and can trust this man."

"Hold on Helen, we don't even know his name," Greg argued.

"Call me Christopher. Can you direct me to Wotton Road?"

"This is madness Helen. Just because he says he knows your father; you don't know him. I could just as easily say I know your father. There is no reason to trust this guy."

Helen turned towards Greg, held onto his hand and smiled,

"Trust me, you know what I am capable of, so there is not much to worry about."

"Trust you, I hardly know you either. I've known you for a couple of days and I am not exactly comfortable placing my life in your hands, I've seen what those hands can do. Helen, we need to step out of this car and follow our own intuition. We've done alright so far, I can't see why we need the help of some overweight, middle aged man we have only just met."

"Done alright so far, are you that stupid Greg? You started off looking for some man who had taken himself off to France as a favour, well to be honest, you'd been thrown out of the paper and needed some money, so if it had been a missing cat you would have taken up the offer. Then somehow or other you have blundered into something, neither of us know anything about really, neither of us know what we are getting into. So if I am going to get into a maelstrom of shit, then I think I would rather be with someone like Christopher here, who seems to know what he is talking about, than a failed reporter like you."

"Fuck you Helen, go off into the night with the old man, I'll take my chances."

Again Greg opened the door, his leg stepping out into the rain, when Christopher looked at Greg in the rear-view mirror and began speaking.

"I will ignore your insults Greg, as I know you are still angry about your sister. Just don't make the same mistake again and walk away. Sticking together we are stronger and better placed to deal with whatever we come up against. William had a secret that we need to find to ensure it is kept secret. Stay in the car Greg and stay with us."

The mention of Greg's sister reignited the memories of those days before she took her overdose, days when Greg was young and immature yet thought he was able to make good decisions. He didn't walk away from her, that much Greg was sure of, but maybe he could have done things differently. Christopher seemed to know too much. Greg pulled his leg back inside the car and slammed the door hard. He did not want to expand the conversation about his sister.

"Just fucking drive," he curtly said.

Christopher was relieved to be finally driving away from McDonald's.

Greg, however, sat in the back, silent as his many jumbled thoughts overloaded his mind. Next to him sat Helen, who he had first met across the table of that French house. She seemed young, enthused, maybe slightly innocent for a national newspaper reporter, with no sign yet of the cynicism that so often took over reporters, and that had been just a couple of days ago. Since then he had seen her kill two men which, so far, seemed not to have touched her emotions. She continued to act as if nothing had happened, yet he knew it had, he had seen the life being pulled out of those men by her. Then, whilst still holding a body in her hands, she calmly removed it from the scene and disposed of it, like a true professional killer. How did she hide that when they first met? He wondered now just exactly who he was sitting next to. Now she admits to knowing, at least as a child, the man driving them to an address in south London. A man he had only just met, although it would seem he had spoken to him on the telephone, when he had given nothing away of who or what he was. For all Greg knew, both Christopher, if that was his name, and Helen were working together. If that was the case, he still could not understand the events of the past few days. Clearly there was something in all this that was attracting a good deal of attention from a number of quarters, unidentifiable quarters. Shadows and hazy images were all that Greg could see hovering around him, not least the shadow of his sister. Yet for all this, he wondered just how he had arrived here in the back of a Golf, between a murderess and a driver who, he still considered to be an abductor. The missing men that had all started this, where was the connection? Where was the logic? Greg wished he could just reason it all out.

NEW ASH GREEN.

Holly Tree Cottage was not an honest description, there was not a holly tree in sight, and it was not a cottage. Holly Tree Cottage was better known as sixty-seven Wotton Road, a small, white-washed terraced house with a fancy name. Once inside, it seemed to be even smaller than it had looked from the outside. The three uninvited guests sat on an odd selection of chairs around the small room. Its ancient two-bar electric fire replaced the open fire that had once been there, when the house was a simple 'two up, two down' house for farm workers, who would have worked at the long since disappeared hop fields, just a half mile away.

Alice answered the door to her late-night guests. The call from Mrs. Usher had irritated her, who did Mrs. Usher think she was, telling her that some people were coming round, it was past nine o'clock. Alice did not encourage any visitors, let alone three strangers during the late evening, but Mrs. Usher was, as ever, pushy and a pain. It was only because of her own curiosity, as to who the people might be who wanted to see a letter that her husband had written for William Lynch, that Alice agreed to answer the door.

Alice was old looking. Her face creased, craggy, with dry and tired skin that clung to her cheeks loosely, her hair, grey and wiry, untidy, unkempt, but just clean enough. As far as she was concerned her guests would have to take her as they found her, she was long past caring about what others thought of her appearance.

She stubbed her cigarette out in an already full ash tray, besides which lay the remains of a sandwich that she had earlier started to eat but not finished. She was a woman who looked isolated and not bothered about living now that her husband had passed away, the shock and grief still etched in her eyes.

"Les told me that when he died, I would need to pass this envelope onto William Lynch, an old school friend of his. At the time we just joked about it, thinking that it would be years yet." She lit another cigarette and drew in a deep lungful of smoke, exhaled into the room and continued her bitter memory. "It was only about five years later that he died, so sudden, so unexpected. He was my life, now that he has gone, I just can't see any reason to be here."

Alice offered the envelope to the three sitting around her, she did not know who she should give it to, although it was Christopher who took it from her nicotine-stained fingers.

"Of course, when he died, I tried to contact William Lynch, I had an address and a phone number, but they had moved. I spoke to some other old school friends of Les, and it seemed that William had just disappeared. Of course I kept it just on the off-chance. So it was sad to hear from Emily that William has also died, people die so young nowadays, leaving us behind. How is his wife taking it?"

"Upset," Christopher answered, he could not be sure, but it seemed the most appropriate response, "so tragic and so unforeseen, a car accident is such a shock, as is any death as I am sure you understand Alice."

Christopher opened the envelope and looked at what had been written on the single sheet of paper that was inside.

"Chess moves, just a number of chess moves," his voice sounded disappointed, as he handed the paper to Greg, he could feel the aggression that Greg exuded towards him and thought he needed to involve and bring him on side.

"Is that what you expected?" Alice asked, having never looked in the envelope. She would not have pried into anything her husband did when he was alive and that had not changed when he died.

"I never knew your husband," Christopher said, taking the paper back from Greg, becoming painfully aware that his clothes would smell of cigarette smoke once he finally left this slatternly house. His look or the tone of voice did not give away his disgust.

"Although I knew William and I would say that William did nothing without it having a purpose, I would guess your husband was the same. These chess moves have a meaning or a message of some sort, we just need to go away and find what that message may be."

Alice had not offered them any form of refreshment, as she did not want to encourage them to stay, the shorter the visit the better in her view. A view shared by her guests, who were all uncomfortable with the surroundings. Still, Alice did want an answer to one question.

"Why would my husband want to leave a message for his school friend?"

It was Christopher again who replied,

"If we knew that we would not need this piece of paper. What we do know is that William hid something from his employers, and this might help us to find it. Thank you for your help." Christopher stood up, Greg and Helen taking his lead also stood.

"Goodbye Alice, again thank you for your help."

SOUTH EAST LONDON.

It was decided, mainly by Christopher and Helen that they should drive back to Greg's flat. There, Christopher promised to spend time telling them what he knew in order to enlighten them both and lead, he hoped, to comprehending the message that appeared to be random chess moves.

They were still a couple of miles from Brockley, when Christopher pulled abruptly into the side of the road parking the car amongst a row of other cars which were parked alongside the road. Watching intently the rear-view mirror, he saw a car pull in and also park, maybe six or seven car lengths behind them.

"Why have we stopped?" Greg asked.

"Interesting, it looks as if they have found us already. There is a part of me that is pleased that our staff are so efficient."

Both Helen and Greg looked out of the rear window not sure what they were looking for. They were both jolted as the car pulled sharply away. Christopher re-joined the traffic and as he expected, the Ford Mondeo, pulled out from its own parking place and continued following them.

"I should have guessed, with so many automatic number plate recognition cameras dotted around our roads nowadays, it would not have taken them long to pick up this car. So, my fellow passengers, it is now down to me to lose them and it is up to the two of you to decide upon another location to go to. I imagine that your flat Greg will now be out of the question as will be your flat Helen, we need somewhere else that we can hold up for a few hours or at least overnight until we figure this whole thing out. I will do my bit now, while you consider, and don't expect much conversation from me until I have shaken off the Ford Mondeo with the two men behind us."

Christopher would not have admitted it out loud, it would just not have been in keeping with his position and status, but the thought of having to shake off a car that was tracking him, stirred up and revived all those memories and techniques he had thought he might have lost so long ago.

Back in the mists of time, in his early days as a civil servant, it was the Russians who were following him or being followed by him. In those days, it was a lot harder for those doing the following. There were no ANPR cameras, no mobile phone tracing, CCTV cameras, speed cameras, all of which were tools that could help those behind the target car. When he had first started, it was a turn of speed, a few sharp manoeuvres, a couple of double backs and a trip through a multi-storey car park and you were home and dry, just as long as Lady Luck was on your side that day.

Today, it would not be so easy to lose the Ford Mondeo, which was now following too close to be polite. Clearly they knew that he knew they were there, Christopher was going to have to start avoiding the major roads, where most of the cameras were placed. Mobile phones took longer to triangulate, so on a moving target it was not the best way to track anyone. Yes, he was going to enjoy this. He wondered if he still had it in him as he pushed his foot hard on the accelerator - he was soon going to find out. First of all he pulled away from the lights, well before they had changed, took a left and moved swiftly down a high street of shops.

"That was a red light," Greg pointed out the obvious.

"I doubt it will be the last one before the night is out, just let me do what I do best."

He turned on his satellite navigation system, its colourful screen projected a glow across his face as he regarded it and considered the streets around him. Modern technology could be just as useful to him. He took a right, between a chicken take-away and an all-night newsagent. The road was narrow, he drove just on the speed limit to see just how good his pursuers were at tracking him. He watched as they sped up and closed the gap between them and their target. Text book stuff, if your target was making a number of quick turns, you need to stay close, as it was clear to everyone both fox and hounds knew of each other's existence. Christopher drove into a small shopper's car park in order to go back the way he had come and back out onto the high street, once again they passed the chicken shop and the newsagent. The Mondeo was still behind him as he made a right turn into the high street to continue in the same direction as he had been driving previously. It was then a short way to a left turn, ignoring the no entry sign, Christopher sped up, hugging the left-hand side of the one-way street and annoying only three cars. Still his speed was not over the top for the roads around him, but it was interesting to see the Mondeo follow going against the traffic in the one-way street. Christopher, then continued left out of the one-way street into what looked to be the edge of an industrial estate. The road was clearer here, so it was easier to ignore the four sets of red lights, as he went through them building his speed, to enter a roundabout, listening to the voice of his instructor all those years ago, "Either brake hard or accelerate hard at roundabouts, anything else is just pussyfooting around." Christopher accelerated hard into the roundabout shocking a small white van. The third exit led onto a dual carriageway, which according to road signs and his satellite navigation screen joined a wider and faster dual carriageway. Now he would see what they were made of. He filtered into, what was in effect, a town motorway, once again he gunned the accelerator, which pushed the car towards the outside lane, then left his foot on the accelerator. There was some traffic around, not enough to hinder him, yet those vehicles that he had come up against in the outside lane were soon intimidated.

They might have been doing eighty miles an hour or maybe a little more, but when they realised there was a car almost touching the rear bumper of their car, they quickly moved out of the way. Again, the words of his instructor echoed in his head, "If you're an inch away from the car in front, at whatever speed they are doing, if they hit their brakes hard, you'll only become part of their car and push them into whatever they are avoiding, you'll have hardly a dent in your car."

Give them their due, Christopher conceded, the Mondeo was comfortable to follow at whatever speed Christopher drove at. They were happy to be there and watch, wondering if he would make a mistake. Christopher heard a few comments and oaths come from the back seat of his car, all of which he ignored. An exit approached, three hundred yard sign, he stayed in lane three, waiting and watching, judging the progress of other traffic. Two hundred yards, still in the high nineties. The Mondeo, now a little way back, wondered if he would take the exit ramp. One hundred yards, lane three, ninety-three miles per hour, Christopher decided. He turned the wheel, without braking, running over the cross hatching, throwing up dust and bouncing his passengers, a little dramatic he thought, but modern cars were rarely driven anywhere near their limits. So it was no surprise that the Mondeo pulled off and followed Christopher up the ramp.

"Well I have had my fun, so now it is time to see if we can shake these people off."

There was more of a country feel to where they were now, and Christopher soon noticed some roads ahead without street lights, now the enjoyment of the chase really begins. The road was now winding alongside field hedges with the occasional house and driveway. Looking at the satellite navigation, Christopher guessed he might have a mile before reaching a village, he looked for bends and evidence of a house soon after. He guessed and hoped it was a bend maybe forty five degrees to the left. There was going to be a house just on the left, he stamped hard on the brakes, turned the steering wheel to send the sliding car into what was a small lane, thankfully it had no gate, a bonus in Christopher's eyes. In the same instant he turned off his lights, bringing the car to a final stop with the handbrake. He did not want his brake lights giving him away. It could only have been a second or two later that the Mondeo flashed by the entrance. As soon as it did, Christopher reversed back out into the road without worrying too much if anything was coming; he knew that he would have to be very unlucky for a car to be coming along at that precise moment, and tonight he felt as though Lady Luck was on his side. Lights back on, he continued retracing his route the way he had come, intent on reaching the motorway before his pursuers realised they had lost him somewhere along that dark lane. He guessed that moment would occur to them when they reached the village and then they would turn around, thus giving him a good minute or two to get on the motorway and get off it before they knew just which direction he might have gone, let alone which exit he might have taken. They would then need to ask for some information from the ANPR, that would give Christopher another three to four minutes at least. By which time he would be only using small side roads and avoiding the bigger junctions. He loved his satellite navigation.

Christopher had not seen the Mondeo in his mirror for ten minutes now, as he drove carefully through housing estates and the back-waters of Kent. He felt a bit smug with himself, and deservedly so, he still had it in him. Part of him missed the excitement of working in the field, outwitting others. His thoughts turned back to the present, as he asked his passengers,

"So any ideas where we can go?"

"I have a friend, Donna, I am sure she'll help us," Greg offered and hoped he was right.

DEPTFORD.

Donna finished the sandwiches by cutting them into quarters, that way, piled high on a plate, there would look more than there really were. As it was, she was using the very last of her white bread and sliced ham, which she had ear marked for her lunch during the rest of week. It was a sacrifice she was happy to make for Greg, who had knocked at her door, looking tired and hungry. She would have preferred it to have been just him, so the two who followed Greg into her compact flat did nothing to endear her to the situation. Especially the young woman who was called Helen, who was possibly a little younger than her, and had both longer legs and a slimmer body. At least her hair was more of a mess than she would have imagined it would be for a woman who clearly had expensive taste in fashion. Her clothes, maybe a little bedraggled at the present, were no doubt designer and a lot more expensive than any hanging in her wardrobe. Donna wanted to know a little more about just how she fitted into Greg's life. For now, she was happy to help any friends of Greg.

Donna rented a small, ground floor flat in an unimportant residential development of twelve similar flats just off Deptford High Street, within a short walking distance of her work. It was a purpose built, one bedroom flat, with an open plan living area with integrated kitchen, sparsely furnished and with plain magnolia painted walls. With this open plan layout, as she made the sandwiches, she could hear the conversation between her three visitors. It sounded intense and hopefully when she learned more, she might find it interesting.

Helen sat listening to the older man, Christopher, as she wiped her hands with some sort of antibacterial gel, in an obsessional manner. Donna hoped that was normal for Helen and not an indication of her dislike of Donna's currently not too tidy flat, which she had truly planned to clean at the weekend but had instead spent most of the time shopping with a girlfriend.

Christopher accepted politely the sandwich that Donna offered him. It looked nothing like what he would have described as a sandwich; the white bread was thin and manufactured, not even medium sliced or wholemeal. From what he could see there was nothing contained within the sandwich but for an equally thin slice of ham, again he guessed manufactured into shape, not cut from the bone. As ever with so many of the lower classes, which on the whole he tried to avoid, there was no salad or green lettuce leaves inside the sandwich to give texture and moisture, just a limp slice of ham. Even so he still smiled politely, took the sandwich and ate it. It had been a long time since lunch and he very much doubted that there would be a restaurant around this area which would suit his taste, or hygiene requirements for that matter. His assumption was based on the large number of fast food shops they had passed as Greg had directed him through the back streets of Deptford. Many of Christopher's friends often spoke of finding small restaurants, offering native cuisines in the back streets of the many run-down areas of London, Christopher, for one, could never see the attraction of that.

Greg ate his sandwich without judging it; he simply enjoyed the sensation of eating and drinking Donna's coffee, and watching Christopher reluctantly eat his sandwich. Greg was still not convinced that Christopher was being as honest as he should be with them. Looking back, Greg felt he knew a lot but not enough, or as much as he should, about R.G. Plastics and just why William ended up in France. He still could not understand if there was a connection with the two missing men, or if this was just another incident that he had stumbled into. R.G. Plastics was destroyed, that was a fact, one of many that Greg started to turn over in his mind. William worked for the company and was not a casualty of the explosion; he was then transported to France. Whatever R.G. Plastics did, it would seem that it was something that was sponsored by the government of the day, and for some reason William was spirited away to France with his family. Now following his death, there appeared to have been renewed interest in, not just William, but Greg as well. His hotel room had been searched, and that had been followed by an attempt to abduct them from the Burger King car park and take them some place, and just a few hours later, once again someone wanted them taken off the street, for whatever reason Greg had no idea. Then at the critical point when Helen and Greg were about to be arrested by who Christopher now claimed were two men impersonating police officers, Christopher arrives on the scene like a white knight to save those in distress. The same man who had, more than likely, been in contact with William in France, and in Greg's opinion, was the person who had moved and supported William when his family were in France. Maybe Christopher did not want William to be found, maybe something that William had, he did not want to be uncovered, and that something could well be hidden behind the clues that had come into their possession. Maybe Christopher was not their white knight at all, maybe one of the white knights ended up under the wheels of Greg's car.

Christopher sat in silence for a moment, still wearing his pin striped jacket, tie and shirt, and still looking immaculate. Having finished his sandwich, he asked Helen for the two sheets of paper, which they had received from the two widows, but as she prepared to hand them to Christopher, Greg spoke out with his concerns,

"Let's be honest here, do we really know who you are Mr. Davenport? Do we know that you have our best interests at heart, or are you in this purely for yourself? If it was you that moved William Lynch to France, then why are you looking for what he seems to have hidden? If you really wanted it, why not ask him for it eight years ago? Why wait until now, when two people have stumbled into this situation? If we find it, will we be whisked away to France or maybe some other fate might await us?"

Christopher leaned back into the chair, relaxing in front of Greg in an arrogant way.

"Greg, let me ask you, do you know what you are actually looking for? Do the chess moves and numbers that you have talked about lead to something or could it be they are the prize that William has concealed? I'll answer for you, you have no idea. True, you may have gleaned a few facts from William's widow, and his friends, yet none of what you know so far helps you understand just exactly what you are on the edge of. You know something is there, what that something is you do not have a clue. That is why you need me, I have a better command of all, or at least most of the facts, so however uncomfortable you are about it Greg, you need to trust me."

"He's right," Helen added, "we need someone to help us through this maze, and if he is a friend of my father, then I think he deserves some trust."

"You forget Helen," Greg tried to counter her reasoning, "the man sitting over there had the power to tell, what appeared to be police officers, although I have no idea just who they really were, but he could tell them to go. He ordered them; he pulled some sort of rank on them. That does not endear me to trusting him, there are normally two sides to a story, I am not sure he is on the same side as ours."

"The trouble with that Greg is..." Christopher, stood up and removed his jacket, folding it carefully and laid it beside him as he spoke, "you have no real idea which side you are on or should be on."

Donna busied herself in the kitchen, wiping the worktops down with a cloth while still listening and taking in the ever increasingly sinister conversation, this resulted in parts of the worktop being cleaned with a vigour rarely seen in her kitchen before.

Christopher sat down again, he was contemplating Greg's dilemma and worries. Granted understandable worries given that they were all hiding from, who Christopher knew to be dangerous men, who were in turn being organised by an even more treacherous and devious civil servant called Reece Campbell. Both Helen and Greg did not have a clear picture as to just what they were implicated in, and he now only planned to give them enough to satisfy their curiosity and illustrate to them both that he, Christopher, was going to continue directing them, ensuring that he was the first to obtain what William had squirrelled away.

"Of course, you have every right Greg, as do you Helen, to know exactly what this is all about, I would just like to make it clear, that once I tell you some facts that I know, then both of you, and Donna who, can I say, makes excellent and most welcome sandwiches, will be under the official secrets act. I know you are both journalists, so if you have any ideas that any of this will appear in any newspaper, you are both being very naive. I have some very powerful people I can call on."

Christopher leaned forward and picked up his mug of coffee, it saddened him that these days young people never seemed to have cups and saucers, just huge thick mugs, which truly belonged with builders on a building site. Even so he smiled at Donna as he sipped the disappointing instant coffee.

"Starting at the beginning, there was a company called R.G. Plastics, a simple company based on the edge of a characterless industrial estate in Sevenoaks. Founded by Her Majesty's

Government, R.G. Plastics employed highly talented research scientists to develop a particular specialist military weapon. So there it was, a small, well-concealed research establishment for the Ministry of Defence, but in practice, for complex political reasons, operated by the Home Office, and hence my involvement."

He saw Helen open her mouth to ask a question, he guessed it would be requesting a greater explanation of the weapon, he was not prepared to give that to her so held his hand up to stop her speaking,

"Questions at the end please Helen."

For a moment Christopher recalled the young Helen playing in the garden whilst he visited her house, she had matured into an attractive young woman, much like her mother had been before her tragic accident. Such a loss, Christopher often wondered if under different circumstances Helen's mother might still be alive. If he had made different decisions back then, not have been as confrontational, or just acted the way any human being should towards another human being.

"R.G. Plastics and its staff worked hard over a number of years, coming close to what they had been tasked with. We were all very excited and pleased with their progress. Then one day a tragic accident befell the company, a fire and explosion resulted in the small but dedicated staff being killed. I would have thought you would have already known that as it was widely reported, the investigation showed it to be a tragic accident. Through a twist of fate on that day, William, did not get to work, he was the only member of the team left and had on his laptop, both relevant and valuable information from R.G. Plastics, which meant that the research could continue, albeit with a year or so delay. As I am sure you are more than aware, Governments are fickle and new Secretaries of State mean new directions and priorities. Sadly R.G. Plastics was no longer one of those priorities. Yet, William had a lot of information that could be of great benefit to, shall we say, those countries who are not enamoured to the ideals of the West. I decided it would be safer for everyone to ensure that William could not be traced, by setting him and his family up with a new identity and looking after them in another country, France was the chosen country. From there William contacted me at least once a month to assure me that he was still feeling comfortable and safe. The problem was that we could not be one hundred per cent sure that our secret research at R.G. Plastics had remained a secret. If information had seeped out along the espionage route, then it would have been highly likely that there was foreign interest in both William's laptop and the knowledge he held in his head. So you see for eight years everyone was happy, William and his family were enjoying a very enviable life style in France, I was happy that each time he called me he had little to say. That was until one day he told me about a reporter, asking about his previous work in the UK, which in itself would not present a large problem, if it was just that reporter."

Christopher gave the look of a dissatisfied headmaster towards Greg.

"But that reporter then decided to ask a few more questions that stirred up interest in R.G. Plastics and highlighted William's existence and where he was, interest coming from groups who do not have our country's wellbeing at heart. As I understand it, his death was a very tragic accident, it has however, left a question mark over what remains of the research R.G. Plastics took part in, and I suspect somehow those clues, in the form of chess moves, indicate just where we might find the information relating to the research that William carried out. I might add, before you ask, his death was an accident. As you know Greg, your arrival that night, revealing that you were fully aware of his real identity, gave rise to a panic in William. He was driving to call me, having already consumed a little too much wine, his driving was not as it should have been. The panic and the wine are not good companions to have when you are driving. If we are looking for those responsible, I would suggest that you Greg, played a part in his death."

Greg thought better than to respond to the barbed comment.

Without any enthusiasm Christopher finished his instant coffee and waited for the questions he was no doubt going to be bombarded with. They would be water off a duck's back for Christopher, fending off politicians could be a little difficult, two lowly and inexperienced reporters should be no problem at all.

"Who was Mick Hayes?" Helen asked, her eyes watching for any sort of reaction from Christopher, she received none at all.

Her eyes were so much like her mother's, crystal clear and incisive. Christopher recalled the last time he had seen those beautiful, alluring eyes, pleading for him to stay, maybe he should have stayed, but he did not.

"Mick Hayes works for me, and would have been in France, finding out as much as he could about Greg Auden, who was poking around in things he could have little idea of. Unless Greg was not a reporter and if that was the case Mick Hayes would find out for me. Talking of Mick, have you seen or heard from him, I have been expecting a call from him?"

Helen spoke first again, "No," regretting her denial as soon as she had spoken.

Christopher came back with the quickest retort, "So how do you know Mick Hayes?"

This time it was Greg who answered, "He was poking around in my room, going through my suitcases."

"Which I would expect as he was trying to find out if you really were a reporter."

"Then he got a little too physical with me, hands around the neck."

"Well that was uncalled for; I will speak to him when I see him next."

"You won't be speaking to him for a long time; Helen stepped in and killed him."

"She did what?" Christopher continued to show little emotion, "you actually killed Mick Hayes?"

Donna, who had now finished cleaning the work top and was now busying herself moving jars around, felt her legs go weak as she heard what Helen had done. A murderer, Donna was starting to feel both a little uncomfortable and nervous, wondering just where this evening might end up. Helen looked almost like a guilty school girl as all eyes in the room fell upon her, before she hauled up her shoulders into a shape of defiance. Donna's eyes widened dramatically when she had heard that Helen was a killer, she was sure such a woman would not suit Greg's mild manner.

"He was murdering my friend; it was self-defence and I would do it again given the same circumstances. Mick Hayes seemed to be willing to kill, he just came up against a superior person."

"He often was a little dramatic. I'm sorry he tried to strangle you Greg, although I doubt if he would actually have killed you that was never in his instructions. If he did overstep the mark then so be it, sad but these things happen. So what have you done with his body? Have you stashed it away somewhere? I am not aware of any communication from the French police."

Donna continued to remain silent and stunned throughout the conversation. Greg's female companion, she still could not work out what sort of relationship there was between them, and now it turns out she is a murderer, who shows little sign of remorse. It was more of a nervous reaction that prompted Donna to ask,

"More coffee anyone?"

Christopher refused, having had more instant coffee than he ever wanted in his life; Greg requested another, keen to learn more of R.G. Plastics and Helen just stared at Christopher and told him,

"I doubt if you will ever find his body, I like to keep things tidy."

"Did you find killing him easy?"

Donna was surprised how calm and uncaring Christopher's voice was when he asked the question. She had read about people being cold and unemotional, but this Christopher guy, well he had just been told that one of his work colleagues had been, not just killed but, murdered by the young lady sitting opposite him and he asks her about it as if he was asking about the weather on her holiday.

"To satisfy your obvious curiosity, yes it was easy, a natural reaction. But now I want to know just who else might be interested in this so-called information that William has hidden away, and I want to know who those people are who have tried to arrest us and are still out there looking for us. If they are some sort of foreign power, would you be able to call up the secret service and get us out of this mess?"

"Interesting," Christopher spoke, his mind distracted; Helen was a remarkable and resourceful young lady that was becoming abundantly clear.

Donna decided that this Helen was only asking as she wanted to kill someone else. At that point Donna wondered how much interest she should show in Greg in case Helen was the jealous type.

"You don't seem to be that shocked or surprised that Helen has just admitted to killing someone," Greg said, knowing how he had felt when he saw Helen kill right before his eyes.

"Helen, I have always known to be a very extraordinary person who is able to do things others of us can only imagine."

"That is an odd answer."

Christopher looked across at Helen and smiled. "Whatever she does, her father, I know, was always proud of her."

Greg decided to stop what was becoming a weird conversation and stood up and walked over towards the kitchen where Donna was boiling a kettle in preparation for more coffee. There he put his arm around her waist, looked into her eyes, and spoke to her making sure his voice was loud enough for all the room to hear.

"There is no foreign power, just those who tried to arrest us, kidnap us or whatever you want to call it, yes, Donna, it has been an interesting afternoon. Those false police officers who had us handcuffed knew Christopher and knew him well. Well enough for them to do exactly as they were told and let him take us. I am starting to wonder just who Christopher actually is and who he is working for. Helen was more than happy to trust him as there is some connection between her father and Christopher, yet I for one, sweet, trustworthy Donna, am beginning to doubt that we are on the right side of the tracks."

He kissed her affectionately on the forehead and took his coffee from the work top leaving Donna speechless.

Christopher looked calm and untroubled by the inference that Greg had made, he treated it as he would any other question,

"From your viewpoint Greg, you are unable to judge which is the right or wrong side, if there is such a thing. If I told you everything that I know about R.G. Plastics and those things that have happened since its closure, it would not help you and you would still be unable to decide who is right and who is wrong. I am bound to portray the other side as the bad one, yet I could equally be the bad one. Meeting the other side and talking to them might help you reach a conclusion, yet I doubt it would be reliable. In the end we have to trust someone or something, my only saving grace is that I knew Helen's father, which I am sure counts for something, and also, I have all the clues here in my hand, what use do I have of you now."

Greg throughout his life had put his trust in people only to be disappointed in the end. As a child his parents did nothing to help him when his sister took her own life, and now the Deptford Chronicle had pushed him away. Every relationship that Greg had placed his trust in seemed to just wash away, so being asked to trust a complete stranger was going to be hard.

"So what have we got to lose?" Helen asked. "The worst thing will be Christopher here gets what he wants, and we get nothing out of it, other than maybe losing a few days of our lives, at least we can tell our grandchildren about it."

Christopher listened to Helen's words, yes, he mostly did get what he wanted, but often others lost out because of it.

"Greg, I can help to fill in some of the gaps, not all, but some and together we can find whatever it is William has hidden away."

Greg looked at Donna, maybe the only person who would not betray his trust. If only he could relax around her and let her into his life; it was just that he did not want to mess up her life like the other lives he had messed up before. Donna sensed that he wanted to ask her a question, an unspoken question that she was happy to answer.

"Greg, we are all just a very small cog in a very big wheel, where not all cogs are created equal, whatever people say. In the end we get taken wherever the wheel goes, and it is always people like that Christopher who are steering us in our lives. 'Posh Un's' like Christopher rule our lives and set our rules and targets, rules that they never seem to obey."

Greg returned and sat on the arm of the chair where Helen sat; he sipped the hot coffee and looked at his watch.

"It's getting late, I am getting tired, and I sense it will be a long day tomorrow, so I suggest kipping down here on Donna's floor, assuming she is happy with that. But first, so that I can sleep, you tell me exactly what this is all about, who the other side are, tell me more and let me make my own mind up. I still might be wrong, but at least I will be better informed."

Christopher took a deep breath, picked up his jacket and started to talk.

"Well if we are going to have to sleep here, I presume there is only one bed, so I might well end up on this reasonably comfortable chair. I had better try and draw some trust from your sceptical mind, or else, Helen might well decide that I would make a second murder victim."

He handed the paper with the chess moves back to Greg, who was tempted to tell him he might be her third victim, instead he just sat back and listened as Christopher started to explain.

"The purpose of R.G. Plastics was to find a simple chemical that could be added to the food and drink of soldiers to strengthen their resolve. Take away the natural fear that any human has, make them fearless, happy to run towards blazing guns. It had been done successfully before for a whole host of things; chemicals to reduce soldier's sex drive, preparations which enabled soldiers to stay awake long hours, even to reduce their need for food, so removing fear was an obvious idea. R.G. Plastics did well and came up with a preparation that was added to daily vitamin pills that soldiers take, food additives. I should explain at this point the name R.G. Plastics came from the fictitious people Ron and Gerry Moss who were directors of the company, in case anyone started asking questions at Companies House, normal procedure for many of our activities. Following the fire, the then government of the day decided that they did not want to continue. Reece mentioned how valuable what we had would be to another country – he was thinking of an Arab country – and that it would be worth maybe millions. Imagine, you would be able to choose your suicide bomber, not just pull one from a pool of fanatics. Potentially you could turn a decent businessman into a fighting machine, a fearless fighting machine. So when Reece heard that not all was lost, William had retained much of the valuable information on his laptop at home, he decided that he wanted to lay his hands on that for the obvious financial gain. Hence, I took William off to France and placed him in hiding, leaving Reece waiting on the side lines like a vulture waiting to pounce. He would happily kill me, but for the reason that I was the only link to where William was. So he waited, a very patient man is Reece, now he knows almost as much as we do about William, and wants the information that is hidden away, with these chess moves being the only clue as to their location."

"Why not report this Reece fellow?"

"He is, like myself, a very influential civil servant, making allegations is one thing; making them stick is another, especially when the subject matter is based on such a secret project. We need to get to the information, laptop, however William has stored it, and I for one, would be in favour of destroying it."

"I'm not convinced," Greg said, "so I am going to sleep in the corner over there and see who has been murdered come the morning. Maybe if we are all still here, I might start trusting you."

*

Donna did not sleep that well at all. Most of the time she laid awake, huddled under her duvet, patterned with bold yellow and black stripes, looking in the darkness like a large wasp sleeping on the double bed. Donna was unsure of what the next few days might bring her way, the main reason was that she had no clear idea as to what she was exactly getting herself involved with. Scared was where she was, scared of the unknown and maybe unimaginable consequences. She was more than a little confused by her current house guests and the topics of their conversations. When Greg had turned up with those 'come to bed eyes' of his, she knew she was not going to resist anything that he might ask of her. So the two strangers that followed him in, were not of too much concern to her, her thoughts were still recalling Greg standing naked in the shower. The elderly man, smart, yet old-fashioned in his dress, carrying his trilby hat, who had a slightly arrogant, haughty air about him seemed friendly enough, although he did seem to turn his nose up slightly as she handed him a mug of coffee. The young lady, who made up her trio of guests, was very stuck up. Waltzing into Donna's flat with a confident stride and looking around the flat as if she was inspecting it for dirt and dust, which maybe she was, given the number of times she pulled out her small plastic bottle of antiseptic gel. Whatever Donna might have thought, they did appear to be friends of Greg's, so they were welcome to share her flat for whatever reason they had. It was only as she listened to the conversation as it developed during the long evening: secret research, government scientists, explosions and fires, tragic deaths, that she wondered just what she had opened her door to. Even now she was not sure if she had heard it right, but was a little too embarrassed to ask more questions. Helen appeared to admit to a murder. That just did not seem right, she didn't look like a murderer, or maybe Donna should just make a new assessment of what she thought a murderer should look like. So she was not that surprised that she had not slept well, thankfully no one had asked her to share her bed, not even Greg. As, however much she would have welcomed him at another time, she would not have been comfortable inviting him to sleep alongside her with the presence of other house guests in the adjoining room.

Donna had begun to wonder if she might have dreamt the whole evening. Searching through some old newspaper reports for Greg in connection with two missing men, had seemed like innocent fun, a distraction from the everyday monotony of the Deptford Chronicle newspaper. With the added bonus of spending more time with Greg, getting closer to him and becoming part of his life, it had felt good. Yet now, with strangers in her house, everything had changed, conspiracy talk, almost being arrested, that was a reality check. A person killed in a car crash, sad and tragic, then an admission of murder, no attempt to cover it up. From a pleasant time spent with Greg helping him, it had now turned into a nightmare, where Donna had begun to fear for her life. She was caught up in a situation, not of her own making, that only her kindness had drawn her into. So now lying in her own bed, she felt scared, scared to a height she had never felt before. She had wedged a chair against her bedroom door, just in case, she had seen that in the movies, and hoped that it would work a lot better than she had seen in the movies.

Helen dozed lightly on the thinly carpeted floor, covered with an old, slightly yellowing duvet that Donna had found deep inside one of her cupboards. Her mind was not letting her sleep, there was too much to digest, excessive amounts of inputs that required processing. She would have liked to have sat down and worked through the chess moves, to try and understand the meaning of the information that William had left behind. Reluctantly she had agreed with the other two that working on problems with tired minds, was not the best way to solve any puzzle. Better wait until the morning, after a good night's sleep, but Helen could not sleep. She looked across at Greg, bent awkwardly in a chair, breathing lightly, then at Christopher, snoring quietly, his head resting against a patterned cushion that Donna had provided.

Then there was the aftershave that continued to drift across the room from where Christopher was sleeping. A fragrance which continued to torment Helen as she tried to place it. She had not easily recalled Christopher visiting her house at weekends with so many other guests, eating, drinking and laughing, in fact she could not recall him at all. The more she tried to place the sensation, the further back she was travelling through her memories. The smell of his aftershave seemed to evoke dark memories, a time of terror; she searched and searched her mind. Finally in the relative darkness of the room, her memory, like an overwhelming tidal wave, flooded back to when she was a child, a young girl. She was out in the garden painting her flowers, when her mother screamed out for her. There was no one else in the house, it was the servants' day off and her sister was shopping. How could she have forgotten, she had only relived these moments a day or so ago with Phillip, memories that she had never shared with anyone before. She had run into the house and found her mother lying at the bottom of the stairs, shouting at her terrified daughter. It was there, she had forgotten, hanging in the hallway unseen was that aroma, that aftershave, heavy and pungent, distinctive. Yet at the time pushed to one side, ignored as she considered the situation of her mother lying injured on the floor and how best to take advantage of her mother's predicament. The aftershave belonged to her mother's lover, Christopher? There must be hundreds of men who have the same aftershave, Helen reasoned with herself. He said he was her father's friend, but men lie, that Helen knew well. Why was that aftershave, hanging in the air at the time, so fresh, so pungent? There could only be one reason, Christopher had only just left the hallway. Had he been there moments before her mother fell. Had he witnessed it? Had he pushed her?

Fear engulfed Helen, if he was there, had he seen her come rushing in, then left, wanting to preserve the secrecy around their affair. Had he presumed that Helen would care for her mother, get help, assistance, help that only later came. If Christopher was there, had he left for his important meeting or only once he heard her coming and if that was the case, then he would have known that the inquest said the ambulance was called a lot later during the day. He would have known that Helen ignored or refused to help her mother. Christopher would know that Helen had caused her mother's death, equally, Christopher could have pushed her down the stairs in the first place. Helen began to wonder if her trust in Christopher might be misplaced. She recalled what Christopher had said about her earlier that evening, 'Helen, I have always known to be a very extraordinary person who is able to do things, others of us can only imagine.' Did he know the truth about how Helen's mother died? That was the frightening question that kept Helen awake until the early hours.

Donna had dipped in and out of a light sleep throughout the night. She looked, through sleepy eyes at the time, five past five. As she turned over, attempting to slip back into her sporadic sleep, she was startled to hear a loud cracking sound, followed by what she could only describe as wood breaking and splintering. It was very loud, in fact it sounded as if it was in her flat. Within the sleepy part of her mind she could not be sure, until the shouts of "Armed Police!" echoed loudly and clearly from the other room. Under the voices, heavy footsteps were moving swiftly through the flat and coming closer to her. A moment later a tall dark figure appeared at her bedroom door, shouting "Armed Police!" and pointed what looked to be a gun at her. Donna felt no fear or indignation, she just held her hands high up extracting herself from her warm wasp like duvet, surrendering and resigning herself to the way her daily routine had changed over the last twelve hours, and felt relieved that she had worn a nightdress last night.

Donna was directed out of her bedroom in just her nightdress, hands held together in front of her with cable ties, into the living area of the flat. She looked at her front door, broken and hanging oddly from the broken hinges, splinters of the wooden door frame across her carpet. Greg, Helen and Christopher sat in a timid row on the settee, hands similarly held with cable ties. Two clearly armed men, darkly dressed with balaclavas covering all but their eyes, stood behind their captives, looking official and in control, no longer threatening, or not as threatening as the one who had come into her bedroom. To her right, standing close to the kitchen worktop, were two men dressed in jeans and padded bomber jackets. The taller one spoke to the armed police officer behind Donna,

"Just the four of them?"

"Yes sir." The answer was not only curt, Donna thought, it was also deep and sexy.

"OK, take her back into the bedroom, cut her ties and let her put a dressing gown on or something, and stay with her."

Donna was taken back into the bedroom; strange thoughts came into her mind, could the day get any weirder. Once she was back in there, she heard the conversation start.

"Well Mister Davenport Wellington, we meet once again....."

The armed police officer closed the door turning the conversation into a muffled sound that she could not hear clearly. As she slipped on a dressing gown, she could hear muted voices and managed to make out the odd word, but none of it made any sense. She sat on the bed, with the police officer standing close to the door, in silence. It was about five minutes later, or perhaps a little more Donna could not be sure, when the door opened and another of the armed officers came into the room, this time his balaclava mask removed, revealing a strong jaw line, lightly stubbed in a fashionable way, and clear blue sensual eyes.

"They've taken the other three, we just need to stay until the local boys get here to sort out the door damage. This young lady is free to go, and we are to assist where necessary."

The officer who had been in the bedroom with Donna removed his mask, revealing an African face whose brown eyes looked apologetic, as indeed they were.

"We're sorry about having to burst in this morning. We'll arrange for the damage to be repaired and if there is anything else we can do to help you, let us know. We have the people we needed to arrest. It would seem our detective friends have no further questions or use for you, so you can go back to your normal life madam."

Donna wondered how life could ever be normal again after she had stood in her bedroom, dressed only in night clothes in the presence of two very attractive police officers, normal was not on the agenda.

BEXLEY, KENT.

The whole room stank of rotten cabbage in addition to other odours which were best not described. Reece Campbell despaired at times at the standards that his two, so called assistants, had, they just did not seem to reflect their correct job title of 'senior executive assistants'. He knew they had access to a variety of places, where they could discreetly take people to talk to them, to resolve any problems that they might be having. They had to be inconspicuous venues, as sometimes the way problems were resolved might not fit well with the Civil Service environment in London. Even so, Reece thought they could have at least chosen somewhere which was not a cold, dank, industrial unit that stank of rotten cabbage. In his frustration, he kicked a lone innocent chair over. The sound of its rusty metal frame echoed around the graffiti strewn concrete walls. The other occupants of the industrial unit just watched without passing comment. Reece walked around the three detainees, examining them all.

Christopher, he knew well, they had both risen through the ranks of the Civil Service very much on a par but for different departments, different job titles, different countries and different morals. They had worked at their closest when they had both spent seven years in a counter espionage unit of MI5. It was a misleading title, as most of their work was identifying leaks within government and watching out for weaker links in foreign embassies and trade delegations. They identified them and passed on information. They had spent time doing exactly what Reece still continued to do. Whisk people away in the dead of night, threaten to expose some dark secret the confused and scared victim might have and which they hoped had been well hidden, in exchange for a few titbits of unassuming information, simple, easy and one off, and their secret would not be revealed to the world. The victim relieved that it was such a simple solution would agree readily, anything to ensure their dark secret remained a secret. But it was never a one off, it was always just the start, just one more slice of information, to add to a deeper knowledge, maybe pass this back to your government. Deeper and deeper the reluctant spy would be dragged until they could never escape. They had been snared and were now a puppet, controlled and directed at the whim of people like Reece or Christopher. The only way blackmail might end would be death or exposure, yet exposure often brought bad publicity to Her Majesty's Government and to a foreign government, so death was always the preferred mutually agreed option of both governments. The poor soul with the dark secret had little choice, unless they had some hold, some leverage that ensured they were needed to remain alive.

In his day he would never have chosen such a dismal place to talk discreetly, he would need to speak to his assistants at a later date, but for now, he looked at the three, lightly manacled with cable ties, and gave Christopher a complacent look. Christopher returned a definite rebellious look, the indignity of being held captive and for now being put to one side. Reece gave a curt glance at Greg and Helen; he would assess them later. They had a value although not of much interest at present for Reece, it was going to be a lot more fun toying with Christopher.

"Well Christopher," Reece began, standing in front of his former colleague, arms folded, his head tilted to one side. "It looks as though I will get my way after all. Notwithstanding your many efforts and maneuvering, I still find myself within reach of all that, you would have us believe, was lost all those years ago at R.G. Plastics. I have always admired your tenacity. Still it would have been a lot easier if at the time, you had simply asked William to hand over what he had and then we could all have gone about our lives in peace."

Christopher looked up at the figure now towering above him in a smartly pressed grey herring bone suit, which Christopher hoped would be reeking of this malodorous warehouse when Reece eventually left, which he would. Reece never stayed anywhere but his office for very long. Christopher was sure that Reece always deep down felt vulnerable, when he was not safely seated behind his desk.

"And you," Christopher added in rebuttal, "will have long since retired, having sold the secrets William held on to, having sold them to the highest bidder. You will be living in peaceful tranquillity in some secluded corner of the globe, whilst the rest of us will be living in a much less stable society."

"Yes," Reece coldly agreed, "yet you were more than happy to hold onto the information and not destroy it. I wonder how tempted you are to sell to the highest bidder; your mere presence here testifies to your interest."

"If I had the details, I would have destroyed every scrap of research, documentation, test tubes and computers to ensure that no one got close to what we had achieved at R.G. Plastics. It was, as you know, a potentially dangerous drug, that should have made the United Kingdom a stronger world force, but if it got into the wrong hands, it would have rocked the very fabric of our society. So when, as you recall, we were jointly told to destroy everything and everyone, I had no hesitation doing so, although when it became clear that we had missed one employee, that employee was very shrewd in using the information as an insurance on his life. He clearly realised that he was going to suffer the same fate as his deceased colleagues. For that reason, he had kept the information that he had well away from prying eyes and ears, especially your prying eyes and ears. I never knew just where he had concealed the information, and hidden it well, he certainty had. He showed me the laptop which he had for some obscure reason, although fortunately for him, he had it at his house. He gave it to me, saying that he had downloaded everything to a safe location."

Helen and Greg listened as the two former colleagues traded words.

"I had no choice but to hide William from you," Christopher continued. "You Reece, who knew exactly what those secrets were worth and would do anything to lay your hands on them, so I acted as a high security fence between you and the secrets of R.G. Plastics."

"So why not simply kill him Christopher, and have done with it? Your hands were already awash with the blood of others, so what difference would one person make, his secret would have gone to his grave."

Christopher negatively shook his head.

"That was always one of your weaknesses, not considering all the possibilities; you just consider the ones you think are important. I could easily have ended William's life; it would have been just tying up the loose ends. There again, I considered that even from beyond the grave, William might just like to ensure everything was exposed publicly, so I could not really dispose of him. These two unfortunate people alongside me are only here because William has left such a trail that will lead, I am sure, to the documentation of all the processes that were carried out at R.G. Plastics. He dies in a tragic car accident, and at once two members of the public have clues to the location of where those secrets are hidden. Also they were our hands Reece, our hands had blood on them, you will recall I just wanted information destroyed; killing fellow workers was never in my comfort zone. You were more than keen to carry out orders, knowing with everything gone, if you did have the information of how to manufacture the drug, it would be worth a fortune to you."

Reece turned his back and walked away from the three seated people towards his two assistants. They looked confused as they listened to the conversation, he wondered at what point his two assistants would realise the more they learned today, the less likely it was they would make retirement.

"To be fair to myself,"

Reece spoke towards his two assistants, who were still standing and watching the three seated hostages, although they clearly understood their boss was not talking to them.

"It was never my original intention to sell any secrets to anyone, I was happy to wipe the slate clean and move onto the next project. So when it became clear that William was alive with a computer full of all the research information and detailed manufacturing data, then yes, I did consider what that information might be worth on the open market. I did my sums and the temptation was too great to resist, any man has his price, even you Christopher. So yes, from that point on, I did want William and his knowledge."

Reece, turned back towards the three. He looked at Greg, there was fear and uncertainty in his eyes. The woman had a different look in her eyes, concern, observing, listening and no doubt planning, she seemed to be an interesting person. If what he had heard was true, she appeared to have shown no emotion when running over and killing one of his staff. She didn't look the killing type and that interested Reece, who was always looking out for people who might be able to help him.

"Christopher, the great thing about all this is that we are both equally guilty, both equally vulnerable to each other, secure in the fact that we are tied to such a tragedy. I could not have you killed, too many questions would be asked. Maybe once I have all the research safely in my possession, and I am positive you can be of no use to me, well it would be no surprise if someone of your age had a heart attack, now would it? So maybe it is best if you go for now. I have these two slips of paper, which are clearly clues as to the whereabouts of William's secret, well it is a government secret really, but that is neither here nor there, I have what I need of that I am sure."

As scared as he was at all the talk of murder and clandestine activities, and in no small part having his hands tied and being held against his will, which did nothing to reduce his fear, Greg still butted into the conversation,

"So can someone explain to me just why Christopher cannot have you guys arrested for abduction to say the least?"

Reece looked down at Greg, noticing a bead of nervous perspiration on his brow.

"Maybe you have not been listening closely enough, fear does that to you sometimes. Christopher is just as guilty as I am. Between us, acting on orders, we in effect wiped out R.G. Plastics and all the staff who worked there. Whichever way you dress it, we murdered those people, not to mention some of those who helped us to achieve our dark goal. We both have a lot of blood on our hands and those whose orders we were following have the power and the protection to deny everything we might say and put us both away for many years in a prison. If I go down, so does Christopher and vice-versa, simple really. So I am happy for Christopher to walk out and go back to his desk and get on planning his not too distant retirement. I, on the other hand, need that something that William Lynch had, and I am guessing one or both of you might have some thoughts and ideas as to what these chess clues mean, or you might even still be concealing something more from me."

This time Helen asked the question,

"So what is the secret that William Lynch has that is so valuable yet so dangerous that the British government would have people killed? You might have it but there was no need to use it." Her voice was steady as she looked at Christopher, who was sitting next to her. Once again she inhaled his cologne, bringing back memories from her childhood, stirring emotions as she began placing the times in her childhood that she had inhaled that sweet smelling cologne. Was he really her mother's lover? Did he know her mother fell down the stairs? And did he know that Helen had allowed her to die at the bottom of those stairs?

Christopher looked into her eyes, his own still had a firm confident look to them.

"A simple drug, as I have mentioned to you. The politics are more complex," he confessed, and repeated to ensure the two faux detectives knew exactly what this was all about, as he doubted Reece would have shared much, if any, information with them. "That would block fear in our armed forces, when added to their food. A little like bromide in the tea that was so effective in the previous world wars to curb sex drives. This drug would make our troops fearless; fear would not be anywhere in their psyche. The drug blocks the fear receptors and we then have an army that would act on instructions without any thought or fear of the consequences. So at R.G. Plastics we developed the drug and perfected it as instructed, a job well done. Yet as ever in politics, things change and the priorities and personalities of the powerful alter. There was faint concern that should this drug get into the hands of any drug dealers or gang leaders, those despicable people who frequent the ghettos of our inner cities, well if they had the drug, how would they use it? Give it to their drug runners and those who do their dirty work, the kids you see, who have no better way of living. Education has given up on them, their parents have disowned them, so the only family that they can become part of is the local gang. Selling drugs and handing out violence, kids maybe as young as ten, being arrested by police. Those kids now with no fear will fight and fight the police, violence on small and large scale would be very likely. The first time a ten year old fights the police and is killed in the process, the papers will have a field day. The second time questions start being asked, the tensions will rise and the consequences could be political suicide. Plus, if it ever came out that it was the government that had developed the drug in the first place, well a lot of MP's and minsters would soon need to look for something else to do. So that was why we were instructed to destroy all traces of it, to ensure that no MP had to face the question of just where the drug had come from. Our Lords and masters considered eight deaths in an explosion to be an acceptable price to pay."

Christopher turned to look at Reece, while still answering Helen.

"I very much doubt that Reece will be selling to any local gang member, I would guess it will be some regime that has plenty of money and ambition." He turned back to face Helen, with just a faint glimmer of a grin, dawning over his mouth, "R.G. Plastics, was just one of those political whims, it seemed like a good idea at the time, cost effective, a cheap way of strengthening our armed forces, so money in millions was pumped into it. Then the political mood changes and the whole thing is cast aside, regarded as a leper and destroyed, people as well, they are of no consequence to our masters. Reece and I are lucky in part, we are the barriers, the defences if you like to those who make the grand decisions. We stay simply in case this thing comes to light, and then we become the scapegoats, it will have been us, our fault. Which to a point it most likely is, we do exactly what we are told to, compliant and malleable, which ensures our promotion and status within the organisation and that becomes our profit. And before you left-wing journalists go on about high morals, you know as well as I do, that is the way of the world, a few very powerful people, whose bidding is done by those who want just a taste of that power."

"Please Christopher, spare us the sermon," Reece signalled that he should be untied. "let the old man go back to his office and prepare for retirement."

Christopher said no more, he rubbed his newly released hands and walked out through the door that was to the side of the roller shutter without turning back, leaving Helen and Greg to their fate.

As if he was at some family social event, Reece sat down on the scruffy wooden chair that Christopher had vacated and leaned close to Helen.

"I have at my disposal some very intelligent cryptographers, who will relish the challenge of these chess notations. I will be interested what they tell me. I don't suppose you have any further information that you might wish to share with me?"

"Even if I did, I wouldn't," Helen spoke so close to Reece's face that he felt her breath on it.

"I guessed as much, but I thought I would politely ask anyway. I will leave you for now, in the very capable hands of my two friends here and they will do their best to make you as comfortable as any deserving abductee deserves, which is not a lot. If I need you, I will call, although I am confident that William was not that clever at writing cryptic clues, he might have been good at chemical expressions but puzzles, not so."

With those few words, Reece left the foul, smelly warehouse and was pleased to walk out into the grey morning with its wintry drizzle, however wet it was, the air was fresher and far better than inside.

*

All four had sat in silence for the best part of an hour before it was broken. Helen and Greg could do no more than sit and stare at a dusty, dirty wall. Their two guards were playing on their mobile phones, some simple-minded game with fruits and sweets, passing the time, a skill they had perfected over a number of years working with Reece. Absorbed in their games, Helen and Greg made facial expressions to talk in silence, Helen nodding and indicating towards a stool just to the left of Greg, which had on its seat a small shard of glass that would be capable of slicing through the plastic straps around their hands. Once Greg had realised what Helen was saying he carefully extended his leg towards the wooden stool. Half watching their sentinels engrossed in their games, his foot moved closer to the leg of the stool. Carefully hooking around one of its legs, he pulled gently, knowing that any scraping sound on the concrete floor might draw the attention of their guards and put paid to the attempt. Slowly and carefully the chair moved, under his direction toward him ever closer, the glass glinting and tempting. He did not see Helen, yet he felt her encouraging looks as the stool was almost against him, its movement silent and careful. As Greg continued to edge the stool towards him, his mind wandered into the scenario, what if the stool fell, echoing around the cavernous room, alerting the two occupied men to what Greg was attempting to achieve. Would they just kick the stool further away from him or would they take a greater retribution, just to teach him a lesson, pain was not a favourite sensation for Greg. Still he continued moving the stool a few centimetres at a time. Just another couple of tugs and he might be able to lean forward and somehow pick up the glass shard and then carefully cut through first Helen's cable tie and then she could cut his own. Hopefully that movement would not bring attention to what they were trying to do. After that he did not want to think just what might happen and what they would do, it would be at that point that confrontation would be inevitable. He knew if he thought too much about the possible consequences of pulling the stool towards him, he might well stop and lose the opportunity of the glass freeing them.

That had always been his problem, thinking of the consequences, of what might happen to him, not what might happen to others. Greg wondered if he had not worried about the consequences when he was a teenager, if his sister would still have been alive today. She did not think of the consequences when she asked him for help, fully expecting that he would give it, stand up for her, after all he was her older, bolder brother, or so she thought. He wished he had been bolder then. 'I'm going to the police, I have to,' that was what she had said, across that cafe table all those years ago, "Will you come with me?" that was all she asked of him, her older brother, a brother she had always looked up to and trusted. He said no, he recalled his exact words, that he had replayed in his mind time and time again as the years went by. 'You're just being silly Brenda, it will only cause lots of trouble and arguments,' there he was again thinking of the consequence. 'You don't believe me, do you?' she accused him. Greg was not sure what he believed, what he did guess was that believing his sister could lead to heaps of trouble, which he would prefer to avoid. 'I'll go to the police with or without you.' And he had said, 'you'll regret it Sis if you do, trust me.' But it was Greg who regretted it in the end, not going with her. When the police did come to question him, he just denied everything, she was mistaken, confused, a misunderstanding, they were the answers he gave. When Brenda heard the police were taking it no further, she felt totally isolated and scared.

The two men playing childish games had pistols, he did not want to consider what they were capable of. The silent journey of the stool was now almost complete. Greg prepared himself to pick up the glass, the extra movement that he would need to twist and pick it up would be harder to do covertly. He had to try now, he had to ignore the consequences, whatever they might be.

Without warning the silence and tension was broken by a muffled phone ringing from within Helen's jacket, which immediately became the centre of attention for everyone in the room.

"Best answer that, it will be my editor wanting to know where I am. I should have been in the office this morning. Some of us have real jobs you know."

The taller one moved across to Helen.

"Top pocket," she said, "and be careful where your hands go," she threatened.

Greg looked as the man approached, would he or his companion notice the small wooden stool had somehow moved and was now within touching distance of him.

As he pulled the mobile phone from her pocket, the ringing becoming louder, he looked blankly at the screen. Old landline phones, you just lifted the receiver, anyone could do that, but modern, slim mobile phones are answered in a number of ways.

"Touch the screen and draw the letter z, then press the green button. Or you could just undo these straps from my hands and let me be free so that I can answer my own phone and not have the phone call answered by one of my jailers."

"Shut up, while I answer it. One word from you and you get a slapping, understood?"

The tall one carried out the unlocking instructions and spoke into the phone, "I'm sorry she is interviewing at the present time and can't answer the phone......I'm her cab driver, can I take a message?"

There was a long silence as the tall one listened to the voice at the other end. He then, without saying anything further into the phone, held the phone to her ear. "He wants a word."

The conversation that Helen had was both short and very one-sided, the only words the others in the warehouse heard Helen speak were:

"Hello, thanks for calling, ...Yes,.... I understand,... I will call as soon as I get a chance, bye."

She looked at the three around her, who were all looking at her expectantly.

"He's happy. Put the phone back and then we can get on with being your prisoners."

The smaller one asked of his accomplice, "So who was it, her boss?"

The tall one sat down, pulled out his own phone and looked for the game he had been playing. "Don't know, I can't remember, I don't think he said."

The two guards went back to their monotonous games. Greg kept giving Helen inquiring looks as he began to turn his head towards the stool and the waiting glass shard, to which she shook her head negatively, silently urging Greg to wait patiently, mouthing the word 'wait'. It was about ten minutes later, when she spoke.

"Greg, are you hungry? I know I am starving, we were dragged out of bed, no breakfast. Do you think there is any chance we might get some food?" She aimed her question at the two men who were still engrossed in their games.

The tall one, who was no doubt the senior of the two, looked away from his phone.

"No, unless we are told. Until I am instructed, we just sit here, hungry or otherwise."

"I see. Do you remember that Sharon Stone film, now she was hungry, and she was fed? Maybe you should take a lesson from her film, Basic Instinct?"

"The film you are talking about," the shorter one now looked up from his phone, "I don't think she was hungry in that sense," he laughed at his own smutty joke, his partner did not laugh.

"Maybe she was not hungry, but I am, so get us a pizza, that is what I really want, a pizza and a fizzy drink."

"Huh, you'll be lucky miss, this isn't a friggin' restaurant," the shorter one mocked her again.

"Get her a pizza and a fizzy drink," the tall one ordered.

"What?" the shorter one looked at his colleague in disbelief, "Reece said nothing about feeding them; we just sit here and wait."

"Get her the pizza and a fizzy drink, didn't you hear me the first time, just go and get it."

The shorter one huffed and tutted, then stood and walked off, muttering to himself,

"Well if she is eating, then so am I," as he left the room, not even noticing that the air was so much fresher outside.

If Greg had looked bewildered earlier, he was now more so. Then, when there were just the three of them in the room, what Helen said next he could not trust with his own ears.

"Untie me now."

Greg did not believe his own eyes when he saw the tall man move towards Helen, take a small knife from his pocket and cut the cable ties that held her wrists together.

"Now untie my friend."

The tall one moved towards Greg and released him.

"Give me your gun and go into that office, and do not let anyone in."

In silence he walked away from her and towards the small, empty office in the corner of the unit, first handing over as instructed, his gun to Helen.

"Come on, let's go."

"But I don't......."

"I'll explain later," she threw the gun into an industrial bin, then pushed open the door. "For now let's get out of here before the pizza man returns."

TO CHARING CROSS.

Mid-morning trains on the South-Eastern service from Bexley to Charing Cross were pretty much empty affairs with seats no longer being in short supply. A couple of hours earlier, the morning rush hour would have seen the services crammed full of commuters, all seats taken and most of the standing space as well, as the trains trundled slowly into London. Now Greg and Helen sat opposite each other, the nearest fellow commuter was at least six or seven seats further down the carriage and out of earshot. The remains of the morning rush hour still hung about the carriage, newspapers were strewn on seats and on the floors, as well as the odd empty coffee carton rolling across the dirty floor with the motion of the train. Greg leaned forward towards Helen, resting his elbows on his knees.

"Please explain exactly what happened back there?"

Helen looked at him; the stubble on his face was dark, his hair disheveled, his breath was stale, his clothes were creased and he looked tired, as indeed both of them were. Helen guessed she might not look a picture of health and beauty at the moment, having been dragged from her slumber earlier on.

"If I say so myself, I am rather proud of what I did, although it was the phone that gave us the key to escape. When it rings you answer it by simply picking it up, I hate all that fussing around swiping screens, putting in passwords, I just want to answer my phone. So, as soon as the tall guy picked it up, I started telling whoever was on the other end of the line that I was tied up and being held against my will; well you heard my side of the conversation. I was just hoping whoever was at the other end would care enough to do something, I just prayed it was not some call centre trying to sell me something. It turned out it was Phillip, the guy from France."

"The weird one."

"No," Helen retorted defensively, "he has a way with people. I think, well I am pretty sure, it is a form of hypnotism because when I got to speak to him, with the tall guy holding the phone against my ear, Phillip said, *'Be casual, give me simple answers. You are being held against your will?'* 'Yes,' I said. Then Phillip says the most mystifying thing, *'Trust me in this Helen, just say these exact words to the person who answered the phone, - Do you remember that Sharon Stone film -, once you have said that he will do exactly what you want. Call me when you get free, which I am sure you will have no trouble doing.'*"

There was something else that Phillip had said, she was pretty sure of that. Something in French, she thought, but could not be really clear, maybe she had imagined it. It was more of a feeling, maybe her mind was confused, which would not have been surprising considering the situation they had been in.

"Do you remember that Sharon Stone film! That is bizarre," Greg repeated.

"Bizarre it may be, but it worked as you saw for yourself. As soon as I had spoken that phrase, he did exactly what I asked, that was a totally weird experience for me. It must have been a sort of phrase, to trigger the hypnosis, that is all I can think, yet Phillip was only on the phone for minutes, how do you do that?"

Greg leaned back into the grubby seat, rubbed his very tired eyes and spoke thorough his fingers,

"As if much of the last couple of days could be deemed to be normal."

Helen tried to catch her reflection in the window of the train. Looking past the phallic shape that had been scratched into the toughened glass, her hair was indeed a mess and she dragged her fingers through it to try and make it slightly more presentable.

"I'm going back to France later, Phillip wants me to and I think it will be a little safer for me."

Greg looked at her with surprise; he had just assumed that she would want to stay with this thing until its conclusion, whatever and whenever that might be.

"Giving the story over to me?" He said almost taunting her, although she ignored the tone in his voice.

"This is not our fight, and even if there is a story, it sounds like it would never get published. Plus, I think I will have pissed off my News Editor enough to prevent any warm welcome home, so I'm going to do something different, Phillip and I talked the last time I was with him, he has some ideas."

"He's a bloody hermit, what can he offer you?"

"Nothing that concerns you at all. I'm going; you're not my guardian, end of story. As I said this is not our fight, so I am moving on, you can do whatever you think is right. We owe each other nothing."

"Well if you owe me nothing, what about Christopher? A friend of your father's, maybe you can still be of help to him."

Helen leaned back into the worn out train seat,

"I don't recall him," she lied, "I recall his aftershave, a very distinctive aroma that I remember from that day when my mother died after her fall. In the car with Christopher, I could not recall exactly how I remembered it, but being with him over night and sitting next to him in that awful warehouse, it all came back to me, like a dream coming to life. It was many years ago that I found my mother at the bottom of the stairs, but I recall there was a distinct aroma around, I have never been able to exactly work out what it was, I always put it down to one of my mother's strange perfumes that she favoured, but I know now it was Christopher's aftershave."

"You're saying he was there at the time your mother died?"

"I don't know what I'm saying, what I know is that I no longer want to be around Christopher and his aftershave."

"So why don't you ask him if he was there, he might be able to throw some light on why your mother fell down the stairs."

"Maybe I don't want to know exactly what happened on that day, maybe it is so long ago. Whatever comes to light, or is said now, can never change the fact that my mother is dead, digging up other facts about that day will only lead to those of us still living to have a greater hurt, some things are best left alone and the history that we have learned to live with to remain unchanged."

Greg got off the train at Lewisham, waving goodbye to Helen as she continued on her journey. He had been unable to convince her not to go back to France. Greg wondered just who Helen was? When he had first met her, she had seemed an average mild reporter, but he knew that in the past two days, she had taken the lives of two people. And now, a new potential fact about her mother's death had come to light, and she did not want to pursue it. So not as mild or as sincere as he had first thought, maybe Greg should reconsider how good a judge of character he might be. Alone on the platform, he needed some help, or at least a change of clothes, he called the only person in the world he knew he could trust, Donna.

MILLBANK, LONDON.

Helen alighted from the train at Charing Cross. She was still planning to go back to France later in the day, hopefully she would make the afternoon flight to Dinard. Now, there was other pressing business she needed to attend to.

A matter that had lurked quietly in her memory from her childhood. Ever since the day she had left her mother to die at the bottom of the stairs, she had successfully pushed it to one side. Over the years, living her life, she had treated it as just one of those childhood memories, albeit a memory that she could not share with any other living soul. Then Phillip had come into her life, somehow he connected with her through that memory, reigniting it, pulling it from the depths of her mind into the daylight of the present. Showing her that some things you repress prevent you from being the person you are meant to be. Helen now accepted the memory knowing the actions that she had taken that day, had changed her from an innocent child, into a criminal who had broken moral and social laws. Helen was an unconvicted murderess. Her sense of survival, her wish to remain free, avoid incarceration, meant that she had to ensure anyone that knew of her crime were contained.

As a child, she was aware that a man visited her mother on many occasions. A man that was never introduced to either her or her sister, a man both siblings guessed was Mother's lover. A man who gave her male company, lightening her often dark moods. His aftershave often hung in the hallway after his visit. He spirited into and out of the house like a phantom.

Helen had detected that same aftershave in the car with Christopher the first time they had come into contact. Now she had to confront him, she had to ask him, was he her mother's lover? Was he there the day she fell down the stairs? Then she would need to find out, exactly when he had left that day, and what he might know.

The Millbank building was a short walk from Charing Cross station, passing through the tourists thronging around Parliament Square to then pass the House of Commons and head towards Lambeth Bridge. The receptionist looked at her suspiciously, her unkempt appearance was not in keeping with the average visitor to the office building, rarely would Sir Christopher see anyone in such a state as that which this woman was in.

"I was with him this morning and now have additional information that he urgently needs. I do need to speak to him in person," Helen was firm in her demand.

The blonde receptionist telephoned the Personal Assistant to Sir Christopher. There was a delay, before she asked,

"So you don't have an appointment?" Helen was asked if she could make one, to which she replied,

"No, although I can assure you that if I am turned away, he will not be too pleased. You need to let him know that Helen Taylor is here to see him."

Again a short conversation with the PA, followed by a longer pause, before the receptionist held the handset towards Helen, gesturing her to take it.

"Helen, this is a pleasant surprise, are you downstairs with the reception?" She recognised Christopher's voice.

"Yes, I am and I need to speak to you."

Following his instructions, Helen waited for Christopher on a park bench in Victoria Tower Gardens overlooking the Thames. She did not have to wait long before he settled in beside her.

"Did Reece just let you go?" He asked without looking at her, instead he watched the tourist boats slide under Lambeth Bridge.

"Not exactly let me go, let's just say, our escape was engineered."

"You are clearly a very resourceful young lady, I am sure your father would have been very proud of your many talents. I must apologise for meeting you here, I just thought it would be more discreet, away from the prying eyes of the many people and cameras that are around the Millbank Building. So, what can I do for you?"

Helen felt chilled sitting there in the park. She looked at Christopher, his aftershave invading her nostrils.

"What aftershave do you use?"

His eyes continued to follow the tourist boats on the river,

"Is that all you wanted to ask me? Well, you could have just called and I would have happily told you, it is a cologne, my dear, English Leather, not exclusive, but certainly not common."

"My mother's lover used the same cologne, I recall it from my childhood."

"As I implied, I am not the only man wearing that particular fragrance."

"Maybe the only man ever wearing that aftershave who visited my childhood home."

This time Christopher turned to look at Helen, the light wind, tossing her hair across her eyes.

"That was so many years ago, times were different, I was different. Having just been returned to a desk-bound job, all that extra time with my wife only put a harsh spotlight on the cracks that our marriage already had. Late night dinners with colleagues and friends can only go so far to satisfy a man's desire. Your mother, attractive, a dry sense of humour and having so much affection to share, it was a natural fit. After the first kiss, there was going to be no turning back. I relished your mother's company, she enjoyed lying beside me, we both enjoyed the clandestine nature of our relationship. Does my bluntness satisfy your curiosity?"

Helen brushed the hair from her eyes.

"You were friends with my father, how could you betray that trust?"

"Your father was a very nice man, I am sure you have many good memories of him. Those weekends that I joined his family, I not only resisted the temptation to embrace your mother passionately, I also saw how happy he made his family, how much you and your sister adored him. Clearly a wonderful father, yet a man who also had a dark side. This might be hard for you to accept, and I guess you do not have to believe me, but your father was very much a 'ladies man' when he was in the city. Your mother might have had an affair with me, for all I know there might have been others. Your father, I know, had countless affairs, which your mother knew about and I know how much it hurt her. Yet, somehow they continued with their marriage, for the sake of you and your sister."

"Did you tell her about the affairs?"

"She asked, many times, I tried to resist, but in the end, I could only be honest with her. She had guessed as much, I only confirmed what she already suspected."

Helen recalled what her mother had said to her, looking up at her daughter, she knew exactly where her husband was that afternoon, and Christopher would have ensured that she knew every move her husband made.

"Were you there, at our house the day she died?"

Christopher turned his attention back to the boats plying their trade along the windswept Thames. His answer was not immediate, he was thinking, and was not going to be rushed, he needed to be careful how he answered Helen's question.

"Yes I was there. I had to leave early, I had an important meeting in town, but your mother wanted to see me that day, so I spared the time and made a brief visit. She was, as ever, demanding and did not want me to leave. So, as I left, she remained upstairs, I had just reached the hallway when I heard her slam the bedroom door, I thought she was going to rush after me. I was late, so continued opening the front door. Just then I heard the dull tumbling sound, which I now know was your mother falling down the stairs. Even though I was late, I am not a monster, and I was about to turn and go and see if she was alright when I heard her call out your name, shouting to you in the garden. If I had stayed and helped, you and I would have met for the first time without your father being there, potentially that could have been embarrassing and might well have exposed our affair. At the time given my position in the Civil Service and the state of my marriage, that would not have been advisable. I reasoned that her daughter, Helen, a very able young lady, would no doubt be on the scene within moments and give whatever help might be necessary. So I left, slipping away as I always did and leaving you, Helen, to look after your mother, who was shouting, so I reasoned, could not have been that badly hurt, at worst a broken bone? There you have it."

Only the sound of the light winter breeze came between them, they both sat ignoring each other in an awkward silence. What could Helen say? He knew that she had gone to help her mother, he knew the time her mother had fallen down the stairs. Christopher was not a stupid man, did he suspect? Of course he did. Did he know? He could not be certain, unless she confessed now. Then would he let sleeping dogs lie or would he report her confession?

"Look over there," Christopher pointed towards the Buxton Memorial Fountain, "that was built to commemorate the abolition of slavery, which is ironic really, given that we are all shackled like slaves to our memories. We can't set them loose, we can never be free of them, they live with us and haunt us. I'm sure you understand, Helen. It was such a shock to me when I heard that your mother had died from her fall, a tragedy. I, at first, regretted not going back to help, I felt I was to blame, leaving her young daughter to cope, while I stepped away because I was afraid of what the consequences might be. Then I learned how she must have fallen down the stairs, hitting her head on the banister, a fact the coroner highlighted in his report. Which left your mother unconscious at the bottom of the stairs, dying, while her daughter continued painting out in the garden. A tragic set of circumstances is how the coroner described it. If I recall correctly you were mentioned, the trauma of discovering your mother lying dead and calling the emergency services, acting sensibly; the Coroner did praise you. The ambulance crew arrived within fifteen minutes of your call. As I recollect, it arrived at eighteen thirty eight that evening, just thirteen minutes after your call." He looked at Helen with accusing eyes before he continued, "I could have and maybe should have, brought to the attention of the coroner, that I knew your mother was conscious at the time she landed at the bottom of the stairs as I had heard her shout. I could also have told him at the time, that it must have taken you, what, about six hours to get from the garden to the hallway. I could have done those things, but I did not. To have shared that information would have torn apart so many lives, mine for having an affair, your father's for the affairs he was having that drove your mother into my arms. Your life would have been ruined, your sister would never have forgiven you, friends and family would slink away from that side of the Taylor clan. None of this would have brought your mother back to life, so I chose not to share what I knew, with anyone. Maybe I should have been more shocked when I heard you had killed Mick Hayes, then you might not have felt the need to confront me. Now I hear that you have another victim, the young man in the Burger King car park. You continue to impress me Helen." Christopher stood up from the bench and towered over the silent Helen. "I need to get back now, I have an appointment. Goodbye."

"What about William Lynch and his secret?"

"Forget it Helen, let us professionals deal with it now, before one of you get hurt."

"Am I a wanted person?" Helen asked, stopping Christopher in his tracks.

"Hard to say. For me, Mick Hayes is just one of those things, in his line of work there are not many health and safety rules. As for Reece, that will depend on what he finds out and what he needs. Knowing the man, like I do, he will keep the knowledge that you drove over one of his people in his back pocket, saving it for a rainy day. Shackled to a memory Helen. Shackled to a memory."

LEWISHAM STATION.

The greasy spoon café was just a few hundred yards from Lewisham train station. Famous for generous large English breakfasts and fresh exciting lunches, it was popular with local residents as well as transient workmen and builders who were in the area. Greg stood at the door way and looked around the café. Even now, during the late afternoon, the chattering of the customers created a blanket of sounds across the tables, only broken by a waitress, holding two plates and calling out, "Egg, beans n' chips, n' a lasagne," as she looked around to see who would claim the freshly cooked meals. Donna sat along the right-hand wall and raised her hand towards Greg when she saw him at the doorway, the waitress for a moment was distracted by the hand, soon deciding it was not a hand calling for food. The tables all looked smart but homely with red gingham tablecloths, on each a small vase contained two flowers, plastic, yet so realistic, you were tempted to touch them just to reassure yourself they were just plastic; the flowers added colour to the image. The rest of the décor reflected the Italian origins of the family that had owned it for the last ten years. Framed, discoloured prints of the Colosseum and an assortment of domestic ceramic plates hung from the wall.

"Thanks for coming Donna; I wasn't sure how keen you might be after this morning's action at your flat."

"Keen? How cool is this, being involved in what would seem to be a TV drama, except it's not that at all. So tell me all so far."

During a full, all-day English breakfast including a large mug of tea, Greg related the events following his and Helen's abduction from her flat. The happenings at the industrial unit, the talk of R.G. Plastics and the secrets that it held. The bizarre escape, which seemed to be achieved with the help of a hypnotist on the telephone. Donna, listened and stared intently at Greg in awe. This was the man for her, if she was not sure before, which she was of course, the cast had certainly been set for her now.

"Here's the book you wanted, the one you were using last night to make notes."

"Thank goodness I like writing things down, now that Reece has the original heirlooms from William and the other guy, I would never have remembered the chess moves and all the other stuff. So, I guess next we visit the Wilmington Woods and then try and figure this thing out. It would seem that we are looking for some sort of chemical formula, or maybe research notes. I would suspect it will be on some USB stick, which seems a little too small to be in the woods." Greg paused to look at the chess moves again, "Maybe we need a chess board and try and work them out. Although it has been pointed out by Helen the moves are not logical, they just don't follow a game."

"So where is Helen now?" Donna asked, keeping a check on the other female in the equation.

"Gone back to France, weirdly. I thought she would have stayed and continued what we had started, but no, she wanted to go back to France. Maybe she thinks that her 'accident' last night might catch up with her."

"Did she really kill two people, I mean like murder and stuff?"

"Yes," Greg answered quietly, "it scared the shit out of me, I can tell you. Thankfully she has left the country now, or at least is about to board a plane. So, are you happy to continue looking with me or should we just give up now? I'm thinking after this morning's experience, maybe we should walk away?"

Donna leaned over, picked up a chip from his plate and popped it in her mouth, quickly consumed it, wiped a smear of tomato ketchup from her lip, and spoke, "Since when do you give up Greg? How many times have you been told to drop the suicide story and how many times have you ignored that instruction? The scientist guy in France, he took a number of steps to protect this secret. If you step away now, you'll always wonder what if I had carried on investigating. Pulitzer prize? Think of the film, 'All the Presidents Men,' they didn't give up, did they?"

Donna leaned forward and held his hand, for no better reason than she had the opportunity. She knew she could, given what she had done for him so far, he would not be so impolite as to remove his hand, and also she wanted to make what she was about to say sound important, even if it was nothing of the sort.

"Those chess moves, I've been thinking. The first set pointed to a map reference, a location in the UK, Wilmington Woods, simple and to the point. The second set, kept separately, doesn't appear to be a simple map location, even so, somehow the two must have a relationship of some sort, otherwise why write them down and keep them separate? Just like the banks tell you, don't write down your pin number and never keep it in the same wallet as your bank card. So here's my thought for what it's worth, if you're interested?"

"Of course I am, Donna, any help is more than welcome."

"My brother is a smartarse geek, always the clever one of the family. He sailed through exams, got the highest grades, top of the class and right pain to have for a younger brother. He was my brother so I was stuck with him all the same. When he was younger, he and his fellow mathematical geeks used to spend hours playing this stupid game, a sort of treasure hunt, a load of cryptic clues leading to the most boring treasure you could think of. One of the systems he often used was chess moves."

From being a little bored, Greg started to listen more intently when he heard the words chess moves.

"Ordnance Survey maps are based, as I guess most maps are, on a system of squares, much the same as a chess board. So each chess move takes you around the map. A knight will take you three squares north and one square east or west, a bishop will take you diagonally across the board or, in this case, the map."

"Makes sense, but how far, well, how far does the bishop move? If you're travelling across a map grid, then you will potentially soon go off the confines of a chess board."

"The pieces always start from the last square indicated by the previous move, as if it was at its game start position, then the square, indicated on the list of moves, determines how far it goes and in what direction. In the end you get a trail leading across a map."

"Well yes, I think, but where do you start on the OS map?"

Before Donna could deliver what she deemed as her dramatic punch line, a voice that Greg recognised spoke from the table behind him.

"Wilmington Woods of course, the Theresa Quinn square!" Christopher turned his chair and joined them. "Sorry for the surprise."

Dressed in a loose-fitting jumper and casual trousers, Christopher looked ready for a lazy weekend in his garden cutting back his roses and sipping gin and tonic on the lawn. Even in his most dressed down clothes, he still had an air of superiority about him, it was an aura he carried however he was attired.

"What the hell are you doing here?" Greg almost spat the words, it was not the face he wanted to see. "Why aren't you with your friend and partner in crime indulging in dark sinister activities?"

"You can be so dramatic at times Greg. Maybe the reason I am not with Reece is that he is not what I would consider to be a friend. I guess I cannot deny being involved in dark sinister activities, although you are both guilty of that crime too. The reason I am here is because whatever William has, the right thing is to destroy it, nothing less, and in order to, I need to reach this thing, before Reece, hence, my best chance of doing so is sticking with you. As both of you are not part of the system, it will take time for Reece to catch up with you."

"If we are so hard to find, how did you know we were not at the warehouse still?"

Christopher swung his chair further round, alleviating the need for him to twist and further strain his back.

"Helen paid me a visit and told me. Finding you was not that hard, I had someone outside Donna's flat, I guessed you'd pay her a visit at some stage."

Without waiting for an invitation Christopher, holding his tea, sat beside Donna, smiling at her as he did so.

"I do apologise Greg, for listening into your conversation, I was very interested to hear about the person who hypnotised one of Reece's employees, fascinating, it gave me a smile, I like to see Reece make errors, certainly a conversation I would like to have in the future. But for now, I am just glad that you are here and need I remind you that time is not on our side, as I know too well, the Government has eyes and ears everywhere." He turned to Donna, "I like you, not many people would come running when called, after their flat had been raided at some ghastly hour in the morning. Now, here you are sitting in a cafe, one phone call later, ready to risk all for Greg, I admire that loyalty, let's hope he repays you one day, I, for one, have little trust in journalists."

"And I have little trust in politicians and civil servants." Greg retorted.

"Then maybe we have more in common than we think. So Donna, tell me a little more about your brother's treasure hunting system?"

Greg was having nothing of the kind; sitting next to her was the man who for over eight years had squirrelled William away in France. By his own admission he was part of a scheme that destroyed a building and the lives within it. He had wheedled himself into the confidence of Greg and Helen who were looking for the secret, had been abducted and then released before once again turning up, Greg was not sure of the motive and just how much he could trust Christopher, and told him so. The reply was as calm as ever,

"If I was sitting where you are Greg, I would feel exactly the same and quite rightly so. You have no reason to trust me at all, yet sometimes in life we need to take a chance, push to one side the logic, just as I am at this moment sharing highly classified information with a journalist, whatever the consequences."

Keen to get on with her adventure, the ever prepared Donna, retrieved a plastic bag from under the table, from which she took out an ordnance survey map, an A4 pad, some coloured pencils, which had no real significance just they were the only ones she could find in the very chaotic flat once the workmen had restored, albeit temporarily, the front door. She also had copied the sheet that Greg had been making notes on last night, containing the chess moves that they had collected from Bert's widow. Fresh tea and coffee were ordered, and the map was spread across the already cluttered table.

Starting at the centre square of Wilmington Wood they worked their way through the moves, Donna calling out the move, then between Christopher and Greg, they marked the progress of the chess pieces across the Surrey landscape. Occasionally the track of a piece proved to be in doubt, this was a result of missing out a colour. The first move was a white piece, the second black, then white. Then there was making sure they were moving the correct piece; this is where Donna referred back to the chess board grid reference. Their first attempt gave a grid reference in the middle of the A20. All of them agreeing something was wrong, tracing back their virtual steps across the landscape, the error arose from moving a rook on a square too far. They continued having corrected their error this time arriving in the middle of an apple orchard, which was not impossible, still Christopher did not see William burying something in the middle of a field. Again they worked their way back, this time it had been a knight they had moved left, two up then one left, when Donna had meant right. Again they moved across the Ordnance Survey map, until the final piece had been moved and that location was in a small village of Kingswood among houses and shops, many options within this one OS square. They looked at each building icon, convincing themselves it would be a visit and wandering around the village, they might be close, yet had no idea how close, until Greg saw a name he recognised, he had heard it mentioned a couple of times in conversations, he was sure he was correct.

"The Ken Dunnett Hall, that was the name of the headmaster at Wilmington Grammar, when William and his chess friends were there, I'm sure I am right."

"Well then," Christopher stood up, "my car is just around the corner, let's go and see what we can find."

KINGSWOOD, SURREY.

Donna watched them both leave the café. She had decided that she would rather not go with them, however much she wanted to stay close to Greg, there was part of her that sensed that this Christopher fellow attracted trouble. But she did mention to Greg, when Christopher went off to pay the bill that she would be close to her phone if he needed her, which deep down she hoped he did. There was another feeling, a darker, more troubled sense that she felt within her, that she might never see Greg again. How foolish was she being, Donna the carefree, slightly eccentric woman at the office, did not accept that such feelings existed, yet however she tried to rid herself of those thoughts, she could not quell them, she hoped Greg would be alright and that he would come back to her.

Christopher had entered Kingswood as the destination into his satellite navigation system and followed its commands as they came to unfamiliar junctions, they were the only speech in the car until Greg asked a question that had been burning inside him.

"So why did you kill the employees of R.G. Plastics?"

Greg thought he saw Christopher smile, but he could have been mistaken. Christopher had indeed allowed himself a small smile that he hoped was not too obvious.

"We do a great many things in our lives that we regret, we all have these regrets, small ones and big ones. I guess if we did not have any regrets, or looking back, thought we could have done things differently, then maybe we have not been living life to the full, or simply just not being true to ourselves. Your government, or in fact any government is always in a state of war, even in the most peaceful of times. The United Kingdom's government might not have troops on the ground fighting a clear enemy as we did in Aden or Korea, even Northern Ireland for that matter, but the government is always at war in a sense. There are many foreign governments who want to learn more about our ways, good old-fashioned spies and counter-spies, like the James Bond films. Then there are the less obvious, the government is fighting a war with industry and commerce. Chief Executives are always pushing for greater tax breaks, changes of regulations to make their businesses easier and more profitable. Then there are the people themselves, wanting better services, less taxation, more freedom. There are the other political parties, pushing and probing for any dirt they might find on their opponents. So government has to fight its corner or else it will be swallowed up under the intense pressures all those forces are inflicting on it and its servants. It's a war and there will be casualties, some obvious, as you say, the R.G. Plastics employees were victims of the war. As are old people, who are considered too costly to treat, so we don't give them a hip replacement, don't take such good care of them, because they are no longer cost-effective. Living in peace and harmony is not an option in today's highly complex capitalist society. So I killed, and I am not proud of what I did, I conspired to kill those employees to ensure the greater good, they were the victims of a battle. Just as my employee Mick Hayes was a victim, and the employee of Reece's who found himself under the wheels of your car. Let's not forget that you too, as a journalist, play a part in this war of societies, journalists never seem to mind too much who they tread on to get their story and win their battle. Take yourself Greg, and your one man crusade against the suicide verdict in coroner courts, that's a war you'll never win, yet you still fight it."

The answer was not what Greg was expecting, even so he did not like the way he was being painted.

"Just because someone has died in circumstances we don't really understand, doesn't mean we should just call them suicides, maybe the reason should be identified and then others might not follow."

Christopher paused as he carefully negotiated a roundabout with an excessive number of cyclists.

"Come now Greg, I know your sister committed suicide. I never work with people unless I know a lot, an awful lot, about their past. Yours is interesting, a sister committing suicide, your mother and father dying soon after. Then your own obsession sees you being released from the newspaper or made redundant if you prefer to call it that. So what war or whose war are you fighting Greg? Whose side are you fighting on, society, your sister, or is it yourself that you are fighting. Or maybe your parents, it was very soon after your sister was buried that you left home. Disowning your parents or were they disowning you? Now there's a question."

"My sister's suicide was a tragedy, an unexplained tragedy that tore my whole family apart, I left home because I wanted to, I couldn't face living in that house any longer. The Coroner had no real reason to say it was suicide, yet he did rubber stamp it. Maybe I take solace in fighting for those who have been driven to take their own life."

"Maybe you left because you felt guilty that your sister had taken her life."

"So why would I feel guilty, what sort of warped theory are you constructing in your head?"

"Greg, I am a well-informed civil servant, I do not construct theories in my head, I take a number of facts and then understand the whole truth, a truth that often lies undisturbed. You do know your sister wrote a note before she took all those pills?"

Greg looked away staring out at the passing countryside as they drove ever closer to Kingswood.

"What the fuck do you know about my sister's death?"

"Now Greg, I have just told you I am a very well-informed civil servant, I have access to many records, many of which never see the light of day. Maybe we should continue this discussion later."

"If you want to say something, just say it," Greg turned to look at Christopher and gave the most threatening look he could, even so it was not that intimidating. Greg found it hard to be intimidating.

Christopher parked the car outside a rundown entrance, which in faded painted letters read: 'Ken Dunnett Memorial Hall', turned the engine off, unclipped his seat belt and half-opened the door.

"There is a police report, made just three days after your sister's funeral, your mother walked into Croydon police station and wanted to file a crime report, about her son who had been sexually abusing her daughter. Sadly the only evidence was that suicide note, which you said did not exist, the police advised that a prosecution would be very difficult, I think it was that night maybe that you packed your things and left. I told you I was well informed. Shall we go in now?"

Greg had always known the truth. It was his guilt that suppressed what he knew, and his parents found out when they discovered their daughter dead from an overdose. The note had been on the bedside table, neatly folded and written in her normal, frenzied handwriting. His mother had come down screaming, hysterical, at what she had seen. Greg's father raced upstairs, hoping that what his wife was saying was a simple error, his daughter would only be in a deep sleep, he held her cold hand and knew Brenda was in an everlasting sleep.

*

The Ken Dunnett Hall, standing alongside the Kingswood Village green, was a seventies brick built single-storey building, that only came about following a long and intense battle within the parish council. Even today's parish councillors now approach requests for planning permission with timid words. Before the hall had been built, the land alongside the village green had been left fallow and unfenced by the farmer who owned it through an act of history. He had left it deliberately fallow, as he did not want to disturb his fellow villagers by driving tractors and large agricultural machinery through the village. He was just pleased that the children of the village and their parents had more space for leisure as well as allowing a large number of stalls to be erected during the annual spring fayre.

His son, Jacob took over the land and dairy farm that Jacob senior and previous generations had managed, with little interest in getting his hands dirty. The property boom of the seventies tempted him to draw up plans for the fallow land which included adding a row of cedar trees, behind which were to be built a block of twenty-four single bed flats that would attract commuters and fresh blood to the village. Many of the parish councillors sided with Jacob, who had in the meantime dropped his biblical name for Jake, which he felt was more in keeping with the social circle he was planning to infiltrate. An equal amount of parish councillors were against the very heart of their village being sacrificed on the altar of property profit and so began a long battle. The parish councillors refusing planning permission had a majority, a small majority, thwarting Jake's plans. He then took the matter to the district council, who not wanting to upset either party, suggested that the parish council should buy the land at market price. If it could not, then Jake could build his flats. Which was as much of a fudge as anyone could make. The asking price for what had become known locally as Jacob's jeopardy, was way beyond the budget of the small parish council. The local bank, who knew that Jake would borrow money from them to build the flats, and also took into account the arrival of a potential twenty-four affluent commuters, could not resist the temptation and so refused any request of a loan from the parish council, there was no security, was their feeble excuse. The situation looked to be a fait accompli, until local resident Ken Dunnett decided to take positive and decisive action, two traits he was well known for at Wilmington school. He sold his not insubstantial house, which stood in an acre of land, gave the proceeds to the parish council, and went to live with his brother. Of course, Jake tried to outmanoeuvre the parish by upping the original asking price, so they went back to the district council planning for them to decide on a fair asking price. A Mr. Usher at planning decided on a reduced price, which more than upset Jake and left the parish council with enough change to build a village hall, which they were happy to call the Ken Dunnett Hall. Of course none of the parties had asked any questions about Mr. Usher of the planning department, if they had, they would have learnt that his son George went to Wilmington School and would in the fullness of time be following in his father's footsteps.

*

Since it had first been built there had been a lack of regular maintenance which had left the building tired looking. Today the front double doors were open, allowing easy access into the small porch like foyer, where Greg and Christopher came across Bert, carefully and slowly wringing out a damp mop, as he cleaned the block wooden floor.

"What can I do for you chaps?" He asked without looking up from his bucket.

Christopher answered without hesitation, "Just a couple of old schoolboys being nosy."

"Old schoolboys, my arse," this time he looked up from his grey metal bucket, full of dirty grey water, "no one came out of Wilmington speaking as posh as you."

This time Greg made use of his more common accent.

"I am the old boy; he is just a friend who likes old buildings."

"Lucky for you I ain't started on the main hall, bloody cubs last night, sticky fizzy drinks all over the floor, so best go in and have a look at the old photos which attract you old boys. I'll be wanting to start on it soon, once I've finished here and had me fag break."

The main hall was lined with large photographs from the Wilmington School archive, some 1930 class groups, various headmaster portraits, the largest being Ken Dunnett on the left-hand wall. Directly ahead was the dark wooden stage, with faded red curtains, a proscenium arch which had on its top a carved school crest. The whole room smelt of children's perspiration and the sweet aromas of confectionery. Along the top of the four windows which gave some light and too little ventilation to the hall, were the remnants of Christmas and birthday decorations long since passed.

"Well here we are Greg, and I suspect that is where it might be." Christopher pointed to the photographs pinned to the wall between the window and the stage.

Amongst the rugby photographs, winning football teams and pupils splashing through mud during cross country races were the innocent faces of four chess champions, having been awarded the cup for 1990.

Christopher stood close to the large, framed photograph that was hung on the off-colour painted wall.

"Well, this looks to be favourite, I wonder what it contains." Without hesitation, he lifted the dusty picture frame from its hook on the wall and inspected the back, brittle brown paper and peeling tape. He visually inspected the edges and nodded towards a patched area in the bottom left-hand corner.

"A repair or a hiding place, what do you think Greg?"

Christopher did not wait for an answer before he placed the picture on the floor and started to tear the brittle brown paper away from the back, there in the cavity was an envelope, with more than just paper inside, something protruded within it.

Christopher withdrew the small yellowed dusty envelope that had been squashed in between the frame and the photograph.

"Well not exactly under lock and key, but to be fair, I doubt many people would feel the need to poke fingers behind frames, unless you thought something might be there."

Christopher held the envelope in his hand; it was, apart from being dusty and yellow, blank without any writing on it. He split the seal and pulled out a black chess piece, a king, along with a hand-written note. Together they read, what William must have written eight years earlier.

*

"As soon as I heard at home on the local radio the first news reports of a large explosion and fire at R.G. Plastics that had resulted in a number of casualties, I understood that my life was potentially going to be very time-limited. Old age would not be a period of my life that I would reach. I could now see that the so-called urgent staff meeting drawing everyone into one place was just a simple ploy to ensure the research we were carrying out would be erased. Those equations and formulae that we had, over a number of years been developing, were no longer needed by our Lords and Masters. Those once hallowed objectives that we were working towards, now were considered too dangerous to exist. So they, and everyone with some sort of knowledge of those equations and formulae had to be erased from the face of the earth. It would not be long before they concluded I had not been present at that last fatal staff meeting, and they would soon be looking

at ways of ensuring I no longer walked the earth. I grasped on to the only thing I had at the time. I had on my laptop - my work-issued laptop - relevant information concerning the research. The knowledge still existed, and all the time I was the only one who knew where it was, I had a chance, an insurance policy which could see me into old age after all.

How well might this work? Well, by the very fact that you are reading this letter indicates that I have either passed away or have been tortured to reveal the location of where I concealed the information and secrets of R.G. Plastics. I suspect and indeed hope it will be the former, so if it is and the year in which you are reading this letter is in the late 2030's, that could mean that I have died of old age and this letter was found by accident when the Ken Dunnett Hall was either knocked down or just fell apart through old age. Much earlier than the 2030's would indicate that my death might not have been so natural.

Soon after the explosion at R.G. Plastics, Sir Christopher Davenport Wellington, my then boss, or at least one of the overlords of the research, called at my house, no doubt to give my wife the very sad news that I had died tragically in a fire. So seeing me answer the door to him must have given the 'old fart' a shock, which did not, sadly, kill him. Flustered, he did compose himself and start to waffle on about the tragic loss. I, of course, reacted as though it was the first I had heard of it. I made a point of telling him I still had all the research on my laptop, which he kindly offered to take away for safe keeping. I decided to play my card at once, making plain and clear, I was not just a brilliant and slightly eccentric scientist, I had common sense. If I gave him the laptop, then I would no doubt be dead within a week, that, I told him, was why the information had been transferred onto a USB stick from the laptop and was already in the Royal Mail to an address that only I knew of, ensuring it would be in safe hands and ready to come to light should anything happen to me. It was my insurance policy, which clearly, as you are reading this letter is a policy that has now expired.

Since that first meeting, I have now placed this letter in its hiding place and Sir Christopher has offered to hide me away in another country for my own safety. I am happy to go along with his suggestion, it sounds as though it will be a very easy life, although I am convinced that by hiding me away, and Sir Christopher being my only contact with the old country, there must be something in it for him.

Thank you for reading this missive. Oh the chess piece, the black king enclosed with this communication, it represents me capturing Sir Christopher's leading piece and winning the game. The information, the valuable research documents that I had, well, they never existed on my laptop or my person. To be honest with you, dear reader, I was never the most diligent of scientists at R.G. Plastics or anywhere else for that matter. I rarely took work home, security you know. But at that moment when Sir Christopher was standing on the doorstep, no doubt thinking about how he was going to extinguish my life, I needed a lever, a small lie, which I hope has given me a longer life than I might have expected had I not created the existence of fictitious research data.

I wonder who you are reading this epitaph. I hope, as I mentioned previously, that you are some builder knocking down the Ken Dunnett Hall, which will indicate that I have lived to a ripe old age. Yet in a perverse sort of way, I hope it is Sir Christopher, even though this would mean that I never did get to see old age. Because if you are reading this, Sir Christopher, I would just love to see your face when you realise there was nothing at all on that laptop and that one of your minions outmanoeuvred and outplayed you. I always told you I was a good chess player. Checkmate!"

Greg looked at Christopher, a wry smile on his face. "Nothing?"

"Checkmate indeed!" Christopher repeated William's written words. "I suppose at the time I did not take all the facts about William fully into consideration. He was a slapdash type of scientist, bright, but disorganised and a little rebellious, if I am honest. Did you know he was on a final warning? We were on the verge of sacking him; although if the research had continued, we would have found it hard to move him off the project. Slapdash he might have been, but he was good at being a scientist. Something maybe that should have made me question if he really would have taken the entire research data home with him. But hindsight is the most useful skill, unfortunately, it is never available when you need it. Sorry Greg, no formula, no news story, and no retirement fund for Reece, he will be disappointed."

Christopher folded up the letter and placed it carefully into his inside jacket pocket. The black chess piece he handed to Greg saying, "A memento of the story you will never be able to write."

Greg rolled the wooden chess piece around the palm of his hand. "Never write, I am a reporter, a freelance in need of a story, what makes you think I will walk away from this without writing one?"

Both men stood in front of the enlarged version of the photograph that Greg had first seen in France and which had led him to a musty community hall in Kingswood, and now holding a black chess piece. Christopher looked at the young man in front of him, admiring his innocence.

"Strong, categorical denials from government departments. Gentle, discreet hints to editors that such a story, although untrue, might have some elements that could compromise national security. Even maybe an unofficial briefing, letting interested editors know that the writer of such a story, had been brought to the attention of the police in previous years. No editor to whom we would have spoken, would want to go anywhere near your story, even if you decided to write it. Your story would be crushed and buried forever. And do not think for a moment of flattering yourself, it would not be the first or the last time a news story had to be buried for reasons of national security."

Christopher indicated towards the door, where the elderly caretaker had now started slowly and methodically mopping the sticky floor clean ready for the next community group to use his hall.

"Maybe it is time we left, before we get mopped up."

Outside a break in the clouds had created a warm shaft of sunlight that pooled the village green in a rare winter warmth, hinting at the spring that would be along in a couple of months. Greg leaned on the roof of the Volkswagen Golf, and looked across at Christopher as he opened the driver's door.

"There should have been a second report at the police station."

Christopher closed the door and leaned on the roof opposite Greg.

"Only one with your name on Greg."

"It was my fault that she took her life. If I had been more courageous, then she might well have still been alive. The morning that she died, my father came down with the suicide note, which told how Greg had abused her and that no one would listen or believe her. She could find no other answer than to end her life. Humans can split the atom, send rockets across the Universe, yet my sister could not find an answer; for her the only answer was death. 'Opprobrious' that's what my mother called me. I was so young; I was not sure what it meant. The whole house had gone mad, shouting, crying, total despair. My father, at the time said that the note should not be made public, it would disgrace the family name. Mother only agreed after a lot of shouting, even so, without his knowledge she did go to the police, who as you said suggested that there was not enough evidence. I had not said anything in my defence until that time, I took the abuse, because I loved my family. I also knew the truth.

Brenda had asked me to meet her in a small cafe, away from our usual haunts, very much a clandestine meeting. She told me that her father, my father, had abused her, forced her to have sex with him. I thought she was imagining it. Now our father was a tough man, but I always looked up to him, I could never think of him doing wrong, he was a righteous man, or so I thought. 'Why not tell mum?' I asked her. You have to understand, when I say tough, maybe dominating and intimidating would be a better description. He ruled the house. My sister might have told Mother, but one word from Father and her allegation would have been dismissed. Brenda was going to go to the police and report the abuse. I told her that was mad, Dad would end up in Prison. 'So what,' she said, 'he deserves it'. But she wanted my help, help to support her to tell the police that Father was a bully, they would be more likely to believe her then. I said I couldn't help her. I pleaded with her not to call in the police. She stormed out of the cafe, and a couple of days later at school, I had a visit from a Police officer, who sat me in an empty classroom and told me about the allegations that she had made. They wanted me to testify against my father, maybe in a court of law. I was scared, really scared, of what he might do to me; it would not have been the first time that I had had a beating. I said there must have been a mistake, told him that my sister was often the sort of person who would make things up. They took no action because I did not have the courage to stand up to my father. I was scared of what was going to happen to me, not what was happening to my sister. I was her big brother; I should have been looking after her. Two days later she was dead. It was my fault; I could have prevented her death."

Christopher played with his car keys as Greg told his story.

"The note, the note your mother handed into the police station, it accuses you."

Greg shook his head.

"Mother was the only one who had the courage to stand up to my father. He had forbidden her to let that note see the light of day. Even so, damning the consequences, she found that note and took it to the police station telling them to arrest me. That night, when she came back, having been told there was going to be no further action taken, she wanted to kill me, thinking I was the one abusing her little daughter. I could not stand by any longer. I told them both what Brenda had told me about Father having sex with her. I won't repeat the words they both used to describe me; lying little boy was the theme. So I pointed to the note, the one that Father had discovered and shown to us all. It was Brenda's handwriting, well most of it was, until you looked carefully at it, the handwriting was not as clear as Brenda would normally write, there were errors and spelling mistakes, well, she was about to kill herself. I can still recall word for word what it said:

" *i'm sorry eveyone, but i cannaot think of what else i can do or who i can turn to. no one beleives me that Greg has been sexually abusing me for several months now. i cannot face his leering breath and eyes as he pushes down on me when we are alone in the house. so i am turning to the only person i can trust, i am sending my self to heaven, where i know jesus will protect me as he does all his children, brenda.*"

"I pointed out to both of my parents to look at the way she spelt the name Greg. It had been spelt with a capital letter, the only one in the whole note, take away that capital G and you are left with reg, short for Reginald, who was not our real father, he was our stepfather. Yet I was still called a liar, even though I could see that I had sown some seeds of doubt in my mother. So I left, I walked out of that house that day and never went back.

Christopher, when you go back to your tall, filing cabinets, look up Reginald Andrews. My parents never married, so both of us kept the name Auden. In his file, you'll see the report from my sister, Brenda Auden, who I let down badly." Greg looked down at the roof, avoiding eye contact. "I've been trying to make amends ever since, not very well, but I am trying."

Christopher folded his arms and rested them on the roof of his car as he listened to Greg relive a time that continued to haunt his life.

Christopher smiled, a fatherly concerned smile at the contrite Greg who leaned tiredly on the car roof.

"We can never wash our guilt away; we can only learn to live with it and learn from that guilt. All those staff at R.G. Plastics, Mick Hayes, Reece's henchman, even Helen's mother, all victims, casualties of the war and conflicts that we all exist in. We just need to learn from our mistakes and hope we don't make them again, invariably we do, but we're just humans, none of us are perfect. Trust me, Greg; forget the last few days ever happened. Find another story to write, go and find those missing gay guys of yours; write their story, whatever that might be. Or just get a boring job, marry Donna, have children and live your life until your body decides it has had enough. Don't choose a lifestyle where someone else can decide that your life should end, let God decide that for you. Now I think a lift back to your flat and then we go our separate ways. Then I must tell Reece the good news," Christopher laughed.

LONDON STANSTED.

Once again Greg found himself gripping the seat, as the Boeing 567 powered up towards its cruising height of thirty-five thousand feet. He thought that having been back and forth a number of times over the last week or so, that he would have begun to relax during the take-off and landing, that was not the case and he imagined it would never be, he would be afflicted with this fear for the rest of his life. Just why he was going back to France he was not entirely sure. It had been a bit of a whim, once he had got back to his flat, showered and changed into a fresh set of clothes, he had thought about Helen going back to France and meeting up with that weird Phillip. He could have just called her, but that did not seem the right thing to do. Then there was still the problem of two missing men, which he had never really found a solution to. Maybe for once he should not just give up, just take the easy way out.

If he had agreed to help his sister, when she needed his help, she might still be alive. Maybe if he had not just accepted his notice at the paper but shouted a bit more, stirred up some industrial action, then he might still have a job. There were times when you should kick up a stink, yet equally there would be times when you should shrink back, it was just a case of what was the right thing to do at the time. He did not doubt that Christopher would prove to be a very sturdy enemy, so the R.G. Plastics story could not be written, that was just common sense.

In fact, he now realised that everything about R.G. Plastics had distracted him away from that very first plea for help that he had received at his leaving do; a young man had just taken off to France without any obvious reason. Looking back, Greg had been very sceptical but he needed the distraction from his own situation so had just taken it on. One absent man on its own, had never really inspired Greg to dig deeper, it was the Bashfords that intrigued him at the time. Then at the Angel Wings club, he heard about two men that had committed weird forms of suicide, then he had really become interested. Walking into the river or pouring petrol over yourself were not, he knew very well from the many news stories that had been written, common methods of suicide. Their bizarre actions had been easy for the authorities to explain, using the simple trusted suicide reason, but much harder to prove was the truth and the motive behind their actions. Even so people do commit suicide, people do elope, and people do just walk away from their lives. Maybe he was starting to put those things behind him and go for a news story he could write. If Helen was to be believed, and he had witnessed some evidence towards verifying it, a man could hypnotise someone at the end of a telephone, and that sounded like a story that would sell to all the tabloids. So that was why Greg found himself on a plane to France once more, still tightly gripping the leather seats as he had always done.

It was during the quiet, stable part of the flight as the plane crossed the Channel and approached the French coastline that lay out below like a living map, that Greg thought once more of those two missing men, who had taken this same flight, maybe sat in the exact same seat where Greg now sat. They had gone missing and whom he had been tasked to find; two men, acting out of character, seemingly on the spur of the moment. It suddenly occurred to Greg they could have been acting as if hypnotised, on a mission, told to do one thing, go to France. The original abandoned car had been found just a few miles from Phillip's house. Greg thought more and more about Phillip and the missing men, had he hypnotised them? Why would he?

What was there to gain? Then there were the others from the club, the other men who had died, why else would anyone just walk into the Thames and just keep walking, maybe they had been hypnotised too. Weird Phillip, there was no crime for being weird. But being in the vicinity of men that do strange things, now there was a possible thought, he had been to the club, circumstantial, maybe?

Greg began to think about those four men, all had acted out of character that was what everyone said and agreed on. A member of the audience, on stage, clucking like a chicken is again acting out of character, but we laugh at them because we know they are hypnotised. Suddenly, if you took away that there wasn't any logical reason for Phillip doing it, you could then explain why these people had done weird things, totally outside of their character, they had had no choice, Phillip had them under his control.

His mind turned to Helen who would have arrived at Phillip's the day before. On the train she had seemed desperate to get to Phillip's house, maybe against her freewill. He now feared for her safety. As the pilot put the plane down and bumped it along the landing strip at Dinard, Greg was too preoccupied to worry about the landing. In his mind he now knew, without a shadow of a doubt, that Phillip was the reason those two men had disappeared. Greg had to find out why, he had to confront Phillip and find the truth, something he had never really done before.

MILLBANK, LONDON.

Christopher sat in his office, picked up the telephone and dialled Reece Campbell's number. He had been tempted just to walk along the embankment and visit Reece in person, it would have been rewarding to see his face, to tell him firstly, that the clues had all been solved and then that there was no treasure, no pot of gold at the end, just a simple letter telling the world there was nothing in the first place. There again, Christopher considered that visiting Reece would only make him feel more important than he really was in Christopher's eyes, whereas a simple phone call would emphasize that Christopher could not be bothered that much, the whole thing was not important enough to warrant Christopher Davenport Wellington leaving his office, as he was far too important.

Reece answered in his usual, curt manner, which became almost hostile when he heard Christopher's voice at the other end.

"Thought I would just let you know it is all over and done with."

"What are you talking about?"

"R.G. Plastics. The clues I have worked out and followed where they indicated, a small nondescript village hall in Kent, run down and pretty tatty, if I say so. In the end there was just a letter from William, explaining that he never had the information or the documents about the process in the first place. He created the illusion that he had something, and we fell for it. We have wasted a lot of time worrying about something that was never there in the first place. So I see that as a chapter ending and then moving on."

"Eight years of you keeping him in the life of luxury in France at the tax payers' expense. Oh Christopher, that might take some explaining in the future."

"I doubt I will ever need to, as asking such a question would invariably raise other questions which I am sure you and others would prefer not to be asked."

"Frankly, Christopher, I am impressed, I am still waiting for an answer from my so-called experts as to what the meaning of the chess moves are. I also understand that you pulled some very neat moves on some of my younger staff. I'm impressed, for a man of your age, you do not seem to have lost any of the skills that we both learned as young men."

"Some things Reece, we never lose."

"Quite. Thank you for letting me know and I guess our paths will cross soon enough at some boring function. Nice speaking to you, goodbye."

Reece did not wait for any sort of reply from Christopher, he just replaced the receiver and stood up from his leather chair, then walked towards the glass window overlooking the Thames. He looked down at the glistening water, today the sun was low in the winter sky and so it gave little warmth, only bright light that reflected off the water of the Thames. Reece took a deep breath, pulled his mobile phone from his pocket and pressed speed dial seven. A man answered, his voice a little timid, as he had seen who was calling him.

"Luke, as I am sure you are still aware, following our discussion yesterday, I am still very upset at you and Harry for letting our two guests go. However, there has arisen an opportunity for you to redeem yourselves. I have a task for you, which I am sure you can understand you will not fail in completing, simply because failure is no longer an option for you and Harry. I need you to go to France, a small village called

La Ville du Bois in Brittany. I want you to find out exactly where William Lynch's widow and two children have gone. I suspect that your paths might cross those of Greg and Helen, our two guests from yesterday, if so, find out what you can from them, as firmly as you want to, their fate is of no consequence to me. All I need you to do is to find out, where William Lynch has secreted all the information regarding the R.G. Plastics project. I suspect his wife; if she has left the area, will have it."

Luke reluctantly agreed, he knew that you never said no to Mr. Campbell, there again, many things appeared impossible at first.

Reece replaced his mobile phone into the inside pocket of his suit jacket and allowed himself a smile which he saw reflected in the glass of the window. Poor, simple Christopher, thinking it was all over, thinking that he was the only one to have visited William on the day of the explosion. Reece was there later that night and listened to William as he talked about having the electronic dossiers and information on the work of R.G. Plastics and the drug that could wipe fear away from a person's psyche. William offered the same story that he had concocted for Christopher, talked about the laptop and the information already in the Royal Mail into safe hands, his insurance policy. Of course Reece was sceptical. He looked at William, clearly scared and afraid, knowing that his life hung in the balance, and told him that he thought he was bluffing. William was quick to prove and show Reece the laptop which had the information on it, screen after screen of chemical formula, processing details, temperatures, proportions.

"So what is to stop me just taking this laptop from you and then tidying up the loose ends?"

William knew exactly what Reece was referring to.

"I told you earlier, everything was downloaded on to an USB stick, in fact two sticks, and posted to two different people, with a short explanation of what they should do if I was ever found dead."

Reece suspected that this again was a bluff, however he could not be sure, and so agreed to leave. Yet he knew that the data was out there, he had seen it, and Christopher had not. Now the field was clear for Reece to track down those USB sticks, which he guessed were now in the company of William's widow, who, if she had left La Ville du Bois a few days ago, should not be that hard to track, the trail being still very warm. She would now no longer have the support of the British Government. He guessed that William would have provided some sort of insurance for his family, those USB sticks could be worth a fortune. Reece just wondered how his widow might go about trying to sell them.

LA BELLE ETOILE.

As Greg walked from his larger than planned hire car - as ever it was all they had available - towards Phillip's isolated house, the cold, biting wind pricked through his shirt sleeves onto his skin. He wondered if it was really the cold wind or maybe just a little bit of trepidation. The ever alert Phillip, wearing dark blue cotton shorts, and sporting a clean white tee shirt (attire Greg thought odd for the time of year), his hands contained in rubber gloves, opened the door before Greg had even reached the threshold.

"This is a surprise Greg, come in, although I am afraid you do find me in a bit of a chaotic state as you can see."

Phillip gestured towards the living room, still tidy and ordered, but which was now dominated by cardboard boxes, a group of six, each with clear white labels describing the contents that had been carefully packed within. The two sofa seats were still present, with a coffee table between them, on which was a folder of documents. The wall cabinets, now bare, had in front of each, two cardboard boxes, again labelled neatly.

"I am moving," Phillip explained, as if the evidence was not obvious enough. "The weather here in the north of France is just too much like the United Kingdom, so I am off south with longer summers and warmer evenings. Can I offer you a drink Greg? I would welcome a break from collecting my belongings together and a little stimulating conversation. Red wine?"

Phillip returned after a few moments having removed his yellow house cleaning gloves, thoroughly washed his hands and now poured them both a large glass of red wine. Sitting opposite each other, Phillip raised his glass.

"Bon sante! What can I do for you Greg? I would not have thought I would be included in your regular social circle; I sensed your hostility the last time we met."

Greg sipped the wine and looked around, even moving home appeared to be an ordered and highly organised operation for Phillip, everything clearly labelled and neatly placed ready to be moved, no sign of any dirt or dust having been discovered behind units.

"Where's Helen?" the question and the tone was deliberately abrupt, which was not lost on Phillip.

"She should be back soon. She insisted on getting some fresh bread and decided that the walk to and from the baker's would do her good. I trust she will be back before it gets dark, as there are no street lights along these lanes, although there are not many places in which to lose yourself. She will be pleased to see you, I'm sure. I know that she was going to try and contact you once we had moved. Oh, I should explain, we will both be moving down to the south of France, I am renting a place near Carcassonne until I purchase a permanent residence. I do not want to pre-empt what she might say to you, but I am sure you can appreciate, after what she has told me you both have been through during the last few days; I think I can understand, I would want to redefine my life, which I think is where she is at. So we, Helen and I, have a lot in common, thus we are going to live life in the sunshine for a while."

Greg sipped his wine.

"Giving up her career for you?" The question sounded sceptical.

Phillip leaned forward and adjusted a small pile of magazines in order to align them with the edge of the coffee table.

"I would not say that she was giving up her career for me, more giving up on journalism. What comes next, she is not sure.

Starting afresh is always a good plan and I can offer her that opportunity. I will be honest with you Greg, there is nothing between us, just two friends who understand each other. I am always willing to help people where I can. Without being too boastful, I did play a part in helping both you and Helen escape, you can thank me later," a wry smile formed on Phillip's face.

Greg could not deny that it was a strange skill that Phillip had utilised.

"Just how did that work, the phone thing, getting that guy to do exactly what Helen wanted?"

Phillip leaned back into the soft leather, smugly smiling.

"He would have done anything for anyone once they had said the correct phrase which I had programmed him with. I just enlightened Helen, she did the rest, more wine?"

Greg took the refilled glass and continued his probing,

"I would not think programming someone over the phone is that easy. What are you, some sort of hypnotist?"

This time Phillip stood up walked across to the six neatly stacked boxes that stood beside the kitchen door, straightened them, looked at the labels and then turned towards Greg, he looked at him, deeply into his eyes. Greg felt he was trying to reach down into his very soul and pluck the very core of his being.

"Not really a hypnotist, but a very similar skill, with much the same result. I have this ability, or talent if you will, that through talking to someone in a certain way, I am able to make a suggestion. I cannot tell them what to do, everyone does really have free spirit, so I can only suggest that they take a particular course of action, which because of the part of their brain I have somehow accessed, is overwhelming and they feel compelled to do it. Very much like a dog, when taught to beg, it is totally unnatural for the dog to sit up and beg, yet it does it, one, because it can, and two, because it wants to please its owner, so it begs for its food. The dog could never be taught to beg if it was naturally unable to. Let me expand, I spoke to that guard or whoever he was, on the phone, and I suggested how much it would please me, if the person who spoke a certain phrase to him, if he would help them by doing whatever they asked. As soon as he heard that phrase, he would have walked to John O' Groats and back if Helen had asked him to. He could not have flown a space craft because he does not know how to, so there are limitations."

Greg looked at Phillip standing beside the cardboard boxes, he looked tall and sinister to Greg sitting on the long leather settee. Yet there was a tone in his voice which was pleased, boastful, happy to share and tell an almost stranger how good he was.

"So, somehow you own that person as you would a dog, and just like any obedient dog, they do exactly as they are told, that is some serious power you have there Phillip. So just how can you turn a complete stranger, even over the telephone, into an obedient dog?"

"Reporters always want to know everything, if I appear to fudge the answer, it is simply because I am honestly not totally sure myself. Before you say anything, I know that is not the answer you are looking for, Helen made that clear when I told her. She was hoping to find a fact she could write about to explain my very unique talent, sadly I cannot offer either her or you a full explanation. I am just able to sense or feel the person's inner most feelings and somehow, maybe my tone of voice connects with them, I then, I suppose, do hypnotise them in a way."

"Show me how you do it, hypnotise me."

Greg laid down a gauntlet for Phillip to pick up, however Phillip glossed over the offer.

"Sadly it does not work with everyone, you have a difficult, maybe impregnable, mind. From our very first conversation I could tell that I could not dip into your mind and turn on your remote control switch. My talent is not perfect or indeed can be applied to the whole population. Maybe if it could, I could become Prime Minister, now that would be interesting, don't you think Greg?"

"Is Helen remote-enabled?"

"Not anymore, she, like you, was interested to see for herself how it worked, just as you are. Thankfully, I could give her a demonstration, as she was one of those whom I could connect with. She knows that I will be talking to you and there is every likelihood that you will write the story that she was planning to write, as she is no longer a reporter, she was not worried in the slightest about what I talk to you about."

"How did you know that we would be talking again?"

"You suspect that I might know something about those men from Gravesend, so you were bound to come back here and speak to me."

Phillip walked over to the side of the fireplace, looking at the now empty cabinet that once housed the music centre, a music centre now packed and protected ready to be shipped to the south of France with the rest of his belongings, he spoke with an apologetic tone.

"I am sorry, I would like some background music, but everything is packed away, well almost everything, in preparation for my move, the men will be coming first thing in the morning. You can take so much with you, sadly my animals will be remaining here, a local farmer is collecting them, my gift to the village."

Greg watched as Phillip moved around the room, clearly recalling the moments of memories that he would be leaving behind. The room was almost bare, empty-shelved, pictures no longer hanging, boxes neatly stacked, a large empty cold fireplace. Greg's eyes travelled to the broad beam that traversed the fireplace and looked at the small trinkets still lined up neatly and yet to be packed. The whole room echoed from the removal of furniture and chattels belonging to Phillip, an ordered, controlled exodus, nothing like the way Greg recalled when he had moved into his flat, following a steady flow of bedsits he had inhabited after he had been cast out by his family. He hadn't noticed them on his first observation of the room, he had been occupied with the boxes, and the cleanliness, almost clinical, of the whole environment. Yet there above the fireplace, a number, six in fact, of small unrelated items, lined up with military precision, which at first mystified Greg as to their significance, a waiter's friend, a blackbird pie funnel, a Roman soldier statue, a small toy bus, a prancing porcelain horse figure, finally a Ninja Turtle figure. Greg returned his focus to the small Roman centurion figure, a cheap looking one, Greg wondered and at the same time knew exactly what he was looking at.

"That is an odd collection of items on the fireplace, what are they?"

Phillip walked over to the fireplace, still holding his glass of wine and stood before them, much like a pilgrim would stand before an altar. Looking at them, he explained that they were simple mementos from times in his life; silly, nonsense items that just helped him trigger memories from his past.

"I am sure, even you Greg, have something similar tucked away in the darkest corner of your flat, I like to have such memories, good memories, out in the open. Much like people have photographs, maybe they represent exactly the same, allowing you to flit back to that moment in time and relive it as completely as one can ever relive history."

Greg stood and joined him in front of the fireplace, standing beside Phillip their shoulders almost touching although Phillip was a few inches taller. Greg decided it was time to show he had no fear, or at least not the degree of fear that was welling up in him and tried to cover it causing him to sway a little.

"Martin, before leaving his car on the other side of the village, smashed the glass window of a small antique shop in

Josselin, and took a worthless Roman soldier statue, I guess much like the one before us now."

"A cheap trinket I bought in Rome during a very pleasant stay, I am sure there are thousands made and sold. I said that you suspected me."

Greg ignored his jibe.

"Martin frequented a club in Gravesend, called The Angel Wings, not far from where you lived at the time. His car was found not far from where you live now. So I am starting to wonder if Martin is still not far from you."

"Well I haven't packed him away if that's what you are thinking." Phillip smiled and calmly sipped his wine, before changing the tone of his voice, a threatening tone designed to intimidate. "So what are you thinking Greg? Are you trying to say something to me in a roundabout way? If you are, please just say what is on your mind, I would be very interested to hear what you have in that narrow, possibly distorted mind of yours."

Greg turned to face Phillip.

"Do you think your special power could force a man to walk into the river and kill himself?"

Phillip turned and walked away from the cold fireplace still holding his glass of wine, he walked towards the window that overlooked the small frontage and looked at the two cars parked there. He stood silently for a moment, as if he was considering if he could force a man to walk to his death in a river, he, of course, knew the answer and guessed that Greg only suspected that he did.

"Interesting thought Greg, I am sure it is possible, given the man could not swim. If he could swim, then I am sure natural instinct would, at the point where he could no longer walk, make him continue his journey swimming. Yet an intriguing theory, although why I would want to do such a thing, I have no idea and before you ask, as you seem to be placing me into the role of prime suspect in the disappearance of your two men, I have been to the Angel Wings club, a gay club. Although I would not consider myself gay, the club did have a pleasant ambience for a drink. Don't tell me you have never been to a gay bar before? Often they have a better atmosphere than other common garden pubs."

Greg ignored the question, instead he thought of the Fox and Hounds in Lewisham and wished he was back there at the bar amongst friends. Here in the present, it was answers that he wanted from Phillip, but he seemed to be getting very few of those. He finished his wine and put the glass on the coffee table, Phillip immediately came over and moved it onto a coaster.

"Why would two gay men visit you if you are not gay, were they just friends, and where are they now?"

"Sit down Greg," Phillip said as he observed Greg's condition, deciding the time was right, he sat back down and motioned Greg to do the same, taking his place opposite Phillip.

"I will be honest with you Greg, not because I like you, but because you deserve to know the truth, and time is getting on, I do have a lot to do here as you can see. Do you want another drink first?"

Greg turned down the offer and settled down to listen to what Phillip had to say.

"Both of them, Martin and Dougie have been consumed by my highly effective pigs; you shouldn't be that shocked."

Greg had to replay in his mind what he had just been told. At first he thought it might be some sort of tasteless joke, yet Phillip always appeared to be the serious type.

"It is the very best solution for disposing of people you no longer have any use for. I should be clear on one point they were long dead before being eaten, I am not that cruel. They both did exactly as I asked, they came all the way from England with a small gift for me." Phillip motioned towards the fireplace, "The blackbird pie funnel from Dougie, and as you suspected and are clearly aware now, the Roman centurion from Martin.

Interesting that he was willing to commit a crime, which surprised me, as I mentioned earlier, people can only be instructed to do what they are able to."

Greg could not help himself but join the somewhat bizarre conversation he was listening to.

"It could be because Martin was not that honest with his expenses a while back and ended up with community service."

"How fascinating, so he did have a dishonest streak in him, just proves my point. I never knew Martin well, or in fact any of them that well, just met up for a few drinks, and unbeknown to them, they were programmed, prepared for the time I would contact them and ask a favour. I can see you are looking somewhat confused, let me expand to help you better understand. Earlier you mentioned a man walking into the river, I would imagine that you were referring to one young man that I was able to convince that he was able to walk across the riverbed of the Thames, right across to the other side. I had met him in the Angel Wings club, and during our conversation, he mentioned that he could not swim, so he was the ideal candidate. I suggested he should try walking along the riverbed to the other side, he agreed that it sounded a good idea, and off he went. I, of course, stayed a while and then left, just to break any association with him. As it happened, the police deduced, in their wisdom, that it was suicide, which was the hallmark of my earlier victim, who had poured petrol over himself and then lit the fluid. I doubt if he knew much more after that, again the police put it down as suicide."

"Just stop there," Greg was feeling his head spin, he could not be sure if it was the wine or the madness he was hearing from Phillip. Was this man really boasting about murder and not just one, but so far, four deaths? "Are you telling me you just killed these people? What on earth could be your reason, whatever did you gain from their deaths?"

"Forgive me Greg, I do get excited when I share my experiences with certain people, it is not as if I could chat about this in the pub with a bunch of friends."

"I doubt you have many friends, you said before that you like being a loner."

Phillip stood up; the early evening had now morphed into night time, he walked across to beside the door and turned on the light, for a moment both men shied away from the sudden brightness.

"I do indeed like being alone, although there are many advantages, there are also some disadvantages, not sharing exciting parts of one's life is a good example." Phillip held the wine bottle over Greg's empty glass, "Are you sure you will not join me?"

Greg picked up his glass and held it against the neck of the wine bottle, to be refilled with St Émilion wine, Phillip poured then refilled his own glass. Greg took a large swallow of the wine; he was thinking about asking for something stronger.

"I do get excited; let me explain more clearly and in a more logical order. My ability to use my voice to direct other people to carry out my requests first occurred to me when I was in my late teens. As a teenager who was a bit of a geek, before the word was ever invented, and being a loner, put me in a perfect place to be bullied by some of the other, not so tolerant, pupils. My weekend homework, unknown to me had been removed from my bag and replaced with another homework paper, which had my name on it and contained a page of obscenities and disparaging remarks about our teacher. The teacher, of course called me to explain. I often look back and try to fully understand what I actually did, in so many ways I think it was like a primitive instinct that just seemed to surface owing to how terrified I was at the time. The tone of my voice changed, the words I used were unusual for me, but most of all, even though I was petrified, my voice, which I could hear as though it was someone else speaking, was clear and confident. Mr. Cook, he was a really hard, brutal teacher, seemed to soften under my words, and agree with whatever I was saying: 'I can repeat the homework tonight', he was happy to agree. Then I recall I only thought, 'I wish you would give them detention for a week' which he did at once. I then said or thought, I can never be sure which it was, about fat David in our class, who everyone knew encouraged the rebellious behaviour of others, yet always stood by innocently, 'He deserves two weeks detention' which Mr. Cook at once handed out to fat David, who of course protested his innocence, so I suggested giving him another week, which was at once applied and shut him up totally. Of course, such harsh punishment being handed out did draw the attention of some parents, in the end they all got just two days detention. But I had found the whole thing so interesting that I continued to use this strange skill I had found within me. So over the next few months, I experimented amongst my fellow pupils, to see just what I could do and to ensure I could control this skill, which in layman's terms is very much akin to hypnosis."

Phillip sipped his wine and continued, "I can now judge very quickly if someone is susceptible to my suggestions, if they are, I am able to implant a phrase in their mind, which will, for want of a better description, switch them on. Hence Martin, once I had programmed him at the Angel Wings club, all that was needed was to call him, speak the phrase and then tell him what I wanted him to do."

"But for what reason?" was the simple question Greg asked of this multifaceted man in front of him.

"I am just interested in how far I can push my talent, our burnt friend and drowned rat, well that was autosuggestion and carried out at the time and place I told them, and they just did it. I then thought, from the point of view of there should not be too many suicides from one club, that I should possibly move away. After the drowned rat, I had been questioned by the police, although they had just asked what they were expected to ask, convinced that they were dealing with a suicide, so not ever thinking about murder. So I decided that if I was going to continue, I should spread things around, so I programmed Martin and Dougie, who were the next stage of my try-out which was programming someone and then to see if I could switch them on from a distance. Thinking about the whole situation it just made sense to move away from the UK, you will have seen how little interest and appetite there is for the British police to investigate men missing abroad. Then once they are here, I took a great deal of pleasure in taking their lives, in a very personal way, not just letting them do the job for me."

"Wow, you are one mixed-up crazy son of a bitch."

"God, you sound like John Wayne, Greg, or some American television actor, actually I should qualify that, bad American television actor."

"So, your trophies up there above the fireplace, six items, four deaths so far, who are the two other victims up there?"

Phillip put his glass down placing it carefully and precisely on the coaster, stood up, and walked back towards the fireplace. Silently he looked at the six items, then pushed the second one from the left, a Lladro Dancing Horse backwards toward the wall. "Nathan."

Next he pushed the third one, a small red die-cast bus. "Thomas."

The fourth a small Roman statue, was also put into the row behind. "Martin."

Finally, the blackbird pie funnel joined them. "Dougie."

Phillip looked at the two left forward of the others, he picked up the one on the left, Greg assumed that this artefact was a souvenir from Phillip's first victim, it was a small toy that he recognised from his own childhood, a Teenage Mutant Ninja Turtle with a purple mask.

"Donnie," Greg spoke, identifying the character toy that Phillip rolled around between his fingers.

"Donatello," Phillip corrected, "smartest of the Ninja Turtles, science and technology are his strong points as well as being an expert with his weapon, a Bo Staff. My favourite character from the series that my parents thought I was too old, at the time, to watch and follow. My younger brother, however, was not constrained in the same way by our parents, he had all the toys, the videos, and was allowed to watch almost all the television episodes. I, on the other hand, was confined to my room doing homework. My younger brother knew how much this annoyed me and played on it. As soon as we started fighting over playing with the toys, my parents stepped in and told me to grow up, act my age, and let my brother get on playing with his toys in peace; I should go back to my studies. He was their favourite, of that they made no secret. One night I stole this action figure of Donatello from his bedroom, I wanted it and was going to take it, come what may. He could not have been that bothered about it as it was almost three days before he noticed it was missing from his bedroom shelf, and not among all his other figures. Of course when he did notice it had gone, he was straight off to our parents complaining and moaning. I denied taking it, passionately denied, to the point that my parents said he must have lost it somewhere and promised to buy him another figure.

I hated him and I think he hated me, although I always thought younger brothers should look up to their older siblings. Just over a week later, my mother, when cleaning and tidying my room, found a figure of Donatello, it was not the one I had stolen, that was still well hidden in my room, it was the one that they had bought to replace the original missing figure, he had planted it in my room to get me into trouble, which it did. I was allowed no social visits, television, or treats, not that I had many in the first place. I was punished for a whole week, just reading, and working in my bedroom, even my Spectrum computer was taken away from me for that period. How I hated my younger brother, so when a few weeks later we were alone, close to the River Hew that ran a few hundred yards from the bottom of our garden, he started taunting me about how he had got me into trouble, I just held his head under the water until he stopped moving. I just did it, it only took a few moments, I had no control over my hand and arms, they just grabbed his head and pushed him down. I was his older brother, stronger and so he learned that you cannot beat your older brother. I let him float, lifeless for a while, before calling for help. A tragic accident, they said, I knew it was justice."

Phillip placed the Teenage Ninja Turtle figure back into the line, adjusting him so that Donatello looked across at the other items on the fireplace.

"Your brother, what was his name?" Greg asked realising that not once had Phillip mentioned his younger brother by name.

"I do not recall; he is gone now so there is no need to remember."

"You don't remember your own brother's name!"

"Pointless, I will never visit his grave and I will never speak to him again and he will never incriminate me ever again, why do I need to recall and remember his name?"

Cutting the conversation short, Phillip picked up the last and sixth item.

"My latest addition, maybe my saddest item, Helen brought it to me."

"You've killed Helen, our Helen?"

Greg's voice had become slow and slightly slurred. Greg noticed this himself, two or three glasses of wine did not normally affect him like that, or maybe it was being in the presence of a madman, that caused Greg to start to fear for his own life.

"I think describing her as 'our Helen' is a little over the top Greg to be honest, I doubt that she was anyone's in reality. She is not dead yet, although she will have to die."

Phillip mawkishly rolled the waiter's friend through his fingers.

"Helen, I had such high hopes for her, but she gives me little choice. I knew from the moment that I met her, she had that murderous gene within her DNA. She had the ability to kill another human being without emotion, yet in her current capacity she was only able to react to circumstances that developed around her. Her mother falling downstairs whom she left to die, which, luckily, she got away with. Then acting in defence of you, killing that Mick Hayes, who clearly was connected to the government and they will no doubt come looking for him, I have reservations that Helen would have ever got away with that one. These were just killings, like you would kill a fox or a rabbit, killing out of need. I am more than just a killer; I am a pure, sophisticated murderer, skilled in my trade, which requires planning, ingenious action, and intelligence in order to commit a murder that will remain uncovered forever. I had high hopes for Helen, yet in the end she would need more training to iron out those little flaws in her technique, to make her the consummate killer that I am."

"So you plan to kill her because she is not good enough at killing people?"

"Oh Greg, listen to what I am saying, few people are immediately good at anything they do, there is always room for improvement, I learn all the time, working towards perfection. Under my guidance, Helen, undeniably, had the raw talent to become a highly effective murderess. That is not the reason I have to kill her. You see I realised, with her around me, I could not control my emotions. With her in the room, I do things which I have not calculated or planned out. She made me smile when she walked into the room. Being close to her gave me a feeling of warmth and being valued, that I have never felt before with another human being. When she was around, I wanted to be spontaneous. I phoned Dougie up on the spur of the moment, called him over here and killed him, just because I wanted to impress her. I never planned to kill Dougie on that day, when normally I would be planning weeks in advance, that is part of the excitement, each action considered, so I would be in control from the moment I called him to the moment I cut up his body. Yet Helen, by just being in the room with me, with that smile of hers and that sweet mole below her cheekbone, took away that control. A control I have to have if I am to continue my lifestyle, something inside of me reared up and I decided that anything that can weaken that control, I would need to destroy."

"It sounds to me that you are going to kill the only thing you love in this world," Greg concluded, voice still slurred.

"I have never loved and never will Greg; it is something I am not capable of."

"I would say being in love was something that you cannot recognise."

"Whatever you wish to call it, I will not let it invade my mind and soul, so I need to extinguish it."

Greg had been dumbfounded into silence by what he had been told, his head spinning.

Phillip continued, "It is ironic Greg, that to be the perfect murderer, you cannot tell a single person or share your experiences with anyone, that is what I will miss in Helen, she understood me. Now no one will ever know how good a serial murderer I am. I often wonder, just how many perfect murderers there are in our society, it is something that we will never know, and can only imagine. As special as I am, if we looked closely enough, I am sure I am not unique in this wide, diverse world."

Phillip turned and walked towards Greg.

"So! First I had best see if your phone is on, if so, it will be turned off."

Greg sitting on the soft sofa, tried to stand, in order to defend himself as Phillip came towards him, but his legs did not move, they remained flaccid. He then tried to move his arms, they too stayed slack beside him. However much he tried to entrust his limbs to move, they stayed still.

"What have you done?"

Greg's words were becoming more slurred as his lips and mouth muscles, softened and relaxed.

Phillip sat beside the limp figure of Greg and dipped into each of his pockets in turn, removing items.

"As I said, I could not hypnotise you, strangely you have one of those minds that seems to have impenetrable barriers built around it, so I needed another way. I am sorry that you even decided to visit me, if you'd stayed on the other side of the Channel, then you would have lived. However as soon as you appeared at my door, I knew I had to ensure that you could not share what you knew at the time, which was not a lot, but maybe enough for the authorities to trace me. Of course now I have enjoyed some time with you, sharing with you all my conquests, so I am sure you understand even more, that you will need to die. I put some Zolpidem in your first glass of wine, commonly known as Zombie Pills, such a crass name, but it is an effective hypnotic-sedative and can be purchased over the counter in the United States, or through the internet if you're in Europe as we are. Zolpidem is used a lot as a date-rape drug, don't look so scared Greg, I'm not going to rape you, just kill you."

Phillip continued going through Greg's pockets as he spoke.

"Oh look, a chess piece, a black king, well, at least you'll know what your monument will be on my next mantelpiece."

Greg indeed did feel like a zombie, his head had become light as if floating, his arms limp and weak as Phillip heaved him onto his broad shoulders and carried him out through the kitchen, into the cold air of the night. Greg watched the ground moving, his head flopping downwards against Phillip's back, he watched the ground move as they progressed into the night. Greg, had no feeling, he guessed he was going to die, but he had no emotion, the drug had dulled his body and his feelings, so there was no pain when he was dropped on the damp soil. He did not respond to the wetness that seeped into his clothes as he was lying there, and was only aware of Phillip moving around, preparing for the sacrifice that was going to be Greg. Looking up into the clear night sky, Greg was surprised at the number of stars that he could see, there appeared to be thousands up there, twinkling and shining across the galaxy, a limitless space. Greg felt peaceful, as he thought of his sister, Brenda, who must be up there on one of those stars looking down at him, he hoped and prayed that she had forgiven him.

Then the night sky was blocked by Phillip, standing astride the wilted Greg, prone on the ground. Greg saw the knife and was surprised he felt nothing as he watched it heading towards him, nor did he feel it being drawn deeply across his neck. Moments later Greg joined the stars in that immense universe.

Phillip looked down at the lifeless body. There had been a lot of death in this back yard over the last few weeks; there was just one more needed. Such a concentration of death is not a good thing, it brings questions from different quarters. Phillip threw the bloodied knife onto the wet ground, he was relieved to be moving on, starting afresh, leaving behind all those clues and forensic evidence. 'That is what makes me such a perfect murderer', he thought to himself, 'adapting, evolving, always one step ahead'. He was not sure what he felt, it seemed, at first, to be like a hot poker had been pushed into his lower back, then he felt a warm fluid against his skin.

*

The walk back from the village bakers had taken longer than Helen expected, she had spent a little too much time watching the colours painted across the sky by the setting sun, so it was almost dark by the time she walked up to Phillip's house. The first thing she noticed was a sliver-grey car, a car that she did not recognise, it was a Renault Megane, new, maybe just a few months old. Phillip had not mentioned that he expected any visitors, and anyway who would even consider paying him a visit in the first place. Unless the visitors were looking for Helen; police, detectives, colleagues of Reece or Christopher. She guessed it would not take them too long to find where she had been when last in France, who she had visited. Did they know she was here, or was it just a speculative visit? Helen stayed close to the hedge that ran along the side of the house leading to the kitchen door. She wanted to avoid being seen from the living room, where no doubt Phillip would be entertaining his guest or guests. Quietly she opened the kitchen door, slipping into the house without a sound. She listened to the voices, first she heard Phillip speak, she waited. Then another male voice spoke, it sounded like Greg, was it? What was he doing here? Or maybe it was just someone from South London who sounded like him. Helen moved closer to the living room door that was slightly ajar, allowing the words from the voices to filter through to her.

She heard Phillip say, "I think describing her as 'our Helen' is a little over the top, Greg, to be honest, I doubt that she was anyone's in reality. She is not dead yet, although she will have to die."

Had she heard that correctly? 'She will have to die'. Helen edged as close to the door as she dared, aware her heart was thumping against her ribs. She hoped it could not be heard above their conversation.

"So you plan to kill her because she is not good enough at killing people?" That was unquestionably Greg's voice, were they plotting together? Helen could not be sure, had the two of them been in this together all the time? Her mind was awash with thoughts, ideas and befuddlement. She listened to the conversation as Phillip boasted of his talents and skills then she heard that Greg was going to be a victim too.

*

Phillip twisted slightly to examine his side, to uncover what had bitten him, which was his initial thought. As he twisted, he saw Helen standing stubbornly, holding a large kitchen knife, glistening with blood, his blood. Instinct made Phillip step back from his assailant, pushing his hand hard against his side, trying to stem the flow of blood.

"Ah, Helen, I assume you arrived a little while ago, while Greg and I were discussing things."

"I heard the important parts of your conversation. Flattering that at least a part of you loved me, it is just a shame that another part of you hated me. I had hoped that we would, together, be a very unique couple. You have just underestimated how unsophisticated your student is. I seem to have a skill in just killing people on the spur of the moment, not taking weeks or months to plan a killing. I just kill. I kill because it suits me or is necessary for me to achieve something."

"You were not inclined to save your fellow reporter?"

"Who, him?" Helen glanced across to the body beside Phillip. "No great loss to the world. His demise is an advantage to me, one less witness to my previous murders, certainly not worth giving up the advantage of surprise that I had over you."

Phillip began to feel light headed, as the flow of blood continued unabated, his hand unable to cover the entire length of the deep injury to his side.

"I was right, we are different, and our modus operandi is very different. I like the sport of planning a murder," he coughed, his legs weakened and crumpled. As he fell onto his knees, he coughed again, this time it brought a trickle of blood onto his lips. "Did you love me, Helen? Did you need me, not just because I could teach you, was there more? Did you really need me?"

Helen moved towards him, still holding the kitchen knife aggressively. She noticed the other knife, well out of reach of Phillip, so moved even closer.

"You'll never know." In one swift motion, she swung the knife across Phillip's throat, exactly as he had taught her, using her foot to push him away from her. He slumped into the mud, blood flowing from his neck.

Helen threw the knife into the mud and said, "Goodbye Phillip."

She turned and walked back to the house. She liked the idea of a memento, so picked up her waiter's friend, slipped it into the pocket of her jeans, then strode out to her car and disappeared into the night.

The End

From the Author

Dear Reader,

Thank you for reading *Sleeping Malice,* I do hope you enjoyed the book. Please, if you could spare the time to leave a review on Amazon or goodreads, this not only helps other readers, I too am interested to hear what you think of it.

Contact with my readers is something I welcome, so please do visit my website - http://www.adrianspalding.co.uk- where you can leave comments, as well as join my mailing list for my latest news. You can also find me on Facebook – Adrian Spalding Books.

Sleeping Malice began as a short writing exercise one very wintry day in France, when the only living creatures moving were Lapwings. It then developed into the story it is today, a story that embraces some human traits that might exist, in that deep shadowy part of the human mind, skills yet to be honed or made full use of. So the 'skills' that Phillip displays during *Sleeping Malice* might not be seen on a day-to-day basis in the local supermarket, but the human mind is as yet an uncharted landscape, so who knows?

Thank you for your support and I look forward to entertaining you again soon.

Best wishes
Adrian

By the same Author

The Reluctant Detective

A humorous crime mystery

The Hayden Detective Agency has no need of clients. The very existence of the Agency allows Martin Hayden to claim his large monthly allowance from the family fortune - without lifting a finger.

Martin's biggest problem is his interfering mother, who understands her idle son too well. She takes steps to find him not just clients but also a personal assistant to keep an eye on him.

Under pressure from the women in his life, Martin agrees to take on his first client. How hard can it be to follow a 90-year-old woman who spends her time losing money at roulette tables? As it turns out harder than Martin ever thought possible, especially with the old lady dying in strange circumstances.

Soon the Reluctant Detective is grappling with shady estate agents, an intellectual artist, missing charity money and an irritating Indian waiter. Luckily for Martin there is help in the form of Colin, a transvestite who, apart from having very good fashion sense, is an expert at breaking into houses.

Available now from Amazon

Printed in Great Britain
by Amazon